Theologian and writer Frederick Buchner wrote that a great story should do three things: Seek, treasure, and tell secrets. Laura DeNooyer has accomplished all three with singularity. Her characters are all seeking something that matters—a place of their own, belonging, family, love, and more. There are dozens of moments to treasure in this story that moves between eras, sprinkling literary references like confetti that will never need to be cleaned up later. As for secrets ... Janie and Carrie each have their own. Even L. Frank Baum, author of *The Wizard of Oz*, unveils a few. This mesmerizing saga is beautifully written, a treasure for all ages, an epic story you won't want to ever leave. I didn't.

— JANE KIRKPATRICK, AWARD-WINNING
AUTHOR OF *ACROSS THE CRYING SANDS*

A tale of forgotten stories and hidden truths, where imagination holds the key to a past that shapes the future. Laura DeNooyer's *A Hundred Magical Reasons* is a journey through time and heart—a captivating blend of history, whimsy, and the enduring power of storytelling. An enchanting story that blurs the lines between past and present, reality and imagination. Laura DeNooyer has crafted a spellbinding tale that reminds us of the magic within our own lives.

— PATTI CALLAHAN HENRY, NEW YORK TIMES
BESTSELLING AUTHOR OF *THE SECRET BOOK
OF FLORA LEA*

This book is a reader's delight, a page-turner that keeps you guessing until the very end, a story that stays with you long after you read the last page.

— OLIVIA RAE, AUTHOR OF *A LIFE RECLAIMED* AND SECRETS OF THE QUEENS SERIES

You don't have to be a fan of *The Wonderful Wizard of Oz* to become fully engrossed in Laura DeNooyer's charming tale, but you might be one by the time you reach the last page. One of my favorite quotes from the book— "Coming here was like indulging in chocolate fudge after months of cold porridge"—perfectly describes my feelings as I turned pages filled with fascinating, well-developed characters and settings that transported me to each location. DeNooyer brings L. Frank Baum, author of the Oz books, to life with such whimsical detail, I found myself wishing I too could have become friends with him. This delightful story is a must-read.

— MICHELLE SHOCKLEE, AWARD-WINNING AUTHOR OF *APPALACHIAN SPRING* AND *COUNT THE NIGHTS BY STARS*

Impressively researched and beautifully told, *A Hundred Magical Reasons* paints a portrait of two true-to-life women who experience redemptive power in their lives. It's a story full of heart, brains, and courage!

— AMANDA WEN, CAROL AWARD-WINNING AUTHOR OF *THE RHYTHM OF FRACTURED GRACE* AND *THE SONGS THAT COULD HAVE BEEN*

Ms. DeNooyer has painted a beautiful, fanciful picture of life with *Wizard of Oz* author Frank Baum with her new dual time novel. The dialog is rich and captivating and pulls the reader and the main historical character away from the harsh realities the little girl faces. Several generations later, another young woman is also looking for escape and freedom from her stringent parents. It's a wonderful story revealing the only source of true freedom. Ms. DeNooyer is a talented author and creates vivid pictures for her readers that will leave them mesmerized and pondering the message of the book long after they close the final satisfying page.

— LIZ TOLSMA, BESTSELLING AUTHOR
OF *WHAT I PROMISE YOU, WHAT I WOULD
TELL YOU,* AND *A PICTURE OF HOPE*

Embark on an enchanting journey as a young woman and an older companion form an unexpected bond, their deep connection rooted in a love for books. Through the pages of L. Frank Baum's tales, they unravel surprising parallels in their childhoods, weaving a heartwarming narrative of friendship and shared aspirations.

— SUZANNE WOODS FISHER, BESTSELLING
AUTHOR OF *THE MOONLIGHT SCHOOL*

Laura DeNooyer blends original characters with the real-life author of *The Wonderful Wizard of Oz* in a wonderful novel of her own. While the relationship DeNooyer's Janie has with L. Frank Baum is fiction, Baum's character rings true—her research accurately capturing the details of his life. But this isn't about him; his influence on a child becomes the catalyst in a family drama that unfolds across generations. I was pulled into the lives of Carrie and Janie, hoping each would find her fairytale ending. By the close of the book, I not only wanted a sequel, I also wanted a companion cookbook and a soundtrack!

— JANE ALBRIGHT, FORMER PRESIDENT OF THE INTERNATIONAL WIZARD OF OZ CLUB

L. Frank Baum comes to life in the pages of *A Hundred Magical Reasons*. So does Janie, his young protege during his years at Macatawa Resort. Even Carrie, coming of age in the turbulent 1970s, falls under his spell. So, who am I to resist the lure of the Wizard of Words? The characters, the drama, and beautiful Lake Macatawa are all worth another visit.

— ANITA KLUMPERS, AUTHOR OF *WINTER WATCH*, *A MURDER OF CROWS*, AND *THE LADY WITH THE ALLIGATOR CASE*

Laura DeNooyer crafts a superb story where generations of characters discover their passions with the encouragement of L. Frank Baum's words and friendship. As imagination leaps from the page, DeNooyer draws wisdom and whimsy from fairytales and allegories to help her characters find their happily-ever-after. Creativity and charm will steal your heart and keep you turning pages in this fresh, inspiring story of remaining true to yourself in the Slough of Despond.

— Barbara M. Britton, Amazon
bestselling author of the Tribes of
Israel series

Laura DeNooyer

Published by Scrivenings Press LLC
15 Lucky Lane
Morrilton, Arkansas 72110
https://ScriveningsPress.com

Printed in the United States of America

Paperback ISBN 978-1-64917-438-3

eBook ISBN 978-1-64917-439-0

Editor: Susan Page Davis

Cover design by Linda Fulkerson - www.bookmarketinggraphics.com

Scripture quotations marked (RSV) are taken from the REVISED STANDARD VERSION, Grand Rapids: Zondervan, 1971. Used by permission. All rights reserved.

Scriptures quotations marked (KJV) are taken from the KING JAMES VERSION (KJV): KING JAMES VERSION, public domain.

With the exception of L. Frank Baum, all characters are fictional, and any resemblance to real people, either factual or historical, is purely coincidental.

To my dear friend Rita Trickel, who makes room for fun and fairies every day. You epitomize a life well lived with both faith and imagination.

"Stunt, dwarf, or destroy the imagination of a child and you have taken away its chances of success in life. Imagination transforms the commonplace into the great and creates the new out of the old ... Man's familiarity with the objects around him reduces him to the commonplace. Imagination and faith alone can keep him above it ... Our success, our progress and achievements depend upon that."
—L. Frank Baum, The Advance magazine, 1909

"Fairy tales do not give the child his first idea of a bogey. What fairy tales give the child is his first clear idea of the possible defeat of a bogey. The baby has known the dragon intimately ever since he had an imagination. What the fairy tale provides for him is a St. George to kill the dragon. Exactly what the fairy tale does is this: it accustoms him for a series of clear pictures to the idea that these limitless terrors had a limit, that these shapeless enemies have enemies in the knights of God, that there is something in the universe more mystical than darkness, and stronger than strong fear."
—G. K. Chesterton, Tremendous Trifles, 1909

"Every man's life is a fairy tale, written by God's fingers."
—Hans Christian Anderson

ONE

PART ONE: LEAVING HOME

Once upon a time, there lived a girl who didn't know she was a princess, or that three dragons pursued her ...

May 28, 1980

Two weeks after college graduation with no diploma to show for it, Carrie Kruisselbrink stormed from her house like a prairie gale. Mom handed her an overnight bag, but Carrie left with an overstuffed suitcase. She wasn't going back.

The storm started brewing in childhood, but this morning the temperature spiked as she emptied the dishwasher, her mother barking orders. As if Carrie hadn't been responsible while away four years at college.

Mom chose that moment to pounce. She thrust a paper under Carrie's chin. Skimming the list of elementary teacher positions, Carrie resisted the urge to rip it up and cast it to the wind. She had her own career goals.

She trudged upstairs to her bedroom and found respite

among her overflowing bookshelves. But not for long. The room shrank, the headboard rattled as Mother barged in. Gusting at ninety miles per hour, she tidied Carrie's desk. "Most teachers have contracts already." In the updraft, Mother rearranged pens. "When will you mail more résumés?"

Never. Carrie winced, thoughts spiraling. "Later." Though she'd walked at graduation, she had no diploma, no teaching certificate, and no intention of retaking Philosophy of Education. She fanned her face and opened the window. Three thousand square feet in this house, yet claustrophobia suffocated like pre-storm humidity.

Her mother slammed the window shut. "Your sister had three teaching offers by graduation. What's your plan?"

Swinging open the closet door, Carrie inhaled. Plan B, in effect: *Take charge of my life. Now.* "I'm going to Oma and Opa's." Two hours northwest on Lake Michigan should be far enough away. She'd planned to visit her grandparents anyhow. Why not the whole summer?

"Fine." Mother left and returned with an overnight bag. "Don't forget résumés, envelopes, and postage."

Carrie plopped her suitcase on the bed. She tossed in sundresses and sandals. Home decorator magazines. Colored pencils, sketch pads. Books from Children's Lit class: *Mary Poppins, A Wrinkle in Time,* Chronicles of Narnia.

"Why the kids' books?"

"I like them." Angry retorts galloped through her like gathering winds, but she bit her lip. As usual. She tucked *The Princess and Curdie* in sideways. Too bad her entire classics book collection wouldn't fit.

"What about your date with Brian on Saturday?"

"I'll call him." According to her parents, dating Brian was her crowning achievement. They'd dated six years, now anticipating a summer packed with fancy restaurants and Brian's baseball games. Like Cinderella, she might finally get to the "palace ball." A wedding and a move to Wolcott.

Then, the deluge. "When're you going to do something worthwhile? For two weeks, you've moped around, cluttered my kitchen baking ..." Words whirled and lashed, twisting into a column of anger.

Carrie rummaged through the bookshelf. "Where's *The Tasha Tudor Book of Fairy Tales*?"

"In the garbage downstairs. It's falling apart."

Panic surged like a thunderclap in a squall. Carrie dashed down the steps and dug through trash. She retrieved the book —ripped binding, pages dangling, egg yolk dripping, coffee grounds stuck. In a torrent of tears, she wrapped it in a clean garbage bag and whisked upstairs to her bulging suitcase. Now topped with résumés.

Carrie scattered the papers and replaced them with bagged book remains.

Mother rolled her eyes. "Figures you'd value dilapidated fairy tales over anything practical." She stalked off.

Surely Mother would regret her words in August when Carrie revealed her intentions—one that included fairy tales. Meanwhile, she slipped a manila envelope with her covert business plan into the suitcase and called Rita at the café to say she'd miss work this summer.

***

Wolcott, Population 945, the sign announced.

A mile later, on the front porch, Carrie's ginger-haired Dutch oma greeted her with a breathless hug that infused life.

All sweat and axle grease, Opa stepped from the garage and grinned, then noted the suitcase. "How long're you staying, Carrie Bell?"

Carrie plopped onto the porch swing. "I'll never measure up to their expectations."

Oma sat beside her. "They're just eager for you to follow

the family footsteps into your first elementary classroom. We're proud of you, *liefje*."

Carrie grimaced and blew her nose. "Any job openings in Wolcott?"

"Burger Flipper's hiring," Opa said.

"Ed, that's ridiculous." Oma swatted the air. "Arlene would throw a fit."

Carrie sniffed. "Maybe that's *exactly* what I want." Even her grandparents didn't know her alternate career plans, though she'd spent spring break here scouting out the perfect location for her future book café—booths flanked by shelves of books, savored with pastries or tea. After six summers of restaurant work in Barrowdale and making a fifteen-page business plan with her mentor Rita, she was ready to obtain financing. Then she'd tell her parents. They'd watch her succeed following her own dream instead of theirs.

After lunch, Carrie called the bank's loan officer to make an appointment—the culmination of Phase One.

She walked McKinley Street, a stroll through yesteryear: Victorian homes with turrets, wraparound porches, gingerbread trim, and perfectly placed pansies as dainty as ruffles on a lady's dress. But the disastrous year of midnight studies and student teaching still trailed her. Critiques and comparisons. Rough, ineffective classroom management skills. Fighting nausea every time she entered the classroom. Carrie couldn't measure up. Just like at home.

Shaking off memories, she meandered through a park and circled back to a shady street. One dark green house with white shutters and plum-striped awnings sported a picket fence. An invitation rather than a boundary, the fence drew her to peek at the yard's secrets.

Four triangles of spring blooms surrounded a winding brick pathway. Similar colors clumped together. Lilac bushes hovered over purple pansies and early irises. Yellow daffodils and primroses cheered in unison. Rosebushes huddled with fading tulips. Blue splashed over violets and late hyacinths.

"I need help."

Carrie jumped at the unexpected sharp voice.

Wearing a large-brimmed hat and sunglasses, an old woman rocked in the porch's stark shadows. "Would you please water the sunflower seedlings along the fence?"

Curious, Carrie stepped through the gate. Was she arthritic? Or even lucid? "Such a lovely garden."

"I'd expect nothing less. The watering can's full."

Carrie picked up the can and spilled. "You weren't kidding."

"I never kid." She drew out *never* like pulling yarn from a skein, teasing Carrie's memory.

Wincing under the woman's stare, Carrie began watering. "Sunflowers are my favorite, the epitome of summer."

"'Ah, Sunflower, weary of time …'" The woman recited eight lines of poetry.

Amazing! "William Blake," Carrie said.

"You know something that counts. Did Mr. Blake inspire your love of sunflowers?"

"No." Carrie squinted toward the sun. "No matter where the sun or how weak the light, the sunflower faces it."

"Mature sunflowers always face east," the woman snapped. "But in this poem, a girl rooted to the ground is scorned, doomed to face the sun, far from reach. No optimism here."

Carrie tensed. If she wanted criticism, she'd have stayed in Barrowdale. "Maybe it's about being trapped on earth while yearning for the divine."

"Hardly. Preoccupation with the divine interferes with worthwhile aspirations."

What was this lady's problem? Anger at God? "Or it's a slighted lover."

"Or any unfulfilled desire. Surely you've heard William

Blake was well acquainted with fairies living near his cottage. Muses for his poetry and art. Alas, logic and reason kills them." She quoted:

> "The good are attracted by men's perceptions,
> And think not for themselves;
> Til experience teaches them to catch
> And to cage fairies and elves."

"The end of imagination," Carrie murmured.

"Each flower whimpers when it's picked, he says. The loss hovers like a cloud of incense."

"I love that image."

"Do you now? Quite admirable. Especially considering my flowers' demise in 1969. Remember, Miss Caroline?"

Carrie jolted at her name.

"Kids these days. Off to college and—poof! The elderly are forgotten. Come here." She hobbled into the house as Carrie climbed two daunting porch steps. The woman returned, shaking a sheet of paper.

Carrie read the childish handwriting: "'I, Caroline Kruisselbrink, age eleven, being of sound mind, do solemnly swear to never kick, hit, bat, or roll a ball into Mrs. Gordon's flowerbed or step foot onto said sacred place, as long as I live, so help me God. June 1969.' Oh, my." Carrie looked up as the woman removed her sunglasses.

Mrs. Charlotte Rose Gordon. Nothing like her beautiful name, except for the thorns. Images washed over her: Carrie with Oma's next-door neighbor Jodi kicking to each other down the sidewalk, the ball rolling into the garden, flattening tulips, then old Mrs. Gordon, who'd always been old, shouting from the house. The fence appeared a week later.

That mishap would have brought their childhoods to a screeching halt, if not for the advocacy of Carrie's grandparents. Carrie deemed Mrs. Gordon a witch of the

Hansel and Gretel variety, the Victorian home of stained glass and gingerbread trim enticing like candy. Carrie never walked that way again. Fortunately, it was blocks away from her grandparents' house, easy to avoid. Until today.

Here, eleven years later, sat a hunched shadow of the woman who'd stomped around the garden, smacking their ball with a broom. "Mrs. Gordon." Carrie smoothed her rattling voice. "Good to see you."

"Is it now?" Mrs. Gordon slipped her sunglasses back on, peering at her over the top.

"I'm sorry for the trouble." Under Mrs. Gordon's gaze, Carrie shrank to age six.

"I'd appreciate compensation beyond new bulbs. Finish reading."

Carrie clutched the paper. "'P.S. If I fail to keep this oath, I'll make it up to Mrs. Gordon as she sees fit.'"

The woman pointed to Carrie's feet. "You've failed your vow miserably. Today, you stood in my garden."

"You invited me."

"No such stipulations in this contract."

"I was eleven when I wrote that!"

"No statute of limitations, either."

Carrie flicked the paper. "I can't believe you saved this all these years."

"I heard about graduation and figured you'd visit your grandparents soon."

Had she perched on the porch for two weeks watching? Crazy lady. "Shall I plant more perennials? Read poetry?"

Belying her witching powers, the woman patted the wicker settee. "Come."

Carrie gingerly stepped up, the creak in each step like a squeal of derision. She sat.

Mrs. Gordon removed her sunglasses. Bags under her eyes stood out where a map of wrinkles had long ago settled in. "You'll help me clear my husband's name, God rest his soul."

"How?"

"In 1918, he was doomed to prison for a crime he didn't commit. He died of cancer before his trial."

Why was she revealing this? And why'd it matter now? "I don't see how to help."

"I need a scribe, good at research. You just graduated, so perfect timing. My eyes aren't what they used to be."

Oh, yes, they are. Just as beady as before. "Mrs. Gordon, I'm applying for summer jobs."

"I'm saving you from a summer of *fast food*." With one tongue cluck, she relegated all fast food to the abyss.

"I accidentally trample your flowers, then owe you my entire summer?"

"You're a feisty one."

Carrie crossed her arms. "*I'm* the feisty one?"

"I'll pay you what you're worth."

Carrie shifted forward. "What am I worth to you, Mrs. Gordon?"

"What you don't realize" —her eyes bore into Carrie's— "is what *I'm* worth to *you.*"

"Meaning what?"

"Never mind. It's money that concerns you graduates." The woman sighed, as if the old days were nothing but cherub children, apple pies, and sunflowers. "I'll pay double minimum wage every Friday for a forty-hour week. *If* I'm satisfied with your efforts."

"How'll you measure that?"

The woman resumed rocking. "One criterion you already meet. Spunk. You don't roll over upon meeting an obstacle."

That obstacle being Mrs. Gordon? She'd surely change her mind if witnessing Carrie's usual demeanor at home.

"Miss Caroline, you're in the right place at the right time."

"That's debatable."

"See? You have spunk. Like me. The only reason the Broderick Resort was so successful."

"That tearoom by the lake?"

"Yes, I take full credit. For what it *used* to be."

No wonder the woman disdained the notion of fast food. Such a fine piece of serendipity! Carrie could pick the woman's brain about best restaurant practices.

"Come at nine tomorrow with notebook and pen."

"I never said yes."

The woman slipped her sunglasses back on, eyes disappearing. "But you cannot say no." Not a command. She spoke as if it were destiny.

Two

May 1980

Halfway through supper, Carrie said, "I saw Charlotte Rose Gordon."

Her grandparents' heads jerked up. They could've gotten whiplash. Oma sniffed. "*Grote grutten!* Charlotte Rose, indeed."

"The thorn part fits." Opa chortled.

"That's not her real name?"

"You'd change your name, too," Oma said, "if it were Lodemia Jane."

Carrie nearly choked on her squash. "Lodemia?"

"Sawyer Broderick owned the farm, cranberry bog, icehouse, peach grove, and tearoom." Opa buttered a biscuit. "Charlotte inherited the Broderick fortune and was sole proprietor of the tearoom for decades."

Oma pointed to Carrie. "Don't get snared by her wiles, *liefje.*"

Opa squeezed Oma's shoulder. "Don't get cranked up, Tanna. Give the benefit of the doubt, like usual."

"What happened, Oma?"

Oma stared ahead as if the past projected on a screen. "Spring, 1920. I was eight. *Moeder* and I drove to Wolcott's general store. When I wandered outside, a young woman bustled out. *Her.* Lodemia Jane Gordon. Didn't know her name, but she was pretty. She stooped over me. 'Tantje De Haan, are you?' She knew my name."

"She heard your mother use it."

"But this woman somehow *knew* me." Oma shuddered. "Then she spoke. 'You must walk. It is a long journey, through a country that is sometimes pleasant and sometimes dark and terrible.'"

Opa patted his wife's arm. "Tanna, it's just a quote."

Carrie nodded. "Yup. The Good Witch of the North, from *The Wonderful Wizard of Oz*." She'd reread it for Children's Lit. "What'd you do?"

"My heart was clanging like a spoon on a frying pan, but I managed to ask, 'What journey?' She replied, 'In a utilitarian age, of all other times, it's a matter of grave importance that fairy tales should be respected.'"

Carrie's eyes widened. "You remember that line? It's Charles Dickens."

"Moeder heard it, too, and explained it."

"Crazy." Carrie skewered squash chunks. "Maybe Lodemia was inspiring you to great things."

"She only inspired fear. She never spoke to me at the tearoom, however, she'd pick me out of a crowd. Those beady eyes ..."

"Beautiful blue eyes," Opa said. "Oma just likes remembering them as beady. Right, Tanna? The woman's reputation spares nothing. Much is hearsay."

"Like her husband's so-called crime?" Carrie asked.

Oma gasped. "How'd you know?"

"She told me. She hired me to help prove his innocence."

"*Nou breekt m'n klomp.*" Hand flying to her forehead, Oma

translated. "That breaks my wooden shoe." When Oma grew agitated, Dutch spilled forth like sand from a pail.

"Takes the cake, all right." Opa sliced his beef. "Newspapers reported Walter Gordon would be found guilty of homicide. Lucky he didn't live to see the day."

"Such a scandal for a pharmacist. Folks still talked about it decades later. Tarnished the whole town." Oma shook her finger. "Save yourself trouble and bow out gracefully."

The full magnitude of Carrie's private summer rebellion swelled within. "She's paying good money, double minimum wage."

"Is your sanity worth only a few hundred dollars to you?" Oma stabbed her beef.

"That's one way to test your mettle, Carrie Bell."

Carrie twirled butter into her potatoes. "I'll ask why she quoted those two lines."

"No, don't mention me," Oma said.

Opa chuckled. "Be back for supper by five-thirty sharp so Oma doesn't think you've been swallowed by that big ol' house. We'll tie a rope 'round your ankle to pull you out."

Carrie giggled. "Oma, weren't you inspired? You read me a thousand fairy tales."

"If I spoke to a child once, it wouldn't be *those* words."

"She'd warn not to overcook meat." Opa smirked.

After dessert, Carrie washed dishes. Her head spun with the novelty of an unconventional job her parents would frown upon, though working for prickly Mrs. Gordon would take all the gumption she had. But gleaning from the woman's tearoom experiences and literary inclination was worth far more than twice minimum wage. What could go wrong?

Outside in Oma's garden, sunflower seeds lurked in the dirt, ruminating—surely the only thing Tanna Groothuis had in common with strange Mrs. Gordon. Why'd she choose Baum's words for young Tantje? *A girl rooted to the ground is scorned, doomed to face the sun, forever from reach.*

Perhaps Carrie was embarking on a fairy tale of her own, which included Phase Two: perfecting recipes in Oma's kitchen.

As much as Brian supported her café aspirations, he wouldn't be happy about her sudden move to Wolcott, spoiling their summer plans.

She'd call him tomorrow. Today, this was her secret.

THREE

Thursday, May 29, 1980

Carrie stood at Mrs. Gordon's door. Oma's dismay echoed through her. Despite having to endure grumpiness and deflation of her precarious self-esteem, this venture ranked ten times better than the Burger Flipper. And her parents would be furious. All the better. She knocked.

"Come in." Spoken as if Mrs. Gordon had drunk castor oil for breakfast.

Carrie opened the door. The bleak interior chilled her. She stared past a bentwood coatrack and carved millwork to the figure rocking in the adjoining room.

"Close the door. You're blinding me."

"I can hardly see."

"You'll acclimate."

Beyond French doors, furniture shapes emerged: a glass-fronted secretary desk, Victorian sofa, golden oak tables. At the bay window, Carrie grabbed drapery ropes. "May—"

"Trying to put me at a distinct disadvantage? I'll need sunglasses."

"But I *need* light."

"'Eagle of flowers! ... On the sun's noon-glory gaze ... Light is thy element ...'"

"More Blake?"

"It's too early to entertain such disappointment." Uttered as if she'd no tolerance for ignorance. "British poet James Montgomery."

Carrie envisioned Mrs. Gordon as a schoolmarm, slapping palms with rulers, directing dunce-capped students to corners. "Were you a teacher?"

Mrs. Gordon lowered her chin, peering over glasses. "Why?"

At this rate, it would take months to discover the meaning of the lines quoted to Tantje in 1920. "Never mind. But I still need light."

"Uncover one windowpane."

Success! Perhaps by summer's end, light would flood the house. She drew the drapery and tugged the shade, allowing a smidgen of sunshine to chase some gray. The marble-top end table went from drab to shiny. Flecks of sunlit dust spawned from the glass, revealing ferns, bookshelves, an ornate railing. Walls of framed silhouettes and botanical prints spared no breathing space between bookshelves.

Spurning potential poetry critiques, Carrie sat and opened her notebook. "Tell me about your husband."

"Excuse me. *I'm* directing the research." Mrs. Gordon tapped a hardcover book. Its gold trim outlined faded scarlet and tattered edges. *The Pilgrim's Progress.*

Seriously? Nothing about Charlotte Gordon suggested a trek to the Celestial City, like that of the pilgrim of the story. *Dracula* seemed more congruent with her temperament.

"You're shocked I own such a book," Mrs. Gordon pronounced.

"Not really."

"Tell the truth. I only want truth."

"Are you a Christian, Mrs. Gordon? Most readers find encouragement from Christian's journey."

"I've been called many things, young lady. *Christian* isn't one of them."

"Yet you only want truth."

"The situational facts." She made a sweeping gesture. "Don't misconstrue my meaning with some invisible, ethereal truth floating out there."

Should Carrie apply to fast-food restaurants? No, this challenge was worth overlooking the sharp tongue. Eventually, this quibbling would benefit her book café.

Carrie opened the book to frail, yellowed pages and read the inscription:

My dear Teddy,

May this story remind you of times we've shared, bringing joy and hope of your final destination, no matter how big the Slough of Despond, no matter how tall the Giant of Despair. Someday we'll meet again, beyond the Delectable Mountains, past the Land of Beulah and the Black River, in the Celestial City itself.

All my love,
Mother
June 1905, P.E.I.

A twist of melancholy knotted Carrie's stomach. "Did you know Teddy?"

"He was my beau. He came to Wolcott from Prince Edward Island."

A flutter of intrigue waved through Carrie. "How'd you end up with his book?"

"That coincides with my purpose for hiring you."

Carrie set the book aside. "So, we start with Teddy."

"You'd best satisfy your curiosity first. You're eyeing my shelves. Put the lamp on the lowest setting."

Relieved to avoid another lighting dispute, Carrie switched on the Tiffany lamp and browsed titles. The woman surely owned every novel by Hawthorne, Twain, and Dickens. If Carrie believed in literary reincarnation, perhaps Mrs. Gordon had revived as jilted Miss Havisham.

Dozens of classics and poetry filled the shelves. "Any nonfiction?" Carrie asked.

"What for? Fiction contains all the truth I need."

Next, a bevy of old picture books, including James Thurber's 1943 fairy tale. "*Many Moons*. These look original."

"Collector's items, amounting to four months' pay. Minimum."

"I read these in Children's Lit."

"So, they *do* teach something worthwhile these days."

"Ah, Tasha Tudor." She pulled out the book and ogled fairy tale pictures. "I could browse all day."

"And not get paid a cent."

"My sister and I read it a million times. But my mom threw it away."

Mrs. Gordon frowned. A speck of sympathy? "You may borrow mine."

"Thanks!" Could she lure a smile from the woman? Carrie needed such assurance before venturing into tearoom inquiries. "I promise I won't spill ketchup on it."

No smile. "If you do, I'll deduct it from your paycheck."

If Carrie survived that long. She scanned Newbery winners. "Children's Lit was my favorite class. Absolutely delightful."

"So, why's an old, ornery woman like me reading children's literature? An oxymoron."

Carrie offered a nervous chuckle as if that deduction lay furthest from her mind. "Look—Gretchen Trumbauer! The whole Wendolyn series." One cover showed a jagged road aiming toward a distant castle. "*Wendolyn and the Gatekeeper of*

Merrimack Castle. I wanted to read all seven, but this one went off the market shortly after release. May I borrow it?"

"What's so appealing?"

"Wendolyn is every girl's heroine. The fairyland of Nickelboggen is so real, I could touch it. I'd read in bed with a flashlight long after Mom turned the lights off."

"Too much reading in bed damages eyes. Put it back."

Like a child caught with stolen candy, Carrie replaced it with another. "*The Wonderful Wizard of Oz!*" She sat near Mrs. Gordon.

"First edition, 1900."

The green and beige cover featured the Cowardly Lion with green glasses. Carrie reveled in W.W. Denslow's vivid illustrations. The inscription's handwriting scrawled in faded ink.

July 1902

To my dear friend Charlotte Rose,
May you ever dwell in the Oz of your own imagination.

Ozily,
L. Frank Baum

"You met the author!" Not Lodemia Jane? Carrie couldn't ask without hinting Mrs. Gordon had been a suppertime highlight, along with beef stew. "The movie—"

"Mr. Baum would've hated the ending, Dorothy's adventure portrayed as merely a dream. Oz is as real as that chair."

"Sure, like children long to believe fairy tales are true."

Mrs. Gordon leaned forward. "Of course you don't understand, with your highfalutin four-year college degree. It knocks the imagination right out of you."

Carrie winced at the word *degree.*

"If thou of fortune be bereft, and in thy store, there be but left two loaves, sell one, and with the dole, buy hyacinths to feed thy soul."

Another Name-The-Poet game? "Beautiful."

"John Greenleaf Whittier," Mrs. Gordon said. "Incidentally, those *without* formal education are better suited to dwell among the hyacinths."

"And never be hungry."

Mrs. Gordon lifted her chin as if impressed. "I see your degree doesn't prevent you from grasping what matters."

Carrie tapped the Oz book. "I love the movie, but wish they'd included more from the book." She watched for hints of recognition in the woman's steel trap memory. "Like that line from the Good Witch of the North. 'You must walk. It is a long journey.'"

"I concur. Perhaps we're kindred spirits."

Hardly! "Have you read all these books?"

"My eyesight's failing, but I'll read them all eventually."

"How?"

"I'll borrow *your* eyes."

A crazy image of the woman plucking out Carrie's eyes struck her with terror, but she doused it with common sense. "You want me to read to you?"

"Daily, for thirty minutes."

Without commentary, Carrie hoped. "Which book first?"

"*The Pilgrim's Progress.* But first, I tell you about Teddy." Staring at a framed print of William Blake's sunflower poem, Mrs. Gordon relayed the tale of fourteen-year-old Teddy. Near North Rustico on Prince Edward Island, his farmwife mother saved up coins for months and sent Teddy away to escape his abusive father. In Teddy's knapsack, she packed a map, a shirt, pumpernickel bread, sardines, sunflower seeds, and money to reach Syracuse, New York.

She also enclosed their well-read copy of *The Pilgrim's Progress.* Bread for his soul, she'd said, to keep him aimed toward the Celestial City, away from the Giant of Despair and Slough of Despond on their farm.

Stomach twisting, Carrie stopped scribbling notes. "I can't imagine giving up your child to a better life, knowing you'll never see him again."

"It's beyond all reckoning." Mrs. Gordon's gaze dropped to folded hands on her lap.

"Did Teddy get to Syracuse?"

"He spent two years there until Dr. Weaver brought him here."

"How'd they meet? And what does Teddy have to do with the false charge against your husband?"

Mrs. Gordon adjusted her glasses as if giving her vision a clearer path to Carrie's soul. "Miss Kruisselbrink, the 1918 event needs context. It's vital you understand what each person brought to that iniquitous deed."

Carrie deflated, the woman's condescending tone pricking the balloon of her self-esteem.

"And don't read newspaper accounts yet."

"Okay." She straightened, refusing to cower, embracing her private rebellion. Hadn't Mrs. Gordon said she had spunk? "What a rough life."

"His father beat him fourteen years, which explains who he was, what he became."

Carrie tapped *The Pilgrim's Progress*. "His life was more than what he inherited from his father."

"Life isn't all happy endings, Miss Caroline. Sometimes, evil wins." Mrs. Gordon's face was grim. "Teddy endured many beatings. My own father meted out so-called divine justice while raging like the devil himself."

Carrie's eyebrows rose at such candor. Older people were usually reticent to speak poorly of family members, as if ancestral ghosts hovered, ready to swoop down and consume.

"But beatings were rare. Father was busy with work.

Mother's weapon was words. Words of my ineptness, horrible sins, impending doom."

Empathy gripped Carrie. Words were her mom's weapons, too. "That's awful. How'd you manage?"

"I had an escape. However, the very thing that saved me also condemned me. It clearly began one summer day in my eighth year." Mrs. Gordon's eyes brightened. "My father owned peach orchards, the cranberry bog, icehouse, and farm. Mother ran the Broderick Resort and Tearoom, drawing people from Holland, Saugatuck, and Douglas, especially tourists. My sisters and I helped in the kitchen, sometimes serving guests."

Carrie reopened her notebook, pen ready.

FOUR

Janie, 8
June 1900

"Lodemia Jane!"

Under the lilac bush canopy, Janie squirmed at her mother's harshness. She squinted at a fragrant blossom. "I must go, Beatrice. I'll be back, Estella."

Those fairies! Such a nuisance, but how delightful frolicking together in that cozy nook. Well, cozy for her. Too big for fairies. They constantly complained.

Janie jogged to the Victorian home with myriad windows, turret poking the sky. She fancied herself a princess, waving from the highest window.

Arms folded, Mother stood guard at the kitchen door, then tugged her inside. "The nerve of you disappearing. Wash up and count twenty eggs. Josephine, watch the griddle. Maggie Pearl, mind the bread dough."

At the dry sink, Janie poured water. Tiny streams of dirt flowed into the basin, creating lacy patterns. "Beatrice, you came!"

"Who're you talking to?" Mother yelled. "Count those eggs."

Josephine swished by. "Janie's in her own world again."

Mother rolled her eyes. "Useless."

At the counter, Janie stepped on the stool, shutting out thoughtless comments discharged as easily as water from a pitcher. Two shutter-like half doors invited listening.

"Let's catch the noon interurban, Maud," a man said sprightly.

A boy whined. "Let's leave now. I wanna fish."

"The water's rough, Harry," a woman replied. "You'll capsize."

"That's what your *mother* says." Janie visualized the man's sly expression. "The real reason is that thumpdoodlums live in the lake, worse than pirates. They lure you deeper."

"Did you see one, Papa?" another boy's voice wavered.

An older boy laughed. "No such thing."

"Never mind your brothers, Kenneth," the man said. "Doubters have the most to fear."

Counting eggs while eavesdropping proved difficult. Eleven? Twelve? "Beatrice, pay attention."

Mother whisked by. "Stop dawdling. Guests are waiting."

Janie counted again. *Splat.*

"Lodemia Jane! That does it." Mother yanked her off the stool. "Take this basket to the table with four boys. And leave your fairy friends here."

Was this how Cinderella felt? Basket in tow, she pushed through doors that flapped behind her. The man faced her. Had he heard the exchange in the kitchen? Her cheeks burned.

He smiled, head at a jaunty angle. Brown hair parted over clear, gray eyes and a bushy mustache. His waistcoat pocket bulged with a fob watch chained to his lapel. "Hello, dear. Are those muffins from the Forest of Burzee? Forest fairies bake the most delectable pastries."

Fairies? She eyed the basket, sparing herself from his warm

gaze, then set it down amidst a hint of cigar scent. "Mother's specialty. Blueberry cream cheese."

"Thank you, my dear." He leaned over. "You know why Miss Mary was so contrary, don't you, though surrounded by beautiful flowers? Silver bells, cockle shells, and all."

Startled, she glanced at the man's wife who smiled, dark hair emphasizing merry eyes. "No, sir."

"Oh, but you do! We're here all morning, so tell me when you've figured it out."

Her mother long ago replaced her nursery rhyme books with *The New England Primer*. But last month, Janie secretly cut the Three Bears pictures from Pettijohn's Breakfast Food boxes and borrowed eight cents from Aunt Sophie for postage to obtain an installment of the popular *Mother Goose in Prose* by L. Frank Baum, one of the books Mother pilfered. Janie swiped *Father Goose* music inserts from Sunday newspapers before her father read them.

As Janie walked away, the youngest boy piped up. "Papa knows how four-and-twenty blackbirds escape the pie and sing even after baking."

Really? Outdoors, she wandered to the maple tree. Lower, beyond the sand, Lake Michigan waves rolled to shore in soothing rhythm. She spun like Cinderella dancing at the ball, everyone below gazing in wonder. Her glass slippers fit perfectly.

She began assembling a fairy habitat from twigs, dandelions, and maple whirligigs.

Soon, the four boys tumbled into the yard. The man dropped his waistcoat on the bench by his wife's embroidery bag and tossed a ball with his sons. Picking clovers, Janie ignored their romps and shrieks. Maybe she'd entice her friends from their fairy den.

The deep voice alarmed her. "Did you discover why Mary's so contrary?" The man smiled, having gone from dapper to carefree, his white shirt rippling in the breeze. Behind him blurred a mosaic of blue sky, green leaves, and filtered sunshine.

"The fairies, sir. They hide when you want them. They bother you when you're not in the mood. You know how fairies are. Don't you?"

"I do. I've had similar frustrations. Such tricksters."

Janie blinked. Only Aunt Sophie ever engaged her this way.

He sat beside her. "What's your name? No, let me guess. With such imagination, it must be Anna Isabella."

"No." Hadn't he heard Mother scolding?

"Agnes Winifred?"

Suppressing a giggle, she wrinkled her nose. "Oh, no."

"How about Charlotte Rose?"

"No—yes, that's it."

"Well, then, Charlotte Rose, how do *you* think blackbirds sing after baking in a pie?"

"The king wanted a pie that sang. So, the royal baker sprinkled magic powder in the sugar so the blackbirds wouldn't suffocate."

"Of course! Magic powder works every time."

"Feathers popped out all over. The queen's nose itched. She sneezed."

"*Gesundheit!*"

"What?"

"German for *bless you.*"

"Gesundheit." Janie smiled with the prize of a new word.

He nodded toward the dandelion pile. "A fairy cottage?"

Dare she tell him? "If I make a nice hiding place, Beatrice might leave the fairy den."

"Hopefully. Those confounded fairies are more stubborn than goats with teeth sunk into your favorite shirt. Can't shake them loose. Like some witches I know."

Janie stiffened. "Witches?"

Crossing his legs, he resettled in the grass. "The one from

the North is a good witch. Like the one from the South, very kind. But the Witch of the West is the detestable sort."

"You mean the witch in Hansel and Gretel? Or Rapunzel?"

"A different domain altogether." He added a dandelion to Janie's creation. "Are the fairies close by? Don't tell if it's secret."

Janie twirled a whirligig. "They'll be angry if I do."

"I know. Like the Munchkins. They grumbled for months."

"Munchkins?"

"In the Land of Oz. Unknown until Dorothy discovered them. And another fellow before her. Soon, all the world's children will know."

"Where's Oz?"

The man made a broad hand sweep. "Across many sands, not unlike that dune."

"A real place?"

"If not, how could I write about it?"

"You wrote a story?"

"A book, soon to be in stores. On the sixth title now, so who knows?" He chuckled. "Funny thing about Oz. Some places are lovely—with rivers, farmlands, and meadows—but other parts are scary. Tree branches fling folks around. Nothing like the trees here."

"Was Dorothy hurt?"

"'Twas the Scarecrow. But nothing hurts him. Except a lit match."

"How'd Dorothy get there?"

"Telling you might steal the fun from reading it." He winked. "The fairies in Oz aren't the usual ones. No brownies or ryls carrying paint pots."

"Dorothy must've been scared, far from home. With mean trees. Witches, too."

"She had to be brave. Fortunately, she had travel companions." He watched the boys' buffoonery. Wind wrinkled his hair. "We all have places to go, dear. Hard roads to travel. Difficult things to learn while growing up."

Confused, Janie squinted at sunshine haloing his head.

He fastened his gaze on her. "As the Good Witch from the North says, 'You must walk. It is a long journey, through a country that is sometimes pleasant and sometimes dark and terrible.'"

Janie's stomach prickled. His tone suggested something different than Dorothy's journey, as if he'd glimpsed her very soul. "What do you mean, sir?"

"Like Dorothy, everybody's on a journey, trying to find the things most important to them. Don't ever give up."

He reached toward her. She drew back, expecting the usual slap from an adult. But he gently touched her arm. "As my friend says, true courage is facing danger when you're afraid. Of that kind, you have plenty."

Which dangers? Drowning in the lake? Fear of the dark or being yelled at?

Voice buoyant, he picked up a twig. "Whether grass becomes a lion's mane or a horse's tail, whether dandelions become fairy caps or feather dusters, whether trees are kind or persnickety, you needn't fear how others view you."

The moment stretched in the shade, sunlight tickling its edges. Its magic reached shimmering Lake Michigan, caught in time, bound to her like an anchor to a boat.

"Papa, come play!" The two youngest boys tackled each other in the grass.

"Ah, my kiddiewinkles. Don't tell them I still call them that. That's Harry and Kenneth. The older boys are Frank and Robert. 'Twas a pleasure talking with you, Charlotte Rose."

Burdened by the charade, she looked down. "My name's Lodemia Jane."

He cupped her chin. "I know. That gives you the distinction of being one of a kind. But to me, you're just as much Charlotte Rose. It's all in how you see yourself."

As Charlotte Rose—building a fairy house together and talking about Oz—Janie saw herself as lovable. "What's *your* name, sir?"

The man laughed, such a jolly sound. "I, too, have a confession. I was christened after my Uncle Lyman, a fine fellow, but with a name I cannot endure. I use my middle name."

"What do I call you?"

"Mr. Baum, my dear. Mr. L. Frank Baum."

<hr>

May 1980

Carrie clapped. "Amazing! So, the thing that saved you is the thing that condemned you. Your imagination offered both escape and judgment."

Mrs. Gordon looked over her glasses. "You're worth your wages."

"The latter 1800s were a Golden Age. Children's stories shifted from moral lessons to food for imagination. You were a witness to literary history."

"In other words, old. I saw him each summer for nearly a decade at their summer home, near Holland. Then we corresponded for ten years."

"More talk of fairies and witches?"

"All manner of whimsy." Mrs. Gordon stared as if observing a distant memory, then wagged a finger. "Tell nobody of my memoirs."

Surely knowing more couldn't impair the questionable reputation she already had. "May I tell people I'm working for you? Or shall I conjure some wild story of why I barge into your house daily?" Maybe she'd evoke a smile.

"Of course, tell them. Otherwise, they'll think *you're* the crazy one." No visible smile, but perhaps it was threaded through the slight alteration of her voice. "You'll want to tell your grandparents how unhinged I am, but I'm entrusting these memories to you." Mrs. Gordon pointed to *The Pilgrim's Progress*. "Let's begin."

Familiar with the tale, Carrie read. Weighted down by a huge burden on his back, the protagonist, Christian, lived in the City of Destruction. One day, a man, Evangelist, warned him to flee from the wrath to come. En route, Christian ran into Obstinate and Pliable, who fell into the Slough of Despond—a murky mire of filth where men got dizzy and confused.

Frowning, Mrs. Gordon gripped the armrests. "What does Mr. Bunyan mean by the Slough of Despond?"

"It's a place of fears, doubts, and discouragement where people get stuck on their way to the Strait Gate. Christian had to press on to get help with his burden of sin. But fears and doubts plagued him, tempting him to return to the City of Destruction."

"Time to go." Mrs. Gordon's face was taut, as if fighting dismay. Was that a tear?

Carrie let herself out the door.

FIVE

May 29, 1980

During supper, despite Oma's undisguised curiosity and tainted commentary on Mrs. Gordon's deficits, Carrie resisted divulging confidences. Afterward, instead of redoing her résumé on the typewriter she'd brought, she typed Mrs. Gordon's memories.

Carrie suspected the former tearoom was key to understanding that enigmatic woman. Time to head there. She French-braided her hair, the way Brian liked it, tidy and proper —certainly not the way she'd left Barrowdale without telling him.

Evening sun suspended over the lake. The Brindlewood Café sign marked the sprawling two-story, red brick Victorian house, formerly the Broderick Inn. A gingerbread-trimmed porch, festooned with hanging plants, evolved into a turret and gazebo. The maple tree guarded the grassy knoll not swallowed by the parking lot. Concrete replacing paradise, as in Joni Mitchell's "Big Yellow Taxi."

Under that tree, Carrie assimilated that magical encounter

when Mr. Baum encouraged Janie's whimsy. Lake breezes massaged her hair.

Inside, enticing aromas of chicken and steak drenched her. Fake morning glories climbed latticework over a checkerboard floor of blue and white linoleum squares. Old farm implements, tins, and pottery lined shelves next to a jukebox. Seriously? A tasteless combination of early twentieth century and 1960s. Carrie mentally redecorated on the spot. Pure vintage 1900.

She'd love to renovate her own Victorian for the book café. But old homes and rezoning were cost-prohibitive. She'd settled on a diner downtown. The owner was selling by August —to her, if she got the loan. Tomorrow's meeting at the bank loomed.

Framed photos of old storefronts and sepia portraits adorned the walls. Tiny brass plaques identified the McKinnons in 1885, the Weavers in 1910, and others.

A middle-aged waitress, brown hair in a bun, set down a water glass at Carrie's booth. "I'm Alberta. We're featuring our famous Blueberry Cream Cheese Muffins in memory of the original Brodericks who started this café."

Resort and tearoom, not café. "One original is still alive." Carrie smiled. "Maybe the muffins should be in *honor* of Charlotte Gordon."

Alberta rolled her eyes. "She'll never step foot in here anyhow. Sold the place fifteen years ago. Rumors abound."

"Rumors?" How would Carrie untangle truth from fiction?

"That scandal about her husband, accused of murder. And bizarre menu items."

Strums of acoustic guitar chords wafted over. A folksy tune suggested a place of great charm, giving the decor something to aspire to. A dark-haired young man, probably late twenties, added melody: Gordon Lightfoot's "Race Among the Ruins." His slim, sturdy build and shaggy hair seemed better suited to mountain climbing. His red T-shirt lent an air of informality.

Carrie ordered strawberry pie. Long gone were the swinging half-doors. The room's atmosphere mingled with music like oil in water. Her gaze returned to the ruggedly handsome guitarist with a tug of guilt. She and Brian were practically engaged.

She jotted questions. What role did Teddy play before Mrs. Gordon married Walter? Where had Mr. Baum sat? When did the resort cease? She landed back on the musician crooning James Taylor's "Country Road." Closing her eyes, she absorbed his mellow voice, then gazed so as not to miss the compelling view. Of him.

Carrie savored pie and guitar picking. The singer seemed to feel the music in his fingers, his tapping toe. Her own foot tapped. She fancied him a man of strength, thriving as a free spirit, just as secure seeking mountain footholds as when standing on firm ground. Yet he immersed himself in the song's spirit, as if owning the weight of sadness. He ventured into the Eagles' tune "Desperado," about a man running from love. Singing to himself?

Carrie dashed to a vacant booth and read the portrait's label: The Sawyer Broderick Family, 1899. Sawyer and Elsa stood stony-eyed. Josephine, Maggie, and two older brothers competed for the "most bored" award. Seven-year-old Janie tilted her head as if seeking fairies.

"Makes you wonder what they're thinking, eh?"

The male voice startled her. The guitar player, smiling. More attractive up close. Vivid blue eyes complemented dark whiskers.

Carrie straightened. "Maybe the photographer just announced the end of the world."

He chuckled. "Why the interest in the portraits? I've got ten minutes. If I may take my break at your table."

"Sure, why not?" Brian, that's why not. But she welcomed the breadth of her summer rebellion.

He asked the waitress for water.

"You bet, hon." Alberta winked. "You always get your way with me."

Carrie scooted into her seat. "On cozy terms with Alberta."

"Middle-aged women love me. I'm Dirk." Evening's wispy light emphasized his sunbaked complexion, laugh lines, and more whiskers, unlike clean-shaven Brian.

His inner forearm revealed a tattoo: a plus sign—or X? MH over CD. She grimaced. Only greasy gas station attendants had tattoos. And other lowlifes. Must be a girl. Or two. Michelle Holmes. Carly Davis. "I'm Carrie. The portraits intrigue me because I'm doing research."

"Town hall and the library's microfilm newspapers have everything. Including Denny McLain's 1968 pitching record in *Sports Illustrated*. For winning a bet with my uncle."

She smirked. "Heavy duty research. What do you do, anyhow?"

"When I'm not pretending to be James Taylor? Easier to say what I *don't* do." He took a swig of water.

"Do you work on cars?"

"Have to with old rattletraps."

"Plumbing and electrical?"

"Did my share on old money pit houses my dad bought."

"Rock climbing and scuba diving?"

"Check. For both."

"You probably don't do heart surgery."

"I've been known to mend a broken heart." He smiled.

A ladies' man? No, his charm was more boyish.

"When my sister got dumped, I held her hand along the way."

"Lucky she had you. Sounds like you're a jack-of-all-trades. What's your day job?"

He checked his watch. "Gotta go play. Will you stay? I'll show you more portraits."

"Do you take requests?"

"Yup. Ones you heard, plus Joan Baez, Joni Mitchell, Jim Croce ..."

"How about 'Big Yellow Taxi'?"

"Consider it done."

Carrie's attention wavered between Dirk's rendition of Neil Diamond's "Brooklyn Roads" and jotting observations. What would it take to restore this room to its early 1900s charm?

Two years ago, Brian's reaction to her book café was a nod, as if patronizing a child's aspiration to be an astronaut. The more he talked, the more she fizzled. Brian, the practical one. The accountant. Fortunately, he'd jumped on board since then. Well, more like holding the rope and drifting behind in a lifeboat. But he'd agreed to move to Wolcott after they married so she could pursue her café dream here. He'd conceded to not telling her parents yet.

Tapping rhythm, Carrie watched Dirk. For a jack-of-all-trades, he was an accomplished guitarist. His tenor voice complemented his fingerpicking of "Both Sides Now."

Alberta popped by. "That Dirk's quite the charmer."

The fishbowl part of small towns. Did Alberta watch Dirk snag every girl who walked in?

Finally, Dirk played her request, then returned. "Thanks for waiting."

"Had to, if I wanted to hear my song."

He laughed. "Kept you here, didn't it?"

"So did wanting to see the portraits." She sipped water. "You play beautifully."

"Thanks. May I treat you to dessert?" he asked.

"No, thanks. But go ahead."

He ordered cheesecake. Impeccably mannered Brian wouldn't do that. She should be home calling him.

Dirk led her to another room with larger tables. "They use this for parties." Sunlight streamed through tall transomed windows between Victorian vines-and-rose wallpaper. Cherry woodwork appeared intact. Two wingback chairs flanked the hearth.

"Beautiful!" Carrie visualized little Janie prancing across the floral rug, promenading with fairy friends, hiding in nooks, spying on brownies and elves.

Dirk waved her to the far wall. More Broderick family portraits: 1895 with Janie at age three; 1904, twelve and bright-eyed, still seeking wonder. When did her demeanor change to cranky? Carrie squinted, as if by closer examination she could absorb knowledge of family dynamics.

Dirk plopped into a wingback chair. His red T-shirt contrasted a fabric of fronds, mauve petals, and gold chenille. He seemed oblivious to the incongruity. "Alberta makes deliveries."

Carrie sat. "So, your day job?"

"Here's the CliffsNotes version of the past nine years. I majored in business awhile but felt stifled. Fortunately, I missed the draft, so I took a cross-country bike trip, visited Germany, then volunteered with a crew sailing from Florida to South America." He fidgeted as if sitting still was a bigger challenge than meeting sharks. "That devoured my bank account, so I came home to Holland to work odd jobs, including construction."

"Did you return to school?"

"Nope. Took a missions trip to Kenya, then managed a Grand Haven restaurant for two years. Two summers ago, I went whitewater rafting and climbing in Colorado, then took a camp job in northern Michigan. We hosted kids' retreats, built cabins, and did maintenance."

Carrie lifted her chin. A college dropout. "So, you work long enough to earn money for the next adventure." Brian would have choice words for such lack of focus. He'd also fit this decor. "A little Peter Pan syndrome?"

"Peter Pan would figure out how to do fun stuff without working in between."

"So, what about your day job?"

"My aunt told me this café was looking for new blood. I've been playing guitar seventeen years, since age eleven."

"You want to go further with your music?"

He put a fist to his heart. "Isn't this the ultimate, right here in Wolcott?"

She smiled. "And your day job?"

"Keep getting off track, don't I?"

Much like your life.

"Can't survive on music alone, so I'm working for Uncle John at the hardware store. I live with him and my aunt. What brings *you* to our fair Wolcott?"

Running away from home. Ha! "Visiting my grandparents." Her eyes darted from the mantel to the windows. "This room is gorgeous, but something is missing. Books."

"Books?"

"A combination bookstore-café. Paradise for book lovers." She paused, testing his reaction. "With chairs by a fireplace."

"Great idea. Reading with a good meal in the bargain."

"Yup. I envision a Victorian house with nooks and crannies, rooms decorated in different time periods, featuring an author. A Dickens room. A Twain room. A Jane Austen room. Even children's authors."

"A Dr. Seuss book nook?" He grinned. "Serving green eggs and ham?" She laughed. "What would you call this delightful place?"

"Bilbo's Bistro. Or Tabletop Tales and Tea."

"I love the concept."

Alberta walked in with cheesecake. "This room isn't officially open."

"You make exceptions, right?" Dirk flashed a charming smile.

"Watch out for him," Alberta said. "He knows how to get his way."

What did *that* mean? Carrie glanced at his tattoo. MH. Did he have his way with Maizie? "Are you a reader?"

"Anything with adventure. Plus, C.S. Lewis, especially *The Screwtape Letters*. And Calvin's *Institutes*." He started eating.

"The *Institutes*? You're kidding, right?"

He chuckled and winked. "You've read them?"

"Parts. For class."

"Let me guess. Calvin College?"

"Yes."

He lowered his voice. "We shouldn't be seen together."

"You went to Hope?"

He smirked. "That, I can neither confirm nor deny."

"Well, good. I'm tired of the rivalry."

"You can't escape it. I'm Dirk Vandenakker. Steeped in three generations of Hope College."

"Besides your Dutch pedigree." Maybe he had Dutch girlfriends: MH for Marta Havenga. CD for Catrina DeGraaf. "I'm wondering what I'm up against."

"Okay. My ancestors came over with Dr. Van Raalte, 1847. I attended Camp Calvin for six summers. How 'bout you?"

"Carrie Kruisselbrink." She offered a firm handshake.

"Can't get more Dutch than that. Hey, what's stopping you from starting the café?"

She couldn't reveal her plans. Not even her grandparents knew yet. "My four-year education in elementary ed. My parents paid for college, with strings attached." Strings she was cutting. "Just graduated." Almost.

"Where do you want to teach?"

"Not sure," seemed safe enough to say without lying.

"Teaching creates a dilemma for the café. Unless you hire a good manager during the school year."

Divert. "Tell me about your restaurant managing experience in Grand Haven."

His anecdotes revealed his expertise countered by staff

ineptness, besides his own foibles. All of which had her laughing. "If you can top those fiascos, please do."

"I can. I worked three summers at Bill Knapp's, then three summers at an upstart café in Barrowdale." Neither of which thrilled her parents. Though they constantly dined out, they took a dim view of Carrie owning her own restaurant. Not suitable for a graduate headed for marriage and a family. Too financially risky, too much staff turnover, too many crazy hours.

And definitely not within her reach. They'd established her inadequacy early on. But she'd win them over once they saw her in action. Meanwhile, the charade continued.

She shared several humorous waitress stories and her own management nightmares, but nothing that made her look incompetent.

Dirk scooted forward. "Skip teaching. A diploma's a springboard to possibilities, not a binding contract. A book café makes perfect sense, if you've a passion for it."

Should she share her plan for 572 Walnut Street? "Look, I've got a lot going on."

Dirk took his last bite. "My problem is balancing too *many* interests. My mom says she followed me from toy to toy. I'm still going from toy to toy."

Like a toddler. "Think you'll ever settle down?"

"Meaning, is there anything that holds my interest beyond a year? Maybe. But we're talking about you. Are you doing family research?"

"I'm working for an older town resident, Charlotte Gordon. Just for the summer. Brian and I will be engaged soon and we're moving here."

"Brian's your lucky guy, eh?"

"We've been dating since high school. He's an accountant in Kalamazoo."

"Perfect. He'll take charge of café finances."

She rolled her eyes. "It's just a crazy idea."

"Who told you that? Accountant Brian?"

She bristled. "Drop it, will you?" Her words came out harsh. What was wrong with her?

"I'm sorry. I overstepped."

Unused to receiving apologies, Carrie sat stunned.

"Hey, I live by *carpe diem*. Life's too short to not pursue goals." Dirk rapped the chair arm. "Where's this fire coming from? Your anger, I mean. Your passion for squelching a good idea." His blue eyes intensified.

"I'm not angry at you. Forgive me for barking. And—okay, here's the deal. I *am* pursuing my book café. The owner of Dunham's Diner on Walnut is selling to me in July when I get financing."

"Seriously? That's fantastic."

"But I'm keeping it under wraps for now."

"Why? That's something to crow about."

He'd never understand her insecurities. She stood. "I should go."

"Hey. If you need a tour of Broderick land, you know where to find me."

Six

Back at home, Carrie waved a five-dollar bill. "May I call Brian long distance?"

"Go ahead." Oma tucked a half-eaten pie into the corner and lined canisters in front. "Got a mousetrap? Your opa can't stay away."

Opa chuckled. "Doing you a favor, Tanna. Pie won't go stale."

Giggling, Carrie ventured to the den, singing "Big Yellow Taxi," guitar strums echoing. That Dirk! He probably had flings, not friendships. The tattoo told all. Thank goodness for Brian's predictability, stable employment, and money in the bank. Settled into the couch, thankful for long cords, she dialed his number.

"Hello." Brian's voice flowed like rich chocolate.

"Brian!"

"Finally. I missed you. Your parents mentioned the sudden change of plans."

"I'm spending the summer with my grandparents and found a job already."

"Why'd you leave so fast without telling me first?" He sounded hurt. "What about Ophelia's?"

"I'm sorry, Brian. I had to go. Rita has enough staff."

"Your mom said you left in a huff."

Carrie grimaced. "They were on my case daily. I couldn't breathe right to suit them."

"They're worried you don't have a teaching job yet. After paying your tuition."

"With stipulations. Educational benefits aren't always tangible." *A springboard to possibilities.* How would Carrie confess not wanting to teach? Or failing a class, lacking a diploma?

"My grad party's end of June," Brian said. "It'd be good to have your job confirmed by then."

So his parents and their cronies could be impressed with her future career snapping into place? She resorted to monotone. "I'm coming."

"Working fast food this summer?"

She chuckled. "No, I'm a construction flagger on Highway 31." Mention of any job henceforth would surely be an improvement.

"What?" His tone hinted she should call Kalamazoo paramedics to administer CPR.

"I'm the only girl on a crew of ten." Silence. Her face heated as the distance thickened between them. "Just kidding."

Relief filled his voice. "Whew, thought you had a touch of fever."

She'd once played Elvis Presley's "Fever" for him, almost got him to the point of snapping his fingers, shaking his shoulders. "You know I only have fever for *you.*"

"Carrie, that's unbecoming for a nice girl like you."

Her face burned warmer, and not with Elvis's "Fever." Brian only used her name in reprimand, never tenderness. He surely graduated *cum laude moral superiority.* "Should I croon 'Amazing Grace' instead?"

"Don't be irreverent. So, what's the job?"

She cringed. He'd question her own sanity for taking

unorthodox employment with the town eccentric. "A lady who ran the Broderick Resort hired me for research."

"The resort's history?"

She inhaled, then let it out in a jumble. "Charlotte Gordon wants me to help clear her husband's name."

Dismay shaped his voice. "What'd he do?"

"She says nothing, but he was accused of murder in 1918. She's paying twice minimum wage for a forty-hour week. She lives in this Victorian house, surrounded by books and rumors. Hundreds of children's books—signed first editions."

"Interesting."

His flat tone chagrinned her. "It's *fascinating*. Plus, I'll have time to test my recipes. Tomorrow, I meet with the loan officer."

He sighed. "But sweetheart, how will opening a restaurant work while teaching?"

Why'd he only call her sweetheart when criticizing? She sizzled. "Come on, Brian, we've talked through this. There's no time to teach."

More silence. "Yes, but the restaurant business is brutal and risky. Sixty percent of them fail in the first year. Staff turnover is high. I hate to see you go through so much trouble only to fail."

"You think I can't succeed?"

"Just considering the odds."

"I can beat the odds, Brian." Her words gathered force. "I have a unique concept and menu. Experience in two restaurants. I have the best mentor and a fantastic business plan. I took two business electives. And I know how to hire the right people."

"But your parents expect you to teach."

Why couldn't she just tell him she hated teaching? "I can't live in their box anymore. I tried, but I need to succeed on my own terms." While desperately craving their approval.

"When will you tell them?"

"After the loan's approved and I buy the building."

"You think they're gonna be happy you're not using those four years of college they just paid for?"

"What? You've always supported my café venture."

"I *do* support you, sweetheart. But you're not seeing clearly. I honestly didn't think you'd take it this far."

Dirk had cracked open the door of possibility. Brian slammed it shut. With the force of stormy Lake Michigan waves. Brian, the one voted most likely to succeed, didn't want to be attached to potential failure. He chatted as if unaware of the stomach punch he'd given. "Can you visit this weekend? I want to take you to Win Schuler's. Prime rib, candlelight."

"When can you come *here*?"

"That'll be tough with full-time work."

She stared at the phone. Mrs. Gordon thought she had spunk. Why'd it dissipate around Brian and her parents? Brian was her knight in shining armor, gallantly dashing in to rescue her from parental control of every move. Now he seemed like a humorless foreign dignitary.

"Love you," he said.

She hesitated. "Good night."

Something was profoundly different.

SEVEN

Friday, May 30, 1980

When Carrie arrived, the drapes were open farther than yesterday. Parquet flooring lightened to honey tones. The oriental rug's blossoms formed crisper edges. Parlor furniture promised fresh apple green, salmon, and ivory in stripes and florals, topped with chintz and damask pillows. Mrs. Gordon rocked in the chair.

Carrie sat by the window. "When's the last time you went to the café?"

"When the tearoom disappeared, 1965." Mrs. Gordon shuddered. "Updated."

"They have antique farm tools, tins, and photographs of old-time Wolcott."

"Oil and water, pearls and swine."

"They serve Broderick muffins."

"They don't have my recipes. A shame customers won't know any better. It's like not knowing Hermes from Hercules." She folded her hands. "Did you see a large, framed Kodak, four boys and a girl? A candid shot near the lake, from 1902."

"No."

"I have the original snapshot. But some history first."

⁂

Janie, 9
August 1901

Janie hosted a doll tea party in the peach orchard. Stuffed with imaginary pistachio cupcakes and gooseberry tea, she returned china teacups to the kitchen, hoping Mother wouldn't notice. She poured water for another drink.

A sonorous voice drifted from the dining room. "We were destined to return, Mrs. Broderick, after eating your most delectable blueberry muffins last year."

Janie squeezed her teacup. *Mr. Baum!* She peered through the door slats.

"I haven't made muffins right since," Mrs. Baum said. "If I hear once more about Mrs. Broderick's muffins, Mrs. Broderick's fried potatoes ..."

The man let loose a hearty laugh. "Maud, you exaggerate."

"Look who's talking about exaggeration."

He lifted his coffee cup. "May I? You brew a sturdy pot of coffee. I like mine strong enough to float a spoon."

"Sugar and cream keep it afloat," Mrs. Baum quipped. Mother poured more coffee.

Mr. Baum sampled it. "Is your Charlotte Rose around? I'd love to see her again."

Janie gulped, frozen.

"We've no Charlotte Rose here," Mother said. Janie's face heated.

"I'm certain you do," Mr. Baum replied.

Mrs. Baum smirked. "There you go, mixing up fantasy and reality."

"Lodemia Jane, that's it," he said. "We had a charming exchange."

Janie cringed. *Don't mention fairies and witches.* Mother would be furious. Janie dropped the teacup. It shattered.

Mother whisked in. "You broke my good china!"

Janie stifled a whimper. "I'm sorry."

"Get the broom," Mother barked. "You're nothing but trouble."

The kitchen doors popped open. There stood tall, dignified Mr. Baum, broom in hand. "Allow me." He swept porcelain chunks into a dustpan. "I traveled years as a china salesman and broke 5,287 cups. Accidentally, of course."

Mother tried to grab the broom. "Mr. Baum, no guest cleans my daughter's mess."

He swept, singing "Polly Wolly Doodle" in a rich baritone voice, then dumped shattered china into the wastebasket. Amusement lit his face. He bowed gallantly as if on stage. "Miss Charlotte Rose, how do you do?"

She looked back and forth between grinning Mr. Baum and her scowling mother, then curtsied like Cinderella. "'Tis charming to see you, sir."

Chuckling, he waved toward the dining room. "May she join us?"

With pursed lips, Mother nodded.

Janie exhaled. "Mr. Baum, will you sign my books?" She raced upstairs and gathered *Mother Goose in Prose; Father Goose, His Book; The Wonderful Wizard of Oz; A New Wonderland;* and *Dot and Tot in Merryland.* All Baum books, courtesy of Aunt Sophie.

Moments later, she dropped the stack on the table with pen and ink. The youngest son dragged another chair over. His hair appeared comb-resistant.

Janie sat. Mr. Baum wrote with a left-handed flourish.

"Charlotte, I'm Mrs. Baum." Her cheerful expression was buoyed by a row of ruffles at her neck. "This is Frank. He's seventeen. Robert's fifteen. Harry's eleven. Kenneth, ten."

"Eleven and a half," Harry said. "How old are you?"

"Nine."

Harry grinned and punched Kenneth. "Told you."

"Boys, mind your manners." Mrs. Baum clasped Harry's shoulder.

Kenneth pouted, pale cheeks the epitome of feigned innocence, as if he well knew how to play the youngest brother role.

"What'd you guess?" Janie asked, charmed by banter over predicting her age.

"Nine," Harry replied, "but Ken insisted you were ten."

Janie smiled coyly. "Then maybe I'm really ten." They laughed, Mr. Baum the loudest.

When Janie's family ate, children speaking was akin to trailing mud through the house. Words muddled inside her. She finally blurted, "Mr. Baum, where'd you get your ideas for Oz and the Emerald City?"

He picked a popover from the basket. "Well, my dear, Oz is a place I discovered rather than invented."

Robert's brows arched over gray eyes like his father's. "Ever hear of the White City, Charlotte? The 1893 World's Fair, bright with a million electric lights."

"Imagine wearing green glasses there," Harry added. "Everything's green."

"Oz looks like the White City?" Janie's father often remarked on the Columbian Exhibition, much like Aesop's fox despising out-of-reach grapes.

"Or the Celestial City in *Pilgrim's Progress*," Frank said.

"Or the City Beautiful in *Two Little Pilgrims' Progress*?" Janie asked. It was about two poor farm twins traveling to the White City.

Mr. Baum explained to Kenneth. "That's Frances Hodgson Burnett's tale about the pursuit of the American Dream."

So much table talk! Broderick dinnertime was a droning dialog of business and social commentary, followed by stilted scripture readings, pious critiques, Janie's yawns, and desire to quickly leave the table.

The Baum conversation, though, bounced between the White City's Ferris Wheel, Mr. Edison's kinetoscope, and Tesla's winning the bid over Edison for the illuminations. "With alternating current," Robert asserted as if he'd made the selection himself.

"Alternating, direct, or upside down." Kenneth shrugged. "Who cares?"

Robert rapped his fist on Kenneth's head before Mrs. Baum deflected it.

"Charlotte," Mr. Baum said, "ideas come from many sources. I've sold china, observed cyclones and hot air balloons. Many events found a home in Dorothy's experience."

"Will Dorothy return to Oz?" Janie asked.

"If so, the Ozians might not tell me. They keep to themselves. Instead, I'm creating a stage experience for her. My associates, Mr. Tietjens and Mr. Denslow, have been with me at Macatawa, composing music for an Oz musical extravaganza."

"Were you in shows?"

Mr. Baum dabbed butter on another popover. "Several. The best was *The Maid of Arran*. But I gave up theater to sell Castorine Oil." He smirked. "Otherwise, I wouldn't have written a book about chickens."

She stifled a giggle. "A chicken story?"

"No, it's about breeding chickens."

Robert patted Janie's book pile. "Unfortunately, you don't have *The Master Key*" —he pointed thumbs to himself— "for which *I'm* the sole inspiration. A boy named Rob experiments with electricity, batteries, motors, wires—"

"Until," Frank said, "the demon of electricity brings him incredible gifts."

"Like a device that helps him fly at any height and speed." Harry's hand sailed across the table and knocked his milk glass. Mrs. Baum swooped in for the rescue. Not a drop spilled.

"And," Kenneth added, "a record of events shows everything happening in the world during the past twenty-four hours."

"A set of spectacles," Rob said, "shows a letter on people's foreheads, indicating their character. *G* for good, *W* for wise, *F* for foolish."

"I see a *B* on your forehead," Harry said to Robert. "For boondoggler." He faced Janie. "His lollygagging always makes us late."

"Lollygagging to you is industry to me," Robert said. "Remember that next time you want to run my railroad."

Mr. Baum poured more coffee. "I see *R* for rambunctious on all of you." He turned to Janie. "I wrote *The Master Key* in mind of boys who love adventure."

"*I* like adventure." Though Janie's were imagined.

"Then read it. A girl may do anything she pleases." To prove it, Mrs. Baum poured a cascade of honey into her peach tea.

Mr. Baum wiped his mustache. "Mr. Lewis Carroll, God rest his soul, created the first modern fairy tale with a girl heroine. Except Alice's elegant adventure is naught but a dream. Dorothy's experience is absolutely real."

"Papa." Kenneth swirled his fork. "This cheesy broccoli reminds me of that menu you made for Grandma Gage." The broccoli spear bounced on the table.

Mrs. Baum leaned over Harry and thunked Kenneth's wrist down. "Manners, please."

Ignoring the projectile, Mr. Baum sliced his beef. "Ah, yes, the Hotel La Femme needed a worthy menu. We had Strong-willed Head of Cauliflower, Undaunted Though Smothered in Cheese Sauce." He reached for his wife's hand.

Mrs. Baum smiled. "Mother's favorite was Chicken Cordon Bleu in the Face."

He explained. "That's because no amount of talking changes a mind in that household."

"What food would you name after us?" Kenneth asked.

"Ragamuffins, no doubt." He tousled Kenneth's hair. "The Gage dessert is Sticky Caramel Angel Food Cake Snare. The sweetness is deceptive, for Gage women rush in where angels fear to tread." The boys laughed. Mrs. Baum offered a satisfied smile.

Thus launched more food talk from the World's fair: the salt Statue of Liberty, the life-size chocolate Venus de Milo statue, a prune knight on horseback, a USA map of pickles.

"'Tis astonishing what one accomplishes with ordinary objects and a little ingenuity," Mr. Baum said. "Let's head to the dune. Will you join us, Charlotte?"

Her stomach fluttered like a blooming flower, petals tickling. "I'd love to!"

EIGHT

1901

Outside, as if carefree breezes conquered all caution, Harry turned cartwheels. "The Kodak is science and magic combined."

"Best combination ever." Mr. Baum fiddled with his accordion-style Kodak. "Ken's camera is Kodak Brownie Number Two, named after those rascally brownies Mr. Cox is so fond of drawing."

Janie tugged at the hat ribbons Mother had tied snugly under her chin. "Can it photograph them?"

His mustache twitched. "We've not succeeded. Point if you see any."

They flung shoes and stockings on the sand. Janie's feet sank into the grains, a luxurious indulgence.

"Papa took a thousand cloud pictures in Aberdeen," Kenneth said.

"We've developed photographs in our basement," Robert added.

At the dune's base, Mr. Baum waved toward a clump of tall

grasses. "Let's take a picture." The boys charged over while Janie examined the Kodak. He pointed out features. "It's nothing like those confounded cameras that take ten minutes for one shot due to opening the aperture to let in enough light. I've never met a grimmer lot, have you?"

"I use that time to make up stories in my head."

"No better way to spend time." He let her touch buttons on the camera.

Her father never allowed her near valuable objects. She peered through the viewfinder to see the boys' silly expressions. Kenneth hopped on Rob's back, Harry on Frank's.

Mr. Baum winked. "Go with the boys." Janie trotted over. Her hat slid off, hanging by ribbons. Aiming, he yelled, "Tarts and tadpoles!"

"Hold still, Robert," Mrs. Baum said. "Harry, stop punching Ken."

They posed with broad smiles. Breezes whipped Janie's hair.

Traversing the steep incline, Janie bounded behind the boys. Kenneth waited, then showed her how to use his camera. "Mother says I'll pay for it if it breaks, a whole dollar. Here, maybe you'll see brownies."

Janie squinted through the hole toward the lake. No brownies. As she snapped the picture, Kenneth popped in front of the camera, laughing.

"Hey! You ruined my photograph," Janie spouted in mock exasperation.

Kenneth gave the camera to his mother and proceeded unhampered.

Sand stretched on all sides, every step a chore. On top, Janie squinted at squawking gulls, sunlight on wings against cerulean blue sky. The boys bounced down the dune, leaving Janie behind. Dizzy, she froze. Her stomach lurched. Such a long way down!

Mr. Baum patted her shoulder. "You've more courage than you think."

Heart pounding, Janie sucked in the breeze, then jumped free as an eagle, arms like wings. She sprinted down, then looked up. Mr. and Mrs. Baum embraced at the top, kissing as if alone in the world. She'd never seen her parents kiss.

The kids scrambled up again. They rolled down partway, then hopped a zigzag line.

Hot and sweaty, they raced to the shore. The boys stripped to tank tops and plunged into the water, creating a ruckus.

"Go ahead, dear," Mrs. Baum said. "I'll hold your hat and pinafore."

Janie discarded petticoats, then dipped her toes in. Cold tingled her feet. Waves slapped her legs. She stepped farther, dress ballooning around her thighs. Kenneth splashed her. She splashed back. The game was on.

An hour later, they dried on the beach. Kenneth flopped by Janie in the sand.

"Look!" Robert pointed up.

A hot air balloon floated. She waved to the balloonist, jumping with Harry and Kenneth, yelling to be rescued. If her parents saw, they'd yank her home to administer a sound thrashing for such unruly behavior.

Back at the house after the Baums left, Mother glared at the sandy puddle under Janie, as if sand were as ruthless an intruder as robbers. "Lodemia Jane, did you bathe in your dress?"

The blooming flower in her stomach wilted. Waves that had refreshed a few minutes earlier now drowned her. She stared at the dry pile: hat, pinafore, stockings, shoes.

Mother dragged her to the tin tub in back. "Your face is sunburned. Your dress is torn, your sleeves filthy." Mother's scrubbing ground sand into her skin. Janie hunkered down in the tub. "What's this Charlotte nonsense?"

"I told him that's my name."

Mother slapped her. "You wicked girl!"

Cheek stinging, Janie bowed her head over scrunched-up knees, hands behind her neck, as if taking cover in a cyclone. Mother tugged her hair. "I labor teaching you manners and morals, bringing you up on the Good Book. You thank me by lying to guests. You make a fool of me every day."

Gritting her teeth, Janie closed her eyes in shame. Mother yanked her from the tub, wrapped her with a sheet from the clothesline. "Get to your room."

Janie sprinted across the yard like Cinderella running from the ball, her beautiful gown in rags, her lovely day dropped like a glass slipper. She'd be doomed to housework. Like Dorothy, too, stuck in the Wicked Witch's castle.

In her room, rolled in the sheet, Janie hugged the Dorothy rag doll Aunt Sophie had made and read Mr. Baum's inscription in *The Wonderful Wizard of Oz*:

August 1901

To my dear friend Charlotte Rose,

May you ever dwell in the Oz of your own imagination.

Ozily,
L. Frank Baum

Cradling Dorothy, she leaned back, arms and legs feeling sand and waves.

Her mother barged in and tossed her a frock. "Get dressed."

Trembling, Janie drew up her knees, book trapped between her thighs and chest. Mother pulled the sheet, seized the book, and charged out.

"No!" Fighting tears, Janie scrambled into a dress.

Mother popped back in and thumped a book on the bed.

"Read *this*." *The Pilgrim's Progress*. "No more devil's fodder." She snatched all Janie's Baum books and dashed out.

Bawling, Janie ran downstairs. The books perched on top of the dining room hutch. Mother lunged from the kitchen, shaking a wooden spoon. "Hush now. Guests are coming."

Janie shrieked all the way upstairs and flung herself on the bed, heaving sobs. She hurled Mother's book across the room. She'd never read it.

She crawled to the bookshelf and waded through titles: *The Princess and the Goblin, The Yellow Fairy Book, The Book of Dragons*, three from the Brownies series. She paged through Walter Crane's *Beauty and the Beast* and Arthur Rackham's fairy tales of the Brothers Grimm. She must hide them. But how would she retrieve the books Mr. Baum signed?

May 1980

Stomach knotting, Carrie sat spellbound. "No wonder you never read *Pilgrim's Progress*. That's unwarranted punishment for having a lovely day, for liking the name Charlotte Rose." Did a troubled childhood explain Mrs. Gordon's grouchiness?

"Mother believed Great-aunt Lodemia would reach her gnarly hand from the grave if Mother called me anything else. She'd say, 'Be glad I didn't name you after Aunt Mehitabel.'"

"How'd you see yourself when you were Charlotte?"

Eyes filmy, Mrs. Gordon gazed across the room. "I was inimitable, unsinkable. Imaginative. Even beautiful." She folded her hands. "I saw myself as loved."

The words fluttered like breezes through laundry. "May I see the photo?"

"I wish I had that enlarged photo, but this will have to do." Mrs. Gordon withdrew the small Kodak image from the drawer. Though faded gray nibbled at the edges of each form, the joy of five exuberant faces shone through as vividly as velvet through lace. Even the lake behind them sparkled.

Feeling pangs of her own rare moments of childhood joy, Carrie wished she could recapture that happiness for Mrs. Gordon, right then, right there.

NINE

Friday, May 30, 1980

Though the bank's air conditioning blew cool air, Carrie's palms sweated. Her dress might as well be a parka.

Mr. Haberfeld scanned her fifteen-page business proposal as if he had better things to do. Not a gray hair was out of place. She hoped he'd say the same for her proposal. Her future depended on this meeting.

He finally looked up. "Miss Kruisselbrink—may I call you Carrie?"

"Of course, sir." Whatever would make him more favorable to her request.

"I've never seen such a unique restaurant concept, combining both books and food. Bilbo's Bistro sounds enchanting. The literary-themed menu is incomparable."

"Thank you. That's my favorite part. I eventually hope to alternate monthly menus based on authors and classics." Perhaps she shouldn't have said *favorite*, as if the uncreative, mundane tasks were beneath her.

"How'd you choose your location and business classification?"

"I've always wanted to be sole proprietor, hands down. I chose Wolcott for its proximity to Holland, Saugatuck, and Douglas, considering tourism. I spent a year scoping out downtown Wolcott and targeted Dunham's Diner after observing their popularity, traffic, neighboring businesses, and customer profiles. The owner wants to sell by August, and I'm the first contender." *Assuming the loan comes through.* "I have my business license and will obtain other permits and certificates upon acquiring the building." She uttered a silent sigh. *Don't state the obvious.*

"So, why are you reinventing the wheel instead of opening a franchise with a proven business model and track record?"

She gulped, despite anticipating such skepticism. "Fair question. As much as I enjoyed working at Bill Knapp's and an upstart café, I loved helping my mentor Rita's brainchild grow into a thriving business. Ophelia's. Besides attending seminars, I learned hands-on from Rita."

"Such as ..."

See page three. "Ordering inventory, evaluating food wastage, dealing with rude customers and disgruntled employees, hiring and firing, managing the books, doing payroll, scheduling, plus cooking, serving, and hosting." Releasing a long breath, she resisted the urge to swipe her sweaty forehead.

"Did you consider *renting* a facility?" His tone brought her father to mind. Questions asked not just to probe the problem but to call attention to her ineptness.

"Yes, but with the literary theme, I'll need renovations I can't do with a rental."

"What about a pop-up featuring signature dishes to ease your way in? Since you're an unknown entity here, a pop-up or catering business could build your clientele and reputation before jumping in full force."

His words expanded like oppressive heat on a blistering day, undermining her best efforts. She forced confidence into her voice. "I've considered those options, but I'm fully prepared to invest myself in the café. Also, my grandparents have been established in this community over thirty years. That works in my favor."

"Yes, it does." He turned a page. "Glowing recommendations, but two business classes with an education degree?"

Degree. She winced. She'd written that months ago, assuming she'd have it. Now wasn't the time to explain her parents' college stipulations with no clue about her café plans. "Teaching's a backup plan, sir." *Was.* But any joy, creativity, and confidence had been squashed to the point of nausea whenever she entered the classroom. *Redirect.* She asked questions about the loan.

He clarified the loan would cover initial renovations and expenses for a year, when she'd presumably break even. Expenses included permits, liability insurance, staff wages, food, and every necessity for success.

Though casually twirling his pen, he homed in like gulls to a fish. "How will you prevent high turnover? Average restaurant turnover rate is seventy-five percent. Plus, restaurant stress is akin to brain surgery."

"I'll offer benefits and competitive compensation. I'll develop a full-time staff of experienced adults aligned with my vision." She caught her breath. "I'll treat employees the way I want them to treat customers, by addressing grievances. I'll require three weeks of on-the-job training with feedback rather than just handing them a manual."

Words spilled out as if she were approaching a marathon finish line. "I'll offer flexible work hours, especially for young moms, plus bonuses and cash incentives, such as quarterly referring contests. All listed on page seven." *Whew.*

"Fine ideas. What else ensures your success?"

His rapid-fire questions unnerved her. "We'll have a soft opening to iron out wrinkles. My marketing plan includes flyers and radio spots. Keeping with the literary theme, I'll stamp guests' passports to Narnia, Middle-earth, Dickens's London, the Mississippi River, and other novel destinations. Ten stamps earn a free meal or appetizer. I also want to host fundraisers by partnering with non-profits, to draw crowds and win community support."

"You've certainly thought of everything." He leaned forward, hands folded on the desk. "Owning a restaurant is not for the faint of heart, Carrie. There's a boatload of challenges to contend with, mostly while thinking on your feet. How will you handle those?"

"With grace and humor." Did he suspect she was biting off more than she could chew? "My mentor saw me in every scenario. She and other references will vouch for me." Did she sound haughty? Did he want examples? Her head was spinning.

He set the proposal on a paper pile. "We'll be in touch in July."

Reeling from the meeting, Carrie moseyed to Mrs. Gordon's. *Breathe.* She fanned her face. Mr. Haberfeld's presence still hovered, suffocating her. She'd done her best. Was it good enough? Was her churning stomach from nerves or Elsa Broderick's harshness toward her daughter in 1901?

Mrs. Gordon was in the kitchen. Teakettle steam rose to a tin ceiling. Cheerful mugs hung from a shelf lined with plates of fairy tale scenes. Folktale figures splashed the tile mural over the stove. The hutch featured Kate Greenaway glassware and pottery. Above the dinette hung a Tenniel illustration of The Mad Hatter's Tea Party.

Carrie reveled in the whimsy. "I love this kitchen!"

"No dillydallying." Mrs. Gordon pulled a wooden box from the cupboard. "Find Elsa Broderick's Blueberry Cream Cheese Muffin recipe. Also known as Munchkin Delights."

"Munchkin Delights?"

"The tearoom specialized in baked goods and desserts. Muffins came in two sizes, regular and Munchkin."

Carrie laughed. "Was that on the menu?"

"Since 1956, when *The Wizard of Oz* entered public domain. With permission, I also served Jack Pumpkinhead Bars, Bunbury Popovers, Rigmaroles, and Cayke's Magic Dishpan Cookies inspired by Baum's other Oz books."

"Anything named for Dorothy?"

"Home Sweet Home Chicken and Dumplings."

"Creative menu." How'd this cantankerous woman contrive such playful names?

Mrs. Gordon squinted at her. "Did you change into a dress?"

Carrie flushed. "Um, yeah. It's so hot out." She was bursting to talk about the meeting and could learn much from the woman. But no. She'd have to confess her college failure, inviting criticism. Mrs. Gordon wasn't safe yet.

"I can't sit idle while the café passes off insipid dustballs for genuine Broderick baked goods. Today you'll experience authentic tearoom muffins."

Carrie lingered over smeared recipes dotted with batter. "Maple Oatmeal Biscuits, Carrot Spice Scones."

"At this rate, nothing will get accomplished." Mrs. Gordon crossed her arms. "They're family secrets."

"Not under lock and key?"

"They've been perfectly safe until today."

Hoping Mrs. Gordon would let down her guard, Carrie bounced *B* words on her tongue. "May I try Brown Butter Bourbon Banana Bread?"

Mrs. Gordon rummaged through the cupboard, plopping items onto the counter. "You can't resist alliteration."

"Guilty as charged. Dirk would appreciate a Broderick special."

Mrs. Gordon looked over her glasses. "Dirk who?"

"Dirk at the café. As a tip for fine guitar playing." Carrie flipped through cards. "Eureka! Found it."

"I named Eureka's Caramel Hazelnut Tea after Eureka, the kitten in *Dorothy and the Wizard in Oz*. Especially good with milk."

"I prefer sugar."

"Sugar distorts the taste. Did they teach nothing useful at college?"

Carrie smiled. "Not about tea."

"Education consists of what's vital. University is overrated and expensive. Ray Bradbury never attended college. After high school, during the Depression, he went to the library three days weekly for ten years."

"Did you attend college, Mrs. Gordon?"

Her voice tightened. "I'm self-taught."

They poured batter into two muffin tins, large and small, a cream cheese dollop between layers. Mrs. Gordon waved a canister of tea leaves. "Dorothy's Red Ruby Raspberry Hibiscus Tea."

Carrie adopted a serious tone. "Dorothy wore silver shoes in the book, not ruby slippers."

"You've proven your worth again." Mrs. Gordon put tea leaves in the strainer. "In Hawaii, girls wear the hibiscus blossom behind the left ear, if spoken for. Behind the right if available. Yours would go on the left? For Dirk?"

Carrie winced. "No, my boyfriend's Brian."

Mrs. Gordon jiggled the strainer. "Jamaicans and Mexicans add ginger and press juice from the flower's calyces, add cloves, cinnamon, even rum, and serve it chilled on Christmas."

Soon they sat at the table topped by a cabbage rose teapot, with matching cups and saucers. Butter dripped over muffins.

Carrie sampled hers. "Delicious. Oma would love this."

"Dirk, too?" Mrs. Gordon's eyebrows rose. "Or Brian?"

"Dirk." Carrie wiped butter off her chin. "Brian's in Kalamazoo."

"So, you love baking?"

"Yup." This was her chance to reveal the café plan and cooking experiments. But she couldn't. Not yet. "My freshman year at Calvin, I baked monthly in the dorm kitchen. Before Christmas break, my roommate and I had a hankering for *oliebollen*, to survive exams. Other kids were using the kitchen, so we made *oliebollen* batter in the bathroom, and deep fried it later on the stove."

Mrs. Gordon shuddered.

"*Oliebollen*'s a doughnut-like Dutch pastry—"

"I know. You obviously didn't meet hygiene regulations."

"The bathroom was part of our suite. We kept it clean."

"Say no more." She cringed.

Did Carrie detect the slightest crescent of a smile? The teakettle whistled. "Sounds like wind. Maybe they boiled water for cyclone sound effects in the movie." She poured water over hibiscus leaves, but after it steeped, one sip wrinkled her nose. "Cranberryish."

"Tart? You're allowed one lump of sugar."

"Only one?" Carrie tried to discern a smile twitching.

Through tea and muffins, Mrs. Gordon inquired about Carrie's family, then set several muffins on a plate. "Take these home and copy this recipe for your grandmother."

"She'll be thrilled." And shocked.

They settled in the parlor for another visit to Janie's childhood.

Janie, 9
August 1901

When Mother left, Janie meandered to the kitchen. Columbian Expo images inspired her: the pickle map, prune knight, and chocolate Venus de Milo. What could *she* make? She surveyed the pantry: Quaker Oats, Pettijohn's, Uneeda Biscuit crackers, and macaroni.

At the table, she sliced bread, onion, and celery, tore broccoli into bunches. She stacked and cut strips, arranging and rearranging. Soon, cracker owls nestled on a plate. Star-shaped cucumber slices hovered like the night sky. Peanut butter fastened raisin eyes, almond feathers, and pecan talons.

Poked with a wooden skewer, ham slices formed sails. A potato sailboat floated in leftover mashed potatoes, lining a pebbly Grape-Nuts beach. Another plate featured a broccoli-parsley forest on a bed of spinach leaf moss. A green pepper monster wore a macaroni-onion necklace and walnut shell hat. Grated carrot hair stuck with peanut butter. Mr. Baum would be impressed.

Horse hooves tripped down the road. Janie rescued a slipping raisin and licked peanut butter off her fingers.

"Lodemia Jane!" Mother plopped down a bag of canned goods. Plates rattled. A broccoli tree fell. "What's this mess?" Mother snatched the pepper monster and scraped off carrot hair. "This was for beef stew." Grimacing, she poked the owl. "Peanut butter?"

Janie was shaking. "I should've used cream cheese."

Mother shook macaroni off the necklace. "Such a waste."

"It's still edible," Janie said meekly.

"How long has the ham been out? There's no salvaging this mess. You contaminated everything." She shoved Janie's sticky hand. It struck the table leg. Janie cried. "I can't abide this nonsense." Mother tore off monster arms, disembodied owls, ripped the sails. She threw hunks on a plate. "Take *that* to your room for supper."

"Janie," Sawyer Broderick called from the parlor, his voice like Lake Michigan waves churning.

Janie gripped the stair railing.

"Lodemia Jane!" Like storm-infested waves.

She peeked around the corner. "Yes, Father?" A fire crackled in the hearth. Why?

Flushed, her mother held *The Wonderful Wizard of Oz.* "I've never been so appalled."

Her father's hair was tinged gray. He had three facial expressions, two for home: stern and angry. The smile lighting his whole face was reserved for friends and business associates. "We're concerned about your propensity to lie and your attraction to fanciful stories."

"What do you mean?"

"First, you tell a stranger your name is Charlotte Rose," her father said. "Secondly, you fill your head with senseless tales of made-up lands, distorting the mind until you don't know right from wrong."

Tension jerked her muscles.

He pointed to a newspaper headline: *Sawyer Broderick's Generous Donations Instigate Church Addition.* "We've a reputation to uphold. Folks trust the Broderick name. Have I built five successful businesses by telling lies? Honesty's the foundation for earning trust. How far would we get if I put rotten peaches in bushel bottoms? What if I fibbed about sanding my cranberry bogs? What if your mother introduced herself as Jenny Lind to the customers?"

Janie squirmed under her father's austere scrutiny.

Mother lifted the Oz book. "This story makes no distinction between good and evil, with both good and bad witches." She tapped a Glinda illustration. "There's no such thing as a good witch. All witchcraft is evil."

"But the good witch uses her powers for good," Janie said.

"See? You're deluded. All witchcraft opposes God, clearly stated in Scripture."

"It's pretend," Janie said. "A story made up for fun."

"Filling your head with delusions," Father said.

"There's only one destiny for this book." Mother stood. "The same end as all witchcraft."

Janie now knew why the fire burned in August. "No!" She lunged to snatch the book.

Brushing past her, Mother walked to the hearth. She ripped out pages and tossed them to the hungry fire, flames leaping with each morsel.

"No!" Janie shrieked, charging forward.

The Scarecrow sizzled, calling for water. Smoke encircled the Tin Woodman. Flames singed the Lion's mane. Janie reached. "Dorothy! Toto!"

Father grasped her arms as she pleaded, trying to escape. Mother ripped out page after page, each one curling, blackening, disintegrating to ashes. She tossed the rest of the book in all at once. The fire swallowed it whole.

TEN

1901

Days later, Janie overheard Mother and Aunt Sophie argue in the dining room.

"I'll not abide you buying any more fairy tales for Janie," Mother said. "Especially by that Mr. Baum."

"Janie's an imaginative girl. She thrives on stories."

"She has all she needs straight from the Bible and *Pilgrim's Progress*." Dishes rattled as Mother sputtered. "Cinderella, Oz, that silly Alice book. It's all twaddle." She stomped to the kitchen.

Aunt Sophie rallied. "The Pansy books have strong girl role models. George MacDonald tales—"

"Such rubbish!" Mother started chopping. "All fairies, witches, and giants are headed for the wood stove."

Footsteps. Janie darted upstairs. Her stealth did little good. Each step emitted a *squeak*. She flopped on the bed with her Dorothy doll.

Aunt Sophie knocked. "Hello, cream puff." She knelt at the bookcase, scooping books into a grain sack. "I'm performing a rescue mission. Find books with elves, fairies, and fantasy lands so they don't follow Oz into the fire. We'll leave enough books your mother will consider harmless."

Janie joined her, filling the sack. "But my favorites are on the hutch."

"Fear not." Auntie pointed to the bag, then kissed her niece on the forehead like the Good Witch of the North kissed Dorothy.

Sack in tow, Auntie eyed the shelf. "You've plenty here. *Heidi, Five Little Peppers, Hans Brinker,* the Pansy books. Even *Pilgrim's Progress.*"

"I won't read that." Janie wrinkled her nose.

"It's for show. Now, dumpling, I'm leaving without fanfare. You'll visit soon?"

Later, carrying her Dorothy rag doll, Janie walked the mile to Aunt Sophie's on Hickory Lane. Upstairs, the bedroom window seat invited sunshine. Calico pillows beckoned. Janie placed Dorothy on the cushion.

"Your little spot." Aunt Sophie opened the wardrobe door.

Janie ogled shelves of books in their snug new home. "Wonderful!" She fingered George MacDonald's *Dealings with the Fairies.* "I need a new *Wizard of Oz.*"

"Look closer." Auntie pointed.

Janie withdrew a new Oz book and hugged it. "Thank you."

Aunt Sophie adopted a British accent. "Shall we have a spot of tea?"

Janie giggled. They sat at the kitchen table with peppermint tea and oatmeal cookies. "Auntie, are you sinning by hiding my books from Mother?"

Aunt Sophie fingered her cup. "Let me worry about that. Reading about Alice, Dorothy, and Cinderella won't harm you."

"What's Mother afraid of?"

"That you won't know the difference between truth and lies." Auntie took her hand. "Your parents mean well, chinchilla, but they're inventing sin where there isn't one." She poured Janie more tea. "Take a sip."

Janie did so, scrunching her nose.

"You know how to make it delicious." She offered a sugar cube. "Books are to your imagination what sugar is to tea. Stir it and drink."

Janie stirred and sipped, then dipped her cookie too.

"Sugar sweetens everything it touches. Like books and stories. They flavor your whole life. They sweeten every day."

"It's not a sin, Auntie?"

"No. We're made in our Creator's image, so we create too. Many great artists and writers through the centuries used their God-given gift for good."

"Doesn't Mother know about them?"

"She clings to her own notions like a drowning man clings to a broken tree branch."

Like a witch to a broomstick. Janie swallowed more sugary tea.

"*The Princess and the Goblin* was written by George MacDonald, a Christian minister. He used his imagination to show something important about God. Princess Irene was the only one who could see the great-great-grandmother and her light, because she believed, remember? Yet the grandmother healed Curdie's leg even when he didn't believe she existed."

Janie dipped her cookie. "Curdie sees the grandmother later."

"Yes, cream puff, because he finally believes. See? The Lord cares for us, even when we ignore Him."

If God cared so much for Janie, why'd she see only disgust in her parents' faces?

May 1980

"Did you believe your aunt, that imagination is good?" Carrie asked.

"I tried. But at home, I was singed by the hellfire my parents warned me about."

Carrie tapped her pen. "Did you know how influential MacDonald was to other fantasy writers? G.K. Chesterton, Tolkien, Madeleine L'Engle. Especially C.S. Lewis."

"That's why I have all the truth I need on that bookshelf of folktales and novels. G.K. Chesterton said the child's imagination already knows the dragon well. The fairy tale provides a St. George to kill the dragon." She eyed Carrie, as if dragons were at hand.

Images flashed of Janie cowering under her father's judgments, crying as fire devoured her book. "I feel privileged hearing about those dragons."

"Dragons are aplenty, for not all are slain. Now, let's continue *Pilgrim's Progress*."

"Last time, Christian and Pliable fell into the Slough of Despond, the place that prevents belief." Carrie read about Christian hoping to drop his burden of sin, a weight worse than pain, hunger, and sword. Mr. Worldly Wiseman warned him that the Slough of Despond would still plague him, causing sorrow, weariness, and peril.

Eyes closed, Mrs. Gordon gripped the armrests.

Carrie proceeded. Mr. Worldly Wiseman sent Christian to Mr. Legality to remove his burden. Climbing the steep hill, Christian feared the mountain would topple over him. Evangelist warned that Mr. Legality had never removed a burden in his life and sent Christian to the Strait Gate instead.

A shadow crossed Mrs. Gordon's face. "The Slough of Despond still bothers travelers going to the Celestial City?"

"Yes, it's a place of fears, doubt, and discouragement that harms everyone."

"Who does Mr. Bunyan say Mr. Legality is, this son of a bondwoman?"

Carrie swallowed. "Anyone claiming the road to heaven is based on good works."

"Mr. Legality cannot remove a burden?"

"He only adds burdens." Carrie paused. "Perhaps Mr. Legality is a dragon, like those who burn a child's book or tear apart green pepper monsters."

ELEVEN

May 30, 1980

After peeling back layers of Mrs. Gordon's life, Carrie went home and handed Oma the recipe and muffins. "From the Broderick family archives."

"*Lieve hemel!*" Oma's eyes widened.

"Good heavens is right."

All concurred the muffins were delectable. After washing dishes, Carrie donned a sundress and French braided her hair, her nod to Brian. She headed to Brindlewood Café to ask about the enlarged, framed dune picture Mrs. Gordon was missing.

Lake Michigan wind swirled. Shades of rosy peach smudged the water and western sky. Carrie imagined Janie scrambling up the dune behind the Baum boys, bouncing down, traipsing into waves. Then the spanking, the food sculpture, the book burning.

Friday night's crowd filled the café, along with Dirk's rendition of "Oh Susanna," James Taylor style. Unfortunately, the owner wasn't there. Neither were tea options—besides black.

Carrie tapped her toe to Gordon Lightfoot's "Carefree

Highway" and poured two packets of sugar into her tea. *Stories flavor your whole life, sweeten every day.*

"This seat taken?"

She faced a smiling Dirk. "Not yet." He sat. She glanced at his tattoo. MH/CD. Melissa Hoeksema? Cheri Dykstra? "I'd like a tour guide tomorrow."

"I'm free before noon. Can you manage Wolcott in two hours?"

"Depends on how longwinded you are," she said.

"I can turn every historical site into a good story."

Carrie smiled. "Here's a tip." She surreptitiously handed over the baggie from her purse. "I baked these with Mrs. Gordon, her tearoom recipe for blueberry cream cheese muffins."

He indulged, then winked. "My compliments to the chef. That wink was for Mrs. G."

"She's too old for you."

"Older ones love me best. How was your day?"

She offered a two-minute rendition of the bank meeting.

"Fantastic. How're you feeling about it?"

Scared to death. Like she'd said everything wrong. "Hopeful. I gave it my best shot." Safeguarding privacy, Carrie shared about Janie's lovely day with the Baums, then asked, "Did you ever want to finish college?"

"I got restless. I had a situation."

She offered a sly look. "Were you in trouble?"

"I feared 'Only the Good Die Young.'"

"That Billy Joel song was your life motto?"

He grinned. "Speaking as a fan?"

"The biggest. I predicted his popularity when I saw him in concert three years ago. Then again in '78." Brian frowned on her inclination for secular music. "You're a fan too?"

"Absolutely."

"Why aren't his songs in your repertoire?"

He presented his guitar pick. "I'm Guitar Man, not Piano Man."

"You're letting that stop you?" She lifted her chin. "'The Entertainer' lyrics are poignant. Forced to cut your genius lines. Compromising your art. But squashing the sublime is like trying to stamp out a cloud."

"Great imagery. You sound like a Calvin prof." Dirk lowered his voice. "Maybe Calvin's not so bad."

She sipped more tea. "You'll soon be a convert."

"The best fiction and art capture the truth of the human condition." Dirk tapped his spoon as if he couldn't sit still. "Like *The Scarlet Letter*. Gets to the heart of hypocrisy, pride, true and false repentance."

Not bad for a college dropout.

"And Billy Joel's 'The Stranger.' We show different faces to different people. Folks are shocked when they learn what we're really thinking."

Carrie bit her lip. She wore a satin face for everyone, including Brian.

"Gotta love the Eagles' 'Hotel California.'" Dirk raised his spoon. "Fantastic extended metaphor for the coming-of-age experience."

Like William Blake's thwarted sunflower.

"Artists capture complexities and beauty. Common grace in action."

"Is this what you pondered during long nights at sea?"

He grinned. "Gotta do something to stay sharp."

"Brian believes all secular books and music are sinful." Much like Janie's parents. "He threw a fit about my first Billy Joel concert. I never mentioned the second one."

"So, he doesn't know Billy Joel's your true love. I'd be upset, too."

That's doubtful. He seemed perpetually happy. "There's a lot Brian doesn't know." *Oh, my! How'd that slip out?*

Dirk raised an eyebrow. "What should he know?"

"Nothing." She stared at her bouncing teabag.

He quoted from "The Stranger," different faces people show.

She met his eye. "I don't want to teach. I'd rather flip burgers."

"But you got your education degree."

Almost. "I had to. Mom's a teacher. So were Dad's parents. Dad's on the school board. As Calvin grads, my folks paid for college, provided my sister Amy and I follow in their footsteps. Kruisselbrink tradition."

"They're not onboard with the café?"

"It's complicated."

"What does your lucky guy think?"

She set her jaw. She could hardly admit Brian's doubts. Besides, why was she sharing her heart with a man she'd known only twenty-four hours? "I never told him I hated teaching."

"Ah." Dirk crossed his arms. "You haven't found the right moment?"

Avoiding his eye, she stirred her tea.

"Let me guess. He's not fond of the book café."

She jerked her head up. "Don't you have to play music?"

"Crumbs!" He popped up. "Will you stay? I'm taking requests."

"'Both Sides Now.'"

He cocked his head. "Interesting choice."

"No commentary, please."

Of course he played it last in the eight-song set, as if to bind her there. But she didn't mind. He poignantly sang Joni Mitchell's lyrics portraying love as a fairy tale, then nothing but illusions.

She chided herself for observing him so closely. He was brotherly—attentive, fun to be with. But surely only capable of summer flings. And she had Brian.

Why'd these lyrics churn her stomach? The melancholy of

love's illusions draped over her. Especially since last night's phone call.

Afterward, Dirk asked, "Wanna head to the beach? Can't beat a Lake Michigan sunset."

Carrie followed him down steps past the dune, visions of Charlotte Rose hopping down, arms like wings, hat swinging. Light still meandered the sky. They dropped their shoes at the bottom step. Loose strands feathered Carrie's face. She combed fingers through her hair, shaking out the French braid. Wind swept through her liberated hair as they walked.

Answering Dirk's queries, she explained how she got her job: the disrupted flowerbed, her sixth-grade oath, the 1918 murder charge, *Pilgrim's Progress*, and decent wages.

He countered by declaring, "You can't put a price on such experiences."

Was he feigning interest? Looking for a fling? Well, he'd be sorely disappointed. Yet he seemed honorable, respecting her loyalty to Brian.

The sun's palette of gold and red melted over the lake. She asked about his sailing adventures. He shared anecdotes, gesturing to the sky, explaining constellations and weather signs. He laughed like merry waves rolling to shore.

At home, she called Brian. After stargazing Dirk, she appreciated Brian's stability. Yet why did being with Dirk evoke such vibrancy?

"Hello?" Brian's rich, chocolatey voice carried a touch of hopeful.

"Brian. Sorry to call late. Hey, when I come to your grad party, I wanna pick up that old rocker at my house. Opa and I will refinish it."

"When we get married, we can afford new furniture. Forget hand-me-downs."

"I love that chair. It's full of memories, snuggling with Mom and Amy. With sanding, varnish, and fabric, it'll be good as new."

"But old-fashioned."

"I like old-fashioned. Can you please pick it up and keep it till I come? Mom's redecorating, so the sooner, the better."

"Okay. Did you give those schools your new contact information?"

"No. Mom'll give them my number here."

"That's unprofessional, Carrie." Again, her name used in reprimand.

Why'd he always put her on the defensive? "You're badgering me." She'd never rebuked him before. Her heart sped from fear and the thrill.

"Sweetheart, I care about our future."

She couldn't push the bubbling tension down this time. "Then ask about my bank meeting!"

"Oh, that's right. How was it?"

"Seriously? You forgot?" Her agitation grew. "Never mind then."

"Carrie, this isn't like you."

"Right, it's not," she snapped. "The Carrie you know always agrees."

He softened his tone. "What's going on, sweetie?"

"Listen to Billy Joel's 'The Stranger.'"

"Why would I listen to *that* music?"

"To understand me. You don't even know me, Brian."

He seemed confounded. "Of course I do."

Not about the second Billy Joel concert. Or hating teaching. Or not graduating. "When I'm with you, I wear my satin face. Go listen to that song. I have to go."

TWELVE

Saturday, May 31, 1980

On the front porch swing, Carrie pointed to the album's faded photograph. "Oma, you're adorable! How old were you?"

"Four, in 1916. That's my baptism picture."

Carrie flipped pages. "Why weren't you baptized as an infant like your sisters?"

"I'm not sure. I don't have baby pictures."

"Call your sisters. I'll make duplicates and organize your album."

Opa poked his head out the door. "Muffin alert!"

"I'll bake more." Oma lifted her coffee cup. "Right after *een bakje troost*. A little cup of solace."

Carrie smiled. Here, Carrie felt plugged into her ethnicity. Dutch lace at the windows, Delft plates and tiles in the kitchen, and original oak woodwork enhanced the Old World look in this early 1900s bungalow—as welcoming as her grandparents.

Carrie climbed into Dirk's 1968 Chevy Camaro in the café parking lot. She hid her cringe. Old photos and furniture she valued, not old cars. Especially rusty ones with cracked leather. Brian's Mustang was pristine.

Downtown, Dirk pointed out previous sites of Dr. Weaver's office, Walter Gordon's pharmacy, and Sawyer Broderick's cranberry shed, now a gas station. Each building elicited a story. After an animated tale about Percell Grocery, Carrie eyed him sideways. "Is that true?"

"Does it matter?" His grinning made up for Mrs. Gordon's dour expressions.

Did he blur the lines between reality and fantasy as Mr. Baum did?

At the café, they started on foot. Periwinkles and Queen Anne's lace swayed against tall, lush grasses. Using a map, Dirk pointed out earlier locations of the peach orchard, cranberry bog, icehouse, and farmland across the Blue Star Highway.

"Here's where I prove my worth as your official tour guide." He gave a spiel on Saugatuck and Douglas on Lake Kalamazoo, four miles north, twin towns that had drawn artsy summer tourists since the late 1800s. Some stayed at the Broderick Resort. In October 1871, a fire mysteriously ravaged Chicago, Holland, and Peshtigo, Wisconsin, on the same day. "Afterward, this area became known for its peaches. Whew." He wiped his forehead, exaggerating the effort. "I'd much rather tell stories than cite facts and figures."

Carrie chuckled. "Charging for the extra labor?"

"No, but I accept tips."

What'd *that* mean? She narrowed her eyes.

"A Coke at the café. Or french fries."

Relieved, she smiled.

Near the shore, vertical posts stood as grave markers for the old pier.

"Imagine hauling ice chunks out in winter," Dirk said,

"then burying them in rock-solid ground to stay frozen. Later, they built the icehouse for storage for the resort and sold ice in summer. The Broderick Resort was a great Sunday school and company picnic spot." He picked a periwinkle and handed it to her. "Summer's the best as long as you don't think about what happens in winter to make it possible."

"How insightful." She examined the flower.

"Same brilliant color as your eyes when you talk about the book café. They stand out like a sail at dawn."

"What song is *that* line from?"

He bowed. "Vandenakker, Minuet in C, opus number seventeen."

Her cheeks warmed. "Thank you, maestro."

At home, Carrie imagined Oma's hutch in her café, stocked with apothecary jars of looseleaf tea. Assuming she got the loan. Tension gripped her again. Shaking it off, she slipped the periwinkle into a vase.

She ducked into the basement to rummage for photo albums or furniture needing refurbishing. Among old book boxes, she found the Wendolyn series. Inside a manila envelope nestled *Wendolyn and the Gatekeeper of Merrimack Castle.* She charged upstairs with the book. "Look!"

Oma slid muffin tins into the oven. "Those Wendolyn stories are the only books I kept from childhood. A shame that one went off the market. Such a wonderful tale."

"Where'd you get it?"

"In the mail, like the rest. Almost yearly."

They sat at the table. Carrie thumbed through brittle pages adorned with whimsical illustrations. "How old were you when you read these?"

"Age eight, initially. Moeder knew English well by then. We enjoyed them together."

Carrie's mother hadn't read with her since Carrie outgrew lap-sitting. "You were twelve, 1924. Look, the author signed it. Gretchen Trumbauer. She was rather reclusive. When'd you meet her?"

"I didn't." Oma left the room and returned with a small wooden box. "After Moeder and I read *Wendolyn and the Lost Locket*, she gave me this." Oma withdrew a silver locket featuring a tiny photo of Great-grandmother De Haan. "The first story's about Wendolyn not finding her mother anywhere. By the end, she knows her mother did everything possible to care for Wendolyn, though the mom had fallen under a wicked spell."

Carrie fingered the locket. "Your mom was assuring you she'd always love you, no matter what." She winced, her own mother's aloofness inflicting a chill.

"After each book, Moeder gave me an object symbolizing the main theme." Oma picked up a miniature ladder. "In the second book, Wendolyn ran into many obstacles. When a boulder blocks your path, find the nearest ladder and climb over it."

Carrie smiled ruefully. Her own mother *was* the boulder blocking her path. No way around her until Carrie moved to Wolcott. She peered into the box. "A paintbrush?"

"From the banned book. The brush of imagination, which magically painted Merrimack Castle walls. As it paints new scenes—doors, rooms, or mountains—Wendolyn enters them."

"Can she return?"

"With the Gatekeeper's help. He unlocks the magic of imagination."

Carrie lapsed into melancholy. She pictured herself painting a *trompe l'oeil* on a huge wall, only to have a wicked fairy snatch the brush, splashing paint on scenes she'd labored over for days. Killing the magic. As her parents did.

Carrie and Oma discussed each object. "See, *liefje*, each one reminds me about something important. Seeking love by giving it. Having courage and perseverance despite obstacles. Fostering imagination when others shut you into a box."

Oma painted the air with the brush. "Moeder picked the perfect object for each. Though I relish the Psalms, I've often reflected on life lessons from these books, finding nuggets of encouragement. Each story helped me *trek de stout schoenen aan*. Put on the brave shoes." She touched the locket. "For years, I had nightmares of being alone in a dark forest. I'd cry in my sleep. Moeder came running, promising to always be there. The next day, she'd make me wear this locket." Oma patted Carrie's wrist. "She taught me God never forsakes. Same lesson in the Wendolyn book, told a different way."

The timer buzzed. Oma pulled muffins out. "I have letters from the author. I wrote her first, through the publisher. We corresponded for years. I'll find them and show you later."

<hr>

After calling her mentor, Rita, about the bank meeting, then helping Opa Zip Strip the bureau, Carrie typed Mrs. Gordon's memoirs. At suppertime, she picked at meatloaf and poked mashed potatoes. *Just say it.* "I didn't get my college diploma."

Oma stiffened. "*Lieve hemel!*"

"*Bliksem en donder!*" Lightning and thunder. Opa nearly spilled his milk.

Tearfully, Carrie divulged her disintegration first semester and dropping out of Philosophy of Education. "I'm not retaking the class. I'll tell Mom and Dad the weekend of Brian's party." Oma and Opa sat stunned. "They'd only pay for college if I majored in elementary ed. I really tried to make it work. I had creative ideas, but I failed. I hated student teaching."

Oma's eyes blazed. Opa's jaw tightened. Carrie numbed. Were they about to spout denouncements? Oma squeezed Carrie's hand. "*Liefje*, you can't beat yourself up."

Carrie's chin quivered. "You're not angry?"

"Not at you," Opa said. "You went through tough times only to discover what you don't like. That's disheartening enough."

"Finishing that class would be *dweilen met de kraan open*," Oma said. "Mopping up while the faucet's running. That Arlene."

Carrie blew her nose. "They'll call it a waste of time and money."

"It's no waste," Opa said. "You got a fine education and grew up in ways that wouldn't happen otherwise."

That's debatable. Carrie pressed potatoes with her fork. Butter rivulets streamed down.

"You've got time to figure things out," Oma said.

Opa straightened. "Oma and I don't have PhDs, but we have a DLE. Doctorate in Life Experience."

"School of hard knocks." Oma nodded. "Worth more than five college degrees."

Carrie smiled. If only it would be as easy telling her parents. And Brian. "One more thing. I've already chosen my career path." She revealed her efforts forming a business plan, pinpointing a location, and meeting the loan officer.

Opa's eyes widened with each new revelation. "You've done all this without your parents knowing?"

Her face heated. "They think opening a café is foolish, so I won't tell them until I purchase the building. I want them to be proud of me for reaching my *own* goals, not theirs. I can't live squashed in their box."

Oma clasped Carrie's hand. "Oh, *liefje*. No box can confine you and all your beautiful creativity."

"Thanks, Oma. But please don't tell my parents. I'll tell them in July."

Oma glanced at Opa as if verifying their coconspirator roles.

"We understand your silence, Carrie," Opa said. "We're here for you."

———

After Carrie and her grandparents attended church and ate a traditional Sunday dinner, a car rumbled into the driveway.

At the front window, Carrie froze. Her father walked up the sidewalk, scowling.

The doorbell rang. She panicked. "Oma, what's Dad doing here?"

"*Lieve hemel!*" Oma flew to the door and opened it. Her calm demeanor belied any frenzy. "Hello, Martin. We didn't expect you. Lucky I have pie left over."

"I didn't come for pie, Tanna. Where's Carrie?" All business, he stepped inside.

Carrie braced herself. "Why didn't you just call?"

"Why'd you take off in a huff? What's going on?"

Every ounce of strength she'd summoned for the bank meeting dissipated in her father's presence, as usual. Always engrossed in his newspaper, her father huffed when she offered opinions. Once, when young Carrie showed her father a drawing, he grunted at the intrusion. But when older sister Amy pirouetted into the room, he watched her dance, smiling. Carrie had slunk away, sketch drooping. "I came earlier than planned to Oma and Opa's."

"Did you quit Ophelia's without giving notice?"

"Yes, but Rita has enough staff—"

"Kruisselbrinks don't quit, Carrie."

"I thought you didn't like my restaurant work."

"But you should honor your commitments. You're coming home and apologizing to your mother."

Childhood incidents rolled over her, all ending the same: her mother's castigation followed by seasons of silence.

Berating her for rearranging furniture, dawdling over projects, paging through decorator magazines. Recurring images burdened her: parents rolling their eyes, turning their backs, leaving the room. Never good enough to warrant attention, she was flawed in a unique way. Besides the weight of any wrongdoing, she bore the shame of being Carrie.

Numbness and tension took turns throughout her body. "I'll call her to apologize." Why didn't Mother apologize to *her*? "But I'd like to stay here awhile."

"You can't quit your job. Your sister would never be so irresponsible."

Amy, always Amy, holding a bar nobody could reach. How would Carrie ever confess to dropping the final college class just short of a diploma? Words clogged her throat. *Don't cry.* "Dad, I need to stay here."

His eyes widened. "You're coming back *now*."

Opa appeared in the kitchen doorway. "Martin, Carrie's twenty-two and can make her own adult decisions."

"That assumes she knows *how* to."

Oma's turn. "She does, Martin. And she's a wonderful help around here and brightens every day."

Dad faced Carrie. "Get your car keys and suitcase. I'm following you home."

Carrie remained stuck as if sinking in quicksand. No use speaking even if she could. He'd pounce on anything she said.

Oma left the room. *Don't abandon me!*

Opa stepped to the front door. "Martin, Carrie's staying here, and you need to leave. That's *not* a suggestion."

Oma breezed back in with a plastic-wrapped dish. "A piece of pie for your trouble."

Muttering, Dad stomped his foot and left without pie. He slammed the door shut.

Carrie fled to her room and flopped on the bed as if back in sixth grade. Is that where it all started? Not just the shame, but her hatred of the classroom. That harsh, wretched year with Miss Nieuwenhuis.

Thank God for her grandparents' advocacy—God somehow loving her through their kindness. But it didn't wipe out shame heaped on by her parents, just for being her. Shame that required a different kind of power to overcome it.

Thirteen

Monday, June 2, 1980

Carrie opened the drapes more, hoping Mrs. Gordon wouldn't notice. Museum-quality opulence and the panache of the carved cherrywood fireplace engulfed her. Lace draped the mantel supporting a clock, brass candlesticks, and exquisite porcelain nursery rhyme figures—like Dainty China Country. Her father's unexpected appearance yesterday seemed worlds away. As was the short but not-so-sweet obligatory apology to her mother.

Canisters and containers lined the kitchen countertop. "Mr. Cinnamon Bunn, Esquire's Caramel Sticky Rolls, inspired by Bunbury in Oz," Mrs. Gordon announced. "Pour warm water into a bowl for yeast. Nothing like your *oliebollen*-in-the-bathroom trick."

They kneaded dough for rolls. "There's no Ginger Apricot Tea at the café," Carrie said.

"The tearoom has been greatly compromised. Never mind that regrettable experience. Today, I'll serve Princess Ozma's Peach Jubilee. Loose leaf. *Real* tea." She lifted a tin. "Rooibus, an herb from a South African red bush. A Dutchman from there introduced it to me in 1952."

They sat facing nautical-themed Delft plates and teacups. Would Mrs. Gordon dock her pay for teatime? Shouldn't they discuss Mr. Gordon's plight? Carrie picked up the sugar spoon.

"Protocol dictates sampling imported tea *before* adding sugar and cream."

Bristling, Carrie replaced the spoon. "Oma loved your recipe. She made three batches."

Mrs. Gordon lifted her chin as if receiving the compliment, but no smile emerged. "I don't want to be held responsible for anyone's weight gain."

"She hopes she captured Broderick magic. She's also handy with knitting and crochet. Did you knit for your children or grandchildren?"

"Nobody to knit for," Mrs. Gordon snapped.

Oops. "Guess what. Oma has *The Gatekeeper of Merrimack Castle.*"

"Now you won't beg to borrow mine," she said tartly.

"Oma has every Wendolyn book from childhood. Mail order. Her mother gave her a treasure box full of mementos for each book."

Mrs. Gordon's eyebrows rose. "Indeed?"

Carrie explained the locket, ladder, paintbrush, and other items. "She remembers each story fondly. The objects helped her remember lessons learned. Even now."

Mrs. Gordon's jaw twitched. "Clever idea, having a treasure box."

"She still has letters from the author somewhere."

"Well, lucky her." Mrs. Gordon thumped her hand on the table. "Gretchen Trumbauer surely got scads of fan mail."

Whoa. The timer buzzed. Carrie served rolls oozing with caramel and cinnamon.

"How'd your beau like Munchkin Delights?" Mrs. Gordon asked.

"Dirk devoured them. My boyfriend's Brian. We've dated since eleventh grade."

"You're not married yet? What's wrong with that boy?"

"We wanted to finish college first."

"Tell me about him."

"He's tall, handsome. Played sports in college. He's an accountant. He's organized, disciplined, great at saving money. He takes me to fancy restaurants and buys gifts."

"Those are extraneous qualities. How does he *treat* you?"

Carrie flushed. "He's well-mannered. He brings chocolate." *Though I prefer caramels.* "My parents love him. When we started dating, everyone cheered us on."

"Sounds 'as sweet as candy made from mustard and vinegar.'"

Carrie balked. "What?"

"A line from *Rinkitink in Oz*. They cheer because he's polite and parsimonious?"

"He's not stingy. He's frugal. He's a great guy. You make it sound like I'm reducing him to a house pet."

"*I'm* not the one doing that."

Exasperating! "He'll be a wonderful husband and provider, stable and responsible."

"Hmm. Tall, handsome. Plays baseball. Polite. Brings chocolate." Proving her steel trap memory. "Does he support your teaching aspirations?"

Should Carrie tell her about the café? Not yet. It would only encourage an inquest. Flustered, she watched her fork drip caramel. "These buns are fantastic with whipping cream."

"I'm not an absent-minded old woman."

"Fine. No tricks. Let's change the subject." Carrie licked caramel off her fingers.

Like a schoolmarm, Mrs. Gordon aimed a penetrating look that challenged Carrie to consider the wisdom of her words. "Please copy these recipes for your grandmother. Sticky Rolls and Billina's Cheesy Egg Strata."

"She'll be thrilled." Carrie surreptitiously added sugar to her tea and offered her words as a test. "*I'm* thrilled, too. I love cooking."

"Beyond *oliebollen* in the bathroom?"

"Far beyond. I've perfected favorite recipes, including the white soup in *Pride and Prejudice*." For the book café.

"Charming." But no smile. "You have a propensity for novel-inspired meals?"

"Absolutely." Carrie rattled off a list.

Mrs. Gordon nodded thoughtfully. "Anything inspired by Oz?"

"No, but with your permission, I'll add your Ozzy recipes to my repertoire."

"For what purpose?"

Carrie shrugged. "Well, in case I run a restaurant someday."

"When? In summers between teaching obligations?"

She gulped. The woman's tone didn't bode well for transparency yet. "I'm looking forward to hearing your next story about Mr. Baum."

Mrs. Gordon perked up, face brightening.

Janie, 9
September 1901

A letter arrived for Charlotte Rose, return address Chicago. Fortunately, Janie retrieved the mail before Mother did. Out slid a letter and photograph: Janie and the four boys by the dune.

Dear Charlotte Rose,

Please enjoy the reminder of our day of merriment and frolicking on the dune. We'd love you to visit us at Macatawa Park next summer. Kindly write to tell me which July day is best for your mother to bring you. Mrs. Baum, the boys, and I promise a delightful time.

Ozily yours,
Mr. Baum

An invitation! With a map and directions. But she couldn't tell Mother, still sputtering about the missing Baum books. So she asked Aunt Sophie to take her.

Three days later, Auntie decided. "I'll do it. But it's our secret. We'll also visit my friend, Alberdina Vanderlaan. That's where I'll say we're going, and it'll be the *truth*."

Janie composed a letter confirming the date and asking Mr. Baum to sign her new Oz book. She said it was severely damaged from a horrible accident, but nobody was hurt.

That was a lie.

***

Janie, 10
July 1902

Janie and Aunt Sophie took the interurban to Holland. After time with Dena Vanderlaan and a streetcar ride to Macatawa Park, they wandered on sand-drifted boardwalks through maples, oaks, and cottonwoods. Janie's clunky black shoes turned silver, like Dorothy's. Wooden plank paths became the road of yellow brick. The buzz of cicadas emerged into Munchkin chatter. Bushes swirled with jewel-winged damselflies and dragonflies, shining as brilliantly as yellow Winkie Country.

The walkways of Maksauba Trail, Mishawaka Avenue, and Nahant Path wound through clumps of half-hidden cottages in a forest that crept toward the sky. Did flying monkeys wait among the trees? Janie plopped on the log fence, swinging her feet and sweeping up the view.

Down Waukezoo Trail stood proud Victorian homes. One wore a wraparound porch, another peaked with a crow's nest. The Munchkin lad Boq might step out. Houses bore signs, such as Uneeda Rest Cottage—like Uneeda Biscuit. Janie giggled. Would Mr. Baum's house look like Hansel and Gretel's gingerbread cottage? Or the dwarves' snug hovel in Snow White? Maybe a dome-shaped Ozian dwelling.

They finally stood at the bottom of his porch steps, lakeside, facing an imposing three-story home with myriad windows, balconies, and railings. A jumble of boxes topped a porch table. Hanging from a beam, a golden-colored oval suspended a wooden goose silhouette. Black letters spelled Sign of the Goose. Paper flapped in the typewriter. Another Dorothy story?

Mr. Baum stepped outside the porch. "Welcome to my Fairyland!" His jaunty gesture embraced the scenery.

Aunt Sophie gripped Janie's hand for their first step up. A loud bell rang from under their feet. Auntie's face paled. Janie popped off the step, heart pattering. Was that a warning of impending doom if Mother discovered her?

Reddening, Mr. Baum chuckled. "I'm sorry to startle you. That's my son Robert's shenanigans. He wired the house, electricity and batteries in places we'd never noticed. Bells and buzzers, wires and widgets. But he was *not* to wire the porch."

"Everywhere else is fair game?" Aunt Sophie smiled, hesitated, and stepped precariously over the stair that rang, pulling Janie up.

"Everywhere except the kitchen. Mrs. Baum won't tolerate

tomfoolery in her domain. Matters were bad enough in our Chicago home, holes and wires galore." His buoyant gait carried him to the table of boxes. "He installed a wire in his bedroom doorknob that gave a shock. His poor brothers fell victim all too often."

Janie stifled giggles. If she tried that trick, she'd be whipped to the moon.

"A lovely place, Mr. Baum." Auntie gazed from the sprawling porch in view of treetops, blue lake blinking between branches. A long, steep staircase led to the beach.

Janie's eyes roved over the boxes. What was all this stuff?

He lifted an empty Quaker Oats container. "Charlotte, I'm planning a window display for the local grocery. You may make your own."

"How?"

He stroked his chin. "Seems to me a certain girl once created a haven to entice two feisty fairies."

"Beatrice and Estella." Did he suspect she'd brought them along?

"Ah, yes. I sold my window showcase magazine last year, but Mr. Colby asked for my expertise. My miniature scene will show him the possibilities. Make whatever suits your fancy. Every object offers free rein for your imagination." He pointed to muffin tins full of beads, buttons, lima beans, and cinnamon sticks. A bucket contained pinecones and pebbles. Boxes held paper lace, wallpaper scraps, and die-cuts. Bins cradled spools and ribbons.

Janie's eyes widened. "Where'd you get all this?"

"Harry and Ken collected it. Mrs. Baum donated food and sewing materials. Consider this tray a theater stage to build upon, or a place you've been in a book."

"Like Oz?"

"Or your own fairyland for your pesky friends." He opened a scrapbook. "This may offer ideas. I pasted my favorite store window displays here. My *Show Window* trade journal helped store owners improve theirs." He pointed out photos: the Brooklyn Bridge made of cotton reels strung together, a Venetian palace devised from cloth origami.

Janie paged through miniature landscapes, buildings, and animals made from branches, rope, sponge, and fabric. "The Tin Woodman!" A wash boiler formed the torso, with bolted stovepipe arms and legs, its face a saucepan's underside, topped with a funnel hat.

"For a hardware store," he said.

Something buzzed inside the house. Janie jumped.

Mrs. Baum peered through the screen door. "Robert!"

"Frank and Rob are golfing," Mr. Baum said. "Our guests arrived."

Mrs. Baum stepped out with a lemonade pitcher, greeted them effusively, and invited Aunt Sophie inside. She nodded toward her husband. "They'll be occupied awhile."

Kenneth bounced out of the cottage. "Hey, Charlotte." Looking more like six than eleven, he swung onto the porch railing like her father's farmhands did on the cow pasture fence. His buttons were crooked, hair uncombed. "Harry and I are having a backgammon tournament. One more game to go." He pointed out scrapbook highlights, including clippings from the 1890 *Aberdeen Saturday Pioneer* columns entitled "Our Landlady" by Mrs. Bilkins.

"Who's that?" Janie asked.

Mr. Baum chortled. "She owned a boardinghouse in Aberdeen and held a considerable number of unpopular opinions."

Kenneth nudged Janie. "There's no Mrs. Bilkins. It's him."

"Fiddlesticks!" Mr. Baum opened a cigar box. "She's as real as this cigar. That woman had viewpoints on everything from suffrage and politics to farmers and technology. Her boarders endured much, considering the preposterous situations she found herself in."

"He was the newspaper editor." Kenneth pointed to a column dated July 1890.

Janie read from Mrs. Bilkins's column on the drought. "'A farmer put green goggles on my horses and fed 'em shavings, and they think it's grass.'" She looked up with a sly smile. "Does Mrs. Bilkins know you borrowed her idea for the Emerald City, Mr. Baum?"

He laughed. "Babe the Blue Ox used green spectacles, too, and brought spring back in a hurry. So, asking where ideas come from is like asking which came first, the chicken or the egg." He lit a cigar. "Let's get to work." Kenneth left.

Janie and Mr. Baum sat side by side. Accompanied by whistling breezes, he sang "Oh Susanna" in his baritone voice, tucking escaped die-cut cherubs under the tray.

Ideas like feathers fluttered through Janie's head. She cut tiny rectangles of wallpaper, folded them into library books. A Pettijohn's Flaked Breakfast Food box formed a fairy throne.

Here, her words were welcome, as if crossing the steps to the porch had evoked confidence, besides eliciting the tinkling of bells. "Mr. Baum, I read *The Master Key*, though you called it an adventure for boys."

"You're a girl who will create plenty of her own ventures."

"Are new inventions bad? In the book, they're used for evil."

"Man does evil, not inventions." He compared two pinecones. "I'm fascinated by new gadgets and technology, though modern inventions aren't conducive to seeing fairies. One must return to once-upon-a-time before trains and telephones." He studied a walnut. "But folks like us aren't daunted by that. The fairies know whom they can trust." He winked.

Janie smiled, happy to be included. She lined up three buttons.

"Though evil performs terrible deeds, good shall always prevail."

She shuddered at her Oz book burning in the hearth. But here she was, beside its author.

She outlined a road leading to a library gazebo of twig construction. Later she'd find a mushroom for the center of a fairy ring, for nightly dancing. She riffled through the muffin tin. Beans and peas would make perfect cobblestones. Hands shaking, she scooped kidney beans. *Lodemia Jane! What's this mess?*

Janie's stomach clamped on the memory. *You're useless ... Nothing but trouble.* She bumped the muffin tin. It clattered onto the floor. Beads, buttons, and beans plinked across the boards. Wailing, she sank to her knees. "I'm so sorry." Tears blinded. For every three buttons she snatched, two fell. Beans slipped through floorboard cracks.

"Charlotte, get up." Mr. Baum's voice filled her head like a foghorn.

Such a waste. Her body shook with sobs.

"Please get up, dear. No harm done. Miss McKinnon!"

Aunt Sophie bustled outside. "What happened?" She embraced Janie, sobs smothering in her chest. "There now, dumpling."

"She picked up beans and started shaking," Mr. Baum said.

Janie's voice unraveled. "Mrs. Baum will be angry ... such a waste."

"It's not your fault, Mr. Baum," Auntie said. "Her mother punishes severely for messes of any kind. She destroyed her food sculpture after an hour's work."

Mr. Baum frowned. "I'll clean up in a jiffy, and we'll start fresh."

FOURTEEN

July 1902

Janie and Aunt Sophie drank lemonade while Mr. Baum cleaned the porch.

He patted Janie's wet cheeks with his handkerchief. "Charlotte, I once knew a boy who refused to touch toadstools because someone told him they'd explode like firecrackers." He launched into a sprightly tale, prompting laughter, then handed her a twig. "This is handy for starting fires. A scientist uses it to study botany. A writer sees a metaphor and creates a poem about shade, roots, or the wisdom of years. An artist paints it or builds with it. But I say, hmm, it functions as a leg for a sawhorse. A tiny one. What do *you* see?"

Janie sniffled. "A fairy king's scepter."

"Ah, yes. As Mr. Twain says, 'You can't depend on your eyes when your imagination is out of focus.'"

"So true, Mr. Baum," Aunt Sophie said. "I see that in the classroom."

"I've worried about children having nightmares from fairy tales," he said. "As a child, I had anxiety and was deathly frightened of scarecrows. They abounded in fields back home and wound up in my nightmares."

Janie straightened in alarm. "Are you still afraid?"

"Not now that I've met a friendly one." He winked, then pointed out the restored muffin tin. "Make anything you wish with all the beans you want." He lit a cigar. Janie sifted through objects.

"Congratulations on the success of your *Wizard of Oz* musical extravaganza," Aunt Sophie said. "The *Tribune* called it 'the best show of its kind' and 'a memorable spectacle.'"

"Indeed, but it has little to do with me. As I said opening night, the play is like plum pudding, combining flavors of many contributors, including comedians David Montgomery and Fred Stone. Nobody can do better as the Scarecrow and Tin Woodman. I bid the audience back for a second helping." He puffed his cigar.

Janie watched cigar smoke rise like fairy clouds. "Did you like seeing your characters alive on stage?"

"Absolutely, but other than Dorothy, the Scarecrow, and Tin Woodman, not much remains of my original story."

"What was different?" Janie wrapped wire around several twigs.

"The Wicked Witch of the West vanished. The Cowardly Lion's role is meager. The Wizard became a Dutch comedian. Instead of Toto, Dorothy's companion is Imogene the Cow."

Janie giggled.

"Dorothy Gale, she is. The Tin Woodman is Niccolo Chopper."

"Did you have a say-so, Mr. Baum?" Aunt Sophie inquired.

"Hardly. Mr. Mitchell completely rewrote the script. The musical comedy I'd envisioned became akin to vaudeville." He explained changes, including Glinda. "Apparently, mice cannot be portrayed on stage, so I changed the poppy field scene. The Snow Queen creates a snowstorm that destroys the poppies' spell. I rather like that touch."

Janie smoothed a piece of velvet. "How'd you show the cyclone?"

"Celluloid discs." Gestures in full force, Mr. Baum explained how a revolving painted disc, spotlight, gauze screen, and shrieking wind machine created effects. "Another disc simulated the snowstorm, as flowers shrank."

"How?" Janie laid out patchwork quilt scraps.

"The poppies were chorus girls, dressed like flowers, with petal hats."

"Sounds thrilling." Aunt Sophie sipped lemonade. "Did you write the music?"

"Mr. Tietjens wrote songs to my lyrics. Sadly, only four were retained. I was anxious about drastic changes but had to trust Mr. Mitchell's experience. I'd have saved myself much anguish by trusting him sooner." He touched Janie's arm. "Like the Good Witch says, 'You must walk. It is a long journey, through a country that is sometimes pleasant and sometimes dark and terrible.' Grownups need courage, too."

Janie smiled, then placed a mossy roof over cardboard pillars, hoping no elves or sprites were lured there first. "Is this where you wrote *The Wonderful Wizard of Oz*?"

"Some I wrote in our rental cottage, but most was written in Chicago. I framed my stub with the words, 'With this pencil I wrote *The Emerald City*.'"

Janie envisioned Dorothy and her companions streaming from Mr. Baum's paper as he penciled the tale. "What're you working on now?"

"Shh," Aunt Sophie whispered. "He may not want to say."

"All questions are welcome. I'm writing about how Santa Claus came to be. Not the familiar legend, but one set in the Forest of Burzee."

Janie's parents would throw that book into the fire, too, proclaiming Santa a fake.

Aunt Sophie's gaze followed his arm's sweep toward the

lake. "I'd be hard pressed thinking about Santa and winter, sitting on this porch in July."

"It's not such a stretch, Miss McKinnon. Though Macatawa Park's the most beautiful summer fairyland, snowflakes are just as clearly in my head as sand piles on the boardwalk. Munchkin Country's no farther away than the shore. And my version of Santa brings toys to all children, not just good ones."

Janie suddenly remembered. "Will you please sign my books?" She delivered them from Auntie's satchel: *The Wonderful Wizard of Oz, The Master Key,* and *American Fairy Tales.*

As he wrote, sweat glazed her forehead as if fire flared nearby. But no more book burnings. Parents must be obeyed, but they couldn't interfere with fairies.

Aunt Sophie stroked her hair. "It's all right, dumpling. Mr. Baum, are you here all summer?"

"Yes. The only drawback is missing baseball games at West Side Park."

"Which team?"

"The team with more nicknames than a dog has fleas. White Stockings, Colts, Orphans. This year, they're dubbed the Cubs. Frankly, I don't know which name will stick. Hmm. With my name, *frank*ly is the only way I can consider things at all."

Laughing, Aunt Sophie collected the books. "I'm headed to Holland. I'll return for Janie—uh, Charlotte, by six. Mind your manners, cream puff." She kissed her forehead.

On tiptoe, Janie whispered, "What if Mother finds me here?"

Aunt Sophie patted her arm, voice low. "She won't. Don't fret. You'll have a grand day." She left, avoiding the bottom step. Janie stared at the typewriter.

"Try it, Charlotte." Mr. Baum placed her hands on the keys. She inhaled his cigar scent. Would her mother smell cigar smoke on her? His pocket watch ticked. Laugh lines crinkled around his clear, gray eyes. Her father's lines were from scowling.

She plunked out *dorothy gail*.

He typed *Gale*. "Like a gale of wind, the cyclone that whisked Dorothy to Oz."

Kenneth burst onto the porch. "I'm the backgammon champ! And dinner's ready."

Inside, viewing the parlor was like lifting the lid of a jewelry box to find shiny bracelets. A stained-glass goose in green glass sparkled in the window, casting flickers of emerald, gold, and turquoise. Surely Beatrice and Estella felt at home, reveling in magical colors that rivaled pixie dust.

Kenneth gestured toward the wall. "Papa painted the geese. Mom made the fans." Stenciled geese flew from corner to corner against grass-colored walls over floral wallpaper fans. Other geese found rest as andirons in the hearth. Wicker furniture accompanied oak pieces and an upright piano. Messy stacks of magazines and games topped the coffee table. Crammed bookshelves, stenciled with characters, braced the wall. "So many books and geese!"

Kenneth smirked. "Some folks here call him Father Goose."

Janie perused titles of Dickens and folktale collections. "You have *Pilgrim's Progress*."

"A wonderful adventure of a hero's journey," Mr. Baum said.

"But I don't see a Bible."

"Ah. But I've a Bible verse framed over my desk back home. 'When I was a child, I spoke like a child, I understood as a child, I thought as a child.' A daily reminder of who I write for." He withdrew a volume of Hans Christian Anderson tales. "I consider Mr. Anderson the Glorious Dane, the first to originate the new fairy tale of our age. The best ones have elements of folklore with familiar modern features. Now, let's make sure Mrs. Baum doesn't burn the blackbird pie."

In the kitchen, strands of Mrs. Baum's long, dark hair hung

loose from her bout with food preparation in the heat. She presented plates of thick rye bread slices, cheese sauce dripping over the edges. Mr. Baum unfolded his napkin. "Ah, my favorite meal."

Nothing but cheese-topped bread?

"It's Welsh rarebit," Harry said. "Papa's specialty. He makes the creamiest sauce."

Mr. Baum winked. "But today, Maud, yours is the best."

"Better than Mrs. Broderick's food?" His wife's eyes flashed merriment.

"Far better." Mr. Baum turned to Janie. "Don't tell your mother I said that."

"I won't." Janie folded her hands. Were they going to pray over the meal first? Instead, Mr. Baum picked up his fork. Janie frowned. "Welsh rabbit? Where's the meat?"

The Baums laughed. Harry explained. "It's *rarebit*. The dish was created in a place where rabbits were scarce. It's a rabbit substitute."

"Consider it a *hyperooden rostratus*," Kenneth said.

"What?" She'd never like it now.

Mr. Baum wiped his chin with a napkin. "*Hyperoodon rostratus* is what one says in new surroundings."

Mrs. Baum passed carrots. "It's Latin for bottlenose whale. There's one in Chicago's Columbian Museum, from the World's Fair."

"What do whales have to do with Welsh rarebit?" Janie asked.

"It's a word we use for anything mysterious or strange," Kenneth said.

"It's what we named our rental cottage," Harry added. "Everything here's so different from Chicago."

"We call this cottage The Sign of the Goose. For obvious reasons." Kenneth nudged the cheese sauce bowl toward Janie. "Have as much as you want. Papa ordered a hundred-pound wheel of cheddar cheese from Chicago. We call him the Big Cheese."

"We indulge in weekly Welsh rarebit parties," Mr. Baum said.

Dinner proceeded with lively chatter and short pretense of good manners. When Harry and Kenneth argued about the distance from Chicago to Aberdeen, Mrs. Baum marched to the parlor and retrieved an encyclopedia. "Stop quarreling. Over 600 miles."

"I win." Harry's chin lifted. "What do I get?"

Kenneth punched him. "That's what you get."

Mrs. Baum grabbed Kenneth's arm before Harry could reciprocate.

Unruffled, Mr. Baum liberally ladled more cheese sauce. "Sometimes all you get for winning is pure satisfaction. Our myriad books, Charlotte, settle frequent disputes."

"Though some shall never be settled, with so much balderdash at this table," Mrs. Baum said. "Taradiddles and bilgewater coming out your ears."

Mr. Baum wiped sauce from his mustache. "Exaggeration can be put to good use."

"Like when Papa won the Biggest Lie contest," Kenneth said.

Janie's eyes widened. "A lying contest?"

"A tall tale, like Paul Bunyan or Pecos Bill. I submitted one called 'The Cold Day on the Railroad.'" Mr. Baum told the story, which evolved into laughter and more tales.

Mrs. Baum set out blueberry pie with a bowl of cream. "Michigan blueberries."

"Ask how blackbirds escaped the pie," Kenneth said as they ate.

 Mr. Baum shared the escapade, a variation of his *Mother Goose in Prose* version. "Why did the pig make a house of straw?"

The children took turns inventing answers.

"How'd the cow jump over the moon?" Harry queried.

Following Kenneth's wacky explanation, Janie asked, "Where'd Welsh rarebit *really* come from?"

Mr. Baum delved into another tale, full of puns, about a creature claiming to be a rabbit, but nobody believed him because he kept mispronouncing it *rarebit*.

Kenneth nudged her. "Papa can't tell a story without puns. Drives Mother crazy."

"I have a pun. From one of my favorite authors." Janie lifted her hand with a flourish and dramatically cleared her throat. "The scarecrow has a husky voice."

They burst into laughter.

FIFTEEN

Janie, 10
July 1902

When Frank and Robert returned from golf, Mrs. Baum relayed orders. "Rob, no dinner until you dismantle wires on the porch. Kenneth, heat water over the stove. Harry, your turn to wash."

"Shall I help, Mrs. Baum?" Janie asked. "Mother calls it women's work."

Mrs. Baum guffawed. "Honey, we don't have boy and girl roles. The kitchen's my domain, but my boys are just as comfortable doing laundry as pounding a fencepost. When I attend meetings, Mr. Baum assumes meal duties." She raised a hand. "My mother worked hard for women's suffrage, alongside Mrs. Anthony and Mrs. Stanton. Someday women will *vote*."

Mr. Baum checked his pocket watch. "This dishwashing interferes with our schedule. How will we have time to fish, swim, build sandcastles, and pull taffy?"

His wife stared at him. "Dishes don't wash themselves, L.F. It's the maid's summer off."

"Perhaps Harry and Ken can show Charlotte around while the older boys and I clean."

Mrs. Baum told the younger two to show Janie the beach but avoid the water until the adults joined them. She plopped Janie's straw hat over her braids and secured ribbons under her chin. Mr. Baum handed Janie the Kodak Brownie camera.

The kids scrambled down creaking steps to the beach, discarded shoes, jumped the boardwalk fence, and forged the half-mile through sand past groups of bathers to the channel where sailboats skimmed from Black Lake to Lake Michigan, stark white sails against sapphire sky. Squinting into the sun, Janie tugged off her hat and faced the wind. Let the sun kiss her skin, leaving a tangible reminder of this glorious day.

They circled the Holland Lighthouse on the south pier. North across the channel, the red roof, white arches, porches, and peaks of opulent Ottawa Beach Hotel graced the foot of Mount Pisgah, a dune. Janie took pictures.

Headed back, the boys splashed at water's edge. Janie stayed on the boardwalk. "Won't your mother be angry you're in the water?"

"It's just our feet." Kenneth kicked a clump of wet sand. "She'll never know."

"Besides," Harry said, "it's nothing like dropping the cat out the window or sliding down the porch roof into the sand." Janie's jaw dropped. He laughed. "The cat was fine. But Mother held Rob outside the window to see how he liked it."

"Oh, dear!"

"I slid down the roof, too." Harry flapped his arms like rooster wings. "With*out* punishment."

"I'd like to slide down a roof," Janie announced.

"Don't try it here." Kenneth kicked another sand clump. "Mom'll blame us."

"Does your father get angry?" Janie asked.

"Once Papa spanked me because Mother told him to,"

Kenneth said. "Later he came upstairs with supper and apologized. He vowed never to spank again. Never has."

"Probably should," Harry said. "Ken's always in trouble."

Kenneth splashed him.

Janie surveyed the cottages along the beach. One huge dune rose in their midst, Old Baldhead, tufted with grass, a distance from the Baum cottage. Mrs. Baum couldn't possibly see them. She slipped off her stockings and splashed alongside the boys.

After donning shoes—and Janie her hat—they climbed the long stairway. Mrs. Baum retied Janie's hat strings. The kids skipped behind Mr. Baum on winding boardwalks between cottages, through sloped foliage to Black Lake's harbor. The *Lizzie Walsh* steamer and electric streetcar ushered summer guests to downtown Holland, at the other end of the six-mile lake. The *Gladys* ferried guests to the Macatawa Bay Yacht Club. Trees hugged the shoreline, punctuated by cottages and hotels.

The incline railway, Angel's Flight, squeaked as it carried riders to the top of Old Baldhead. Down the shore rose a ruckus from Jenison Electric Park: cheering baseball fans, screeching children, clanking merry-go-round gears, and shooting gallery bangs.

At the boathouse, they launched the *Maybelle* and motored away on Black Lake. Mr. Baum pointed out luxurious Hotel Macatawa, sitting primly near the harbor. Janie's hat slid off again, held to her back by ribbons. Grinning, Kenneth handed her a worm and hook.

She grimaced. "I can't kill a worm!"

Mr. Baum intercepted. "Me neither. You and I shall cast the line."

She delighted in holding the pole, feeling fish tug, and reeling them in with Mr. Baum's capable arms guiding her. An hour of fishing produced a plethora of bass and pickerel.

They rode through the channel as Mr. Baum and the boys

churned out a hearty rendition of "Sailing, Sailing, over the Bounding Main," preface to catching perch. Janie grasped the boat's edge, peering into choppy waters. When the craft swayed and bounced, swelling over the wake of motorboats, her grip tightened.

Mr. Baum dropped the last fish in the bucket. "We were rewarded well despite our chatter. Plenty for supper." In the channel, he turned off the motor. The boys rowed as he belted out, "Row, row, row your boat ..."

Janie relished the wind's breath on her face, tangling her braids. "You'll have to throw a perch party, Mr. Baum, instead of a Welsh rarebit party. Does fish taste good with cheese sauce?"

He chortled. "Cheese goes with anything. We must name it. Hmm. How about Parmesan Pickerel Perfection?"

Janie giggled. "Or *Cheesy Cheddar Perch Enchantment.*"

When he snorted with amusement, the boys pitched their own ideas.

At the cottage, they donned bathing attire. Wearing black bloomers and a large-collared sailor shirt, Janie grinned at the guest room mirror. At home, mirrors were considered vanity, offering no reason to smile.

Mrs. Baum joined them in her dark serge suit with a full skirt, black stockings, canvas shoes, and floppy hat, similar to most women on the beach. The males wore shorts. The boys had tank tops, Mr. Baum a short-sleeved shirt.

Janie, Harry, and Kenneth tossed a ball in the water. Wearing his straw hat and puffing a cigar, Mr. Baum trekked into the lake up to his waist. Janie punched the ball while watching him. He swam, cigar butt in teeth, then turned back. A wave overtook, knocking off the hat. He shook water from his hair, donned the hat, and ambled back to sand. The ball bonked Janie on the head.

"Pay attention!" Harry said. "That's just his daily swim."

Frank and Rob joined them in tag. They heaved the

younger children into the lake amidst shrieks. Janie, Harry, and Kenneth built elaborate sandcastles, christened the Emerald City. They buried Kenneth in the sand.

When afternoon shadows lengthened like stretched taffy, Harry and Kenneth draped over wicker chairs on the porch, eyeing kaleidoscopes. Mr. Baum wrote on his clipboard. Janie finished her fairy library gazebo. He handed her some paper. "Have you considered writing about your fairy friends?"

"No, but they invited me to a very festive party once. They danced around the fairy ring, playing ring-around-the-rosy, telling stories, and drinking ginger ale."

"Sounds jolly."

"But Beatrice complains and gets so furious, lavender steam comes out her ears. So, Estella hides in the lilac bush."

"Such squabbling! You know them like I know the Scarecrow and Tin Woodman."

"How'd you learn about them?"

"Characters are inspirations that strike unexpectedly. But I suspect they've percolated a long time."

"Like Mother's coffee?"

"Yes. The process takes time but results in a delicious brew. The process of creating characters happens constantly, without my awareness. Then, suddenly, I see them."

Janie squinted, aiming to see them herself. "Do you see chickens?"

"Not yet." He chuckled. "I was long ago inspired by Mr. Charles Dickens and his marvelous characters. Someday you'll read *Great Expectations* and understand why. He said, 'In a utilitarian age, of all other times, it is a matter of grave importance that fairy tales should be respected.' Utilitarian has to do with being useful. But life is far more than practicality." He slurped lemonade. "But you already know that. When we add a little magic and imagination to everyday objects, we breathe new life and meaning into them."

She gazed at the bird on the railing, wondering what character it might be. "Do story ideas pop into your head, too?"

"No, the plot takes longer to develop. So be patient when writing. You can add more later, as ideas come."

Ideas already flitted, igniting her imagination, for he'd spoken as if he saw in her a story she'd not seen herself.

Mr. Baum shook his cigar. Ashes flew. "No matter what happens, there's poetic justice. Good always triumphs."

"Like when Cinderella marries the prince, but the stepmother dances in red hot shoes?"

"Exactly." He tapped the typewriter. "You'll need this someday, as a teller of tantalizing tales. I knew it when I first learned about your fairy friends."

He spoke as if knowing fairies was a wonderful bit of serendipity.

He lit another cigar. "Imagination's a fine place for characters to reside, but it's just the beginning. Start your own story. Choose from sprites, elves, nymphs, ryls, knooks, gnomes, brownies ..."

"A ryl and a brownie, please."

"Add three objects. First, a glider. Those Wright Brothers experiment with flight, but fairies get confused by it. The second object ..." He stroked his mustache.

"A rabbit," Janie said. "The Welsh rarebit's sister. Or a chicken!"

"Splendid. The third is a pinafore with a magic pocket."

As he rocked, writing on a clipboard, Janie penciled, *Once upon a time.*

She wrote, amazed at how a string of words in her head could take shape on paper and sound better than if spoken. Perhaps writing was a grander way for preserving words that would otherwise disappear in the atmosphere. She incorporated all three things, including a ryl with five paint pots and a brownie who lived under the stairs.

Mrs. Baum stepped out with a tray. "Time for taffy pulling."

After washing up, they smothered their hands in a bowl of butter. Harry and Mrs. Baum worked on one hunk of red taffy, while Kenneth took another. He pulled, folded, and twisted, then handed Janie an end. She stepped back, pulling on the warm, sticky blob.

"Not so far, Charlotte," Kenneth said. "You'll fly off the porch if it snaps."

Aerated taffy went from red to opaque pink, stiff and shiny. They pulled off sections to roll into ropes. Mrs. Baum cut them into pieces for a strawberry-flavored late afternoon snack.

The boys played checkers. Mrs. Baum stitched pansies on a silk doily.

Mr. Baum handed Janie the Brownie camera. "Take this home. Perhaps you'll have better luck catching a brownie unawares. I'll give your aunt instructions for sending film to Rochester for development. Now then, which three objects for a story?"

"A train," Kenneth replied.

"A toad," Harry said.

Janie smiled coyly. "A hundred-pound wheel of cheddar cheese."

They laughed. "Please make Mrs. Bilkins a character," Janie added.

"Hmm, why is Mrs. Bilkins on a train with a toad and a wheel of cheese?" He slowly repeated his question, then spun a tale about the conductor Mrs. Bilkins and her adventures with a toad, trapped by a hundred pounds of gooey melted cheese, transported on a hot summer day. At the story's conclusion, Aunt Sophie arrived, avoiding the first step.

Janie's heart dropped. Kenneth jumped up, toppling the checkerboard. "May they stay for supper, Mother?" Mrs. Baum extended an invitation. "Yay!" Kenneth grabbed Janie's hands. They hopped around the porch. "Can she come back for the regatta? She *must* be here for Venetian Night. Better than Fourth of July."

"There are boat races and fireworks," Harry said. "The whole lake is lit with lanterns."

"Like a boat parade," Kenneth added. "It's Papa's idea. He's on the committee."

"He's on every committee," Harry said.

Mrs. Baum turned to Aunt Sophie. "We'd love to have you overnight, Miss McKinnon. Charlotte was delightful. She minded me in everything."

Janie winced. Fortunately, Mrs. Baum didn't know about unsupervised wading.

"Most importantly," Mr. Baum said, "she brought her imagination."

Aunt Sophie faced her niece. "You had a good day, chinchilla?"

Janie grinned. "As amazing as a *hyperooden rostratus*."

Sixteen

Tuesday, June 3, 1980

Carrie entered Mrs. Gordon's kitchen. "What're we baking now?"

"Aunt Em's Apple Crisp with Emerald City Green Tea." Mrs. Gordon waved a peeler. "Please gather the ingredients." The teakettle purred.

Stifling a yawn, Carrie complied. Last night, she'd spent two hours typing up yesterday's episode with Mrs. Gordon's commentary. Janie and Aunt Sophie had attended Venetian Night in August though Janie's sunburn nearly sabotaged future outings. Favoring appearances over a daughter's bruised soul, her mother claimed it made Janie look like a poor field hand's child.

Mrs. Gordon needed her story preserved. Carrie wanted to know more, wanted to make her smile, wanted her trust. But why were they baking instead of investigating her husband's charges? The thought of paying for companionship saddened Carrie. She glanced around the kitchen, a baker's heaven. Tea sets galore. Delightful fairy tale tiles and plates. But nobody to share them with. Except Carrie.

Mrs. Gordon filled the sugar bowl. "Moroccan tea is made with gunpowder green tea. Tiny pellets open during the brewing process. Moroccans traditionally add sugar as they brew, but you may add sugar after trying it."

Carrie's skin prickled with agitation. Mrs. Gordon's mandate mimicked her parents, requiring her to fit their mold, whether clothing, social opinions, or college major. "Mrs. Gordon, I'll take sugar when I want it."

"You'll miss the full tea experience."

Bristling, Carrie, presented an envelope. Mrs. Gordon opened it and gave the card to Carrie to read.

Dear Mrs. Gordon,

Thank you for sharing your well-guarded Broderick family recipes. I look forward to baking cinnamon buns. My husband, Edward, couldn't resist the temptation to take another muffin whenever he entered the kitchen.

Sincerely,
Tanna Groothuis

Blinking, Mrs. Gordon held the letter to her chest. When was the last time someone thanked her?

Carrie copied the recipe for her grandmother, plus Gayelette's Golden Scones, referencing the magical Golden Cap that compelled the Winged Monkeys to obey.

While apple crisp baked, they drank tea. Hand-painted lilac sprigs graced a white china tea set against a lavender tablecloth and floral cloth napkins. Mrs. Gordon handed her a trifold booklet: The Broderick Resort & Tearoom Menu, 1957, featuring a photo of the inn, Est. 1885.

Carrie read aloud. "Square Meals offered in honor of the Highly Magnified Woggle-bug, T.E. (Thoroughly Educated). He created the six-course dinner in one pill, which the Shaggy

Man carried on his journeys. Here we serve the actual food so you can enjoy your dining experience longer." She smiled. "Prince Karver's Parmesan-Sage Pork Chops. Tollydiggle's Mutton-chops with Gravy, topped with a Story. Uncle Henry's Farmer Omelette, courtesy of Billina the Hen. Bristle of Bunnybury's Welsh Rarebit. Of course, you had Welsh Rarebit."

Vegetable dishes featured Cowardly Dande-Lion Greens, Scarecrow's Corn and Potato-Sausage Hash, and Nick Chopper's Forest Gusto. Carrie read from the bread section: "In *The Emerald City of Oz*, Bunbury is a village made of flour and meal. Houses, fences, and sidewalks are comprised of crackers, breadsticks, waffles, or crusts. People are formed from buns and bread."

The dessert menu included Emerald City Mint Squares, Princess Ozma's Birthday Cake, Captain Dipp's Ice Cream, Scraps's Peach Bread Pudding, and Winkie Surprise—cobbler featuring the fruit of the day. Tea was served in cups from Dainty China Country: The Great Elixir's Orange Jasmine Tea, Glinda's Passionfruit Papaya, and Spiced Jinjur Plum.

Carrie chuckled. "Such a creative menu." She sipped tea and grimaced. Needed sugar.

"When I left the tearoom, the new owner changed the menu, but I've had worse disappointments," Mrs. Gordon said.

Teddy? Thwarted goals? Her parents? This journey fascinated her. "Did you return to Macatawa the next year?"

"That's where I'm taking you today."

Janie, 11
July 1903

Janie took the Baum's porch steps with exuberance, then disappointment. "No bells—oh, look!" A tarp covered the porch floor. Apron-clad with rolled-up sleeves, Mr. Baum stood behind a black iron contraption on the table, surrounded by ink bottles, papers, and a tray over a faded tablecloth. Wind swayed a painted oak rocker with goose-shaped sides.

"Welcome to paradise!" His hands were dark with ink. "My seventeen-year-old niece Matilda is visiting this summer. She's golfing with Robert. Harry and Kenneth left with bows and arrows, but perhaps got waylaid by bandits. They can handle themselves, though. Now choose an engraved picture and a poem."

Janie viewed metal plates with images of flowers or animals. She picked a chicken, then paged through Mr. Baum's *Father Goose, His Book.* "What're you making, Mr. Baum?"

"Better yet, what are *we* making?" He handed her a paint-splotched apron, which Auntie tied. "We're printing book pages and typesetting a poem engraving for a book of your own." He slipped the chicken engraving into a metal frame. "This is a chase. The image goes in just so." He handed her a slim metal rod. "This key tightens shapes so nothing slips or expands."

Gritting her teeth, Janie turned the key in the tight slot.

"Good. Did you find a poem?"

"How about the Good Witch's line? 'You must walk. It is a long journey ...'"

"Help me find letters." He pointed to the tray, each section filled with tiny metal figures, symbols, and punctuation.

Mrs. Baum appeared bearing a tray of glasses and a pitcher. She hugged Janie, poured lemonade, and invited Auntie in. At the door, she shook her finger. "Frank, I'd better not find one tiny ink spot on my porch."

He snickered. "I laid tarps so thick an elephant can't gnaw through them."

Janie giggled. "Or a Cowardly Lion?" She'd be careful to not bump letters or spill paint. "Is this how people make books?"

"It's a smaller version of what publishers use, like mine at age fourteen. My brother Harry and I printed several newsletters." He handed her a four-page paper, *The Rose Lawn Home Journal*. "Rose Lawn was our family property."

Janie read through riddles, jokes, and poems. "'True Origin of Cardiff Giant'?"

"The great hoax of the petrified Cardiff Giant, dug up fourteen miles from our home, a ten-foot man of stone. Its discovery inspired this poem. I imagined the giant jumped overboard from Noah's ark, then stuck in the mud until someone dug him up centuries later."

Janie quavered, "Maybe Jack the Giant Killer attacked him. How was it discovered?"

"A man secretly had the stone giant built and buried on a farmer's property to be found later, supposedly by accident. When news circulated, the farmer charged fifty cents per view. Thousands came. Finally, the man claimed it was a hoax." He puffed the cigar.

"Were people upset?"

"Absurdly enough, even more folks came. Such a sensation that P.T. Barnum offered good money to feature it in his Greatest Show on Earth." He rearranged letters. "When the Syracuse men refused to sell, Mr. Barnum made his own petrified man, claiming it was the Cardiff Giant."

"A fake of a fake." Janie spelled out *dark* on the table.

"No wonder Mr. Barnum is called the Prince of Humbugs. It occasioned the line, 'There's a sucker born every minute.'" He tapped the cigar on the table. "My sister Mary Louise wrote poetry for our journal and created a Rose Lawn alphabet. Each letter stood for something in our household." He set down four Ts.

"Can I make the Macatawa ABCs book?" *H* and *K* would stand for the Baum boys.

"Splendid idea. Right after this one." He arranged the last word.

They sorted and set letters on the type stick, then tightened it into the metal frame.

"Your parents didn't mind you making newsletters?" she asked.

"They encouraged my literary interests, though my father hoped I'd have a mind for business too." He smirked.

"My dad wants me to get better arithmetic grades. But I'm not good in schoolwork."

"Learning goes beyond textbooks, my dear. Remember what the Wizard told the Scarecrow? Only experience brings knowledge. Today you're having a new one."

She grinned. "What else have you printed?"

"Cards and programs. And my own newspaper in Aberdeen."

"With Mrs. Bilkins?" She offered a sly smile.

"More of a nuisance than a help." He snorted. "I printed a poetry book called *By the Candelabra's Glare*, with my own poems. Now, pick a color."

She chose yellow. He helped her apply a golden blob of ink on the metal plate. Her hand shook. What if she dropped ink? Mrs. Baum would be furious.

He let her use the foot pedal to see how ink coated moving rollers. Tentatively, she pressed the pedal. What if it broke? She cringed. *You broke my good china!*

He operated it, showing her how to feed paper to the machine, one at a time. Her mother's voice cackled in her head. *Useless, in her own world again.*

They printed a dozen sheets and set them aside to dry, a vibrant row of chickens. No spills, thank goodness. She admired detailed feathers. "Did you print your chicken book?"

"No, I wrote a pamphlet called *The Book of the Hamburgs*, about managing Hamburg chickens. My father, brother, and I bred them."

Her father's chickens were leghorns and buckeyes. Her mother considered serving hamburger. "You mean those sandwich things from the World's Fair? I thought they were beef."

He laughed. "Those are. *These* Hamburgs require fastidious care and are exceptional egg producers."

"You must love chickens."

"We had fancy roosters and hens, developed new strains, and won prizes across the county. So, yes, I have a fondness for our fair fowl-feathered friends." He sniggered at his pun, waving his cigar with a flourish.

"Wonderful alliteration, Mr. Baum." She'd learned the word in fourth grade. "Can we make the ABCs now?"

"Absolutely. Mix and match letters as you please." He washed ink off the plate and rollers and stacked dried papers. Janie inspected styles and sizes, settling on a pleasing arrangement. They refilled the type stick, leaving room for handwritten words.

She selected blue and carefully dotted ink on the plate. Again, he operated the foot pedal and guided her trembling hand as she inserted and withdrew pages. Her hand finally steadied. Taking the last print, she bumped the table. An open jar of blue ink crashed onto the floor, forming a puddle on the tarp.

Janie gasped, covering her face. Her mother's voice barked. *You're nothing but trouble!* She dropped to the floor, weeping. *You make a fool of me every day.*

"Charlotte, it's an accident."

Aunt Sophie appeared and pulled Janie into a hug. Mrs. Baum stepped out. "A good thing you laid this tarp, L.F. So thick an elephant can't gnaw through it." She patted Janie's wet cheeks. Janie's crying reduced to sniffles.

Mr. Baum handed Janie the dried pages. "Time for making ABCs." He took the printing press inside and cleaned up as she listed words. *B* could be Baum, Black Lake, Blackbird Pie, Boardwalk, or Boat. *F* could be Father Goose, Fish, or Fireworks. *L* could be Lake Michigan, Lighthouse, or Lemonade.

He returned and refilled lemonade glasses. "Have another

dose of ozone, Miss McKinnon." He pointed to the goose-sided rocking chair.

Aunt Sophie sat. "I hear the Oz extravaganza is doing well in New York City. What are you working on now? Or, should I say, discovering?"

"Like these cigars, one good thing has ended for another to begin." He lit a new cigar from the old. "I finished *The Enchanted Island of Yew*, along the lines of old-fashioned fairy tales, to be published this fall. Mr. Tietjens and I are working on another musical comedy."

"Island of *You*?" Janie wrote *Enchanted Island* by the printed *E. C* for Cheese.

"Y-E-W. It's a tree. I'm dedicating it to Kenneth, as it's his turn. *The Master Key* was inspired by Robert. The *Santa Claus* book was dedicated to Harry." She wrote *Master Key* by the *M*. "Frank might need a book dedication, too. He's nineteen, stationed in the Philippines after graduating from Michigan Military Academy. Robert will attend this fall. An irony, for I couldn't abide military school myself. Teachers were as human as a school of fish, ever poised to slap a hand or poke with a cane to enforce senseless rules." He offered Janie a sober look, as a kindred spirit. "I struggled to not see myself how they viewed me. I left mid-year. But Frank copes well."

Janie's gaze meandered over treetops. Were yew trees good hiding places for fairies?

Mr. Baum inquired about Aunt Sophie's teaching experiences.

"Times have changed, Mr. Baum. Educators finally determined that childhood is an important time of development, that children are to be nurtured, like seeds, as taught by Rousseau and Locke. Education should be pleasant."

Janie wrote Welsh rarebit, Waukezoo Trail, Wizard, Wicked Witch of the West.

Mr. Baum said *The Master Key* was listed in *St. Nicholas* magazine as one of the most popular books, though sales disappointed. *American Fairy Tales* was not well received. To his chagrin, nobody viewed Chicago and familiar settings as a fairyland capable of magic. But *A New Wonderland* was being reissued under another title: *The Surprising Adventures of the Magical Monarch of Mo and His People.*

M for Magical Monarch of Mo. *D* for Dorothy. "Will you write another Dorothy story?"

Mr. Baum chuckled. "So many children ask. I received a bevy of letters from girls named Dorothy and folks ages five to seventy."

"Seventy?" Sign of the Goose, Sailboat, Sandcastle, Scarecrow. *T* for Tin Woodman.

"My books are intended for all whose hearts are young, no matter their age. I'm so touched by every letter that I reply to each."

Janie scooted forward. "So will you write a Dorothy story?"

He exhaled, watching smoke rise as if seeking an answer. "I haven't heard news from Oz. So many projects pull me in different directions. But I promised a young Dorothy that if I receive a thousand letters from girls requesting a Dorothy story, I'd write one."

"A thousand!" Janie set down her pencil. "Since Dorothy lives on a farm, she has animal companions. First, Toto. Then Imogene the Cow. What about a chicken friend? You know so much about chickens, especially those Hamburgs." She cast Aunt Sophie a smug look, as if possessing secret information.

He picked up his glass. "Hmm."

"Are you thinking about it, Mr. Baum?"

Aunt Sophie frowned. "Don't pester."

"She's hardly pestering, ma'am. All questions are welcome. Pestering is hiding my cigars or playing Wagner's 'Ride of the Valkyries.'" He shuddered. "Matilda has abominable taste in music."

Aunt Sophie murmured to her niece, "Better to err on the side of caution."

"Fiddlesticks! Exercising caution would mean no Father Goose, no Oz, no Macatawa Park." He eyed Janie. "It's risky letting your imagination run free. But it's necessary." He shook his cigar, ashes drifting to the floor. "Vital, actually, though living with fairies takes more courage than jumping down dunes."

Especially at home. *D* for dune. *F* for Fairy. *B* for Brownies. *T* for Taffy.

He gestured to the Goose sign. "Let me take a gander." He examined her list. "Marvelous. Remember *C* for Camera. Did you finish the story you started last year?"

"Yes, it's at home." Pages for wood stove fuel if her parents read them.

"Bring it next time, Charlotte. Let's create a story now. No more difficult than cooking a savory pot of soup." He put a finger to his chin. "Name a Grimm Brothers tale."

"'The Bremen Town Musicians.'"

"That's the basic broth, but switch ingredients. Instead of a donkey, dog, cat, and—"

"How about an elephant, monkey, parrot, and lizard?"

"Instead of going to Bremen, they're on their way to ..."

"A boat race."

"Instead of aspiring to be musicians, they wish to ..."

Janie watched the lake through tree branches. "Be sailors."

"Toss in trouble, for zest."

"Pirates!"

"Stir in poetic justice at the end."

Janie told a story of how four friends found a battered ship for the race and headed out on the ocean. Pirates came up from the hold and attacked, claiming stolen treasure. The four friends used their unique animal talents to capture the pirates and return the treasure to its owner. Poetic justice was served when the friends were handsomely rewarded with half the treasure.

Mr. Baum and Aunt Sophie applauded. "It's ripe for writing," he said.

She grabbed the pencil and wrote while Mr. Baum and Auntie talked. Soon, Janie asked, "What's your new show about?"

"Which one?" He snorted. "I've difficulty focusing on just one thing. Mr. Tietjens and I are writing about new Ozian characters. I wrote 'The Alligator Song' for the annual vaudeville night here, also for *Prince Silverwings*. I wrote a play for gala night at Ottawa Beach Hotel."

"Do you prefer theater to writing books?" Auntie asked.

"Theater's my first love. I acted in Shakespeare and dramas that I penned, performing on stages across the States. My best musical script was *The Maid of Arran*, an Irish melodrama, based on William Black's novel. One of my numerous plays that was actually produced."

He whirled his cigar. "I would've continued in theater forever, but alas, when little Frank's birth loomed, Mrs. Baum felt I should have a job that paid the bills, rather than gallivanting by my creative whims. So, I went from *The Maid of Arran* to selling Castorine Oil. In my soul, job-wise, it felt like going from Welsh rarebit to stale breadcrumbs."

Aunt Sophie nodded. "Some things are to be valued more than money. John Greenleaf Whittier says"—her voice took on the theatrical—"'If thou of fortune be bereft, and in thy store there be but left two loaves, sell one, and with the dole, buy hyacinths to feed thy soul.'"

Mr. Baum clapped. "Wonderful! Money merely helps to avoid creditors, while funding projects of destiny. Money's for living well. A miser's never content." He raised his glass toward Aunt Sophie. "I subscribe to Oscar Wilde's philosophy, 'Anyone who lives within their means suffers from a lack of imagination.' So, if you need financial advice, speak to my wife. She encourages my flights of fancy with her own feet on the ground. A superb combination."

Mrs. Baum appeared in the doorway. "How long does it take to shoot arrows? Dinner's almost ready."

"Perhaps the boys ran into Robin Hood and his merry men," Mr. Baum said.

Unamused, she returned to the kitchen. Talk concluded with banter over the Chicago Cubs and Detroit Tigers. Aunt Sophie kissed Janie and left.

"Are we having Welsh rarebit again, sir?" Janie asked.

"We'll eat whatever Mrs. Baum dictates." He sniffed. "Smells like roast chicken. I dare not order cheese without permission. I learned the hard way with the Bismarcks."

SEVENTEEN

July 1903

Bismarck doughnuts? Janie frowned. Whatever happened?

She wrote Bismarcks after *B. H* for Harbor, Holland, Harry, *Hyperooden Rostratus*. How would she decide? *V* for Venetian Night—no competition there.

"Hey, Charlotte!" Harry and Kenneth, thirteen and twelve, bounded up the porch steps, toting bows and arrows.

"Dedicate your story to me." Harry posed with his bow as if aiming for a beast.

Hair sticking out in multiple directions, Kenneth jumped in front of him. "I'm more worthy." His show of muscles emphasized his ragged shirt.

Mrs. Baum called. Inside, the parlor was more magical than before. While stenciled geese still flew across green walls, brass goosehead nails trimmed leather upholstery.

Kenneth pointed to a rocking chair. "Father's been woodworking. Besides the goose-shaped chair on the porch, he built all this furniture."

"My doctor prescribed a less strenuous hobby than theater

production." Mr. Baum waved his cigar. Janie traced a burned-in goose on the rocking chair back. As adept with wood as with words.

"He also built a dining room shelf for a dictionary, atlas, and encyclopedia," Harry said. "We got tired of traipsing to the parlor to settle disputes."

"When I was a baby," Kenneth said, "he rigged a jumper in the doorway that bounced when Mother pulled a cord."

"Using electricity?" Janie asked.

"We had no electricity," Mr. Baum said. "And still don't in our Chicago house."

"Though we just moved to a nicer place," Harry added.

"I prefer kerosene lighting," Mr. Baum said.

They bustled into the kitchen for a meal of roasted chicken, mashed potatoes, green beans, and something called Jell-O. Did Mother know about it? Mrs. Baum explained that it was strawberry-flavored with fresh peaches stirred in. Boiled first, then cooled in the icebox.

Harry told Janie he was six before realizing chickens didn't have four legs.

"Really?" Janie offered a coy smile. "Even though your father's a chicken expert?"

"Frank and Robert got the chicken legs since they were older. Mother handed us wings. We didn't know better."

"Why do you prefer kerosene, Mr. Baum?" Janie's parents wired the inn for electricity years ago, praising its brightness.

"With electric lights, edges are sharp and clear, unlike the fuzziness of gaslight." He leaned forward. "Darkness is just as alive as daylight, but electricity banishes darkness." He slashed a line through the air. "Kerosene illuminates it." His wiggling fingers spread, hands following an arc.

"Like fireflies." Janie squinted as if peering into a summer night. "Or candlelight."

Mr. Baum gestured. "Imagine hazy moonlight rippling over treetops."

"Reflecting on the lake," Janie said.

"God created both day and night. Nature's darkness has its own beauty. Picture evening delights of bonfires."

"With popcorn," Harry said.

Mrs. Baum chimed in. "Rest from the day, warm quilts."

"Croaking frogs," Kenneth added.

"A cricket chorus," Mr. Baum said, "all under the umbrella of twinkling stars and velvet backdrop." He kissed his wife's hand. "And sitting on the porch swing with your sweetheart."

"You need a dark sky for fireworks," Janie added.

Mr. Baum sliced chicken. "The White City's lights, three times more than all Chicago, couldn't be appreciated in daylight."

How did electricity disperse the darkness? Janie visualized dark dots swirling and whooshing away like wind, as streetlamps turned on, one by one.

"For those who dream of great futures," Mr. Baum said, "night is essential. Mr. Oscar Wilde put it perfectly. 'A dreamer is one who can only find his way by moonlight, and his punishment is that he sees the dawn before the rest of the world.'"

Janie frowned. "Punishment?"

Mr. Baum chortled. "A fancy way of saying that dreamers see how things can be long before others are ready. They're chided by those with no imagination."

"Dreamers are ahead of their time," Mrs. Baum said. "Suffragists like my mother."

"And authors, artists, musicians, inventors," Mr. Baum added.

Janie jiggled her Jell-O. "So, punishment is the Wright brothers being laughed at for their ideas about flying heavier-than-air craft."

"Exactly." Mr. Baum scooped potatoes. "Stories arise from the enchanting blend of dreams and memories in that magical place between slumber and wakefulness."

"Is that when you discover ideas, Papa?" Kenneth asked.

"Perhaps, for when I wake, I can't write them down fast enough."

Mrs. Baum smirked. "That's when he writes on the bedroom wallpaper."

The children restrained giggles through impish smiles.

"In our Chicago home," Mr. Baum continued, "we gathered around a kerosene lamp to read and talk. That's when I told nursery rhyme stories that eventually became *Mother Goose in Prose*. Neighbor children came too. After dark, Patrolman Jamieson saw them home safely."

"On cold nights," Harry said, "we pulled taffy or made popcorn balls."

"On warm nights, we made ice cream," Kenneth said. "Harry and I had a contest to see who could crank the most."

"It was no contest," Harry said. "I always won."

Mrs. Baum placed an arm between the boys before Kenneth could react. "Enough."

Why didn't Janie's family tell stories, pull taffy, or eat popcorn balls together?

"In summer," Harry said, "we rode bicycles to Humboldt Park for Sunday picnics and music in the bandstand."

Janie and Aunt Sophie walked to the park to hear bands and quartets.

Kenneth stabbed a peach. "Once Father got an advance for—"

"No," Mrs. Baum snapped. "It's impolite to speak of finances."

Kenneth pouted. Janie predicted he'd relay the story later in private. Instead, he told about his dad dressing as Santa, sneaking a tree into the house every Christmas. Holidays were celebrated in grandiose style regardless of finances.

Mr. Baum asked for suggestions, then conjured a tale from a seashell, magnet, and hammer, concluding with, "After swallowing the magnet, the boy attracted many friends with his magnetic personality."

Mrs. Baum groaned. Janie giggled. Harry and Kenneth exploded into fits of hilarity, holding out their hands. Mr. Baum pulled a dime from his pocket and held it over Harry's palm, then Kenneth's, going back and forth, producing louder guffaws. He finally dropped it into Harry's. Kenneth frowned.

Mrs. Baum rolled her eyes. "Charlotte, we're outnumbered by three *boys* at this table. Their antics are worse this summer with our dear niece Matilda here."

"I'm proud of Matilda," Mr. Baum said. "She passed muster for pun mastery."

Mrs. Baum plopped a chicken breast on her husband's plate. "I worry about you stretching the truth, especially with journalists."

Kenneth whispered, "He doesn't know the difference between fantasy and reality."

Janie smiled. Her parents said the same thing about her.

While Harry and Kenneth washed dishes, Janie added to her ABCs on the porch. Nearby, Mr. Baum smoked and typed. She stared at the rising smoke. Was that how night dissipated when lights turned on, circling to the sky, hovering until light was extinguished?

D for Dragonflies, Darkness, Dreamer, Dawn. *K* for kerosene.

Mr. Baum, Janie, and the boys boated on Lake Michigan. Janie pushed her hat back, inviting sunshine to caress her face. Robert and Matilda joined them on the beach. Matilda waded while Robert played water games with the younger ones. They built sandcastles. Mr. Baum took his customary swim, identical to last year's, hat and cigar intact.

Afterward, Kenneth asked his father for three pennies. Mr. Baum scraped his pockets for loose change, muttering about his money disappearing, though it jingled with each movement. He finally opened his hand to reveal three shiny nickels. The children ran to Colby's Pavilion and bought candy. Outside, after Harry emptied half of Kenneth's Good & Plenty, Kenneth tricked him out of a Tootsie Roll. Janie hugged her Cracker Jack box.

They ate while watching the railcar climb Angel's Flight, the incline railway sloping up Old Baldhead Dune. Fishermen lined the pier. Down the shoreline, at Jenison Electric Park, boaters and bathers abounded, the circular swing spun. Shrieks rivaled the rumbles of the new wooden Figure-8 roller coaster. Janie hoped to ride it sometime.

Walking back, Kenneth relayed the banned story with such animation that Janie suspected extreme exaggeration. His father had reluctantly picked up an advance paycheck for *The Wonderful Wizard of Oz* before Christmas, pocketed without looking at it. At home, when Mrs. Baum saw it, she screamed, so excited that she forgot her iron and burned a hole in the shirt. The check was for more than three thousand dollars. He framed the canceled check as a souvenir of good fortune.

At the cottage, Mrs. Baum collected the remaining candy to be rationed and surreptitiously handed Janie a chocolate drop. "This is worth the indulgence, but don't show the boys. Mr. Baum gives me a box of candies weekly." With a sly smile, Janie promised silence.

On the porch, the boys played Old Maid. Mr. Baum read while Mrs. Baum showed Janie embroidery stitches. "In our early Chicago days, I gave lessons, ten cents a visit."

Relishing the chocolate, Janie admired the French knots and lazy daisy stitches. "What're you making?"

"Flowers on these pinafore pockets." Mrs. Baum handed her scrap muslin, a needle, thread, and thimble. Janie's fingers fumbled through numerous attempts and finger pokes, then managed a row of cross stitches.

After supper, they strolled on the beach boardwalk with Rob and Matilda. Setting sun sparkled over Lake Michigan, spawning rosy clouds through an orange sky. Before the lake swallowed the sun, Mr. Baum brought them inside around the piano. "We play at the Yacht Club, so the boys have their instruments here, with their robust voices. Let's have music hour without electricity as dusk settles in."

On the piano, he performed "The Traveler and the Pie" and "When You Love, Love, Love" from the extravaganza, his deep baritone voice filling the room. Mrs. Baum lit the kerosene lamp, illuminating the dusk. The smoking flame mesmerized, casting shadows that moved like shaggy gray beasts over terrain.

Out came guitars and mandolin for rousing versions of "She'll Be Comin' Round the Mountain" and "I've Been Working on the Railroad." Matilda requested "Daisy." The boys outdid each other volume-wise for "Clementine" and Stephen Foster's "De Camptown Races."

Twilight moved over for night to slip in. Mr. Baum made hand shadow shapes against the wall as the children guessed: a kangaroo, elephant, and giraffe. He and his sons concluded the evening, singing "Good Night Ladies" in harmony to Mrs. Baum, Matilda, and Janie.

Janie followed Mrs. Baum and the kerosene lamp up creaky, shadow-filled steps, shivers tingling her. In her nightdress, she slid into cool sheets. Fresh air spun through the windows, tickling her face. As Mrs. Baum left with the lamp, flames of light diminished. Particles of darkness jumped in to take their place.

Remnants of waves, sandcastles, Cracker Jack, ABCs, and jaunty tunes filled her, preventing sleep. Last year, she'd slept here with Aunt Sophie on Venetian Night. But tonight, the room felt like a cavern in this big, raspy house. *The dark is just as alive as the daylight.* She gazed out the window. Moonlit clouds scudded across the sky.

The door cracked open, revealing silhouettes of Mr. and Mrs. Baum. "We heard you tossing and turning." Mrs. Baum waved her husband toward the corner rocker. Sitting on the bed, she took Janie's hand, stroked her hair. "Close your eyes, dear. Sleep well so your aunt will bring you again."

Janie wanted next time to be tomorrow. She wanted to live here.

Mr. Baum sang, "Hush, little baby, don't say a word. Mama's gonna buy you a mockingbird ..."

Eighteen

June 3, 1980

"Another wonderful day," Carrie said.

"Also," Mrs. Gordon said, "Auntie surprised me with a visit to Jenison Electric Park with her friend Dena Vanderlaan and sixteen-year-old sister Katrina."

After lunch, they watered flowers and weeded, penance for 1969's trampled tulips. Bluebells swayed. Hollyhocks started their climb to the sky. When would Carrie hear about the homicide charge? Yet no use hurrying a woman who likely hired her for companionship.

Mrs. Gordon fell asleep on the porch. The previous week, Carrie saw this place as Hansel and Gretel's gingerbread cottage, housing a witch. But now, looking over the fence, she viewed the world from Mrs. Gordon's eyes. Lonely. Distant.

She went inside to peruse books, gravitating to the forbidden *Gatekeeper of Merrimack Castle*, pulled from circulation, symbolized by Oma's treasure box paintbrush.

Carrie read on the shady porch, breeze tufting her shirt as the story's tension festered. Wendolyn had one goal: to reach Merrimack Castle, the place of wonders. But three troll-size dragons—Lieso, Shamea, and Fearat—chased her. They thwarted her efforts by barricades or evil magic, stretching an hour-long trip into days. Finally, she arrived, greeted by the jovial Gatekeeper. Chapter Seven. Mrs. Gordon stirred. "I'm reading *Wendolyn and the—*"

"Put that back." The woman's voice was sharp.

Carrie deflated. "Okay. But I'll just read my grandma's book."

"It's pure trash."

"It's very well written."

"Not speaking well of your tastes."

"Then why do you own it? I have excellent literary taste." Fuming, Carrie took the book inside. No doubt what her bedtime reading would be.

She returned with iced lemonade. Only fifteen minutes left, thank goodness. *Now apologize for snapping at me.* But Carrie was used to no apologies.

Mrs. Gordon stared across the porch. "I asked Mother about serving Jell-O to guests. She warned that if I wanted to return to Holland with Auntie, I must stop bothering her with silly ideas. I constantly feared displeasing her."

"Surely one of many fears."

"That year, my uncle's collie died. Pepper followed me everywhere, tail wagging. But one day, a rabid fox attacked her. My uncle shot her. While I watched."

"Horrible!"

"I vomited, cried all day. Father discussed it at supper, as if predicting weather. I ran upstairs. Father came to fetch me. I was sobbing." She winced. "I said Pepper was my friend. He replied, 'Get downstairs and quit fussing.'"

Like the freshwater turtle Carrie put in the saltwater tank. She wept when it died. Her parents berated her. "What'd he do?"

"I went downstairs to avoid a whipping. 'You act like a city

girl,' Mother said. 'So feeble-minded, I'm ashamed of you.'"
Mrs. Gordon grimaced.

The castigation of Carrie's own parents gripped her.

Mrs. Gordon's voice quavered. "'Eat your carrots,' she said, "or you won't go back to Holland.' That was the clincher. Fighting nausea, I ate. Mother didn't speak to me for days."

Carrie kept her eyes on Mrs. Gordon. The woman glanced at her, then blinked, as if she couldn't take in the concern on Carrie's face. Carrie tried to dismiss images of being shamed by silence, parents walking away, blind to her pain.

"Aunt Sophie and the Baums understood and accepted me, but that didn't sustain me through spiteful treatment at home. My siblings were competent, levelheaded, not plagued by vivid imaginations. But I was a bafflement to my mother. Forgetful, given to flights of fancy. I didn't work fast enough, couldn't sit still in church. I mismatched socks. Cried over dead animals. Mother was determined to set me on the path to righteousness. Everything, from daydreaming to forgetting chores, was on the sin spectrum." She looked crestfallen.

How would Mrs. Gordon's life have been different without parents invoking false sins, punishing without love? "Sounds like a normal child. Your folks only understood Mr. Legality." Carrie fought off images—her own father's gruffness, Mother's sharp tongue.

Carrie touched the woman's hand. Mrs. Gordon flinched and withdrew it. Yet Carrie hovered, eyes fastened on the wrinkled face, willing her to turn in Carrie's direction. Something instinctively told her to keep looking, that *looking* was what Mrs. Gordon needed most. Someone *seeing* her. With acceptance. *Look. At. Me.*

Finally, Mrs. Gordon reciprocated, but couldn't meet Carrie's steady gaze. Was she fighting tears with each blink? Shame. The shame of being invisible.

Not the shame that accompanies true guilt. This kind

nibbles, saying you can't measure up, you're not worthy of love. The kind that unhitches you, with no remedy.

The kind of shame you feel when you cry, and no one notices. When you accidentally kill a turtle. When parents criticize your desire to reupholster furniture. When you work up courage to share your soul, but they leave and close the door.

Carrie grasped Mrs. Gordon's wrist. "You're not invisible anymore." The old lady's heartbeat pattered rapid fire under Carrie's fingers.

"Time to go." Mrs. Gordon stared at her lap.

Carrie shuffled home with leaden footsteps, as if carrying Mrs. Gordon's pain instead of dessert. Surely the story of her husband's murder allegation would prove more gut-wrenching.

At home, Oma told her Brian had called. He was coming to town Saturday. Good. Surely talking in person would compensate for two phone disasters. Maybe she'd take him to Mrs. Gordon's. Show him the café. Introduce him to Dirk. On second thought, maybe not. She imagined struggling to help him understand the café's value. And Dirk, well, likewise.

Carrie gave Oma the recipes, mentioning how touched Mrs. Gordon was by the thank you note. Oma's face lit. Apple crisp and Opa's chatter about car engines accompanied supper.

Afterward, weary, Carrie washed dishes.

Oma dried. "Why's my *liefje* so quiet tonight?"

Oma's notice felt like salve. "Whatever happened to my mother? You've always been happy, thoughtful, and generous. You're patient and don't mind messes. You fix scraped knees with a smile. People in the community admire Mom, but at home, she's harsh. And cold. I can't meet her expectations. What happened?"

Oma sighed. "She wasn't always that way. No, ma'am. My sweet Arlene. Just a little high-strung. Our kids were happy as clams in Holland. Your opa worked for Van Noord Motors. Very respected in business. Then a car they'd repaired crashed, near-fatal. Three people from one family were injured. They sued the shop for damages. It was the mechanic's fault. He and Opa went to court. The judge ruled it negligence. Opa got blamed too, and accepted it, because he'd trusted the mechanic instead of double-checking things.

"It was awful. Opa took on financial burden for things insurance didn't cover. Hospital bills were astronomical, and Van Noord Motors lost business. Their reputation took a tailspin. The only way to recoup was to fire Opa and the mechanic. Every time Opa blinked, he was criticized. We couldn't afford to stay in our house, so we started over in Wolcott."

"Mom must've been horrified."

"*Ja*, she was only fifteen. She constantly ducked snide remarks. Opa handled the fallout tolerably, but Arlene lost friends. Right in the middle of high school, we picked up and moved here. She hates this town because of it. She hated us too." Oma dried a pan. "We hoped Wolcott would give her a fresh start, but this town became symbolic of everything she'd lost. Especially friends. She felt humiliated."

"Wow."

"She turned bitter. Your Uncle Jim and Aunt Patty were in college, not as impacted. Here, Opa worked for Howard Motors, repairing engines and later buying cars at auction for dealerships. I went to market without running into folks who used to be friends." Oma stopped drying. "Others have faced hotter fires. But this was ours."

"Can't imagine."

Oma stared out the window. "I shouldn't judge Mrs. Gordon. Some of her reputation springs from that murder charge against her husband, a blight on the Broderick and Gordon family names since 1918. But there's always more to the story." Another sigh. "I'm sorry for my criticism. I overreacted." Oma wiped a plate. "It took a while to mend. We had to forgive folks. The only way to start *de wind in de zeilen hebben.* Start catching the wind in the sails. We made new friends. Though I missed our old church. Still do." She paused. "Your mother vowed she'd never look stupid again."

"Is that why I can't measure up?"

"*Ja, liefje,* that started her perfectionism. Appearances above all. She needs her family to be above reproach, to succeed. Or *look* like they do."

Like Amy's right choices—college, career, clothes, even coffee. Successful husband, perfectly scheduled toddler.

"During that dark time, I had a childhood nightmare again. Alone in the woods, abandoned. Crying for help. Psalm 27 took on new meaning. 'The Lord is my light and my salvation. Whom shall I fear?'"

"Did a treasure box object help you?"

"*Ja,* the ladder from *The Meticulous Meddling of Madame Throttlemeier* reminded me of Wendolyn's courage in facing an obstacle. If a boulder blocked her, she'd climb over it with her magic ladder to see a new perspective." She dried the plate. "It reminded me to *trek de stout schoenen aan.* Put on the brave shoes. Incidentally, the Vandenakkers in Holland, Dirk's grandparents, were among the few supportive folks. We knew Dirk's dad Roy and Dirk's Uncle John before John moved here to buy the hardware store in 1966."

That evening, with the librarian's help, Carrie discovered two books by a minister and Oz admirer, Frederich Buechner. In *Telling the Truth,* she read about his analogy of the Gospel to a fairy tale, where good battled evil, good won and lived happily ever after. Not just once upon a time, but continuously. Carrie puzzled over the author's analogies, how the marvel and mystery of the Gospel faded when preachers tried to make it rational and manageable. One ended up with a humbug wizard, or an Emerald City that only sparkled green while the viewer wore tinted glasses.

In Buechner's other book, *The Magnificent Defeat*, he used the road analogy for life—and Dorothy's journey—to explain how travel unmasked people, stripping away roles. *Masks*.

After typing Mrs. Gordon's 1903 memories, Carrie read more of the forbidden *Gatekeeper* book. Alexandre Dumas's quote prefaced it: "Happiness is like those places in fairy tales whose gates are guarded by dragons: We must fight in order to conquer it."

She continued in chapter seven. Though still hunted, Wendolyn finally reached the Castle, amidst the wonders of the magic paintbrush that opened doors and new vistas. As the gatekeeper led the tour, voices called Wendolyn to turn around. Someone desperately claimed to need her help. Was it a trick? Was it those dragons Lieso, Shamea, and Fearat?

That was where Carrie left off, reading herself to sleep.

NINETEEN

PART TWO: SEEKING HOME

Wednesday, June 4, 1980

Upon arrival, Carrie beelined to the window and opened the drapes. Crown molding outlined the coffered oak ceiling. In the center hung a brass lamp with etched globes. Silver-laced valentines gleamed from shadow boxes beside a gilt-framed mirror.

In the kitchen, Mrs. Gordon was making Scraps's Peach Bread Pudding. Petite Fleur Porcelain teacups topped a lace tablecloth. "We're having Spiced General Jinjur Plum tea with ginger and cinnamon. The flavors' vim and vigor represent the power of a woman's influence. Jot Scraps's recipe for your grandmother, plus Winkie Surprise."

"I read Oma's *Gatekeeper* book last night," Carrie said with a hint of sass. "Voices are calling Wendolyn back from the castle. Must be those nasty dragons, out to steal happiness."

"I hope you survive the suspense."

"I found an article by Mr. Baum, 'What Children Want.' He

said children need adventure and fairy tales over sentimentality, with action moving swiftly like a current.”

“He’d no use for dull, prosy pieces. Children loved his stories, though librarians didn’t.”

“Why?”

“High on entertainment, low on moral instruction. In 1957, the Detroit Public Library sent denouncements that spread over the nation. It’s reminiscent of Ray Bradbury’s story, where books are banned by non-dreamers of the world. When the last Oz book goes into the fire, the Emerald City falls.” Mrs. Gordon explained the progression of Oz acceptance over the decades, naming author fans and biographers who gave Baum credibility.

“I found another Oz fan,” Carrie said. “Frederick Buechner, a minister. He calls *Oz* our nation’s greatest fairy tale and one of its great myths.”

Mrs. Gordon peered over her glasses. “Indeed?”

“He says fairy tales point to our longing for restoration, good overpowering evil. How we’re powerless to save ourselves from evil, but God redeems by *His* power.”

“Turning fairy tales into some Christian analogy is preposterous.”

Later, in the front room, Mrs. Gordon said, “Put the drapes back. Too much light fades the books.”

Even her books abhorred daylight. Carrie trudged to the window as if regressing into shadows, further from prying open Mrs. Gordon’s life. She moved the drapes two inches.

Carrie sat. “Albert Einstein said, ‘If you want your children to be intelligent, read them fairy tales.’” Hoping to draw a smile, Carrie spread her arms in a grand gesture. “‘Knowledge is limited, but imagination encircles the world.’”

No smile. “Baum’s Oz successor, Ruth Plumly Thompson, said, ‘Imagination is the magic that accomplishes the impossible.’”

"Too bad your aunt didn't have such quotes to reason with your mother," Carrie said.

"Auntie gave up. We continued going to Macatawa without Mother knowing. The next Holland trip started with an overnight at Dena and Katrina Vanderlaan's, then taking the *Lizzie Walsh* steamer to Macatawa Park."

Janie, 12
July 1904

A jangle of shouts emanated from the Baum porch as Janie and Aunt Sophie approached. Dioramas, the printing press—what now? Coming here was like indulging in chocolate fudge after months of cold porridge.

Janie patted her satchel. More than anything, she wanted Mr. Baum to like her story.

Harry, Kenneth, and four neighbor boys gathered around Mr. Baum.

"Hurry, Charlotte. We need General Jinjur." Looking more eight than thirteen, Kenneth wore a scrappy shirt stuck with straw, hair messier than usual.

"Stand over there, dear." Mr. Baum handed her a script and two knitting needles. "Your weapons. You're marching as head of the girls' revolt."

"Revolting against what?"

"Housework." Harry wore an oversized vest, hardly looking his full fourteen years.

"Against minding the children, too," Kenneth added.

A flurry of activity bubbled as the children performed, following Mr. Baum's script. Scenarios included Jack Pumpkinhead, Tip, and the Sawhorse played by neighbors, and Kenneth as the Scarecrow, Harry as the pompous Highly

Magnified Woggle-Bug, Thoroughly Educated, and the flying Gump constructed of cushions, branches for wings.

After the revolt, Mr. Baum placed a crown on Janie's head. "Now you're Glinda, the good sorceress. Work your magic."

Discovering that evil magic transformed Ozma, the true ruler, into another form, Glinda stepped on a wooden crate, waving her wand. "I never deal in transformations, for they're not honest. No respectable sorceress makes things appear to be what they're not. Only unscrupulous witches use the art," she read from the script.

Janie changed into Jinjur, appalled to find herself floor scrubbing and butter churning. The boys cast off their aprons. With another crown, she became Princess Ozma.

"Bravo!" Mr. Baum said. Aunt Sophie applauded. Mrs. Baum offered Jinjur cookies and lemonade.

Basking in the palace, Janie held her cookie, pinkie up, the way Princess Ozma might. Nibbling, she lifted her chin. Boys romped, wolfing cookies. Fancying herself as queen and actress, she viewed them smugly as her pitiful subjects.

As a stage celebrity, she'd bloom as a vivid morning glory rather than a pale thistle. Father, Mother, teachers, and classmates would adore her. She'd star in an extravaganza, adoring fans arriving in droves. Her Royal Highness, Annabella Esmerelda. She took another dainty nibble and lifted her glass. She'd be sorry if the neighbors left. She'd lose her entourage.

Boys jostled her arm. Lemonade spilled on her lap. "Sorry, Charlotte. Didn't see you."

Didn't see her? How dare they!

As lady-in-waiting, Mrs. Baum tied on a clean pinafore with embroidered flower pockets. How lovely! Charlotte lifted her chin higher.

Mr. Baum presented a book. "Hot off the press. The story we performed."

Janie reached as if receiving a gift from a visiting dignitary.

Holding *The Marvelous Land of Oz*, she tingled with excitement, almost forgetting she was queen. "Another Oz story!"

"No Dorothy, but plenty to delight."

She almost hugged the book, but such a display was beneath her. Preparing for her future, she regally replied, "Thank you, Mr. Baum." He cocked his head in amusement.

The dedication was to Fred Stone and David Montgomery, still touring with the Oz extravaganza. As simple Janie, the closest she'd get to the production was viewing the book's endpapers. But now, as queen and future renowned actress, she must attend.

Prolific drawings by John R. Neill blinked with color, irresistible to touch. She invoked her most mature voice. "Lovely pictures, but why didn't Mr. Denslow illustrate?"

"Time for a change." His voice had an edge.

Janie pointed. "This must be the Woggle-Bug, though most people wouldn't know."

He eyed her keenly, surely noting her pretension. "The name came to me on the Coronado beach when a little girl showed me a crab."

Janie delicately turned pages, voice ringing with authority. "You called Glinda a sorceress, not a witch."

Mr. Baum's eyes widened at her uncharacteristic tone. "Our friends needed her magical help. With too many negative connotations for witches, she's better suited as a sorceress."

Janie nodded as if approving his best royal political strategy. But the royal parents wouldn't approve of sorcery either.

"Acting is an exhilarating escape to imagination." His gaze intensified, his voice kind. "But offstage, even Glinda, with all her magic, won't change into different forms, nor change somebody else." He clasped her shoulder, as if delivering Glinda's message solely for her benefit. "So, it's vital to be content as yourself. And you're one of the brightest, most imaginative girls I know."

His touch strengthened her. The famous actress-queen Annabella Esmerelda vanished with the strike of a magic wand, like dandelion seeds disappearing into the wind with one puff.

"You can't be someone else to escape being yourself. And why should you? You're an engaging story writer. Your journalistic skills rival none. If I had a dollar for every thoughtful question you asked, I'd have the riches of Ozma."

With him, she was happy to be herself, queen or not. "Why'd you write the play?"

"For another extravaganza. My new publisher's planning the promotion." He dropped a round yellow pin into her hand.

She read the button. "'What does the Woggle-Bug say?'"

"In September, you'll see these buttons everywhere. A newspaper Woggle-Bug contest and comics will promote the book and show." He pulled a folded newspaper from under the typewriter. "All the official Oz news here in *The Ozmapolitan*."

Janie eagerly scanned Ozian headlines: "A Swell Dinner," "Farewell to Jinjur." Edited by H.M. Woggle-Bug, T.E. How exciting!

Mr. Baum lit a new cigar from the old one. She read while he asked Aunt Sophie about educational systems. Soon, Kenneth might attend the experimental Interlaken School in Indiana. After Auntie left, Janie handed him the Macatawa alphabet book from her satchel.

He read aloud, sentences like tongue twisters. "'Mr. Baum Bounced from the Boardwalk to the Boat, Balancing a Blackbird pie on the Backgammon Board.'" He chuckled, continuing through the alphabet. "'On Wednesday, the Wonderful Wizard Wolfed Welsh rarebit on an unWieldy Wheel of cheese While Wandering West on the *Lizzie Walsh* over Windy Watery Waves toward the Wide Waukezoo Trail.' They're charming, full of ingenuity. Your pictures sparkle with Crayola color."

She blushed. "It's yours. A small way of saying thank you for inviting me."

"A *gargantuan* way of thanking me. Did you bring a story?"

She fished a manila envelope from her satchel. He opened it, and her muscles tightened.

"Sit down, dear. Don't fret. Ah, 'Camellia of Lavender Lane.' I like it already."

Janie giggled. "I named her after tea. A Chinese emperor discovered tea when a camellia plant fell into boiling water." What had Mother said? "He said the tea gave vigor, contentment, and determination."

"Then I expect great things from Camellia." Smoking, he read. Janie scanned the *Ozmapolitan*, glancing for telltale signs of his pleasure or dislike. Lips twitching, he nodded, burst out laughing, then read more. "Superb! I didn't guess Camellia would find the key in the clover field. Very clever."

Janie squeaked out a "Thank you."

"How fortuitous of that urchin Maxwell to discover the box. And that Beatrice, feistier than most fairies. I can imagine Maxwell eating hot peppers." He puckered his lips like a fish.

Janie laughed, then pouted. "The action didn't go as planned."

Mr. Baum tapped the papers. "In telling the stories of such obstinate characters, you must let them do as they please."

"How do I decide who plays the trick on Maxwell?"

"Know your characters like you know your left hand. In your case, right hand. Remember their idiosyncrasies. The Woggle-Bug considers himself a real crackerjack. Whatever spews from his mouth shows off his education, prodigious vocabulary, and facility with puns."

"That's why he doesn't get along with folks."

"And his solution to problems will be jim-dandy."

"According to him. Hmm. I have an idea ..." *The Ozmapolitan* caught her eye. "Time to write a fairy newspaper. With news about Fairy Chasm where Beatrice and Estella live."

"Splendid!"

"You said your characters percolate, but how do you choose their names?"

"Sometimes the way you chose Camellia. Or variations of words."

"I start with flowers. Daisy turns to Daisilea. Buttercup becomes Flutterup."

He stroked his chin. "Let's conjure more. What name derives from lemonade?"

Janie wrote *lemonade* on a paper tucked under the typewriter. "Hmm. Elmoneda?"

"Perfect." He took a swallow. "Try the word *group*."

She experimented with letter combinations. "Gorup, Grupo, Progu, Rugpo.I'm picturing a funny-looking man called Mr. Gurpo."

"Me, too. Now consider the word *slumgullion*, with multiple meanings. Meat-and-potato stew, a weak beverage, or the refuse from processing whale carcasses."

"Ugh!"

"But it's a wonderful word, isn't it?"

"Yes. So is Saskatchewan. Or Schenectady."

Mr. Baum's amused laughter blended with waves rolling to shore. "I'd include Chittenango in the same category of blissfulness. My birthplace."

"Chittenango." Janie tasted the word. "Or percolate. Tapioca. Pumpernickel."

"And skedaddle, verb or noun. We skedaddle out of Chicago. We're on the steamer with a skedaddle of people."

"I like discombobulated, too."

"Have you ever wondered about thumpdoodlums?"

Mrs. Baum called them for dinner. At the table, she ceremoniously presented frankfurters and a basket of elongated buns. "Since we're not attending the St. Louis World's Fair, we're having popular fair food." She pulled Dr. Pepper bottles from the icebox.

Janie gaped. Gordon's Pharmacy carried carbonated beverages. But Elsa Broderick refused to support her competition.

"Nobody will suffer from lack of sweets. I have a plan."

"Does it involve Fairy Floss?" Mr. Baum inquired. "Spun sugar. All the rage at the fair."

"I've no machine for that." Mrs. Baum set down a huge plate of pickles.

"Really, Maud? You're figuring twenty for each of us?"

"Charlotte, these pickles are manufactured in the Heinz factory here in Holland. It's essential to support the community."

Harry handed Janie the Heinz 57 ketchup bottle. She turned the bottle over. Ketchup splotched over her frankfurter, spilling into a big puddle. To her relief, everyone laughed.

"Now Ken's not the only butterfingers around." Harry smirked as Kenneth punched him.

Twenty

July 1904

While the boys washed dishes, Janie sat on the porch with Mr. and Mrs. Baum. They asked about school, chores, and the inn, busy with tourists. She bemoaned the drudgery of picking beans and shelling peas. "My hands hurt so much, I asked for different chores. Mother made me dust." She sighed.

Rocking, Mr. Baum snickered. "Yes, the rain leaves us nothing to growl about."

Mrs. Baum looked up from her needlework. "Mrs. Bilkins?"

"Mrs. Bilkins noted that when rain relieved the drought, farmers were no happier. Creditors bothered them about debts, no excuses. Always something to complain about."

Janie recalled his scrapbook. "Mrs. Bilkins the landlady? Why'd you write that column, Mr. Baum?"

"Ah, Sairy Ann Bilkins. With her nose in everyone's business, she commented on railroads, drought, farmers, suffrage, prohibition, and her three boarders. Aberdeen was up and coming. Much to write about."

Janie took up her journalistic role. "Why'd you move there?"

"For a better way to support my family than selling axle grease."

"My siblings' families lived there," Mrs. Baum added.

"Dakota Territory prospered with the railroads. Aberdeen was a hub city. Citizens seemed prosperous, so I opened Baum's Bazaar, a store selling fancy goods—"

"L.F." Maud tilted her head. "She asked about Mrs. Bilkins."

He cleared his throat. "Yes, well, I'll tell you about the store and baseball club later. Sorry to put you through that rigmarole. There should be a place for folks who drone on and on. Hmm. Anyhow, Mrs. Bilkins is boisterous. She constantly tells her boarders what's what. Her malapropisms get her in trouble."

Janie wrinkled her nose. "Mala-what?"

"Malapropism. Oh, bother. I sound like that hifalutin Woggle-Bug, dropping fancy words like fleas off a dog. Rather, she misuses words, mixing them up. She'd say flustration, combining flustered and frustration."

Janie giggled. "Maybe, instead of giving someone a big hug, she'd give him a big hog."

"A historical monument would be hysterical," Mrs. Baum said.

He chortled. "When the grocer couldn't sell vanilla extract or brandied peaches due to prohibition, Mrs. Bilkins reported" —he adopted country dialect— "'The town was as riled up as if you'd stirred them with a stick like you would a hasty pudding.' The druggist said, 'Lay in your stock of pickles before May, Mrs. Bilkins, before they decide vinegar's intoxicating and can't be sold without a license.'"

Janie laughed. Harry and Kenneth strolled to the porch, checkerboard in tow.

"Mrs. Bilkins expounded on foibles of human nature," Mr. Baum said.

Mrs. Baum smirked. "Like someone I know with plenty to say about merchant trade lies, gullible customers, western versus eastern women, *The Daily Anythin'*, *The Daily Nothin'* ..."

Janie smiled. "Some folks wonder what the Woggle-Bug says. I'm more curious what Mrs. Bilkins says."

"That's how you think from someone else's viewpoint," Mr. Baum said. "It guides your characters' actions."

"Ken and I were born in Aberdeen," Harry said.

"That's the best thing about it." Mrs. Baum tied a knot.

"Did Mrs. Bilkins get in trouble?" Janie asked.

"Constantly. But as editor, I wrote that if her column was so aggravating, skip it. Instead, invest your money in a dime novel and get some real good out of life."

"Oh, Frank. Charlotte doesn't want to hear that nonsense." Mrs. Baum faced Janie. "Mrs. Bilkins was inspired by Mrs. Anthony. She even ran for mayor."

"She was a far better cook than politician, Maud."

Mrs. Baum wiped her brow in a dramatic gesture. "As Mrs. Bilkins says, 'The conceit of men is the biggest stumbling block to the universal suffering of women.'"

"Men's conceit didn't stop her. She was determined to outdo Nellie Bly's trip around the world in seventy-two days and proved considerably superior by circling Aberdeen in seventy-two minutes, asking for money for the missionary society. With no success, mind you."

Janie gasped. "I have Nellie Bly's Round the World board game. Someday, I'll beat her record."

"Some have." Mr. Baum nodded. "When you're older, it'll be by aeroplane, in a jiffy, instead of steamship and railroads."

"I'll write about it in the newspaper," Janie said.

Mrs. Baum clipped a thread and offered a litany of Nellie Bly's accomplishments, ending with her undercover investigation of the Women's Lunatic Asylum. That report made her famous and instigated improved conditions. Janie listened in awe.

Harry popped up. "Time for fishing!"

Mr. Baum checked his pocket watch, singing, "You get a line, I'll get a pole, we'll go down to the crawdad hole ..."

He motored them around Black Lake. "Hotel Macatawa reminds me of Hotel Del Coronado, where we wintered after exploring southern California." Janie gazed at the steep roof, gables, dormers, and eternal porch railings. "Imagine, Charlotte! The Coronado glitters like a fairy palace on a magical island, with nine hundred rooms and thousands of lights."

Brighter than a million candles, dispelling darkness. "Which fairies live there?"

"Ryls and knooks, of course. And a fairy named Nelebel, banished from the Forest of Burzee."

He drove the *Maybelle* through the channel to a pier he'd built off their Lake Michigan property. Harry caught perch from the dock while Kenneth and Janie jumped from the boat.

They played water tag and built sandcastles. After carving finishing touches on a turret, Janie, with recent niggling concerns, plopped on the sand next to Harry. "Do you go to church?"

"We attend Ethical Culture Sunday School."

"For what?"

"Adults hear lectures. Kids learn about social problems. We do service projects."

"Is it a religion?"

"No. We're united by dignity for all." Harry scooped sand that drained through his fingers. "We don't argue about theology. We encourage everyone to be better people. Our motto's 'deed before creed.'"

His words nibbled, like a worm crawling through her. "Don't you believe in God?"

"Sure. Whatever you believe is fine. My parents want us to think for ourselves." He tossed a stone. It plopped before her.

She picked it up. The burrowing worm expanded, taking a bite. "My church teaches that we do good 'cause God first loved us and paid for our sin."

"We all make mistakes. So, we help each other do better." Sand sifted through his fingers. "We have a sign: 'The place where people meet to seek the highest is holy ground.'"

But that highest should be God, right? The worm took another bite. She squeezed the rock. Even without church, the Baums seemed happier than her parents. Perhaps because they didn't worry about tedious rules.

She should chuck the stone into the lake. Instead, she tucked it into her bag.

Late that afternoon, Janie browsed through Fannie Farmer's *Boston Cooking School Cookbook*. Mrs. Baum said Miss Farmer's recipes were the first to use standard measurements.

Mother made Neapolitans, parfaits, and ice cream cakes from store-bought ice cream, rivaling Gordon Pharmacy's soda fountain. Due to Sawyer's insulated icehouse, Broderick Resort was known for year-round ice cream desserts.

Mouth watering, Janie leafed through desserts. "Baked Alaska? How come ice cream doesn't melt in the oven?"

"Mr. Baum calls it magic. But it's simple. Meringue insulates it. We'll try it next time. Today, we'll make chocolate sauce."

They stood side by side at the stove as equals.

The children took turns cranking the ice cream maker as Mr. Baum dumped in chunks of ice and salt. While they ate, he explained legends regarding the invention of the ice cream sundae. Supposedly, town Blue Laws forbade the sale of ice cream sodas on Sundays, since soda water was too bubbly for Sabbath rest. "So, kiddiewinkles, what's the real story?"

The hour merged into rival tall tales amongst peals of laughter. Afterward, the boys played dominoes. Mrs. Baum had

Janie practice stitches. She showed her the chain stitch on a handkerchief with an ivy border. Janie suggested pink and yellow for flowers.

At suppertime, Janie requested a real chicken leg for Harry, not a wing, since he was probably old enough to notice the difference. At dusk, after card games, they sang "Yellow Rose of Texas" and "Buffalo Gals" with piano, guitar, and mandolin accompaniment. The children belted out "On Top of Old Smokey" and "Billy Boy," concocting rhymed verses, then bellowed "Home on the Range" with their best twang. Only in this magical place would two teenage boys act as silly as their father and not mind.

The clock struck ten as Janie slipped into bed. At home, her family rose with the sun, tending to guests, cooking, farming. Evenings brought exhaustion. But here, nighttime unfolded with as many wonders as daytime, while kerosene lit the darkness.

Streaming fireflies and stars lit her mind. Spots and dots spiraled. Kerosene blurred the edges of night. The preacher said even darkness was light to God. Was He gazing upon her now?

She blinked, her eyes riveted to the moonlit window, then rose. Light-tipped waves lapped the shore. Breezes rustled leaves, weaving through the window, caressing her face. Adventures crystallized before her as Nellie Bly cruised oceans on her whirlwind trip. Undercover, she shed light on evil's darkness, exposing it in the newspaper. Her counterpart, Mrs. Bilkins, spoke of social ills, uninhibited through Mr. Baum's pen.

Could Janie accomplish as much good by pen? Perhaps she'd be a journalist, poking and prodding the darkness, inviting light.

Which pen name? Margaret Weathersby? Violet Ellsworth—

"Charlotte?" Mrs. Baum's worried voice floated from the

doorway. "Come along." At the bed, she patted the pillow. Mr. Baum eased into the rocker.

Unable to stifle a yawn, Janie climbed in. Mrs. Baum stroked her hair.

Mr. Baum crooned, "'Lavender's blue, dilly dilly, Lavender's green …'"

Nobody tucked her in at home. Janie closed her eyes, comforted by God's watch over her. Like Mr. Baum laughing with her, eyes crinkling in amusement. Was that how God was?

Her father's face flitted before her, scowling. Mother's shrillness echoed. The china cup broke. *You're nothing but trouble!* Hands ripped off the green pepper monster. Pepper's bark, a gunshot slicing the air, then stillness. Janie twitched. Mrs. Baum squeezed her hand, settling her.

Somewhere up there, God saw her. Even the darkness was light to Him. He was near, through two people who knew her and cared.

Twenty-One

July 1904

The next morning, Janie woke with a thunk to the head. She grabbed the thrown pillow and chased the culprit. She smacked Kenneth with it until the smell of bacon enticed them.

In the kitchen, Mrs. Baum eyed bubbling pancake batter. "With my husband's appetite, not even Grape-Nuts saves me from cooking."

"Try Bismarcks." Eyes gleaming, Mr. Baum gulped coffee. The boys sniggered.

"Humph." Mrs. Baum flipped pancakes. "I thought we buried the hatchet on that."

"All in jest, sweetheart." He poured streams of sugar and cream into his cup. "Perhaps Charlotte would like to hear about it."

"Good heavens, if you want her to know about your indulgences, go right ahead." Mrs. Baum scooped pancakes onto a plate, then plopped Aunt Jemima's pancake mix on the table. "Another time-saver from the Expo. It gives me more time to sit on the porch."

Janie's mother refused to use box mixes with choice words for those who did. No shortcuts allowed. Maybe that was why Mother was so crabby.

Mr. Baum shared how he once bought a dozen jelly-filled Bismarcks. Maud was insulted that her food wasn't good enough. He ate everything she served for breakfast, besides two pastries. Next day, same thing. With eight left, now stale, his interest waned.

Nevertheless, she set them on his plate each morning, even after he stashed them in the cupboard and buried them in the garden on days four and five. She couldn't bear the waste. Finally, they called a truce when he agreed to never buy food without consulting her.

Janie drizzled more maple syrup. "Mrs. Bilkins would be pleased you learned your lesson." The boys guffawed.

Mrs. Baum pulled a pan from the oven. "Charlotte, whenever I try to replicate your mother's muffins, they fail to live up to her legacy."

"Do you have the right baking powder? Mother has a secret supplier."

"I prefer blaming baking powder rather than my culinary skills when something turns out like concrete. But this puzzles me."

"I'll check Mother's pantry for her brand."

"I'll not have you be a spy in your own house, dear."

Mr. Baum licked syrup off his finger. "What she means is, go ahead and check, but be stealthy, so Mrs. Baum gets no blame." His wife rolled her eyes.

Janie tried a muffin. Good, but Mother's were delicious. Nobody left Elsa Broderick's inn hungry—though the soul might wilt and the spirit flounder. Yet here was plenty of nourishment for both body and spirit.

On the porch, Mr. Baum noted a sparrow. "That little fellow flies without thinking about it. Such a marvel! Imagine all the Wright brothers did to emulate what this creature does naturally." He lit a cigar. "When the Oz comics begin, Charlotte, the Scarecrow, and his friends encounter considerable adventures in America, finding it just as marvelous as we'd find Oz. Americans do by inventions what Ozians do by magic." He patted *Marvelous Land* atop the *Ozmapolitan*. "Take these. And this box of paper to fill with inspirations."

Mrs. Baum handed her the pinafore she'd tied on Janie yesterday. "This, too. I made it bigger last year to fit you now."

Janie hugged Mrs. Baum. "Thank you. I love it. I'm taking home more than I brought."

"No, you're not," Mr. Baum said. "We have wonderful memories and the ABC book full of your imagination. That's worth much more."

June 4, 1980

Mrs. Gordon pulled *The Marvelous Land of Oz* from the drawer.

Carrie found the faded inscription. "'Dear Charlotte, Enjoy this story with its trove of distinct individuals inspiring you to celebrate your own uniqueness.'" She looked up. "Glinda doesn't deal in transformations." *The Stranger. Masks protect.* That was how Carrie survived at home. Frederich Buechner's words: *Travel unmasks.* The journey, the walking. "Did Mr. Baum's words encourage you?"

"Sometimes, but other voices interfered. At home, Mother belittled my idea of putting Baked Alaska on the menu. She was too busy worrying that commercial refrigeration would make Father's ice business obsolete."

Carrie aimed for a smile. "I'll bet she never served Fruit Loop sundaes either. Kellogg's used to serve them after tours."

"I thought I knew every possible confectionary." Still no smile. "Years after her husband's death, Mrs. Baum sent my

ABC book back after cleaning the attic. That's when she found his handwritten manuscripts. She burned those."

Carrie gasped. "Why?"

"Practicality. They were published. No sense wasting space."

"Such a loss for archives, museums, libraries."

"Her family wasn't happy, either."

"May I see the ABC book?"

"It's in a different room." The woman's jaw tightened.

Why such a visceral response? "I want to hear more about your Nellie Bly aspirations." When Mrs. Gordon pursed her lips, Carrie changed course. "I found a book by Jack Zipes. *Breaking the Magic Spell: Radical Theories of Folk and Fairy Tales.* About how fairy tales evolved into literary tales. It discusses utopian function, political climates—"

"Is that what college did?" Mrs. Gordon snapped. "Consult your Frederick Buechner."

Again, chastised for her education.

"Fairy tales are about killing dragons. Your preacher man had it right. Fairy tales are about defeating evil. G.K. Chesterton said that the terrifying enemies in fairy tales have enemies in the knights of God. There's something in the universe more mystical than darkness, and stronger than fear."

Carrie leaned forward. "Have you found that thing stronger than fear, Mrs. Gordon?"

"If I had, we wouldn't be reading *Pilgrim's Progress*."

"Are you afraid of reading it?"

Mrs. Gordon delivered another Chesterton quote. "'Fear doesn't come from fairy tales. Fear comes from the universe of the soul.'"

Which inner demons did Mrs. Gordon wrestle with? Were her dragons awake and haunting? Or dozing, tucked away in memories she feared to relive?

Twenty-Two

Janie, 13
July 1905

Piles covered the porch: sticks, twigs, wooden blocks, hunks of clay, containers of nails, screws, string, and fabric.

Mr. Baum plunked on his typewriter, paused with an eye to the treetops, then bent over the keys, so lost in his own world that Janie could probably yell without him flinching. When he looked up, he grinned, cracking out of his otherwise austere visage. He rose from his chair like a bloom rising from a garden. "Welcome again to my Macatawa fairyland!" His arm encompassed the lake.

The boys charged out, now fifteen and fourteen. "We're having a Lilliputian Regatta," Kenneth said.

Janie laughed. "Are you Gulliver?"

Mr. Baum handed her a foot-long boat. "Robert built this. The boys want to make one."

Robert's boat had twine rigging, white sheet sails, and a carved captain's wheel, the hull shaved smooth. "Lovely, but where are the sailors?"

Mr. Baum pointed to the piles. "They need the loving touch of a creator."

Janie and the boys rummaged through boxes, choosing materials. Minutes fluttered with boatbuilding and chatter. Her stomach clenched, her mind swirling with questions she wanted to ask him about newspaper articles she'd read. Aunt Sophie asked Mr. Baum about his work.

Janie glanced at the typewriter. "Is Dorothy in it?"

"Possibly, after receiving hundreds of letters clamoring for a Dorothy story. They advise on how Dorothy should arrive at Oz, or what adventures the Scarecrow and Tin Woodman should encounter. Some tell about their baby sister named Dorothy."

"No surprise," Aunt Sophie said, "the way your books sell like hotcakes."

Janie cut twine. "Does anyone want her to have a pet chicken?"

Mr. Baum's laughter rivaled sprightly Lake Michigan waves. "Only you, Charlotte."

She compared gingham and calico scraps. "I read about Queen Zixi in *St. Nicholas*."

"It'll soon be gathered into a book." He poured lemonade. "Dedicated to Frank Joslyn."

Would Beatrice and Estella want to stow away? Janie selected spools and wires to construct sailors.

Mr. Baum shared other projects. Nine animal stories, like beast fables, were serialized in *The Delineator* magazine. A Father Goose calendar will be issued in October. Two novels for adults, and a story— "Nelebel's Fairyland"—for a San Diego high school newspaper.

"The Scarecrow and everyone had grand adventures in America," Janie said.

"Charlotte, stop talking." Kenneth tied a sailor's knot. "You'll never finish at this rate."

"I can talk and work simultaneously." To prove it, she

snipped more calico and addressed Mr. Baum. "I have the Woggle-Bug Game of Conundrums."

"Ah, such promotional efforts. Comics, contests, buttons, the Woggle-Bug picture book. Talk of converting Pedloe Island into the Land of Oz amusement park. All for naught."

"Isn't the book selling?" Aunt Sophie asked. Janie wrapped wire to connect body parts.

"Yes, but the Woggle-Bug extravaganza closed after three weeks." A wave of weariness etched his face. "I couldn't bear staying in Chicago for the duration. Truly a disaster."

"Three weeks!" Aunt Sophie gasped. "Devastating."

The fresh wound pricked his voice. "We worked so hard."

Alarmed by his sadness, Janie dropped the wire. "Why'd it close?"

"Apparently, I never learned my lesson. I couldn't sacrifice personal preference as scriptwriter. Secondly, Stone and Montgomery couldn't appear as the Scarecrow and Tin Woodman, so Mr. Woggle-Bug took over. Critics hated his puns." He sighed. "The Woggle-Bug lives on in print only."

"Perhaps imagination is the best place for him after all," Aunt Sophie said.

He managed a weak smile. "An appreciated consolation, Miss McKinnon. But embarrassments are public. My reputation and livelihood are at stake. I counted on income. This failure tops never finding producers for other plays. I've collaborated with Mr. Hough on several abandoned projects. *Prince Silverwings, The Maid of Athens, Montezuma.*"

Janie went over and took his hand. "You must walk, Mr. Baum. It is a long journey, through a country that is sometimes pleasant and sometimes dark and terrible."

He smiled. "A perfect reminder, Miss Charlotte."

"Your other endeavors thrive," Aunt Sophie said.

"I'm always on to the next thing. No time to waste, given all my plans. I'm seeking a producer for a slapstick play, and promotions for next year's book begin soon. *John Dough and the Cherub*."

"Another Oz book?" Crouching, Janie watched Kenneth make rigging.

"No, a different fantasy. The Cherub's gender is determined by reader ballot. Children may write their opinions. Reilly and Britton will offer prizes."

Mrs. Baum appeared as Mr. Baum and Auntie launched into their Cubs-Tigers rivalry.

"Off to the regatta!" Harry held his boat high.

Just in time to escape baseball talk. Neither team was in contention for first place, so why quarrel? Janie followed the boys on the boardwalk's loose boards and sand piles to Macatawa Bay.

Beyond the marina, they removed shoes and stockings to chase their boats in Black Lake. Kenneth's flipped until he rearranged his cargo. Harry's ran in tip-top shape, only capsizing once. Janie's lagged, but she relished breezes rippling over turquoise calico sails. The fairies shed glimmers of light through the hull, enjoying porthole views without seasickness.

Harry revealed three nickels for candy. "Don't tell Mother." He eyed Kenneth. "Don't gorge yourself before dinner."

The boys bought NECCO wafers and Hershey bars. Janie bought Cracker Jack to hide in the guest room. As they dangled their legs off a pier, Harry babbled about the new automobile for Rob's high school graduation. Kenneth related his spring travels to California with his parents, his birthday party, and the ocean in La Jolla and San Diego—story after full-blown story. Like his father.

For dinner, Mrs. Baum set a slice of cheese-topped bread at each setting. Mr. Baum poked his with a fork. "Skimpiest portion of Welsh rarebit sauce I've seen. Economizing, Maud?" He tucked his napkin into his shirt. "Mrs. Bilkins once commended a man who economized by chewing both ends of his toothpick." He compensated for less cheese sauce by doling out extra riddles and puns.

Afterward, Janie helped Mrs. Baum bake brownies. As the boys washed dishes, Mr. Baum and Janie escaped to the porch. "My own newspaper." She handed it over.

Scanning the first page, he chuckled. "A gem! *Laurel's Lark.* Fitting for fairy news." He cited headlines. "So much happens on Lavender Lane."

She shared the next installment of her Camellia story. He commented on catchy phrases that evoked images without being prosy. "Very few puns, but not everyone relishes them as I do. Out of fashion to all but the absurdly merry-minded." He winked. "Such wondrous names. Half the fun, isn't it? Running around my head is a story about a king named Rinkitink."

"Another Oz book?"

"Not necessarily. But let's discuss details that make places and characters seem real. For example, the Scarecrow can't easily pick up nuts wearing his gloves."

Janie contemplated. "The Tin Woodman can't stand in the rain, or he'll rust. The Scarecrow's always tripping. Dorothy gets tired without food and sleep, but the Scarecrow and Tin Woodman could dance all night."

"What about Camellia and her pesky friend Maxwell?"

"Camellia doesn't like to be bossed around, but Maxwell bosses anyhow."

"Causing good or bad outcomes?"

"Sometimes Maxwell's right. But Camellia follows her own ideas just to be stubborn."

"You have the makings of a riveting scene when characters disagree."

After hours at the beach, the boys played Snap on the porch, Mr. Baum wrote on his clipboard, and Mrs. Baum showed Janie feather and blanket stitches. Mrs. Baum worked on a fanciful pillowcase with crocheted lace edges, bordered by a garland of embroidered flowers. "Real lace is imported and much too expensive. But this turned out well. Willow leaf edging. I used to make and sell Battenberg lace."

Janie stabbed herself with the needle. "Ouch! I'll never be as good as you are."

"It takes practice. Someday, you'll want to make your own daughter something special."

"Did your mother make you things?"

"Yes, but she was so busy helping *all* women. She, Susan B. Anthony, and Elizabeth Cady Stanton founded the National Woman Suffrage Association, spoke at conventions, and collaborated on books. Mother researched and wrote books and articles, including women inventors. She visited the Iroquois in New York. They believed in equality for men *and* women. Iroquois women could even veto a decision for war. In fact, Mother was initiated into the Wolf Clan of the Mohawk Nation and received the name *Karonienhawi*. Sky Carrier."

"Really?" Janie envisioned a woman on a mountaintop, arms to the clouds.

"Our house was part of the Underground Railroad. Mother proudly refused to cooperate with the Fugitive Slave Law." Mrs. Baum described the 1851 rescue, when Matilda Joslyn Gage was young. Abolitionists broke into a Syracuse jail to free fugitive slave William Henry, known as Jerry. Later, the Townsend Block in Clinton Square was renamed the Jerry Rescue Building.

Mesmerized, Janie froze, needle in hand. How thrilling! Someday she'd rescue somebody, stand for justice, write about it for the newspaper. If she had that kind of courage.

"Sadly, Mrs. Anthony and Mrs. Cady later excluded Mother. Her views were too extreme, even for them. She believed *all* people should have freedom to vote—women, blacks, even Indian nations. She was adamant that church and state be separate." She shook her head. "After my father died, Mother moved in with us for many winters. She kept writing and never gave up. She'll always be my inspiration."

Mr. Baum paused his typing. "That woman had more brains than five men put together. She inspired me, too, insisting I write down my children's stories."

Mrs. Baum threaded another needle. "Mother didn't want me marrying Mr. Baum, a penniless traveling actor. Yet he won her over."

Janie eyed him slyly. "I'm sure Mrs. Bilkins has plenty to say about it."

He chortled. "Mrs. Bilkins agrees I'm the best match for her."

Mrs. Baum raised an eyebrow. "She'd also say you need me to keep you in line."

TWENTY-THREE

July 1905

Mrs. Baum went inside. Janie stood beside Mr. Baum. "Sir, I read the newspaper about your religious beliefs, about seances and Thee ..."

He stopped writing. "Theosophy?"

"Yes. Believing God's only in nature, not a personal God."

Mr. Baum frowned. "I no longer have seances, nor subscribe to theosophy. What do your parents teach you?"

"We attend the Methodist Church. My parents are ... Christians."

"I, too, grew up Methodist. My dear parents were devout churchgoers." He tapped his cigar. "They loved us, persevering in faith even through hardship."

She sat beside him. "But you didn't continue in church?"

His jaw twitched. "Charlotte, I don't want to interfere with your parents' intentions."

"I just want to understand why you went a different way."

He cocked his head. "I highly regard the Bible. Archeology confirms its stories." He eyed her intently. "Only imagination and faith keep man above the commonplace. Consider battles that Bible heroes fought. Martyrs suffered due to faith in a higher power. I admire that faith, those martyrs. Progress and achievements depend on that. Thus, I refer to God as the Supreme Master in *The Life and Adventures of Santa Claus*. In the introduction for my Christmas Stocking series, I acknowledge the birthday of our Lord Jesus Christ. But I can't abide a vindictive God who casts people into hell for not doing things His way."

"You believe He's harsh, though He made a way for people to be saved from sin?"

"Bible teachings are restrictive, though my convictions grieve my Bible-believing mother. I greatly respect her, even abandoned Sunday baseball games when she visited."

Janie's stomach twisted. "Harry says they attend Ethical Culture Sunday School."

"We've found it superior to religious training. Mrs. Baum's mother ranted about the church being responsible for more bloodshed than any other cause, the Crusades and such. She was appalled that southern Christians justified slavery with Scripture. I agree. The boys must make their own informed decisions about religion. That makes us free thinkers."

"Some say you attacked the church."

"In Aberdeen, years ago, as newspaper editor, I challenged the status quo." As if for emphasis, he gestured with the cigar. "I've *no* tolerance for hypocrisy."

"Your books have good witches." Flames devouring her Oz book sizzled in her memory.

"Individuals should be judged by their own natures, how they use their powers, whether humans or wizards. In *The Master Key*, the demon of electricity isn't inherently evil. I realize this opposes Christian teachings."

Her hands quivered. "I'm confused."

He blew smoke, watching it rise over treetops. "You're thirteen, growing into a fine young lady, so I'll be forthright. Knowing many Christians in Syracuse and Aberdeen, I've found Christianity to be mindless. They disregard science. Christians revere Christmas, but the Yule Feast predates Christ as a pagan ritual. Some Christians have no more use for imagination than a hog does for a bath. They've discovered evil in more places than Old Testament prophets ever did. New sins are created daily, things never considered offensive before."

He leaned forward. "Some folks are appalled at the notion of women attending college. Skirts just above the ankle are still too short. And you know how drinking wicked, bubbly soda water on Sunday leads one astray." He winked. "These folks frown on anything innovative. It may take fifty years for Christians to accept such benign concepts, then embrace them as nostalgia, accepting them for the harmless frivolities they are, rather than dark sins."

So, her parents might someday accept fairy tales?

"In Aberdeen, churchgoers were a sad lot. They gave huge donations for church furnishings for their own comfort, but nobody, not even Mrs. Bilkins, could wring money from them for the underprivileged heathen." He paused. "You know exactly what I mean."

Tears pooled in her eyes.

"There now. I didn't mean to alarm you."

"Mother says I'm doomed for liking fairy tales, or not folding laundry right, for daydreaming."

He reached toward her. She jerked back, covering her face, so used to movements prefacing a slap. She eyed him through her fingers. He took her shaking hand, wiped her tears with his handkerchief. "I can safely say that if there's such a place as hell, one does not get there by daydreaming or mismatching socks. Maud!"

Mrs. Baum returned. "What's wrong?"

Sniffling, Janie stared at her lap. He lifted her chin. She closed her eyes.

"Look at me," he said.

She couldn't. Her mother's mantra penetrated: *I'm ashamed of you.*

"Look at me."

Her eyelids fluttered open. His clear gray eyes revealed compassion. Cicadas hummed. A boat horn honked.

"You've a heavy heart, Charlotte. When parents teach one thing and do another, that's something to contemplate. You'd do well to ask your aunt about this. She's a tender soul who loves you deeply."

Harry and Kenneth poked through the doorway with the ice cream maker. Mr. Baum added ice and salt. Janie composed herself as they cranked peppermint-flavored ice cream.

When Mrs. Baum dropped scoops of ice cream atop brownies, Kenneth's eyes widened. "Jumping Jehoshaphat! Double dessert!"

Harry got the biggest possible bite on his spoon before his mother could change her mind. "It's against the law here," he told Janie.

"Your mother has spoken!" Mr. Baum raised his spoon high. "What she has declared acceptable, we shall enjoy without commentary." A twinkle flecked his eye. "But without her permission, even one measly Tootsie Roll is an abomination."

Janie stretched under the bed's cool sheets. Today she'd gazed into the face of a man who wiped her tears, who laughed with her, reveling in simple pleasures and spinning yarns. She couldn't picture her parents without disapproving scowls, tongues clucking in rebuke.

What was God like? More like her parents? Or Mr. Baum?

Ruminating, she tossed and turned, then crossed the creaky floor to the window. Crickets chirped, waves sloshed. Moonlight stilled her soul as she scrutinized darkness, searching for God. Mr. and Mrs. Baum appeared at the doorway.

Mrs. Baum led Janie to bed and tucked her in. At thirteen, Janie still relished this late-night appearance. It made up for a hundred lonely nights when nobody tucked her in.

Mr. Baum crooned from the rocker. "'You are my sunshine, my only sunshine …'"

The next morning after breakfast, Mr. Baum dropped an object into her hand—a whimsical wooden chicken-shaped ornament, painted yellow. "Recalling your partiality to chickens, I made this for your journey. 'You must walk …'"

They chanted the familiar line together.

"Let this chicken remind you of pleasant times here, helping you through dark times later. Like Dorothy's companions, you have all the brains, heart, and courage you need, wherever the road takes you."

She dangled the chicken by its ribbon. Such memories! Running the printing press, making an ABC booklet, performing a play. Kindness in exchange for spills. Newfound courage to jump down the dune, write a fairy adventure, and blossom as herself. At the Baums' dinner table, she felt the acceptance of a true home.

Janie embraced him. "Thank you."

He took her hand. "Your journey is discovering more of the beauty inside you. Remember what Glinda says."

"She doesn't deal in transformations."

"So be yourself, Charlotte. Make room for fun and fairies every day."

Yes, living with fairies took more courage than jumping down dunes. But she'd do it.

She left with another stack of fresh paper and the embroidered handkerchief from Mrs. Baum, flowers stitched with pink and yellow threads Janie chose last year.

June 4, 1980

Carrie jotted the final note. "Did you talk to your aunt about your confusion?"

"Yes, but her faith wasn't tested by hardships *I* endured. She'd been the favored sister, the teacher's pet. Mother did poorly in school, received much criticism. Which explains a lot."

On the porch, Carrie embarked on *Pilgrim's Progress*. At the Strait Gate, Goodwill directed Christian to the place of Deliverance. Christian ran up the highway of Salvation, to the cross at the top. His burden fell off and rolled into the sepulcher. His heart was light and merry.

Three Shining Ones appeared. The first one proclaimed peace and forgiveness. Another man stripped Christian's rags and covered him with a new Robe. The third man marked Christian's forehead and handed him a sealed roll to give at the Celestial City Gate. Christian praised the Man who'd died on the cross, put to shame in Christian's place.

Swinging stopped. Mrs. Gordon stared across the porch, frowning. "Why did Goodwill let Christian in? He'd fallen into the Slough of Despond."

"People weighed down by burdens are always welcome," Carrie replied.

"Dorothy had a mark on her forehead from the kiss of the Good Witch of the North, allowing her to see the Wizard. She was greeted by three Munchkins, then met three folks who became her companions."

"Similar to Christian's experience."

"The Good Witch gave Dorothy the Silver Shoes. They held great power." Mrs. Gordon eyed Carrie. "Is there great power in this Robe, Mark, and Roll?"

"Yes." Fortunately, Carrie knew the story. And the Heidelberg Catechism and John Calvin's *Institutes of the Christian Religion* that espoused this very concept. "The Roll is the certificate to be presented at the Celestial City Gate. The Mark on the forehead identifies a person as belonging to the King. The Robe is the righteousness of Christ."

"What is Mr. Bunyan saying? Robe, righteousness ..."

"It's a metaphor. God takes our dirty, sinful rags and exchanges them for the perfect white Robe of Christ. A gift."

The woman stared at the railing as if seeking understanding in peeling paint.

Twenty-Four

Thursday, June 5, 1980

After supper and typing the day's memories, Carrie settled into a café booth.

Alberta handed her two menus. "Need one for him yonder?" She tossed her head toward Dirk.

Carrie blushed.

"He'll be over sooner than later since his tip jar's full," Alberta said. "His tips go to Hope Haven for high-risk kids."

Surprising, considering his self-serving adventures. "One menu. Is the owner here?"

"Yes, I'll send her over."

Carrie ordered salad, fries, and a Coke while Dirk sang "King of the Road." How fitting.

An older woman in a purple blouse reached Carrie. "I'm Pearl Donahue, the owner. Alberta mentioned you want to see me." She sat.

Carrie judged her to be sixty. "How long have you been the owner?"

"Fifteen years and worked here thirty before that."

"I'd love to know more café history."

"I'm steeped in it. Sawyer Broderick owned half the land around here a century ago, opening the resort in 1885. His wife Elsa ran it with her daughters, Josephine, Maggie, and Lodemia Jane, till 1916. Then Lodemia ran it like a Navy ship forty-nine years. It survived two World Wars, the Korean War, halfway through Vietnam, and Lodemia's harebrained schemes."

"Till 1965?"

"That's when she sold it to me. Lodemia's my Aunt Jane. AKA Charlotte."

"Your aunt?" Why hadn't Mrs. Gordon mentioned this?

"Mother's a Broderick, Maggie Pearl. I'm her namesake."

"That's why you serve Broderick specials."

"Keeping the spirit alive. Mother and Aunt Josephine passed away years ago." Pearl rolled her eyes. "Aunt Jane did odd things with the menu, renamed items for *Wizard of Oz* characters. When I signed papers, I changed it back. Now it's more café than restaurant. The inn is long gone."

"Ever see your Aunt Jane?"

"Every Saturday. Duty calls like screeching cats in a rainstorm. I take her to the grocery store and doctor. Run errands. Plant annuals. Call throughout the week."

"She hired me this summer."

"She mentioned having help." Pearl shook her head. "She insists on keeping up that garden. She can't do half the work. With the fence, nobody else enjoys it either."

Carrie hardly wanted to mention her role in putting up the fence. "Do you have the large, framed photo with four boys and a girl on the dune?"

"She pestered me about that a while ago. I don't have time to sift through eight rooms of clutter upstairs."

"May I look for it? It means a lot to her."

"Maybe later." Pearl leaned forward. "Don't knock yourself out to please that old grouch. She'll bite you in the back."

Carrie withdrew from the rancor in Pearl's eyes. "She's always been that way?"

"She's the scary aunt, for sure."

"How'd she inherit the tearoom?"

"With no children, Aunt Jane could devote all her energy to it. Financially, she didn't need the place, but it was her pride and joy. She never let anyone forget it."

"She probably had income from her husband."

Pearl lowered her voice. "Initially. That murder scandal did nothing but disgrace the Broderick name. I grew up hearing about it. He died from cancer before his trial, but they knew he was guilty." She shuddered. "Humiliating!"

Maybe Carrie could prime the pump without flexing the handle. "Possibly a mistake."

"I'll say," Pearl snapped. "Marrying Walter Gordon was her mistake."

Time to end this enlightening dialog. "Thanks for your time, Mrs. Donahue."

Pearl stood, speaking as pleasantly as if they'd chatted about the Fourth of July parade. "Nice meeting you, Carrie."

Pearl left as Carrie pondered, chin in hand. How had Janie changed from a bright, imaginative girl to the grumpy old lady people avoided? Something kept her from blossoming.

She ate salad while Dirk played Dan Fogelberg's "Longer." During his break, he buzzed over. Alberta swooped in with Coke and fries.

Dirk's face brightened. "You've a heart for the starving musician."

"It's from me," Carrie said. "Your tip for Saturday's tour."

"Thanks." Dirk guzzled some Coke. "You met the boss."

"Yup. Failed miserably at getting her to find an old photo. No powers of persuasion."

"Borrow mine. I have a way with the over-forty crowd." He grinned. "How was your day with our Mrs. Gordon?"

She loved how he said *our*, as if her days were just as

important to him. Brian wouldn't say that. "I'll bet you don't know what *hyperoodon rostratus* is."

"Got me there. Sounds Latin. Scientific. Species of turtle or elephant?"

"The scientific definition refers to bottlenose whale. The creative version is a place of wonder, or new landscape."

"It's what I'd say when I reach the top of Mount Everest." He munched fries.

"Exactly. Or eating caviar at a fancy restaurant instead of hot dogs at the root beer stand." Nothing would look more out of place than Dirk at an upscale restaurant.

He chuckled. "How'd you find this intriguing trivia?"

Careful to safeguard Mrs. Gordon's family dynamics, Carrie summarized Janie's Macatawa visits. "She came alive at the Baums. He inspired her. She was a dreamer."

"Like you with your book café."

A dream in Dirk's book probably didn't include a quiet summer rebellion refusing to retake a class. Or starting up a café behind her parents' backs. Her muscles suddenly ached with tension. What if the loan didn't come through? Her parents' scowls materialized. She bristled. She'd been squashed too often, especially since sixth grade. Was that where this anger bubbled up from?

Dirk invaded her thoughts. "Say, how 'bout a turtle sundae? Saturday at Captain Sundae in Holland. It just opened. They use Hudsonville ice cream. We'll go to Macatawa Park, see where the Baums lived. I'll talk my buddy Gerrit into sailing."

Her heart fluttered. "I've never sailed."

"It's high time you did. And visit Holland hotspots of interest. Mount Pisgah, the dune. Laketown Park dune. My parents' for a home-cooked meal."

"Is this a date?"

"Strictly business. Gotta know the territory to serve Mrs. G. well. Her old stomping grounds."

She couldn't admit how thrilled she was. Not just for Mrs. Gordon's sake, either. His eyes sparkled. His enthusiasm, kindness, and humor captivated her. His good looks, even his bristly chin. Guilt poked her.

"Your lucky guy doesn't need to worry."

"Of course not." She wouldn't have a fling even without Brian. She glanced at his *X* tattoo, MH/CD. Margaret or Christy?

"We'll go as friends. For research purposes. Sound good?" He finished the fries.

"Not this weekend. Brian's coming."

"Great! Bring him to the café. I'll sing a request." He slurped the last bit of Coke.

Fat chance. Brian preferred Win Schuler's. Or Great Lakes Shipping Company in Grand Rapids. Even informal Bill Knapp's was a step above this hodgepodge decor.

"Good hiking trails nearby." He stood. "Or visit the hardware store."

"Ha!" She requested James Taylor's "Shower the People."

Dirk performed it near the set's end, then returned. "Whatcha working on with your opa?"

"We're sanding the bureau. Oma's in baker's heaven with Mrs. Gordon's recipes. And Oma has a book I've always wanted to read. *The Gatekeeper of Merrimack Castle* from the Wendolyn series by Gretchen Trumbauer. She has all seven, signed by the author."

"Cool. Why do you love kids' books so much?"

"True confession—I'm a kid at heart."

He grinned. "Like me. I go from toy to toy. You go from book to book."

She winced. *I'm nothing like you*—no career goals, no direction, just following the wind, like a sailor. And that tattoo. MH/CD. Margie, Carla. Seriously?

Dirk was a guy she'd pretend to like to spite her parents—

tattoo, shaggy hair, T-shirt wardrobe, no education—everything they despised. If she didn't have Brian.

"Children's lit was my favorite class." She rattled off favorites. "Oz books, too. Folktales and fairy tales."

"Magic spells and heroic quests?" Puffing out his chest, he struck a gallant pose.

"And ones with noodleheads, or tall tales like Paul Bunyan. Tricksters like Brer Rabbit."

"Wait. I'm stuck on noodleheads. That's a genre?"

"A simpleton. Numbskull."

"Ah, numbskull. Now you're talking my language. What's a noodlehead example?" He pulled out a napkin. "Got a pen?"

She handed him one, then listed titles as he jotted them down.

"Will these be in your book café?" He twirled his napkin. "This story talk stirs you."

"Possibly. I'll have adult and children's lit. An Edwardian section includes *The Secret Garden*. A Victorian section will have the Alice books."

"What're your favorite folktales?"

She listed several.

"Whoa! Back up the train. I can't write that fast. Why are they favorites? The happily ever after part? The hero's journey? Like Joseph Campbell's *Hero With a Thousand Faces*."

"Wow, I'm impressed. I'll loan you a folktale book." Brian wouldn't read one. "I need to check the bookstore for an old favorite. *The Tasha Tudor Book of Fairy Tales*."

He wrote the title.

She sipped water. "Did you have favorites as a kid?"

"*Call of the Wild* and the Hardy Boys. But reading was only an excuse to avoid sleep. Later, I chose real-life adventures over books, from snorkeling at port to predicting whale sightings." He relayed an anecdote about tracking iguanas in Panama.

"What's your next enterprise?" she asked.

"After this wild and crazy summer selling paint and

moonlighting?" He chuckled. "Whitewater rafting, a climbing expedition, or hiking the Appalachian Trail. Gerrit wants to do the trail. The camp wants me back, too. But that's too tame after a tame summer."

"Maybe you need a weekend bike trip."

"I work most Saturdays. Sundays, I have dinner with my folks after church."

"Nice you enjoy your family so much." A pang of jealousy twisted through her.

"Yeah, they're great. How about yours?"

She bit her lip. "I've never been gone long enough to miss them."

He seemed to sense her reticence. "So, may I show you around Holland? In three Saturdays. I'd be honored to take you."

She tilted her head with a coy smile. "Is the Macatawa tour guide reliable?"

He grinned. "You'll get all the facts, plus multiple bonus features."

Carrie smiled. "All right then. But remember—strictly business."

TWENTY-FIVE

Saturday, June 7, 1980

Brian canceled, needing to meet a client. At least Carrie could avoid conflict. Instead, she helped Oma pick strawberries, then sanded the bureau with Opa. Tonight she would make her au gratin potatoes recipe. Keeping busy mitigated worry about her father possibly showing up again.

Carrie asked Opa about stenciling the dresser with nursery rhyme characters, like Mr. Baum's folksy touches on his woodworking. He agreed. Reluctantly, she accompanied him to the hardware store. Dirk might discover Brian was a no-show.

Opa spotted him crouching at an end cap. "Hey, Dirk, how's it going, my man?"

Dirk gestured down the aisle of wrenches and hammers. "Living the dream, sir."

Opa hooked thumbs in his pockets, inhaling as if invigorated by paint smells. "You're the envy of every retired codger in this town."

"Best affirmation I got all week."

Carrie ducked down the paint aisle, leaving Opa to his

prattling. She picked antique white and flipped through yellows. Would Oma let her paint the bedroom? Painting could help her discern effective colors for the café. Pineapple Mousse, Tangy Lemon Twist, Butterscotch Cream—hues as delicious as their names.

The dining room needed a facelift, too: Dawn's Promise, Honey Glaze, Sea Tickle.

"Hey, are you hiding?"

Startled, Carrie faced a grinning Dirk. "Unsuccessfully."

He laughed. "Where's Brian? Introduce us."

Her cheeks warmed. "He's not here."

"Hardware store's not on his itinerary?"

"He's in Kalamazoo."

"Oh, sorry."

She shrugged. "Had to meet a client. I'll see him next Saturday."

"No doubt." He glanced at her samples. "Redecorating?"

"If Oma allows."

"Take all the samples you want and use your magical powers of persuasion."

"First, I have to *find* my magical powers of persuasion."

"Let me try mine on you." He adopted a serious tone. "I wanna meet Mrs. G."

"No, you don't." She rolled her eyes. "She's prickly. Unpredictable. A trap waiting to clamp down, chomp you in two."

"I'm not afraid. She's intriguing. She knew L. Frank Baum. She ran the tearoom. She's lived here forever, with decades of stories."

Carrie headed down the aisle. "It won't work. Too awkward."

Dirk followed. "What's wrong?"

"Look, it's hard enough with just her and me. Like going through a minefield. I don't know when the next criticism will be lobbed." Carrie examined the stain display. "You don't get it. Nothing bothers you."

"Actually, dead fish on the beach bother me. And toast crumbs floating in my coffee. How 'bout Monday morning?"

"No." She squinted at the stains.

"I have yet to meet a woman over forty who doesn't love me. Right off the bat."

She glared. "You're supposed to be *working*."

"I'm schmoozing with customers. That's highly encouraged."

"Is annoying them highly encouraged, too?" She waved paint strips near his chin.

"Please."

"Okay, Tuesday, so I can give her fair warning."

"Tuesday won't work."

"Seriously? You're like a kid begging for candy. You finally get it, only to toss it in the trash."

"I'm busy Tuesday afternoons, so Uncle John wants me here all morning."

"What's on Tuesdays?"

Dirk shrugged. "Stuff."

She tightened her jaw. "Okay, Wednesday. Wear something besides a T-shirt." *Preferably long sleeves.* She glanced at his tattoo. MH/CD. Marcy? Charlene?

Dirk bowed. "Yes, Your Majesty. Any other requirements?"

"Come at ten. Bring an appetite."

"No problem there." He grinned. "I see *my* magical powers of persuasion worked."

She punched his arm as Opa moseyed around the corner. "Time's a-wasting. Can't get a lick of shopping done with all the gabbing."

After Dirk's treatise on stain brands, Carrie picked maple for her chair.

With more babbling about hammers and paint, Carrie had

to pry them apart to get Opa out the door. "Looks like you and Dirk bonded."

"Hardware does that for a guy," Opa said.

That afternoon, Carrie and Opa painted the bureau as Oma made strawberry jam, then baked scones from Mrs. Gordon's recipe. Carrie's casual mention of painting walls—without employing Dirk's obnoxious tactics—was greeted with enthusiasm.

In Opa's shop, Carrie sanded and stained an old frame, then wrote calligraphy, in large letters for Mrs. Gordon's dim eyes: "Imagination is the magic that accomplishes the impossible." Maybe it would bring a smile.

* * *

Monday, June 9, 1980

Monday morning, the drapes were open farther. Success! Lace lightened pillows and damask furniture. Tapestry runners garnished pedestal end tables. Fringed lampshades swished as Carrie walked by, fingering them.

In the kitchen, Carrie handed Mrs. Gordon a wrapped gift and a jar of strawberry jam. "Oma made jam. I made this."

Mrs. Gordon held the jar close before unwrapping the gift. Holding the frame, she blinked. "The Ruth Plumly Thompson quote!" She seemed pleased but no smile.

"My calligraphy's not the best."

"Don't make excuses for things you do from the heart." She asked Carrie to hang it beside the Mad Hatter's Tea Party illustration.

They made Tik-Tok's Mechanical Chunky Oats Bars. Mrs. Gordon brewed Princess Gloria's Peach Brulee: black tea with mango, marigold, peaches, and coconut, served with a lesson on marigold's health benefits. She gave Carrie Mr. Popover's Cheesy Garlic Popovers recipe for Oma.

Over tea, Mrs. Gordon asked more about Oma. Carrie shared how Opa lost his job in Holland, how the tough situation strengthened her grandparents' faith while driving Carrie's mom to obsess over appearances.

"It takes mettle of a different kind to live with misjudgment and criticism."

How much gossip about her was true? "Oma says trying to console my mother was like *water naar de zee dragen,* meaning—"

"I know. Carrying water to sea. I lived with a Dutch family. Your mother's response surely impacted you while growing up."

Should she reveal the sixth-grade catastrophe? Carrie's heartbeat quickened. No, she'd never told anybody. "Mom favored my sister Amy, who made the family look good. I had to cover for her mistakes, even forfeited a weekend in Chicago when she double-booked herself for babysitting. I was devastated." She swallowed. "I know it doesn't sound like much."

"Don't minimize what feels like a great weight," Mrs. Gordon murmured.

Surprised by kindness, Carrie continued. "Life revolved around Amy, her peppy personality, dramatic talents, and good grades. I was quiet, awkward. I sketched in my room, made crafts, or read. When we had company, my folks asked Amy to sing for guests. They'd ask me ... to clear dishes."

"You're Cinderella in your own home, but never get to the ball."

Carrie blinked. "Exactly. Amy was the star. When we'd play-act shows with neighbors, she was always Cinderella, Dorothy, or Mary Poppins. And star of the dinner table."

"As if you weren't there."

"My parents made me take the college track in high school when I wanted to take home ec. They belittled my interests."

She'd inadvertently paid them back by not finishing her degree. But she couldn't admit that.

"Does Brian know how you feel?"

"Mostly, but some things he doesn't understand."

"Like what? Your heart's desires?"

The words fell with a *thud*. "No, I mean, he doesn't even like my music choices. He has no patience for family drama."

"What's wrong with your music preferences?"

"I like variety. He listens to religious stuff."

"Indeed?" Mrs. Gordon narrowed her eyes. "Are you dating Mr. Legality?"

"No, uh ..." *Change the subject.* "Mrs. Gordon, my friend wants to meet you." She braced herself.

"Mr. Legality?"

"No. I mean, not Brian. Dirk."

"Does Brian know about Dirk?"

None of your business! "Look, Dirk's all business. And underqualified as a beau."

"Why does he want to meet me? Antique hunting?"

"He's interested in local history. I told him you're a Broderick."

"That's *all* you said?" She tipped her head forward, looking over her glasses.

"He knows you ran the tearoom. I told him you visited the Baums at Macatawa Park."

She pursed her lips. "You shared what I expressly said to keep in confidence?"

"Nothing about your personal life. He's from Holland and invited me to sail and visit Macatawa. I want to see where you sat on the porch with Mr. Baum."

"The Baum cottage burned down in the 1920s."

"I'd love to see where you swam and fished with the Baum boys."

"Humph. Go sailing. With a boy who's not your boyfriend."

"Strictly business." The words fell flat.

Mrs. Gordon added sugar to her tea, probably to sweeten bitter words ready to fly from her mouth.

Finding herself in typical apology mode, Carrie fumbled her cup. "I'm sorry. I shouldn't have said anything. I'm really sorry. I want your trust, and I blew it—"

"Enough," Mrs. Gordon snapped. "Are five rapid-fire apologies better than one *sincere* apology?"

Carrie froze, about to apologize for profusely apologizing. "You're right. But I want to earn your trust."

"You're talking too much, young lady. Did I *say* I don't trust you?" She peered over her glasses again. "Why does this Dirk fellow have any thought for me or the tearoom?"

"He sings at the café."

"Then he had those miserable rocks that pass for Broderick muffins. We'll serve a genuine recipe with vanilla pear tea. Does he drink tea?"

"He'll drink whatever you offer. He's available Wednesday."

"We'll have tea at ten." Mrs. Gordon hobbled to the recipe box.

"Should he wear a suit and tie?" Carrie smirked.

"No need for pretension."

Carrie called the hardware store and told Dirk he got his wish. She and Mrs. Gordon bought groceries, dusted, swept, and polished silverware and candlesticks. Dirk surely wouldn't notice polished silver, but Mrs. Gordon seemed happy preparing for a guest. Perhaps it would occasion opening drapes.

Wednesday, June 11

Carrie helped prepare biscuits, then The Sawhorse's Streusel-topped Grilled Peaches on a griddle. Mrs. Gordon filled the bowl with sugar cubes for more controlled portion sizes, especially since Dirk lacked teatime experience. Heaven forbid Dirk should suffer from such lavish indulgence.

Carrie set the dining room table with Kate Greenaway napkin rings, glass goblets, and a vase of zinnias. Ropes of glass beads shimmered on the antique chandelier. Blue Willow china lined the elaborate sideboard. Walter Crane fairy tale prints adorned the walls. The swag valance hung over billowed lace, which Carrie adjusted to allow more light.

Mozart played on the Victrola. Peach and vanilla aromas permeated the house when the doorbell buzzed. Letting Dirk in, Carrie smiled at his black sports coat, white T-shirt, jeans, and sneakers. "You've captured the Billy Joel concert look!" With long sleeves, his tattoo didn't show.

He winked. "Had to wear something special for my first tea."

This wouldn't happen with Brian. She led him to the dining room where Mrs. Gordon stood. Carrie introduced them.

Dirk walked over. "Glad to meet you, Mrs. Gordon."

"*Are* you now, Mr. Vandenakker?" She looked at him over her glasses. "Made your day, did I? An old relic from the Broderick Tearoom, still alive and kicking."

Carrie wanted to end teatime *now*, but Dirk seemed unruffled. "Please call me Dirk. I'm glad to meet someone from the tearoom's early days. So many family pictures."

"Caroline mentioned you play there." They sat as Carrie poured tea.

"Caroline?" Dirk arched his eyebrows. "Oh, you mean the queen here."

Mrs. Gordon smirked. "What repertoire do you employ?"

"Contemporary folksongs. Music by Gordon Lightfoot, James Taylor, and others."

"They're unfamiliar." Mrs. Gordon unfolded a floral linen napkin. "I hope they're worthy."

"They are." As if on cue, Dirk placed a napkin on his lap. "They're quite popular."

"Popularity doesn't always denote quality." Mrs. Gordon dropped a sugar cube in her tea.

"True." Dirk dumped four cubes in his cup. So much for portion control. No protest from Mrs. Gordon?

"Did you bring your guitar?" Mrs. Gordon asked. "I'd like to hear a song."

"It's in the car." He hesitated. "Here's the deal. I never play without knowing the territory first. I'm here to get to know *you*, Mrs. Gordon. If you still want me to play later, I'm happy to."

"Fair enough."

How'd he manage to win Mrs. Gordon's affections already? Carrie would never get away with multiple sugar cubes. To prove it, she dropped two in her cup. Conspicuously. *Plunk, plunk.*

Mrs. Gordon stared over her glasses. "You've made your absurd point, Caroline." She turned to Dirk. "What do you do when you're not playing guitar?"

"Work at Vandenakker Hardware, after a year of camp work up north."

Mrs. Gordon handed him biscuits. "These don't compare to anything at the café."

Dirk took one. "I concur. Carrie shared your muffins last week."

"These are Betsy Bobbin's Bountiful Buttermilk Biscuits. She and Trot are the only American girls besides Dorothy who went to Oz and became her good friends. Did you read Oz books as a child, Mr. Vandenakker?"

"The first three." He dribbled honey over his biscuit.

"A mere fraction. Mr. Baum wrote fourteen. After he passed away, the publisher hired Ruth Plumly Thompson to continue the adventures, yearly through 1939. Five other authors brought the series to a close for a total of forty in the official Oz canon. But enough of that. Tell me about your aspirations."

Dirk offered his culinary endorsement for the peaches. "Frankly, Mrs. Gordon, with multiple interests, I'm a bit unconventional." He summarized his bicycling, sailing, and climbing ventures, interspersed with Mrs. Gordon's comments.

"So, such gallivanting takes priority over pursuing a career?"

"Absolutely." Dirk wiped his chin with the napkin as if not wanting to soil it.

"It's refreshing to meet someone following his heart without pretensions, comfortable in his own skin."

Carrie winced. A little *too* comfortable, unencumbered by the world's cares.

Mrs. Gordon squinted. "Did you leave a broken-hearted girl at every port?"

Are you kidding? That tattoo. MH/CD. Martha. Cynthia.

"No, I've never been one for flings. Doesn't seem right for a rolling stone."

"When the right girl comes along, she'll join you on your ventures?"

"Depends on the girl, and what world she thrives in. Two people in love ought to be part of each other's worlds, but neither should dictate which one they settle in. Right, Mrs. Gordon?"

"Well put, young man." Another compliment? Looking satisfied, Mrs. Gordon sipped tea. "Apparently no time for Prince Charming pursuits."

"I'm more of a court jester. Speaking of aspirations, Carrie surely told you about her book café idea."

"Indeed?" Mrs. Gordon's eyebrows arched.

Carrie's eyes bulged. Unbelievable! She drew fingers across her throat in a cutting motion until Mrs. Gordon faced her.

If Dirk saw her gesture, he ignored it. "It's amazing. It's all planned out. Literary themes galore. Quite innovative. With your background and love for books, you'd appreciate it."

"Tell me more."

Carrie kept her voice light. "It's nothing. Honestly, Dirk. What's gotten into you?"

He leaned toward Mrs. Gordon. "She's bashful because of your vast experience. But take my word for it, this idea is taking wing."

Mrs. Gordon nodded. "The turtle only moves forward by sticking his neck out."

Turtle, indeed! Thank goodness the record stopped so she could turn it over.

"Haven't seen an old record player like that lately," Dirk said.

"You young people with your new-fangled ways." Mrs. Gordon flicked her hand. "You have eight tracks, right?"

"Obsolete now," Dirk said. "Cassette tapes."

Mrs. Gordon set down her fork. "Mr. Baum was fascinated by *and* concerned about advances in technology. Tik-Tok is a mechanical man in *Ozma of Oz*, 1907. Mr. Baum was ahead of his time. We discussed it in Macatawa Park." She folded her arms on the table.

Carrie balked. Was she launching into a story with Dirk here?

Twenty-Six

Janie, 14
July 1906

"Welcome to my summer haven!" Mr. Baum greeted Janie and Aunt Sophie for the fifth summer in a row. Harry and Kenneth immediately took Charlotte to the boathouse. Next to fishing rods was the automobile, purchased last year.

"May I introduce you to the Model F?" Kenneth gestured broadly. "From Ford."

The boys pointed out its finer features: steering wheel, roof, running board, sleek green paint, and brass carriage lamps on both sides of the dashboard. Harry tapped the chassis. "Every morning, Father puts gasoline in here to prime the engine before it starts."

"It starts by cranking." Kenneth went through the motions. "Be careful this lever isn't too far forward, or the motor kicks back on the crank. You'd break an arm."

"Oh, my! Why's it called the Model F?" Not very creative for something so exciting.

Kenneth grinned. "*F* for Fantastic."

Mr. Baum arrived with Auntie. He cranked the engine, so dreadful a roar that Janie covered her ears. He donned goggles due to insects. "Hold onto your hats!" He drove to Holland. Squished between the boys in back, Janie's hair flew. The mileage needle poked its way to thirty.

In Holland, Mr. Baum mentioned the Chicago Cubs dominating first place since May 9 while Aunt Sophie's poor Tigers lagged ten games behind, even with this promising Ty Cobb fellow. They left Auntie at Dena Vanderlaan's near downtown.

Back on the cottage porch, Mrs. Baum shooed the boys into the house for chores while she embroidered. Mr. Baum drummed the table. "Automobiles make me wonder if my predictions for the year 2090 will occur sooner."

"Which predictions, Mr. Baum?"

"In 1896, my article 'Yesterday at the Exposition' predicted life with airships, high-speed pneumatic cars, telepathy, even magical fertilizer that grows from seed to wheat in a jiffy."

Janie imagined Jack's beanstalk multiplied in a garden of giant vegetables.

"My poem, 'The Latest in Magic,' toyed with the notion of X-rays having the ability to see into human hearts and illuminate minds."

"A step too far with your imagination, dear." Mrs. Baum poked a needle through cloth. "I thought Robert's dumbwaiter was a great achievement. But it inspired laziness."

"Fiddlesticks!" Mr. Baum said. "That freed him to do more important things and get to Lewis Institute on time. Like the automobile, though such things might overtake nature." Mr. Baum sighed. "We definitely live in wonderstruck days."

"I wonder what Mrs. Bilkins would say," Janie said.

"She applauded such advancements," Mr. Baum replied. "She visited the Downditch farm where everything happened with the push of a button. The front door opened automatically. A table appeared with a nineteen-course meal.

Electricity even did the dishes. A chair wheeled her to a theater. Later, electricity popped her into a preheated bed."

Janie gaped. "I wish I had electricity that washed dishes. Don't you, Mrs. Baum?"

"Yes, Charlotte. Sewing machines and such work in our favor." Mrs. Baum snipped a thread with extra fervor. "But my boys must wash dishes. It builds character like button-pushing never will."

Janie visualized the boys lazing on the floor, playing backgammon, and pushing buttons that washed dishes, cleaned the automobile, and tidied their rooms.

"True, my love," Mr. Baum said. "No magic wand should replace good hard work. But as long as button-pushing doesn't supplant striving for worthy goals, I welcome it. Mrs. Bilkins speculated that airships would bring the cows home or fly to Africa."

Janie clasped her hands. "I want to fly in one."

"I know what Tik-Tok would say. He's a mechanical man made of copper that runs on clockwork springs that wind up. He speaks haltingly. 'Good-morn-ing-lit-tle-girl.'"

Janie mimicked his bland tone. "How-do-you-do-sir?" It dawned on her with a gasp. "Is this another Dorothy story? What's it called?"

"*Ozma of Oz*. I'm still working on it. You'll be quite satisfied. Dorothy is swept overboard with her companion Billina, a yellow hen, capable of considerable feats, more than you'd expect from most chickens."

Janie grinned. "You used my idea!"

"You were right. I can't resist chickens. A storm at sea thrusts them into another world where they must use their wits against the Nome king. Nomes with no G. No child need wrestle with silent letters."

Mrs. Baum snickered. "Sparing much aggravation across the country."

"Are you working on anything else, Mr. Baum?"

"Several things, even on vacation. With Harry in Orchard Lake and Kenneth at Interlaken School in Indiana, Mrs. Baum and I took a six-month trip to North Africa and Europe instead of wintering in Coronado."

Would Janie ever travel outside Michigan? "How thrilling! What'd you see?"

"The Sphinx, Tower of London, the Eiffel Tower. I'm publishing my wife's letters to people back home, adding my photographs, for friends and family."

"My favorite was Egypt," Mrs. Baum said. "I climbed the Great Pyramid."

Mr. Baum blew out smoke. "In Italy, Mt. Vesuvius had quite an eruption. That crater's the only thing that smokes more than I do." Janie laughed. "On the ship, I wrote *Aunt Jane's Nieces* for older girls like you, Charlotte. Three spoiled girls go to their Aunt Jane's estate for her to decide who inherits the property."

"I can't wait to read it."

"You won't find it under my name, though." Mr. Baum waved his cigar. "Look for Edith Van Dyne. Two novels for adults are written by Schuyler Staunton. *Sam Steele's Adventures on Land and Sea* is penned by Captain Hugh Fitzgerald."

"Perfect author name for a sea adventure."

"*The Twinkle Tales,* for younger readers, is a series of six illustrated books crafted by Laura Bancroft. *Annabell*, for older girls, has similarities to the popular Horatio Alger rags-to-riches plot. By Suzanne Metcalf."

"Five names!" Janie said. "How'd you write so many stories?"

"*I'll* tell you how," Mrs. Baum said. "I manage household business, sparing him much bother. Like that automobile, another time-saver."

"Will you drive to our inn?" Janie asked. "You can tell Mother about Welsh rarebit."

He laughed. "Heaven forbid I dictate the menu, already exuding excellence."

Mrs. Baum imparted a tender expression. "Your aunt thinks it best we meet here."

Janie knew why. Her shoulders drooped.

Mr. Baum lit a new cigar from the old one. "I understand disappointments, Charlotte. For years, Mr. Hough and I collaborated on musical comedies, yet nobody's interested in producing *Montezuma* or *The Maid of Athens*. I also fear my slapstick play will never reach the stage, either. But Mr. Hough used my ideas and characters in his own book, without crediting me." He took Janie's hand. "My point is, 'You must walk. It is a long journey, through a country that is sometimes pleasant and sometimes dark and terrible.'"

TWENTY-SEVEN

Wednesday, June 11, 1980

Carrie fumed. Why'd Mrs. Gordon tell stories previously entrusted only to her?

"Ahead of his time," Dirk said.

"Regarding women's rights, too." Mrs. Gordon nodded. "After *Ozma of Oz*, reviewers called him the 'greatest inventor of modern fairy tales,' and said he'd rather write fairy stories than eat. But having sat with him for many meals, I know that cannot be true. Then, from 1913 to 1915, and 1908, he made his own Oz films. He should be credited with the earliest documented original film score. In 1910, he moved to Hollywood, nothing but orange groves. They built a house a mile from where Graumann's Chinese Theater is now."

"Sign of the Goose Two?" Dirk said.

"No. Ozcot."

Dirk took two biscuits. "Was the film industry doing anything then?"

"Somewhat. The first Hollywood movie played in 1910. Mr. Baum and friends raised funds to start a film company."

"Let me guess," Dirk said. "It was Yellow Brick Road to Hollywood."

"No."

Dirk rattled off a string of silly Ozian names, employing Munchkins, Winkies, and winged monkeys.

Mrs. Gordon's smile broadened with each guess. She broke into laughter.

Stunned, Carrie stared at her.

"You've proven me an utter failure at guessing games," Dirk said. "What's it called?"

"The Oz Film Manufacturing Company."

"I like my ideas better." Dirk spooned peaches over another biscuit. "Today exceeds my expectations. When Her Highness Caroline first summoned me—"

Carrie kicked him under the table.

"Ouch! Well, you did dictate the dress code."

Mrs. Gordon looked over her glasses at Carrie. "Dictate?"

"I suggested he wear something besides a T-shirt."

Mrs. Gordon eyed the sports coat. "But rue the day such coats over T-shirts are teatime protocol."

A smile in his voice, he winked at Carrie. "She threatened to cut my guitar strings if I didn't cooperate."

"She has spunk," Mrs. Gordon said. "Ever since she kicked that ball into my yard."

"Seriously?" Carrie lifted her hands in a plea.

Mrs. Gordon offered her rendition of that event, interspersed with Dirk's jests. Her jocularity was a breakthrough, but how'd he do it—magic dust?

At Dirk's request, Mrs. Gordon explained Baum's revisiting Oz on stage and screen. Thus, the *Fairylogue*, three musicals, and various film ventures took wing. After closing the OFMC, Baum returned to Oz through books, foreshadowing future technology with Princess Ozma's Magic Picture Screen and *Glinda's Great Book of Records*.

Mrs. Gordon pointed out photos from *The Annotated*

Wizard of Oz. Fascinated, Carrie browsed as Dirk and Mrs. Gordon chatted.

Dirk buttered a biscuit. "How'd Mr. Baum's view of women's rights influence you?"

"He encouraged me no differently than his sons to pursue my dreams, walking with confidence and kindness."

What happened to kindness? Did she pursue her dreams?

"Because of him and Auntie, I developed untapped skills, turned flights of fancy into reality, even took trips. Yet some things weren't overcome." Dragons not yet slain. "That's vague as bread dough, but I'm sharing chronologically with my scribe, Miss Caroline. If you've explored the territory to your satisfaction, I'd like to hear your music."

After Dirk retrieved his guitar, they sat in the front room. He'd shed his coat, exposing the tattoo. MH/CD. Carrie hoped Mrs. Gordon couldn't see it, especially after his gallant proclamation of leaving no broken hearts behind. Ha! What about Maria and Cecily?

Dirk tuned his guitar. "Kenny Rogers adapted this from an old hymn, 'Love Lifted Me,' a country chart hit. It has personal meaning, especially after God picked me up from the mire."

What mire? Despite stewing, Carrie enjoyed his pleasant tenor voice. Mrs. Gordon was riveted. Afterward, she said, "Simply felicitous."

Three compliments in one day?

"Please play another," Mrs. Gordon said. "Ending our morning on a pleasant *note*."

Dirk smiled, picked at strings, then strummed. "Written by Carole King, sung by her and James Taylor. 'You've Got a Friend.'" His face entered the song's spirit.

Mesmerized, Carrie leaned forward. His voice sent sweet shivers down her spine. His warm gaze melted her as lyrics promised friendship through each season.

Mrs. Gordon smiled. Again.

Carrie walked Dirk to his car. "You did in two hours what I couldn't do in two weeks."

"Huh?"

"You made her smile," Carrie sputtered. "Laugh, even."

"Honestly? The first time?"

"Yes. Every day I'm cajoling, poking, prodding—"

"Are you kidding? The only reason she warmed up to me is because you spent two weeks with her first. She's like a jar lid. Someone else loosens it, but the one who removes it gets the glory."

"Yup, you get the glory." Carrie crossed her arms. "You made her laugh."

"So, I tapped into her humor. But you're the one plumbing the depths of her soul. You should be happy she's laughing."

"I am. But she allows you *four* sugar cubes and saves her crabbiness for me."

"It's a facade. Crabbiness holds you at arm's length."

"I can't believe you wooed her like that. And you told her about the book café!"

"How can a guy say so many wrong things in just two hours?" His tone was light-hearted. "Wooed her? That's far-fetched, though I have a way with the over-forty crowd. Women, that is. Let's see. Alberta, as you know. Aunt Barb, but she's my aunt. Betty at the grocer's."

"You think you're funny."

"I try. But you're angry at me."

"I'm not angry." To prove it, she uncrossed her arms.

"Yes, you are."

"No, I'm not!" Her eyes widened.

"Then you're jealous."

"That's ridiculous."

"If you're not angry or jealous" —he circled a hand over his head— "then what's this frenzy?"

She wanted to smack him. "I'm just flabbergasted."

"No, you're upset."

She waved her arms. "Good grief, do you *want* me to be angry?"

"No, but if you *are*, just say it. Scream and holler, but don't hide it."

"I'm not."

Dirk threw up his hands in surrender. "This Hope-Calvin rivalry's gone far enough."

"Seriously? You didn't even stay at Hope long enough to—never mind. You're turning this into a big joke."

Dirk lowered his voice. "What're you *really* angry about?"

"I'm not angry!" The echo rang through the street. "That is, I *wasn't*, but now I am because you've provoked me by *telling* me I am, over and over!"

Dirk quietly replied, "You've never been allowed to be angry, have you?"

His words stunned her. Tears burned her eyes.

His hand rested on her shoulder. "Look, I'm just a guy, but pretty good at reading emotions. Don't hide who you are."

She sniffed, tears brimming. Her shoulder tingled where his hand brought warmth.

"Hey, I loved being with you and meeting Mrs. G. Even though she cuts to the chase. Thanks." He dropped his hand.

"You invited yourself," she snapped. "You pleaded till I gave in."

"You're right. I shouldn't have pushed. I'm sorry."

An apology! Softened, Carrie steadied her voice. "It's okay."

"I'm trying to know the real Carrie. If there's anger in there, let it out. We need to talk. Can we meet later tonight?"

Her voice wavered. "Okay."

"Pick you up at eight. See you, Caro*line*." He hopped in his car and drove off.

Inside, she carried the teapot to the kitchen and inhaled courage. "You reprimand me for taking two sugar cubes but say nothing when Dirk dumps four in his cup."

Mrs. Gordon turned on the faucet. "He was our guest."

"While I'm chopped liver, just your employee. Why'd you tell him about Mr. Baum? That's what you and I are doing together."

"You're jealous." Mrs. Gordon dunked plates in the sink.

"No, I want equal treatment." Carrie kept her anger front and center to empower her next words. "You realize I can quit anytime."

Mrs. Gordon turned around, face serene. "I had a wonderful time today and am grateful for you making it happen."

Carrie's anger fizzled, mixed with surprise. "You're welcome, but if I want to put *five* sugar cubes in my tea, I'll do it."

"All right." Mrs. Gordon picked up a dishrag. "But you're still jealous."

Carrie sighed. "Mrs. Gordon, *why'd* you open up to Dirk so easily?"

She gazed across the room. "He reminds me of my Walter."

"Was he a sailor, free spirit, and jack-of-all-trades?"

"No, but he was kind, thoughtful, made me laugh. Dirk's sport-coat-with-jeans attire reminds me of Walter's dislike of stuffy people who put on airs. So, when are you two getting married?"

Carrie fumbled the teapot but caught it. The lid rattled. "What?"

"No gawking at teatime."

"I'm with Brian, remember?"

"Well, you'll have to do something about that. All he does is play baseball, keep financial records, and bring chocolate. Mr. Vandenakker's a good one."

"Because he reminds you of Mr. Gordon?"

"He doesn't go after glitter and gold and others' expectations."

"Exactly. He follows whims with no commitments. He's

unstable. Untamable. Not suitor material. Besides, he doesn't care for me the way you think."

"Open your eyes. As Rinkitink in Oz would say, his sweetness puts honey to shame. That second song was *yours*." She leaned against the counter. "And you have a lilt to your voice when talking about him. Unlike with Brian."

"You're imagining things."

"Some things I see clearly. You may share my stories with Mr. Vandenakker. I trust him. He's also charmed by your book café." Mrs. Gordon looked over her glasses. "Because he's captivated by *you*." Carrie's cheeks warmed. "So, what about this book café?"

Mrs. Gordon would surely shoot down her dream, questioning her sanity.

"Literary themes galore ..."

As a test, Carrie explained—*if* she were to do such a thing—how she'd incorporate literary eras and authors into café menus and decor, a bookshelf in every nook. "It's something I've thought about while working summer restaurant jobs."

"A dream takes more than experience. It requires passion. Do you have passion?"

"You sound like Dirk. Did you have passion for running the tearoom? Or was it duty?"

She pursed her lips. "Once I realized the inevitable, I embraced it."

And barreled over everyone else. Pearl's rendition of her aunt's leadership style, a replacement for children. "What was your first choice? Becoming Nellie Bly? Having a family?"

"We'll get to that. How have you prepared for this venture?"

"By making *olliebollen* in the dorm bathroom." Carrie crossed her arms.

Mrs. Gordon speared a gaze over her glasses.

"Actually, besides working six summers at two restaurants, I created a business plan. Last week, I applied for a loan to open a café on the site of Dunham's Diner." Carrie cringed, awaiting judgment.

Mrs. Gordon's face expanded with incredulity. "Indeed? How will you accomplish this with teaching obligations?"

How long could Carrie maintain the facade? She sighed. "Mrs. Gordon, I'm never going to teach." She confessed to the failed class, no diploma, refusing to retake the class. Not yet telling her parents. Pursuing the café behind their backs. Embracing her private rebellion.

"What does Brian think?"

Another sigh. "He doesn't know about failing school."

"You're afraid to tell him."

"Yes." There, she'd said it. Why was she revealing her heart to this woman?

"And you fear your parents' denouncements while craving their approval."

"Oh, my word, yes."

Mrs. Gordon retrieved an object from a ceramic jar. "Do you want to live by your passions or your fears?" She handed Carrie a yellow wooden chicken ornament. "For your journey. Through both pleasant and dark places."

Carrie fingered smooth edges, turned it over to carved initials: LFB. "Did Mr. Baum make others?"

"He never mass-produced chicken ornaments."

"Then this is a real treasure. Sure you want me to keep it?"

"To recognize the value of such a gift is a virtue. And defies questioning."

TWENTY-EIGHT

Janie, 14
July 1906

On Black Lake, the children took turns naming captive fish according to presumed personalities. Later, Mrs. Baum couldn't tell Sigfried from Estralia, or Nocknorton from Hespetunia.

After swimming, Mrs. Baum and Janie made Baked Alaska, served it, then sat on the porch. Mrs. Baum stitched flowers on an apron pocket, demonstrating the herringbone stitch.

Janie's needle barely missed her finger. "How'd you and Mr. Baum meet?"

Mrs. Baum's lips twitched in amusement. "'Twas 1881. A woman can never forget the day she meets a man like Frank Baum. He was twenty-five, so handsome. I was twenty, a Cornell student in Ithaca, New York, planning to study law." She pulled threads taut in rhythm. "My mother was determined that I be the first woman in the family to get a degree. Only nineteen of 131 in my class were women. Boys knew Mother was a suffragist and cruelly mocked me. My first taste of traipsing through a male-dominated world.

"My college roommate Josie was Mr. Baum's cousin. I was in Syracuse at Christmastime at his sister Harriet's home. His aunt introduced us, saying, 'Frank, I want you to know Maud Gage. I'm sure you will love her.' He replied, 'Consider yourself loved, Miss Gage.' My reply? 'Thank you, Mr. Baum. That's a promise. Please see that you live up to it.'"

Janie envisioned charming Mr. Baum, taking his future bride's hand.

Her laughter sparkled, needle paused. "He never stayed interested in a girl before me. The next summer, he visited in Fayetteville often. My father was a merchant. Mother was busy with suffrage efforts. From her, I inherited my stubborn streak and progressive ways. Though a problem at Cornell, it didn't bother Frank one bit.

"When he proposed, I happily said yes. But Mother was furious. He waited in the parlor while she and I argued. She called him an impractical dreamer, unable to support a family as an itinerant actor. Did I really want to sacrifice college for him? But I did. So, Mother gave in.

"We married on November 9, 1882, in our home with a Baptist minister. We exchanged identical vows, without the nonsense of obedience to husbands. Then we traveled with *The Maid of Arran* acting troupe. Before our baby was born, Frank left his beloved stage and rented a home in Syracuse." She gazed across the lake, as if peering back in time. "He constantly rocked Frank Joslyn, singing, and he doted on all the boys. He spent more time with them than most fathers did, especially when I was ill after Robert's birth."

Mrs. Baum sighed. "But he undid my best efforts disciplining four whippersnappers. When he was gone for weeks as a salesman, I single-handedly drilled manners into those rapscallions. But their father couldn't bear my spanking or sending a boy to bed without supper. He'd offer food and tell him a story. That man doesn't have a stern bone in his body."

"Yet you get along so well."

"We love each other, dear. He wrote an editorial about how a happy home lies in men's hands. He lived what he wrote, with empathy for me, working to be cheerful in everything." Mrs. Baum knotted a thread. "We have unconventional roles, which helps. I'm his business manager. He assigns copyrights to me, royalties from books and plays. I fill his checking account, keeping better track than he does. It suits us both."

Would Janie be as fortunate in finding love? "Do you wish you'd finished college?"

She chose another thread color. "Rarely. I'm raising four boys as my contribution to society. I have free rein at home, allowing Mr. Baum time for projects he enjoys. He must create. He knows the heart of a child, even becomes one when writing. So, I accept the times his imagination overtakes him. He's humble, kind, and pleasant, rarely angry. He loves meeting people. Yet when his mind's active with some story, he'll meet his best friend and not see him."

Janie smiled. "Sounds like me. That last part."

"You are two peas in a pod." Mrs. Baum rotated the fabric. "Early Chicago years were lean, but nightly we'd be satisfied with a good day, because we had each other and our boys."

"Sounds lovely." Unlike home. A cloud of sadness overtook her.

"I've no regrets, except not having a daughter. But I have wonderful nieces—Matilda, Magdalena, and Leslie. Since my boys have grown, I've enjoyed the girls' company immensely. And yours, too." She touched Janie's hand, inviting her into that mystical realm.

Mr. Baum appeared and set down a fat manila envelope. "For you, Charlotte. My *Ozma of Oz* manuscript. I often test my stories on young readers. Considering your insistence on having another Dorothy story—with a chicken, no less—I'd relish your opinion."

That was prize enough. But additionally, Mrs. Baum gifted

Janie a new pillowcase, the one she'd made last year, edged in lace and dainty embroidered blooms.

1980

"What a privilege to read his manuscript," Carrie said.

"I loved Billina's feisty antics. She had no trouble putting a rooster in his place." Mrs. Gordon smiled. Smiling might be easier now that Dirk had pried off the lid. But Carrie still sizzled. How could Dirk do in one hour what she'd labored over for two weeks?

"A dozen Dorothys came out of the woodwork, claiming to be inspiration for his Dorothy. It's more likely she was named after their baby niece Dorothy Gage, Matilda's sister. Mrs. Baum was devastated by her death."

"Very sad. So, love at first sight for the Baums."

"I had a similar fate the following spring. Teddy was sixteen, I was fifteen."

Finally! The runaway from Prince Edward Island. Did he break Janie's heart and shroud every joy? Was he the reason she pitied the fated sunflower bound to earth?

Janie, 15
May 1907

Five young men entered the dining room: Jared and Thomas Broderick, hired hands Joe and Ron, and the new boy. He wore long sleeves, despite the heat.

Sawyer Broderick's eyes crinkled in a winsome smile, a rare sight at home. Mother was napping with a headache. He introduced Janie and her sisters. "Girls, this is Theodore Callaghan. Just in from Syracuse with Dr. Weaver last week."

Syracuse! Where Mr. Baum had lived.

"Pleased to meet you." Freckled, redheaded Theodore nodded stiffly, his accent pleasant. He didn't look formal enough to merit such a distinguished name. As suitable as Clarence for a piglet. Endearing but casual.

"I'll check the cranberries," Father said. "The girls'll take care of you." He fed employees dinner for someone's first day on the job.

Josephine and Maggie Pearl returned to the kitchen. Janie wanted to hear the new boy speak again. "How are you, Theodore?"

"I've been better, but it costs more."

The hired hands smirked.

"Your accent sounds more exotic than Syracuse," Janie said.

"Landed in Syracuse from Prince Edward Island two years ago."

Costs more? Landed? Was that P.E.I. talk?

Joe chortled. "What'd you do? Drop in with a hot air balloon?"

Theodore's jaw tightened.

Something about him enticed her, much revealed in simple words. A determined boy who cared about making his way in the world. Green eyes exuded kindness—and deep sadness.

He limped to a chair and rolled up his pant leg, revealing a huge gash. Janie gasped.

"First-day-on-the-job clumsiness," Jared said.

Freckles standing out, Theodore's face darkened. The guys joined him at the table.

Janie hurried to the kitchen. Teasing would stop only if she, the boss's daughter, attended his leg. Time to enter hostess mode, an art she'd perfected by graciously yielding to whims and complaints.

She made a poultice, grabbed a wet cloth, liniment bottle,

and cotton balls, then returned to the dining room as her sisters served food. Janie tipped the back of Jared's chair enough for him to falter and pop out. Hushed laughter rippled around the table as she slid the chair to Theodore and set his leg on it. Jared cussed and grabbed another chair.

She wiped blood from the gash. He grimaced. "Theodore, this'll feel better before you can say *hyperoodon rostratus.*"

"Call me Teddy." He cringed as she took another swipe.

"Call me Janie."

Ron whistled and Joe whooped.

She set the sweet clover poultice on his calf, amidst numerous scars. Why so many?

His lips twitched. She happily received the effort in lieu of a smile. After applying liniment, she gently rubbed his leg, producing a thrill. She ignored the lovey-dovey faces her brothers made between bites of chicken pot pie. "This'll soothe muscle aches."

"You've a knack for making a fellow feel loads better."

Jared stuffed his mouth with potato cakes before spouting a reply. Thomas nearly spit out chicken in a guffaw.

She finished rubbing. "Now, eat up hearty like these others with hoglike manners. Doctor's orders." She returned to the kitchen and watched through the door slats.

"Ooohwee." Thomas howled. "How do you rate catching her fancy?"

"Boss's daughter, too." Ron snorted.

Teddy took some potpie. "Showing kindness, is all."

Dinnertime dialog turned amiable. Soon, the four left while Teddy stayed.

Janie joined him at the table with a cup of tea and a book. "Sorry for my brothers' rudeness."

His face flashed a scowl before relaxing. "I've heard worse twitting."

"How's your leg?" She peeked under the poultice.

"Fair to middling." He shifted with a grunt.

"You've been better, but it costs more?" She pointed to the book, *Great Expectations*. "The perfect antidote. Ever read it?"

"No. Only have one book. *Pilgrim's Progress*."

Unfortunately. "Time to broaden your horizons with Charles Dickens." She pushed the teacup his way and opened the book. "What else have you read?"

"Plenty in school, till age fourteen. Being Scottish, we read Scottish poets, Sir Walter Scott, Robert Louis Stevenson, and such. But no school lately."

"Why?" After no reply, she flipped through pages. "I'll begin—"

He cleared his throat. "Let's talk instead."

She slapped the book closed and gazed at him, waiting.

"I lived in Syracuse two years. Worked the Erie Canal and other places, eventually met Dr. Weaver. He talked me into moving here with him."

"You knew Dr. Weaver?" They surely didn't run in the same social circles.

"I got injured. He was the doc. I didn't have family there. He figured Wolcott would be tamer, so he unofficially adopted me. I'm living with him and his wife."

"How'd you get to Syracuse?"

"Left Prince Edward Island to find work." Wincing, he looked away.

"Ever hear of L. Frank Baum?"

"All Syracuse thinks he hangs the moon nightly."

"'A dreamer is one who can only find his way by moonlight,'" she quoted.

"I like the cut of your jib." A smile etched his face.

"What?"

"Sailor talk, meaning I agree. I know that quote." He shifted. "I never saw the beat of one like you, so many questions in one sitting."

Was she just imagining the poetry in his eyes? Perhaps she could veer from her strict hostess role. How'd he feel about girls with career goals? "I've got journalism in my blood."

"Your relatives work for the newspaper?"

"No." She issued her next words as a test. "I might be a changeling."

He chuckled. "Shhh. The fairies'll hear."

Satisfied, she envisioned Teddy as a young boy chasing fireflies in the meadow, in search of brownies and leprechauns. "I should be safe from scheming fairies now."

"They could still put an enchantment over you. By the way, what's a hyperoo ..."

"*Hyperoodon rostratus*. Latin name for bottlenose whale. It also has a secret meaning. Any perplexity. A mystery or strange new landscape."

"Perhaps *you* are a *hyperoodon rostratus*. Does it apply to a person with mystery? Someone who's intriguing?"

Janie's face warmed. "Have Dr. Weaver check your wound tonight."

She left the dining room in love. He wasn't sophisticated but had savvy. Not wealthy, but he exuded a richness in spirit with a sweet touch of humor.

Would her father disapprove of her liking a foreign boy he'd probably hired as a favor to Dr. Weaver? Never mind. She didn't care what Father thought.

TWENTY-NINE

1907

On Saturday, Mother allowed Teddy to walk Janie to Aunt Sophie's. Jared chaperoned until they arrived. Teddy's leg was "fair to middling." What were the scars from?

Though sweat slicked his forehead, he didn't roll up his sleeves.

They sat on the porch swing with lemonade and books: *Treasure Island*, *The Jungle Book*, *Robin Hood*, *King Arthur and His Knights*. "I prefer to see good triumph and bad punished, don't you?" Janie asked.

"Always. Though sometimes tragedy points us in the best direction."

She tilted her head. "That's deeply profound."

"With Scottish Highlander blood in my veins, I prefer the legendary feats of Robert the Bruce over King Arthur or Robin Hood."

"What's your fancy? Pirates, revenge, jungle animals ..."

He held up Pyle's *King Arthur*. "I'm indulgent."

She read about Merlin, Morgan le Fay, and young Arthur

213

pulling the sword from the stone, musing about poetic justice —or lack of it.

Jared approached. "No poetic justice in that," Teddy said.

Another week, on Aunt Sophie's porch, Teddy asked about Janie's journalistic ambitions.

"I want to be the next woman to travel around the world, beating Nellie Bly's record."

"That's more adventure than most women get. Back home, the only travel a single woman can hope for is becoming a missionary."

"Abominable!"

"My mother wanted to be one. But Pa's a farmer. She had family to care for."

"She served God by loving her children." Unlike Janie's mother.

"Just me. She did missionary work with the Church Aid Society, helping orphans."

His voice was so tender, Janie felt the mother-son closeness. A pang of loneliness prickled through her, a gorge between her and her mother. "You miss her."

He nodded, pressing his lips as if a barricade. "So, you love writing."

"Besides journalism, I want to write fiction. Like Jo March. Fanciful stories like E. Nesbit's *The Enchanted Castle*. Fairy tales so long you get lost in them."

"Then you'd like *Pilgrim's Progress*. Required reading for us Scottish Presbyterians."

"I prefer *Two Little Pilgrims' Progress*. Two children venture to Chicago's White City, thinking it's like Bunyan's Celestial City."

Teddy frowned. "They're nothing alike. The White City's

about earthly gain, the American Dream. Opposite of Christian's hard journey with rewards in the afterlife."

"Confirming that I never want to read *Pilgrim's Progress*. Such gloom and doom. It's the only book my parents allowed." She awaited his judgment.

"I hope you change your mind."

Relieved at no verdict, she sighed. "What do *you* want to do?" He gazed at her, wind ruffling her dress, threading her hair. Her pulse raced. She swallowed. "In the future."

He cleared his throat. "Own a business. I grew up farming, wanting to attend Prince of Wales College, learn agriculture and business. But Charlottetown's a far piece from North Rustico. Tuition's low for rural kids, but there's boarding school, books. Anyhow, I had to leave. In Syracuse, money went to room and board." He looked away, wistful.

"Here you are, farming again."

"Reckon so." He scowled. "Pa taught me how to farm. Surprising, I like it anyway."

"Meaning?"

"Nothing." Instead, they talked about Robert the Bruce until Jared returned.

* * *

1980

"Even Teddy couldn't get you to read *Pilgrim's Progress*," Carrie said. "No wonder he loved it so much. His mother's gift."

"I envied their bond." Mrs. Gordon fidgeted. "Even across the miles, he felt her love."

Envious herself, Carrie could offer no comfort.

After gardening, Carrie read aloud on the porch. Christian, free of his burden, proceeded to the Palace Beautiful to receive a sword, shield, and armor. Not seeing their chains, he was fearful about the lions.

The Lord of the Hill was a great warrior who'd conquered the evil beast Apollyon. But in the Valley of Humiliation, the foul fiend Apollyon found Christian. Apollyon had scales like a fish, wings like a dragon, feet like a bear, mouth like a lion. Fire and smoke rose from his belly. Apollyon accused him of being unfaithful to the King, for Christian had failed miserably by falling into the Slough of Despond and seeking Mr. Legality.

Mrs. Gordon jerked or grimaced with every mention of the Slough, the big murky place of filth that prevented pilgrims from getting to the Gate. Why?

Carrie continued. Every accusation by Apollyon was true, but Christian insisted the Prince was merciful and forgiving. As Apollyon raged and fought, Christian used his shield to ward off Apollyon's fiery darts.

"Enough," Mrs. Gordon said. "I wonder if Mr. Baum thought of Bunyan's Narrow Way when he created the road of yellow brick."

"Both have 'a long journey, through a country that is sometimes pleasant and sometimes dark and terrible.' There'll always be hardships." Parents heaping on shame and criticism.

"Apollyon is made with animal parts like some of Baum's creatures."

"Like the dragon in the Bible that symbolizes the devil. The accuser."

Mrs. Gordon looked over her glasses. "Accuser? Like Apollyon?"

"Yes. He tries to make Christian think he's beyond mercy. But it's a lie."

"Apollyon can't steal Christian's Robe?"

"Never."

"Then perhaps he's no more worrisome than a chained lion."

Carrie rapped the table. "Right. Apollyon's already defeated."

Mrs. Gordon appeared thoughtful—considering unslain

dragons? "Mr. Bunyan uses fairy tale creatures and settings to show how he believes life goes for the Christian."

"Yes, through allegory," Carrie said. "Christian uses his shield of Truth to deflect lies. Fiery darts of accusations."

"Was the shield a gift or a reward?"

Great question. "A gift. Christian uses it to fight, not to earn the King's favor."

Light crossed Mrs. Gordon's face. "So, trying to earn favor is worthless. Like rubbish."

"Exactly."

"Hmm." Mrs. Gordon stared at her lap. "In Oz, Dorothy and her friends were given their gifts after defeating the Wicked Witch. They received symbols of virtues they already possessed. Brains, heart, and courage." She looked up. "But Christian receives gifts *before* his journey. He's given something he can receive in no other way."

Carrie raised her pen. "Therein lies the difference between our own abilities and God's grace."

THIRTY

Wednesday, June 11, 1980

That evening in Dunham's Diner, Carrie loaned Dirk the folktale book and scanned the room, picturing future renovations. She'd been tweaking her plans nightly with colored pencils. Which corners should house the Dickens and Twain nooks?

Dirk drank coffee. "This is it, right? Your future spot."

She startled. "Oh, yes. You caught me daydreaming."

"That's why I picked Dunham's. Tell me your rehab plans."

She'd love to if she wasn't still sizzling from this morning. But that was foolish. "I'm sorry for blowing up, Dirk. I'm glad you got on Mrs. Gordon's good side so quickly."

"I didn't bring you here for an apology."

"But I overreacted. It's good you made her laugh."

He smiled. "Honestly, *you* inspire me to my best efforts."

She felt flushed. "I was jealous. I'm not good at drawing people out."

"*Bzzz,*" Dirk said with the force of a game show button. "Wrong! You have exceptional talent for drawing folks out. That's why Mrs. Gordon confides in you. And I don't tell just anyone about my repulsion of beached fish and floaties in my coffee.”

She managed a weak smile. “Her confidences are payback for the ball incident.”

Dirk smothered fries with ketchup. “No, she deems you trustworthy.”

Carrie sipped bland tea. “You too. She says I can share her stories with you.”

“Really?” He straightened. “Well, open the coop. This rooster’s gonna crow. You know, she’s got me thinking about ‘The Stranger’ and masks. Under the hard exterior is the real person, tender and fragile. Nobody knows the real hurt.”

“I’m starting to. She grew up in a so-called Christian home where she couldn’t measure up. Flights of fancy were sinful. Her parents cared more about appearances.” Like Carrie’s. She shared incidents.

Dirk dragged a fry through a ketchup puddle. “You’re a safe person for her.”

“I suppose.” She fingered her cup. “Again, I’m sorry about this morning.”

“Told you, no apologies. I only want the real Carrie.”

She froze. Nobody wanted the real Carrie. Not even Brian.

“Mrs. G. hides behind a wall of anger. But *you* won’t let anger through. You’re afraid nobody can like you with your true feelings, so you apologize or defer.”

“No, I don’t. I’m easygoing.” A pushover, actually.

“You’re doing it now. You fear letting folks down.”

“Well, who doesn’t?”

“There’s a difference between kindness and ignoring true feelings.”

His words sparked anger. She opened her mouth then shut it.

Dirk dangled a French fry as if hypnotizing her. “What do you wanna say? Don’t worry about my feelings.”

“Are you my counselor?” she snapped.

"No. Your friend."

"Did you read psychology books to figure me out?"

"Nope. Took one college psych class."

"You know just enough to be dangerous."

"Do you talk that way to your lucky guy?"

Her pulse raced. She dove in. "You float from job to job, live from thrill to thrill. You don't stay in place long enough to develop friendships, but you lecture me on honesty? You can speak your mind, then hop on the next plane to Colorado or Brazil or Timbuktu!" She glanced at his tattoo. "With Mollie or Myrtle or Monica!"

He sat back, dazed.

Lyrics from "The Stranger" danced before her.

His palms gripped the table as if preventing him from reeling backward with her blows. "How'd you know about Monica?"

"See? I'm right! The name was a lucky guess." She pointed to his tattoo. "You told Mrs. Gordon you never had a fling."

Dirk's jaw tightened. "She wasn't a fling."

Suddenly aware of her newfound ability to mimic a loose cannon, Carrie blinked back tears. "I'm so sorry." She picked up her purse. "I gotta go." But they'd driven together. "I'll walk home." How ridiculous did *that* sound?

"Please don't. It's natural you're venting, but who're you *really* angry at?"

"Nobody!" The word flew out. A complete lie, but she'd no idea where all this anger bubbled up from. "I'm a wreck. Why do you want to stay here with me?"

His voice soothed. "I'm up for the challenge."

"Am I your summer project?"

He seemed taken aback, then his face relaxed. "Absolutely not. But I wonder if your lucky guy considers you *his* project." She gaped. "Have you told him you don't want to teach?"

"I can't." Why wasn't he yelling about the hurtful arrows of accusation she'd flung?

Instead, he said, "Why not?"

She swallowed hard. "He'd never approve."

"Doesn't he care how you feel?"

"He'll be upset. My parents, too." She set her purse down.

"So, you can't make choices? Besides ordering burgers medium or well done."

Did he somehow see her failed class and no diploma? Or her summer job as a private rebellion? "I live like a turtle. I'm picked up and moved by others. But I can't protest. It's only safe inside the shell."

"That's why you were so mad at me twisting your arm to meet Mrs. G. And you got the degree to meet your parents' approval."

She'd never confess to the college dropout that she had no degree. "Is that worse than spurning education the way you do? You and your gallivanting." She pursed her lips, daring him to prove her wrong.

"There's a reason I gallivant." He folded his hands on the table. "In high school, my best friend was killed in a skiing accident."

"Oh, I'm so sorry."

"I saw it." He stared at his coffee before looking up. "Spring break senior year, with his family in Colorado. We took a risk on a dangerous slope. No guts, no glory. We both lost control. He slammed into a tree, died instantly. I was devastated. We were both foolish but paid for it in different ways. Mine was survivor's guilt."

"Can't imagine."

"That started a downward spiral. I was depressed, lost gumption for everything. My girlfriend hated my floundering and broke up. Daily, I saw Mike flying into that tree. I partied, stayed out late. Part of it was a spiritual rebellion. Where was God when my buddy died? I couldn't follow my parents' beliefs anymore. Figured God wasn't on my side."

"Tough to grapple with."

"I was the epitome of Billy Joel's 'Angry Young Man,' that song, angry at *every*thing." Dirk raised a fist. "I partied through my first year of college. Me and my abundance of stupidity. Too much alcohol. Anything to escape, to ignore the voice telling me *I* should've died, not Mike. I totaled my parents' car, got a DUI, spent a night in jail, lost my license."

Carrie's eyes widened. Brian wouldn't resort to such behavior if something terrible happened to him.

"Those disasters should've been wake-up calls, but I was over the top with underage drinking. When I got booted out of college, my parents died from embarrassment."

Carrie gasped. "Booted out?"

"I deserved it. Finally, after a year of counseling and meds, my depression leveled out. I learned how to grieve and let it go. I made peace with my parents."

Carrie couldn't fathom telling her parents about one failed class, let alone all this. Her father's voice infiltrated. *Kruisselbrinks don't quit.* "How'd your parents handle everything?"

"They went to family counseling, learned how to deal with my feelings, which, being Dutch, wasn't their forte. They also gave me tough love. Didn't bail me out of jail, wouldn't let me drive their car again. They even booted me out once. I was supposed to be gainfully employed or attending school. Didn't keep my end of the bargain."

"Wow, that *is* tough love."

"Yeah, but it doesn't feel like love on the receiving end. My father was a trouper. Later, I said, 'You suffered a fool." He said, 'I considered it loving my son.'" Dirk's voice cracked.

Carrie couldn't envision such kindness from her own folks. If she committed a fraction of Dirk's transgressions, her parents would deliver a sermon of condemnation, then the silent treatment. Forever. "It's all good now?"

"Definitely. With my siblings, too. My dear mom told me

later how her knees wore out praying for me. Every day, she'd ask the good Lord to redeem the time the locusts ate."

"Locusts?"

"Straight from the Old Testament pestilence. Joel chapter two. A prayer passed down from my great-grandmother. The Israelites worshipped foreign gods and oppressed the poor. The Lord warned about consequences, but gave promises, too —how He'd still love them and restore them." Dirk quoted lines. "'I will restore to you the years which the swarming locust has eaten ... You shall eat in plenty and be satisfied ... my people shall never again be put to shame.'"*

"Beautiful."

"It's full of grace." He smiled. "He pulled me out of the mire."

Ah, the mire. "Now you really look ready to crow. So, did God redeem the time?"

"Absolutely." He toyed with a fork. "Mike and I planned to ride our bikes cross country after high school. Take a jar of sand from the East Coast and pour it out on the West Coast. I felt guilty doing stuff without him. But I finally took that bike ride, in his memory."

Dirk displayed his forearm. The tattoo plus sign—MH over CD. "It's not Monica. Mike always said *carpe diem*, seize the day. When I realized locusts didn't have to get the best of me, I had his initials tattooed, MH for Mike Hoogendoorn. CD for *carpe diem*. In the middle is a cross. Only Jesus redeems. I see this daily and think of locusts, think of Mike, of forgiveness, the blessing of living."

No Megan or Claire. A new respect for Dirk blossomed so vividly, it pressed her ribs.

"That summer, I took sand from Holland, then sand from Jersey, and rode to California with a bike tour. I cried like a

---

* Joel 2:25 (RSV)

baby while pouring it out on Malibu Beach. I collected sand there and brought it back to Mike's parents."

Carrie wiped her eyes.

"For two years, I wasted opportunities and friendships. Didn't get anywhere with schooling or a career path. Lost chances for a semester overseas, college tennis, and whitewater rafting with buddies. I wanted to squeeze as many experiences from life as possible. So, after the bike trip, I got a job to fund my next adventure."

"Your folks weren't upset about not finishing college?"

"They were so thrilled I finally engaged life, they would've been happy to see me take up alligator wrestling. My voracious appetite for adventure was a life I was running *to*, instead of running *from*." Dirk knuckled the wall. "I also discovered my parents' faith was sturdier than this building. Having experienced grace at home, I owned the faith for myself."

She sipped tea. "Then had more adventures in eight years than most people do in a lifetime. You've definitely outdone the locusts."

He grinned. "Now, can you tell me about your renovations?"

Finger roving around the room, she pointed out her vision for each area.

Afterward, at his suggestion, they strolled the beach near the café, through lapping waves under moon and stars. "Why aren't you furious with me right now?" she asked.

"Should I be?"

"I misjudged you."

"You could work on tact, but that's what my life looks like to the average person valuing the four-year degree."

A pang of guilt swiped her. She couldn't admit she was no better than he, with no degree, lacking what her parents valued. She couldn't even have an outright rebellion. Just dug her heels in, pursuing the café, taking an unconventional job.

As she stumbled on a rock, he grabbed her hand. His touch

rocketed through her. She squeezed his fingers, wanting to hold on. What was happening? Wait. Dirk was a friend. Brotherly. She loosened her hold. On cue, he let go.

After exchanging Lake Michigan childhood memories, they faced the water, the tide washing their feet. If Brian were here, they'd be kissing.

Dirk could only be a good friend. Great guy, yes. Sensitive and kind, yes. Deeper than she'd realized, a man of faith. Funny and light-hearted, too. But too spontaneous. Wild and carefree. If her heart gravitated his way, he'd break it the instant he pulled up roots. Did he really have no flings? Was Monica the high school girlfriend or someone else?

Either way, Brian was her man, stable and sturdy. Solid. Secure.

Yet when she eyed Dirk's profile, his moonlit face, she appreciated his finer features. She'd yelled at him, thrown accusations like fiery darts, yet here they were. Her heart felt safe.

But Brian was the link to her parents' approval. They'd been together six years.

The moon pulled her gaze. *A dreamer is one who can only find his way by moonlight ...* Dirk embraced his dreams, seizing each day. Hers were undercover.

He drove her home, one hand on the wheel, another playing air piano as Bruce Springsteen belted out "Thunder Road." Brian would never do that. Carrie swayed to the beat.

He walked her to the door. "Thanks for a glimpse of the real Carrie."

"Thanks for a bigger glimpse of yourself."

"Hey, wanna tackle that dune Saturday? Hit Saugatuck's hiking trail?"

She looked at him sideways. "A date?"

"No trespassing for me. Just exploring the area, given Mrs. G.'s history. Part two of our Wolcott tour." He winked. "Strictly business."

"I'd love to, but Brian's coming."

That night in bed, Dirk's words wavered through her. *I'm up for the challenge.* The adventurous part of Dirk. The one who preferred scaling heights, backpacking, and sailing. How could she compete with his constant need for adventure? And his attention span of three months.

Besides that, if she ever opened up, her inner turmoil would scare him away.

THIRTY-ONE

Thursday, June 12, 1980

Dashes of light winked on tile backsplash and copper pots amidst the sizzle of sausage. Mrs. Gordon waved a spatula. "Scarecrow's Corn and Potato-Sausage Hash."

Carrie chopped potatoes, then wrote recipes for hash and Braided Man Breadsticks.

The table held a visual feast: a whimsical tea set featuring Alice in Wonderland. They sat down to Great Elixir's Orange Jasmine tea, yesterday's biscuits, and hash. Mrs. Gordon relayed the finer features of jasmine tea from China, how leaves were harvested, the best time to pick the flowers, best way to release the fragrance.

Carrie sipped. "Every night, I record your tea tips and recipes." *While typing your stories.* "I'd love to use them in my book café. I'm constantly tweaking my menu. But some nights, I wake up in a cold sweat envisioning restaurant disasters."

"But you're choosing your passion over your fears, right?"

"Yeah, but I'll be the fall guy for every bad decision. Hiring, firing, allocating funds."

"'The moment you doubt whether you can fly, you cease forever to be able to do it.'"

Carrie smiled. "Peter Pan wisdom?"

"What did it *feel* like when you were student teaching? Metaphorically speaking."

Carrie briefly closed her eyes. "Like walking through mud and sludge in a thunderstorm. On a road with no end." Sixth grade all over again. "No solid ground, just slipping and sliding, all grays and browns. No trees or umbrella."

"What do you feel like when planning renovations, creating your menu?"

"I feel alive. I'm walking through green rolling meadows with periwinkles and Queen Anne's lace. The sky is cornflower blue. Storm clouds come but don't rule the day."

"Then you've chosen the right path."

"But if the loan is denied, what'll I tell my parents when they expect me to teach?"

"You're borrowing tomorrow's trouble. But whatever your heart's desire, experiences you encounter along the way are grist for the mill. Mr. Baum taught me much in that regard during my sixth Macatawa visit."

———

Janie, 15
July 1907

On the porch table sat two typewriters, old and new. "Working on two books at once?" Janie asked.

Mr. Baum chortled. "Quite a feat, side by side. A job for Mr. Split from Merryland."

Aunt Sophie remarked on the lack of sand drifts on the boardwalks, then offered condolences for the Cubs' loss to the White Sox in last year's World Series, the first-ever Chicago crosstown championship.

"A shame to fall to those hitless wonders," he huffed. "We had a hundred and sixteen victories to their measly ninety-three. But your Tigers are to be pitied above all, losing more than they won."

"Our new outfielder Ty Cobb is batting .316. He stole over twenty bases last year."

"One whippersnapper cannot outdo our infield. We've been first in our league for weeks. If your Tigers get ahead, their winning margin will be nothing to brag about."

Such vehemence—my, how athletics brought out the beast in folks!

"We're still suited to win the pennant." Aunt Sophie turned demure. "What'll become of our friendship, Mr. Baum, if my Tigers are destined to play your Cubs?"

"Fear not, Miss McKinnon." He displayed a teasing smile. "We won't have to find out." He picked up a book: *Ozma of Oz.* "For release next week. Note the preface."

Janie scanned his reference to the child who'd read the book before going to print, stating, *Billina is real Ozzy.* "Oh, Mr. Baum!" She hugged him, her face in his cigar-scented shirt. "You quoted me." From the letter she'd sent last summer.

She thumbed through the book. Aunt Sophie asked about his projects. He cited *Policeman Bluejay* for younger children, written as Laura Bancroft, and *Father Goose's Year Book*, a diary spotted with adages and poetry. "What of *your* stories, Charlotte?"

As Aunt Sophie went inside, Janie said, "Last year in ninth grade, I was on the school newspaper staff." She handed him an issue.

"Splendid!" He paged through it. "Surely you'll be editor someday."

"Only boys get that honor."

"Nonsense." He asked more questions.

Soon she pulled out chapter one of her next Camellia tale. As he read, she riffled through *Ozma of Oz.*

He blasted a laugh. "That Camellia, outsmarting the fairies! Poppi's a pleasant fellow, but he and Camellia talk alike. How are they different?"

"Poppi's afraid of toadstools, like that boy you told me about. He won't take risks. Camellia never admits fear."

"Remember when Jack Pumpkinhead met the Scarecrow? They asked Jellia Jamb to interpret though they spoke the same language.

Janie laughed. "Jellia Jamb was ingenious, twisting their words."

"See? I used conversation to show character." He tapped a page. "Have Camellia and Poppi discuss their options. Their motives and fears can lead to considerable squabbling."

Janie skimmed the scene. "An idea's percolating already."

"Raise the stakes. Throw in more danger, but not enough to cause nightmares."

Mrs. Baum and Aunt Sophie stepped out. Auntie waved a card. "Your wife showed me the invitation you wrote for your twenty-fifth-anniversary party. Such a tidy way to sum up the years." She handed it to Janie.

Janie read the couple's achievements: "Raised four boys. Quarrels—just a few. Wife in tears three times (cat died, bonnet spoiled, sore toe). Husband swore one thousand one hundred eighty-seven times—at wife, zero. Broke occasionally, bent often, future prospects good."

"No matter the prospects," Mrs. Baum said, "life's never dull with my husband."

How would Janie's parents write such an invitation? *Raised five children. Favored boys. Banned books. Youngest child a nuisance. Attended church, forgot teachings. Wife fills stomachs, drains souls.* A wave of sadness rippled through her.

When Aunt Sophie left, Harry and Kenneth returned from golf. Mr. Baum set a box on the table. In dramatic fashion, he withdrew small glass panes and special paint. "We're making a magic lantern show. Charlotte, have you seen travelogues?"

Travelogues whetted her appetite for travel. "Aunt Sophie and I attend monthly."

"Instead of documenting a trip, you three can illustrate a story on these glass slides. Tonight after dark, we'll watch the show."

Janie picked up a blank slide. "Which story?"

Harry struck a heroic pose. "Daniel Boone or Davy Crockett. If you need a model, I'll volunteer."

Kenneth punched his arm. "She needs muscles." He pointed to his own biceps.

"Let's create our own story," Janie said before the boys were in fisticuffs. They concocted a tale and painted pictures on thirty slides.

After a pork chop and ambrosia dinner, they fished from the *Maybelle*, jumped from the pier, played dodgeball in the lake. Mr. Baum made his daily trek into the water, cigar butt intact, wind and waves swiping his straw hat. With her Brownie camera, Janie accompanied the boys to the new Holland Lighthouse, its steel tower recently completed. She took snapshots.

Late afternoon, Mrs. Baum invited Janie to embroider. She worked on a two-foot rectangular piece of muslin outlined with ivy.

"What's going inside?" Janie maneuvered stitches on scrap muslin.

"Words. I haven't decided yet. Now, I'm guessing you have a beau. Tell me about him."

Blushing, Janie relayed Teddy's P.E.I. roots, time in Syracuse, his encouragement of her writing. Despite forfeiting his education, he was learning business from her father.

"Seems he truly cares for you and treats you well. Accept nothing less. My husband always inquires after my needs and accommodates our family, sometimes at great sacrifice to his own goals."

Janie jabbed a needle into cloth. "You still don't mind his risky projects?"

"He must be who he is. I support them because I know I'm the one closest to his heart."

Only time would tell with Teddy. He didn't even know about her Macatawa visits yet.

After Mrs. Baum left to prepare supper, Janie asked Mr. Baum, "Why do you publish under so many different names? Edith Van Dyne, Captain Hugh Fitzgerald ..."

"One reason is to avoid being in competition with myself. Sometimes I reduce myself to potboilers for money."

"Potboiler?"

He chuckled. "Even inferior work boils the soup pot." He flicked his hand. Ashes flew. "My real name's attached to my fairy tales. But how many Baum books will a parent put under one Christmas tree?"

"But how many girls will buy girls' fiction written by a man?"

"So, call Edith Van Dyne to the rescue, for *Aunt Jane's Nieces*. Mr. Reilly requested a sequel. A series looks promising. But poor *Annabell* by Suzanne Metcalf didn't fare well."

"Will Captain Hugh Fitzgerald write another Sam Steele adventure?"

"Indeed. *Sam Steele's Adventures in Panama* releases this year."

"I'd never thought Edith Van Dyne would have an easier time," Janie said. "Women fight ten times harder for anything they want. Except housework."

He laughed. "Regardless, my publisher promotes my work under any name, though Mr. Reilly was unimpressed with my stories for adults. He said to stick with children's fantasy."

"Were you disappointed?"

"Immensely. But he's right. I'm most proud of my fairy tales." He drank lemonade. "You noticed the boardwalks are improved. The reason is cloaked in a new story." He leaned forward, elbows on knees. "Here's a secret, slightly scandalous. I published a novel called *Tamawaca Folks: A Summer Comedy*. By John Estes Cooke. Names are changed. Ottawa Beach is Iroquois Bay. Holland becomes Kochton, and so forth. Tamawaca's an anagram."

"Macatawa!"

"A little satire of the folks here, including a stubborn, loud-mouthed author with the diplomacy of a cannonball." He pointed to himself.

"Won't they catch on?"

"They have already, but it's to make a point. Time to face problems head-on, starting with sand on the boardwalks."

"I thought you loved it here."

"I do. It's an enchanting fairyland, the best place for a dose of ozone. The *Grand Rapids Sunday Herald* is publishing my poem about it." He struck a dramatic pose and chanted a verse. "But southern California rivals this place. Whoever thinks Coronado isn't beautiful would hate heaven, too. The ocean invigorates. La Jolla and San Diego offer plenty of inspiration. I write every morning there."

"How fortunate you've made a living doing what you love."

"After exploring a considerable number of occupations." He gulped more lemonade. "As Mrs. Billkins says, farmers should know business so they can withstand one bad season. In my case, when theater doesn't pay the bills, a man must sell whale oil or china to support his family. Yet each experience prepared me, as grist for the mill."

"How?"

"Besides building character, such incidents found their way into my stories. When I sold fireworks in Chicago, we had the best displays in the neighborhood. So, of course, a firecracker sent John Dough to Oz."

"I'd be disappointed selling firecrackers instead of becoming the next Nellie Bly."

"Don't despise the mundane. Let it launch your imagination."

"The way I created a forest monster from a green pepper?"

"Precisely. Consider the yarns you'll pull from years of tearoom tasks. Who would've thought breeding chickens would benefit our sprightly Billina on her way to Oz?" He blew cigar smoke. "So live life in every respect, retaining its wonder. Learn daily. You must watch a cyclone to write about it. You must see rural poverty to care about it."

"Did you go to college, Mr. Baum?"

"I learned more running my own printing press. Experience breeds knowledge better than textbooks do. And nobody can steal that from you."

"You certainly learned a thing or two from Mrs. Bilkins."

"She learned a thing or two from me." He smirked. "Life will throw curve balls, but dust yourself off and keep going. Failure serves you later. I should know. I need extra fingers to count mine." He tapped each in succession, reciting a silent list. "I kept a file of failures. Some were circumstantial, some my own fault. First, myriad plays I wrote were never produced. I sometimes failed to make a decent living for my family. Aberdeen was the worst. My cloud photographs show the grandeur of endless prairie. But its beauty belies the devastation."

Janie noted the tremor in his voice. "What happened, Mr. Baum?"

"Good things at first. Aberdeen was prosperous. Mrs. Baum and I attended card parties and dances. I participated in plays, headed the Fourth of July baby show, was secretary of the Equal Suffrage Club, and founded a financial magazine." He lit another cigar. "I opened Baum's Bazaar, specializing in fine novelty items—crockery, glassware, lamps, toys, sporting goods, and more. Some was practical, but most was not, and quite pricey. A thousand folks visited opening day. We made a bundle. But my holiday goods sank in Lake Huron."

"Terrible!"

"Perhaps an omen. Meanwhile, I organized the Hub City Nine baseball team, raised funds for the new diamond and grandstand, arranged schedules, and ordered uniforms. Even with a winning season, we couldn't support a team. We lost thousands. By December, they leveled the grandstand, hauled off the lumber."

After a wave of gloom, he brightened. "At the store, I built an elaborate soda fountain and opened another bazaar, Santa Claus Headquarters. But Aberdeen suffered from drought and cyclones. Farmers couldn't afford my products. I sold so much on credit, one hundred sixty-one accounts were past due. I couldn't accept money from floundering folks with hungry families. So, Baum's Bazaar closed on New Year's Day, 1890, a month after Harry's birth." He sighed. "Mrs. Baum said my store wasn't practical. Why'd farmers need brass spittoons or Grendon Velocipedes? She was right. After closing, I had under a hundred dollars and no job."

"What'd you do?"

"I bought the newspaper, ready to usher the town into the twentieth century." He perked up. "I renamed it *The Aberdeen Saturday Pioneer*. I gathered local news, wrote editorials, and ran the press. For extra money, I printed invitations, fliers, and programs."

"What'd you write about?"

"Current events and musings about business, home, and religion. I was outspoken about women's suffrage and eliminating gender prejudice. The South Dakota vote for women's suffrage was held in November 1890. But all efforts failed. *That* was a fine kettle of fish. Imagine the cloud of melancholy in my household, with Mrs. Baum and her mother."

"Maybe I should read your columns." In her reporter role, Janie straightened.

His shoulders drooped. "First, I must confess a terrible

regret. Years earlier, Sitting Bull wiped out General George Custer's troops at the Battle of Little Big Horn. In 1890, the threat of an Indian uprising shadowed the whole town. I wrote two editorials denouncing the Indians. I wrote harsh things about the Sioux, echoing everybody's fears."

Janie sat still, appalled and not daring to speak.

He stared across the railing. "Folks were so hysterical that the Seventh Cavalry stepped in to return the Indians to their reservation. They slaughtered three hundred Lakota—men, women, and children—at Wounded Knee, resulting in Sitting Bull's death."

Janie scowled, pushing bloody images away.

"My mother-in-law wasn't pleased by my outspokenness. She hated oppression by Indians but had high regard for the Iroquois in New York."

"Sky Carrier."

"Yes. But other regrets linger. I used editorials to attack the church, as hypocrisy ran rampant. I promoted theosophical views and spiritualism, making more enemies than friends. I criticized the banker, fire department, school superintendent, and other editors. Even furious high school students wrote me. So much outrage ensued, folks were deeply hurt. I became ill." Twittering birds belied the angst. "My subscriptions went from 3,500 to 1,400, not just from the economy. One man said my soul was smaller than a mustard seed."

Janie couldn't picture him that way.

"If we choose to live in the cellar, the sun is not likely to seek us. And if we meet trouble halfway, it accepts the invitation. Well, I found myself in the cellar, with trouble galore. By March 1891, I couldn't keep the newspaper afloat. The sheriff took over. Three days later, Ken was born, as farming and businesses failed. I left Aberdeen defeated. And angry." Cigar smoke curled above their heads, like dissipating dreams.

Janie touched his wrist, voice hushed. "'You must walk. It

is a long journey, through a country that is sometimes pleasant and sometimes dark and terrible.'"

Mr. Baum uttered a throaty chuckle. "Perhaps Aberdeen prompted that line. See, my dear, life is nothing if it doesn't test our mettle. Now, through my books, I promote understanding and acceptance, exposing petty differences and false notions of superiority."

"Is that why you wrote about Hilanders and Lolanders in *John Dough*? And the wall between them?" In that story, the law forbade asking questions, so each thought the other barbarous.

"Definitely. All people have value. Rivalry is ludicrous, based on absurd assumptions. Like that Scarecrow and Jack Pumpkinhead episode. I greatly dislike mass-produced items, whether furniture or people. In Oz, one is judged by character rather than conformity." His face weighted in sorrow. "I've written several tales set in Aberdeen's nature fairyland, my animal stories in *The Twinkle Tales*. In *Policeman Bluejay*, published this year, I espouse kindness to animals and share history of the Sioux tradition. But it hardly compensates for my previous gross error in judgment."

"Did things get better after Aberdeen?"

"Not immediately. We moved to Chicago in time for the Columbian Expo. After selling china, I started *The Show Window* magazine. When my mother-in-law encouraged me to write my stories, *Mother Goose in Prose* was born, with Maxfield Parrish's illustrations. Mr. Denslow's superb drawings for *Father Goose* created another masterpiece. Though the publisher stipulated that we pay for *Wizard of Oz* illustrations ourselves, by Christmas, it was a bestseller. I could justifiably focus on creative pursuits. Finally."

"What would Mrs. Bilkins say about *that*?" Janie said.

"She'd shake her finger and say, 'Don't you dare let success go to your head, Lyman Frank.' That woman sounds like my mother. In August, the Grand Rapids *Sunday Herald* will publish an interview called 'How the Wizard of Oz Spends His Vacation.'"

Janie smiled. "Now *you're* the great Wizard of Oz."

"Is it a reference to first being a humbug?" He winked. "I told the journalist that writing fairy stories to amuse children seems of greater importance than writing grownup novels. I never aspired to be a children's author. Yet look." He tapped the typewriter. "As our friends learned when venturing to the Emerald City, what we want is within us, has been there all along."

His hand covered his chest. "Truly my own journey. After raising chickens, acting, editing, and selling dry goods, Castorine Oil, and china, I found my purpose with storytelling." He gazed with kind, gray eyes. "That's the achievement that matters. Sharing your God-given gifts with the world, no matter how long and rocky the road, is the highest accomplishment."

THIRTY-TWO

1907

After dusk, Mr. Baum set up the magic lantern projector and hung a sheet in the parlor. "I'm working on a travelogue for Oz," he told Janie. "An Ozologue. For next year."

With lights off, they watched the colorful story of a Welsh rabbit hopping into a garden looking for lettuce and finding Bismarcks instead.

Later in bed, Janie sighed. Spirals of fuzzy light speckled outward, attracting fairies. Mr. Baum's words rolled over her like Lake Michigan waves. *Sharing your God-given gifts with the world, no matter how long and rocky the road, is the highest accomplishment.*

What roads lay ahead? So many fabulous possibilities. She'd work for a newspaper in Chicago or St. Louis. She'd go undercover, exposing evil to light, like Nellie Bly in the asylum, or join a cause to liberate someone, like Jerry's rescuers did. She'd travel, interview fascinating people, promoting equality for all, as Mrs. Gage did. No rocky roads. She knew what she wanted, starting with college writing classes.

She'd create worlds as wonderful as Oz, populated with her own characters. Children would write, asking about Camellia. She'd answer them all, as graciously as Mr. Baum did.

The next morning, when Aunt Sophie arrived, Mrs. Baum handed Janie a gift—a kitchen apron, with pockets Mrs. Baum stitched last year.

"It's beautiful!" Janie hugged her. She'd use it at Aunt Sophie's.

"My publisher insists I have a new typewriter," Mr. Baum said. "The Ts are worn out." He typed on the older one, then handed it to Kenneth. "This'll prevent writer's cramp, Charlotte." Kenneth carried it in a box with a stack of paper to the interurban.

Janie read the typed words: *A gift for a fine writer and friend, Charlotte Rose. Ozily, Mr. Baum.* The Ts were slightly faded.

Janie and Auntie stopped by the Vanderlaans, the perpetual excuse for Holland visits. This time, Dena's sister Katrina was engaged.

In Wolcott, Janie's brother Jared picked them up from the interurban in his horse-drawn carriage. Immediately, Janie switched topics from the Baums to the Vanderlaans—maintaining her Macatawa secrecy.

Jared paused at Auntie's house and waited as they gathered the open box of gifts. Headed toward the front steps, Janie stopped short.

On Auntie's front porch, Mother stood like a shadow rising from a graveyard.

Janie clutched the box.

Startling, Aunt Sophie nearly dropped her satchel. "Elsa! Slow day at the tearoom?"

"Hardly. But I must borrow a pot and had to make sure Janie came home immediately. We're shorthanded. Jared dropped me off, but your door was locked." She walked over and peered into the box. "What's that contraption?"

"A typewriter," Janie said weakly.

"I know, but why? Have you been haunting junk shops?"

Beads of sweat frosted Janie's forehead. "No." She couldn't lie point-blank to Mother. Sneak behind her back, yes. Lie, no. She glanced at Auntie, fumbling with the key.

Mother squinted at the paper still rolled into the typewriter. "'A gift for a fine writer and friend, Charlotte Rose.'" She looked up. "'Ozily, Mr. Baum?' The author who writes about witches? You *saw* him?"

Janie shook, her mouth clamped shut.

Mother lifted a stack of paper. "What's this?" Some sheets fluttered to the sidewalk. "Now *you're* writing fantastical stories?"

"I can explain, Elsa," Aunt Sophie said.

"Explain what? How you've seen Mr. Baum behind my back? That he knows you well enough to give Janie a typewriter? That he still calls her Charlotte?" Mother's face darkened. "How could you, Sophie? I trusted you. I thought you were in Holland with the Vanderlaans."

"We absolutely were," Auntie said.

"That's obviously not the whole story." Facing Janie, Mother formed a formidable wall. "You, young lady, are in big trouble. How will we ever trust you? Your father and I will decide what must be done. Meanwhile, I forbid you to ever see that man again."

***

Father sold Mr. Baum's typewriter for seeds and saplings, grounded Janie from seeing Aunt Sophie and Teddy for two months, and enforced Scripture memorization. Mother worked her extra hard at the tearoom.

Finally, Janie and Teddy sat on Aunt Sophie's front porch swing after a two-month absence. "What happened, Janie? Your mom wouldn't say."

Weary from concealing her true self, she couldn't hide from

Teddy anymore. "I had a secret." Trepidation set in. "Auntie takes me to Macatawa Park to visit author L. Frank Baum."

"Really?"

"Yes, he knows how four-and-twenty blackbirds got baked in the pie. We talk about fairies and imaginary worlds, the grandest of speculations. He critiques my writing. We swim and boat with his sons, Harry and Kenneth." She fingered her sleeve. "Mother hates his stories. Aunt Sophie said to read them anyhow."

His face registered alarm. "You went behind your parents' backs?"

"Not anymore." Would Teddy understand? Tremulous, she explained how Mother discovered their clandestine visits.

He frowned. "You disobeyed."

Exactly what she'd feared. Fighting tears, she blinked at her lap.

Warm flesh covered her fingers. His hand. "I understand."

She looked up. "You do? You're not condemning me?"

"I left my father's household without his permission. How can I judge you?"

She threw her arms around his neck, nestled her head on his chest. "But I fear I'll never see him again." She wept. He held her tight.

After calming, she shared about the book burning, her Macatawa visits, the Baums calling her Charlotte Rose. How she felt loved with them.

He tucked strands of hair behind her ear. "Charlotte Rose is beautiful. Inspirational. Intriguing. Charlotte for Charlottetown, sounding like home." He nuzzled her cheek. "I love you, Charlotte Rose. With all your dreams and imagination, you're a rose beginning to bloom." He cupped her chin. "I want to be with you always, as you blossom."

She reveled in his touch, grateful for his response to her open heart. "I love you, too, Teddy." Their lips met briefly, a first kiss. "What if Aunt Sophie peeks out the window?"

"She's baking." His mouth found hers again.

Only fifteen, she wasn't wearing her hair up yet. He gently stroked her long locks. If Mother saw them together, she'd pin up Janie's hair on the spot.

She hungrily lifted her mouth for more. This time, longer. Warmth filled her from head to toe. Her head reeled. They ended a kiss to breathe.

A pan dropped inside. Aunt Sophie appeared at the screen door, long enough to hinder racing hearts. "Just an old pan." She stepped out and babbled about pie-baking challenges.

***

1980

Carrie charged into the foray to grab the plunder of nuggets Mrs. Gordon offered, ready for more. "I'm glad Teddy understood."

Mrs. Gordon's brow wrinkled. "Yes, but greater concerns arose."

"What happened? How'd you end up with Walter?"

"There's no simple answer." Case closed.

"Did you get to see Mr. Baum again?"

"You'll find out."

"So ironic. It's all about appearances with your parents, no admission of wrongdoing. But Mr. Baum was open about his own failures." Hot shame struck her. Carrie dreaded admitting her college failure to her parents or Brian. Would she be like Mrs. Gordon in sixty years—alone and bitter? Or would she accept all as grist for the mill? "Did you find strength in his words?"

"Yes. Until I was in a predicament unlike anything Mr. Baum contended with."

Her husband's criminal charge? "Mrs. Gordon, I've never

read accounts of the charge you hired me to help clear. Yet it seems we're nowhere closer to discussing it."

Mrs. Gordon squinted. "I should reward patience by revealing events out of context?"

"No."

"You're bored and want me to rush?" Her voice cracked.

"Definitely not bored. I enjoy our time together." *Mostly.*

Lips quivering, Mrs. Gordon stared at Blake's sunflower poem. "You're free to leave anytime. I'm not obligating you, oath or no oath."

"I'm staying," Carrie said without hesitation.

After lunch, they weeded the garden. Each week displayed a lavish treat of color. Irises, petunias, salvia, geraniums, and cornflowers bloomed within triangular patterns of purple, yellow, red, and blue. Sunflowers made steady progress, seeking sun.

They sat on the porch as Carrie read. Christian's new companion, Faithful, escaped the Slough of Despond but faced other troubles. In the Valley of Humility, a man called Shame asserted that the Mighty, Rich, and Wise reject Faithful's beliefs. Shame refused to leave, whispering in his ear about the infirmities of religion.

Christian said Shame was wrongly named because he didn't cower but followed boldly, never leaving people alone. Shame made people feel ashamed of what's good. They must resist Shame and his bravado.

A tremor rattled Mrs. Gordon's voice. "Faithful never fell into the Slough of Despond."

"No, but he was pursued by Shame."

She closed her eyes. "Shame will never be silent."

Carrie swallowed. "Is Shame the dragon not yet slain?"

Looking away, Mrs. Gordon nodded.

Yet another hard-won nugget. But shame for what? Being imaginative and loving fairy tales? Failing to be the next Nellie

Bly? Shame for some deep, dark sin? Or enduring the stigma of her husband's homicide charge?

***

Friday, June 13, 1980

Carrie opened Mrs. Gordon's drapes several inches. On the coffee table rested a floral decoupaged tray next to crocheted doilies and a scrapbook of pressed flowers, Victorian Valentines, and die-cut figures.

She noted the recipe on the kitchen counter. "Rigmaroles?"

"An Ozzy version of rolls from Bunbury."

Carrie jotted the recipe and another for Flying Monkey Cinnamon Bread.

Soon they sipped Glinda's Passionfruit Papaya Tea with Rigmaroles. Carrie peppered her with questions about metrics, bookkeeping, and advertising. Though Mrs. Gordon never started a restaurant from scratch, she offered plenty of insight.

"Oma bought a box for your recipes," Carrie said. "Cooking up a storm while crocheting an afghan for my wedding."

"Jumping gingersnaps!" Mrs. Gordon dropped a spoon. "You're engaged?"

"Not yet. She wants a head start. Opa and I refinished a bureau. I painted it white for stenciling nursery rhyme figures. Baum-inspired for the book café. A children's nook."

Mrs. Gordon smiled, more common since teatime with Dirk. "Is Brian onboard? You'll need his support. Starting a family might interfere."

So would Brian rolling his eyes. "I thought he was, until he recently told me he never thought I'd take it this far. He wants me to teach."

Mrs. Gordon sighed. "Teddy and I also had difficult talks about our aspirations colliding."

Janie, 15
August 1907

As soon as Janie heard about Teddy's fight with a coworker, she went to the Weavers' house.

Teddy sat in the parlor, eye blackened, cloth wrapped around his chest, shirt draping his shoulders. Evening shadows hovered. On the coffee table lay *The Pilgrim's Progress*.

"Look." She held a book. "Let's read about Robert the Bruce." Light revealed a long scar down Teddy's forearm. Was that why he never rolled up sleeves even in beastly heat?

"Don't wanna read. Was in high dudgeon today."

"High dudgeon?"

"A dagger. From Highland Scots, ready to draw. Just a way of talking."

"What happened?"

"Nothing. Just wanna forget it."

She sat beside him. "Forget what?"

Cicadas buzzed. Late sun streamed through the window. The purplish blotch hollowed his eye. "Can't hide it anymore." He held out his arms, revealing long scars. Pushed off his shirt, showing more on his shoulder and chest. "My father used to beat me."

Janie gasped.

"After drinking a spell, he used the horsewhip. Ma told me to leave home, saved up a long time. She sent me away with money, food, and *Pilgrim's Progress*."

Taking his hand, Janie numbed. "How?"

"I left at midnight, crossed the strait to New Brunswick, on down to Syracuse. Took the ferry and train. Limping a lot. Worked along the way."

"You couldn't work on Prince Edward Island?"

Fidgeting, he winced. "Pa would've found me, dragged me home, making it worse. Or I could've been stuck in an orphanage."

"Syracuse is so far."

"I worked odd jobs, mostly on the canal. One day, a guy kept mocking me for working too slow. Mean as second skimmings, like Pa. I finally slugged him. He beat me to a pulp. I ended up at Doc Weaver's." Teddy shifted, gritting his teeth. "Doc sees I'm in dire straits. I'm sixteen then, no parents around. He convinced me to come here. No fighting allowed."

"Did you fight a lot?"

His eyes dropped. "I tolerate loads of hard work, but not insults. It's like Pa screaming."

Janie rubbed his shoulder. "Did your pa hurt your mother too?"

"He hollered, worked her hard. I fear he's beating her now without me to pound on. I feel horrible guilt for leaving."

"She *made* you go."

"But I shouldn't have."

"Can't you bring her here?" Janie wanted to, but how? She had little money.

"She'd never leave my father. She's faithful."

"It's faithful to stay with a man who beats her?"

"She wouldn't make it far striking out alone. She's got strong faith, but she's fragile. And trapped. No matter where she goes on the island, Pa'll find her."

She must get off the island. Janie picked up *Pilgrim's Progress* and read the inscription:

My dear Teddy,

May this story remind you of times we shared, bringing joy and hope of your final destination, no matter how big the Slough of Despond, no matter how tall the Giant of Despair.

Someday we'll meet again, beyond the Delectable Mountains, past the Land of Beulah and the Black River, in the Celestial City itself.

All my love,
Mother
June 1905, P.E.I.

Janie choked back a sob. She couldn't imagine her own mother writing such a loving note. Or missing her if she were gone. Or sacrificially sending her away.

"This book is my most valuable possession, reminding me I'm a pilgrim in this world." Tears escaped. "Reminds me of her."

"Do you write her?"

"I send letters to the neighbors. She said never say where I am, in case Pa finds out."

"If God is good, why'd He let your father beat you fourteen years? He did nothing while your father crushed you."

"Janie, it's like Christian. He goes through the Valley of Humiliation and Vanity Fair. He's devastated by Giant Despair. But in the Celestial City, all will be well."

"It's not right, so much tragedy now."

"That's where faith comes in," Teddy said. "Faith that God has mercy for sinners and keeps His promises."

Janie stared at his scars, over a dozen. How many more hidden? In his wounds, she saw her own. Scars on her soul. Fire burning her Oz book, Mother smashing the food sculpture, Father shaming her tears. Shame for wanting to be called Charlotte. Their pronouncements of her hellish destiny just for being her. They didn't even know her real sins of doubt and coveting.

Teddy interrupted her thoughts. "Got a good scolding from your pa, but he'll give me another chance."

"What'd Ron do?"

"Needled me all day. I wasn't good enough or fast enough. When he called me bastard, I couldn't take it anymore."

"But you're not one."

"Bastard's as low as you can go. Where I'm from, there's nothing more shameful than an illegitimate child. You never outgrow it."

THIRTY-THREE

Janie, 16
1907-1908

The next winter, Janie acquired more tearoom responsibilities and took over Saturday baking. Teddy helped Sawyer Broderick enlarge the icehouse. Sawyer grumbled that newfangled refrigeration appliances weren't going to beat him yet.

Upton Sinclair's book *The Jungle* led to the new Meat Inspection Act. Sinclair had worked incognito in meatpacking plants to uncover immigrants' poor working conditions. Like Nellie Bly's report on the asylum, the power of the written word enacted positive change. Janie longed to be that catalyst —with her typewriter.

Such gleams of hope materialized in February. As a sophomore, she became a candidate for Wolcott High School's newspaper editor. The Baums would be thrilled.

Elsa welcomed the first electric toaster for $1.45 and a Maytag washer—thrilled to abandon the washboard for a crank. Had Mr. Baum predicted toasters and crank washers?

Weekly at market, Janie sought ingredients for culinary

experiments. She succumbed to Kellogg's new advertising campaign, obtaining a free box of cereal by winking at the grocer. Crushed Corn Flakes made perfect coating for fried chicken. But Elsa still reigned in the kitchen.

In spring, the Broderick women canned strawberry preserves, tomatoes, beans, and pickles. Trailed by Jared, Janie and Teddy rode bicycles to the park for Sunday picnics and bandshell concerts, indulging in Hershey's chocolate Silvertops. Porch swing book discussions stirred musings over the influx of orphan characters: Oliver Twist, Jane Eyre, Tom Sawyer, and Heidi, the poor orphan rising in stature. Teddy insisted it wasn't realistic. No orphan rose to stature in P.E.I.

But above all, Janie feared never seeing Mr. Baum again, wrestling with guilt for her sneakiness. When she broached the subject of Macatawa, Aunt Sophie squelched it. Until June, when they anticipated his next invitation.

"I've talked to your mother, cream puff. But it's no use."

"I'll go to Macatawa by myself. You needn't be involved."

"Traveling alone's not proper."

"Neither is sneaking around."

"True, but there's something more important at stake." Auntie patted Janie's hand. "Somehow, we'll find a way. In your home, you wilt and flounder. I don't condone disobedience, but I know a hundred magical reasons why you should still see Mr. Baum. With him, you blossom, full of life and wonder. Like hyacinths to feed your soul."

One hot Saturday, Teddy took Janie to Gordon's Pharmacy while Jared ran errands.

Janie whispered in the doorway. "Mother'll be furious! It's her fiercest competition."

"Welcome," a hearty voice burst from the counter.

Janie faced Walter Gordon, the pharmacist's son, six years

older than her. His friendly face matched his voice. He held an ice cream scoop like a gavel.

Walter's eyes widened. "A Broderick graces our humble pharmacy? Don't be bashful. We *treat* you right. Pardon the pun."

Candy jars featured peppermint and butterscotch sticks. Ceiling fans spun. Breezes cooled her perspiring face. Walter's father filled prescriptions as Walter monitored the soda fountain. Teddy nudged her to the stools.

Janie's voice lowered. "Mr. Gordon, my mother mustn't know."

"We keep secrets." Walter pointed to the menu. "Dozens of possibilities, from sundaes to milkshakes. Mix and match soda waters and sixteen flavored syrups. We have the newest ginger ale, Canada Dry. Teddy, want your usual?"

"You're a regular?" Janie said as if he'd just announced this as a gambling establishment. "Traitor!"

As Teddy and Walter jabbered, Janie scanned the wall menus, glancing over her shoulder, concerned Mother would pick up medicine that minute. "A Black Cow, please."

"With chocolate soda, sarsaparilla, or root beer?" Walter asked.

"Dr. Pepper, please."

"I've taken unusual orders, Miss Janie, but yours is the first of its kind."

She smiled. "I'd like that distinction."

Teddy wrinkled his nose. "Does it carry a money-back guarantee? Risky combination."

"When I begin my world travels, I must adapt to eating unconventional dishes."

Walter handed her the Black Cow and Teddy a strawberry milkshake. Janie took a guilty sip. Delicious! She declared her drink satisfying. "Assuming you keep my secret."

"Absolutely, Miss Janie." Walter struck a gallant pose, finger across his mouth as a promise. "Though I can't credit you with the first Dr. Pepper Black Cow, I'll be silent till the very end."

After Teddy's year in Wolcott, Sawyer Broderick started grooming him as his future business partner. He'd grown in ability and confidence, keeping his temper.

One Saturday on Auntie's porch, Janie waved a book, *Anne of Green Gables*. "A new novel, set in Prince Edward Island. Does this sound like P.E.I.?" She read portions. "I love Anne. She's an orphan, but unafraid of anything, like Rebecca of Sunnybrook Farm."

"Poetic justice for the orphan girl?"

"Definitely." She read more passages for his review.

"Avonlea sounds like Cavendish," he said. "Many allusions to Scottish poets and authors. We Scots value our literary roots. Celtic folklore's in our blood. From dryads to banshees."

"I constantly pulled my fairy friends out of mischief."

"You weren't the *cause* of their mischief?" He grinned. "Like Anne, we had recitations from the Royal Reader series." He stood, bowed, and delivered "How Sockery Set a Hen," about a man's misfortunes putting eggs under a high-roosting chicken. Janie laughed.

He sat. "Odd that Anne names places, not animals. Especially horses. I named mine Robert, after Robert the Bruce. For decades, laws about prevention of cruelty to animals took priority over safety laws protecting destitute children."

Janie's jaw dropped.

He took her hands. "A man would be hard-pressed to choose between his wife and his horse if they both fell into a pit."

"What about choosing between your horse or your sweetheart?" She displayed her best smile.

"It's a toss-up. Bets are stacked against the girlfriend."

She crossed her arms. "Despicable!"

He enveloped her hand in his. "But I'd choose you, above all."

"What about orphans? Surely your people care for orphans like Anne."

"Yes, but Anne's vocabulary exceeds her station. She takes first place in the exam, completes teacher training, and gets a teaching job. That wouldn't happen."

"Why not?"

"Orphans must stay in their social class, even when adopted, so they wouldn't get as much schooling."

"That's not right."

"Neither is hating the French and English, but some habits are deeply rooted. Abandoned children under twelve sign up as working apprentices till age twenty-one, to be useful."

"Useful? What about being loved?" Without Aunt Sophie, she'd feel like an orphan herself. Maybe someday she'd help an abandoned child. Find her own poetic justice.

"I'd be considered an orphan if I'd stayed on the island after leaving home. Another reason for me to leave. But I might've been treated decently since I was legitimate."

"What?" She recalled his fight with Ron over being called *bastard*.

"Highlander Protestants have high criteria for orphans they take. Orphans must have married parents. Unmarried mothers and their children are servants for life."

Janie frowned. "Aren't they forgiven? Christian charity should extend to all."

"I like the cut of your jib, but it doesn't work that way." He set her book down. "Anne rose above everything, but I'm more interested in Janie. Of Broderick farms." He leaned closer. "Marilla had an amethyst. Beautiful blueish-purple. Your eyes are like two amethysts."

They kissed, oblivious to the world. Till Aunt Sophie peered through the screen door.

1980

After pulling weeds, Carrie poured lemonade and settled into the wicker chair. In *Pilgrim's Progress,* Talkative spoke of repentance and mercy so sincerely that Faithful was beguiled. But Christian recognized the masquerade. Ugly Talkative was best when seen afar, like certain paintings. He noisily condemned others' sins, without recognizing his own.

Mrs. Gordon nodded. "From a distance, an Impressionist painting forms beautiful haystacks or waterlilies. Up close, it's a debacle of streaks and slashes."

"More obsession with appearances. Like poor orphans in P.E.I. Beyond help unless they're legitimate."

"My parents appeared upstanding in town, but their faults couldn't be hidden at home." Mrs. Gordon folded her hands. "Knowledge without grace."

THIRTY-FOUR

Saturday, June 14, 1980

Friday evening, Brian called to cancel for Saturday. Again. Rebuffed, Carrie avoided the café Friday night. She tested her green bean almondine recipe for supper, then accompanied Oma to the hobby store for stencils and the fabric store for her childhood chair upholstery.

Saturday, Opa sanded a rocking chair while Carrie stenciled figures on the bureau. Oma baked Flying Monkey Cinnamon Bread, courtesy of Mrs. Gordon.

Needing sandpaper, Opa coaxed Carrie to the hardware store. She ducked into the paint aisle and reveled in colors. Blues included High Seas, Plumberry, and Magician's Cloak.

"Here's one closest to your eyes." Dirk popped out of nowhere. "Dazzle. Maybe Pixie Dust. Or Misty Morning Dew." He held one by her face. "Pixie Dust it is. I see the magic."

Embarrassed, she grabbed the paint strip. "Will it work on a bedroom wall?"

He laughed. "Where's your lucky guy?"

"Brian canceled. Another client lunch. Boss's orders."

"On Saturday? Hey, I know it's not my business, but he's oh for two."

"Yup. No big deal. He doesn't have much say-so."

"Sounds like you don't either."

Carrie bristled. "He's busy. And I enjoy weekends with my grandparents." Did he wonder why she never went home on weekends?

"Up for a hike? I'm off at one. Saugatuck Dunes has miles of trails."

Why not? After all, he knew her plans had capsized. "I'm game."

"Great. Bring another folktale book. I finished the first one."

Later, Dirk showed up in his messy, rust-lined car. The Allman Brothers' "Rambling Man" blared from the cassette player.

"Seems apropos." Carrie climbed in and handed him a folktale book. His blue T-shirt matched his eyes. High Seas or Magician's Cloak.

Four miles north, they hiked through wooded dunes, discussing folktales. His observations and questions delighted her.

On the back dunes, the mosaic of blue sky peeked through branches of oaks, maples, and white pines. A fallen tree opened a piece of sky that shorter trees leaned into on their reach for sunlight. *Ah, Sunflower, weary of time.* Why didn't Brian make her a priority?

"How was your week with our Mrs. Gordon?" Dirk asked.

"She talks about you constantly now."

"No kidding?" He looked smug. "Well, I do have a way—"

"Don't start crowing." She shared how Janie met Teddy, about his temper, orphan discussions, Mr. Baum's hardships, and *Pilgrim's Progress* episodes. They arrived at a perch on the dune's shadier north side, overlooking the shoreline. Carrie leaned on the railing.

Dirk dug thermoses from his backpack. "Baum's time in Aberdeen sounds harsh. The store, the newspaper, the baseball team. Nothing paid off."

Carrie drank from a thermos. "But he talked openly about failures." Like Oma relaying the Holland fallout. Carrie's parents would never admit deficiencies. She couldn't even admit her college fiasco. "Janie learned much from him that her parents failed to teach."

"How does Mrs. G. respond to *Pilgrim's Progress*?"

"She has a visceral reaction whenever I mention the Slough of Despond."

"Maybe she's thinking of things that kept her from God over the years. My Slough was anger and despair, loss of trust in God. How could Mike die so young?" He squinted toward the sun. "My religion was handed to me on a silver platter. Actually, a paper plate. I couldn't own my faith till after hard times."

"You had to learn for yourself." Carrie was stuck in her own Slough. Of fear, shame. "Janie tired of hiding her lively imagination. Mrs. Gordon said, 'Shame will never be silent.'"

"She's trying to tell you something." He twirled grass. "When shame yells, it *causes* silence. Retreat."

She looked at him askance. "About to quote a psychology book?"

"Hardly." He chuckled. "I learned more in counseling. False shame comes from folks telling us we can't measure up."

"Like Mr. Legality and Talkative. Like a painting. The closer you get, the messier it is." *Like my family.* "Made-up rules." Wave tips frothed, rolling to shore, mesmerizing. Buoys bounced without a care.

"So, what are the locusts eating Carrie?"

She snapped around to face him. "Seriously? I've only known you two weeks."

He smiled. "Just tell me to go take a hike."

They walked through the mid-dunes, among jack pines

and cottonwoods. Stepping through a stand of sand cherries, they arrived at the beach. Carrie wiped her brow. *Can't measure up.* She wanted to cower.

"In high school, I was a class clown," Dirk said. "My teacher reprimanded me constantly, without improving my behavior. When he ignored me, that shut me up in a hurry."

"Good classroom management tactic." She avoided his eye.

"More than that. I learned that being reprimanded was better than being unseen."

Unseen. Images flooded. Her father leaving the room when she talked. Her mother paging through files. Letting Carrie take the fall for them in sixth grade. Silence, even after she told them about Miss Nieuwenhuis, the sixth-grade teacher. Scolding, then weeks of silence. Carrie bowed her head, cowering, shame shouting in her ear.

Her stomach knotted. *Unseen.* Was Brian any different? Six years she'd followed him from game to game, at the expense of her own interests. He didn't know about the second Billy Joel concert, the failed class. Didn't know her fears and feelings.

What was she losing out on? *Do you want to live by your passions or your fears?*

She jumped when Dirk touched her shoulder.

"Hey, didn't mean to send you into melancholy. You okay?"

Nodding, she looked away. *How much more fake can I be?*

Carrie tried to shake off her gloom under the canopy of oaks, leaving it for the sassafras, birch, and beech trees on the back dunes.

In Wolcott near the café, Carrie stared at the imposing dune—a steep climb, sand with grassy patches. "We've already walked three hours today!"

"You mean we've *only* walked three hours today." Dirk grinned.

"Okay, Mr. Show-off. Beat you there." She charged toward the base, Dirk in her wake.

"No, you don't!" He bolted after her, elbowing her as he ran ahead, enough to antagonize. She sprinted, sheer grit. "Give up?" he said.

"Never." She forged ahead, but not for long. He nosed forward until they reached the bottom of the path, panting. Trudging uphill in sand, she paced herself, stopping every thirty seconds. Her feet sank with each step, like Shifting Sands around Oz. Her calves ached.

"Ready for the view?" He held out his hand.

Brotherly, right? She reached. He grasped. They plodded up. At the top, he held on. They scanned the cloudless periwinkle sky. His laughter tangled with the wind. Birds swooped and glided. People below spread on towels along the lazy beach. Was this like the day Janie climbed the dune with the Baum boys?

She focused on their entwined fingers. "Strictly business, I see."

"I'll not have you falling down the dune on my watch."

She smiled, but, wanting a clear conscience, withdrew her hand. Breezes invigorated, freeing her hair and spirit. "Let's jump down like we're flying."

They took a running leap, arms like wings. At the bottom, inching out of his shirt, Dirk ran across the beach into the lake. Carrie admired his sturdy shoulders. When he turned around in waist-deep water and waved, she couldn't resist. She jogged over and splashed in.

Oma invited Dirk for supper. After a meal of pork chops, scalloped potatoes, Rigmaroles, and Scraps's Peach Bread Pudding, Carrie showed him Opa's shop and the half-done furniture.

Oma followed them. She fingered the stenciled rabbit on the bureau, chanting:

> "'Did you ever see a rabbit climb a tree?
> Did you ever see a lobster ride a flea?'"

"This rabbit's from 'Bye Baby Bunting,'" Carrie said.

Oma stroked the stencil of a boy jumping over a candlestick.

> "'There was a boy from Kalamazoo,
> who ate too much hot celery stew.'"

Carrie giggled. "Cute, but it's 'Jack Be Nimble.' Not from Kalamazoo. Where'd you get those rhymes?"

"Childhood somewhere."

Carrie showed Dirk the chair fabric. "Just realized I can't fit that chair in my car."

"I'll drive you to Barrowdale in Uncle John's truck, hang out with my buddy in Marshall, pick you and the chair up on the way back." She thanked him profusely.

At the front door, Dirk said, "Considering today was strictly business, I had a great time."

Carrie shook his hand as if closing a deal. "Me too, Mr. Vandenakker. Next item of business, Holland." In one week.

He walked to his car. Befuddled about her feelings, she wanted to invite him back in. She felt safe, *seen* by Dirk. But she couldn't fall for him. Too unpredictable. Not a penny in the bank. Sighing, she watched him drive away. After hiking and climbing, she was as weary as the Twelve Dancing Princesses celebrating all night in magic shoes. Exhausted, but happy.

Oma gathered plates in the dining room. "If you weren't with Brian, *liefje*, I'd say catch that Dirk. He's a charmer."

"You're only saying that 'cause you're over forty." Carrie brushed crumbs into a saucer. "He's twenty-eight and sells hardware. Sails the seven seas. His life philosophy is all fun and no responsibility. How do you say it?"

"*Voor een dubbeltje op de eerste rang.* Best seats in the house for a dime."

"That's it. Expects the world for a small payment."

Oma tilted her head. "I don't see Dirk that way."

"What other way is there? He doesn't stay in one place long enough to have troubles."

In the kitchen, Carrie set mugs in the sink, then dug the chicken ornament from her bag and hung it on a cabinet doorknob.

Oma stopped short. "Where'd you get that?"

"Mrs. Gordon. Mr. Baum made it."

Oma fingered the yellow wood. "This seems familiar. Hmm." She frowned. "I talked to Helen and Florence today. They don't have my baby pictures. The earliest one is age four, 1916. My baptism photo."

"Odd. Why weren't you baptized as a baby, like your sisters? Especially with your parents being Christian Reformed."

Oma shrugged. "*Waarom zijn de bananen krom?* Why are bananas crooked? "My parents probably didn't have a regular minister for the baptism."

Thirty-Five

Monday, June 16, 1980

Carrie and Mrs. Gordon sipped chamomile citron tea. Indulging in Scarecrow's & Jellia Jam's Blueberry Cornbread Streusel Bars, Carrie presented a note:

Dear Mrs. Gordon,

I'm overwhelmed by your generosity. Sharing in turn is like giving scraps to the queen, but please accept my humble gift as thanks.

Sincerely,
Tanna Groothuis

Carrie handed her an index card. "A recipe for *achjes*, Dutch figure-8 cookies we make at Christmas with my aunts. Oma grew up making them with her mother."

Mrs. Gordon squinted at the card. "We'll make *achjes*, if allowed in July. But first, a trip to Chicago and Grand Rapids."

Janie, 16
July 1908

Though Mr. Baum spent the summer at Macatawa, he was so consumed by preparations for *Fairylogue and Radio-Plays*, that the Baums invited Janie and Aunt Sophie to Chicago instead. He wired money for train tickets. The invitation included a Cubs baseball game at West Side Park, if Aunt Sophie could lower herself to attend.

Janie was relieved her parents let her go to Chicago with her aunt. Clueless about Baum's home, Sawyer and Elsa were glad it was the opposite direction of Macatawa.

Aunt Sophie's words affirmed their furtive excursion. *I know a hundred magical reasons why you should still see Mr. Baum. With him, you blossom.*

Everything thrilled Janie, from the elevated train in Chicago's Loop to the Windy City's soaring buildings. They rode escalators and visited the tearoom at the opulent Marshall Field & Company, toured the Chicago Art Institute, and browsed at the Field Museum.

The previous year, the Tigers and Cubs, both pennant winners of their respective leagues, played each other in the World Series. The Tigers lost.

At the ballpark, Mr. Baum kept reminding Aunt Sophie she was on enemy territory.

"Mr. Baum, if you lose today, you'll remain in third place. If the Tigers lose, we'll still be in *first*."

Rolling her eyes, Janie tugged hair off her sweaty neck and turned to Kenneth. "It's too hot to endure such cutthroat banter."

He flagged down a boy selling Coca-Cola. "This'll revive you. Pay them no mind."

After numerous smashing bats and relentless roaring, the

Cubs won five to four over the Giants, putting the Cubs into second place behind Pittsburgh. Newspapers reported that Detroit lost, but as Aunt Sophie said, the Tigers maintained first place.

That evening, Janie and Aunt Sophie basked in the Baums' hospitality with French dip sandwiches in their Chicago apartment on South Michigan Avenue. Though this wasn't Kenneth's childhood home, Janie imagined his boyhood, story hour with the neighbors around the kerosene lamp. How different her life would've been with a family who allowed imagination free rein. Thank goodness for Aunt Sophie.

On Sunday, Mr. Baum invited them to tour Selig Studios downtown where he'd filmed the *Fairylogue* moving pictures. On the *L* train, he asked, "Have you been to a nickelodeon?"

Aunt Sophie replied, "Yes, in Holland."

"What?" Janie balked. "Mother calls them godless places."

Auntie blushed. "She exaggerates, dumpling. It's merely an indoor theater for telling stories through motion pictures."

"So *that's* what you and Miss Vanderlaan do? You never let me see shows at Jenison Park." Pouting, Janie crossed her arms. "Auntie, I'm sixteen!"

Mr. Baum chuckled. "I never dreamed of witnessing a family feud between you two ladies. Over nickelodeons, no less."

"I saw that western, *The Great Train Robbery*," Auntie said.

"The *Fairylogue*, or Oz travelogue, has moving pictures and magic lantern photographs."

Janie narrowed her eyes at Auntie. "Mr. Baum, since I've never stepped foot in a nickelodeon, please explain how it works."

He snickered, then summarized the development of filmmaking. With a friend's loan, he maintained artistic control of the *Fairylogue*. "You'll see how fairies come alive in magical ways, much like radio waves mysteriously carry voices across the miles." He winked.

He showed them around Selig Studios, a grand glass building ablaze with sunlight. In a darker room, he ran the projector for a preview. Pictures sprang alive with movement. Dorothy grew, stepping from a book page, changing from black and white to color.

With celluloid film, he demonstrated double exposures and the layered effect. "By the simplest of tricks, a camera is made to be a fine liar, making fairies jealous of such magic."

"Astounding ingenuity," Aunt Sophie said.

Mr. Baum charmed them with a demonstration of stopgap techniques. He described filming processes that utilized invisible wires, overexposed film, and two scenes filmed separately, then overlapping. He'd filmed stormy sea pictures in Coronado, then Billina's chicken coop on rockers, moved by wires in the studio, and then combined them.

Before leaving Chicago, he handed Janie an envelope. Folded inside his Oz-emblemed stationery were two dollar tickets to the *Fairylogue*'s opening night in Grand Rapids, including backstage passes.

Janie, 16
September 1908

On September 24, Aunt Sophie and Janie took the interurban to St. Cecilia Hall in Grand Rapids for *The Fairylogue and Radio-Plays*, planning to stay overnight with a family friend. Janie's parents knew about the visit, not the show. A twinge of guilt needled her.

Mr. Baum, dapper in a stark white suit with silk lapels and red carnation, welcomed everyone in his deep, sonorous voice, then stepped offstage. The lights lowered. A scarlet curtain opened, unveiling a screen with a Land of Oz map. Suddenly, the picture changed to a storybook. A medieval page opened it to reveal Dorothy. Mr. Baum appeared onscreen in the same white suit, as if he'd magically stepped from stage to film. He called Dorothy, who stepped from the page and grew into a life-size, full-color girl, as in the preview at Selig Studios.

The book closed and reopened to show the Scarecrow stepping out in color, then the Lion, Tin Woodman, and others. Mr. Baum returned to the stage and narrated *The Wizard of Oz, Marvelous Land,* and *Ozma of Oz* as the screen alternated moving pictures and fanciful drawings on magic lantern slides, accompanied by a full orchestra. Fourteen scenes took them through an Ozian cornfield, the Nome King's underground realm, and the Emerald City's throne room.

The audience squealed in delight as the Gump took flight, Tip transformed into Ozma, and Dorothy rocked on stormy waves. The dissolving slides of intermission gave a preview of Mr. Baum's next book, *Dorothy and the Wizard in Oz,* not yet in stores. He autographed books the children brought. Aunt Sophie said they'd see him afterward.

The second half featured *John Dough and the Cherub* in six scenes. The two-hour show flew as quickly as every hour spent with Mr. Baum. Seeing his vision on screen proved exhilarating. The audience burst into applause.

Janie and her aunt went backstage. Mr. Baum's face brightened. "Miss McKinnon, Charlotte Rose!" He took Janie's hand. "What'd you think?"

"Fabulous," Janie said.

"I'm so glad you came. We're traveling from Syracuse to St. Louis, Chicago, Milwaukee, and St. Paul, booked through December and hopefully beyond. Come summer, I'll need the refreshment of Lake Michigan with its own fairyland wonders." He turned to Aunt Sophie. "'Tis a shame Detroit's in third place, while the Cubs thrive in first."

Aunt Sophie lifted her chin. "We've been first all month, Mr. Baum, bound to win the pennant again."

"If you do, your sorry excuse for a team will face us."

Aunt Sophie put a finger to her lips. "Now *you're* on enemy territory."

He gazed at Janie. "How's school, Charlotte?"

"I'm the newspaper editor! And I've a brilliant idea for a column."

He clapped. "You're a trailblazer. Anything you can reveal to an old friend?"

She grinned. "Just think Mrs. Bilkins."

"Splendid! Who gets the credit?"

"Captain Bilgewater, the janitor. And substitute teacher Mr. Taradiddle."

He blasted a jolly laugh. "Clever! I look forward to meeting those alter egos in print."

Mr. Baum's son Frank walked over. Janie hardly recognized him. "Charlotte!" He shook her hand.

"Frank's the film projectionist," Mr. Baum said. "He inspired this Ozologue, due to his own travelogues."

"I work the film and slide projector in a hidden room," Frank said.

"To conjure the fairy magic?" Janie asked. The men chuckled.

"Consider this." Mr. Baum drew an arc across the air. "In America, we do by science what Oz does by magic. Think of all that's invisible, what scientists do with wireless telegraph, sending electromagnetic waves across the ocean from ship to ship. Fairies wait to be known by us through magic, similar to how radio waves work. A *Fairylogue* makes it happen."

THIRTY-SIX

Monday, June 16, 1980

Carrie and Mrs. Gordon started *achjes* and refrigerated the log dough shapes.

After lunch, they weeded among peonies and geraniums. On the porch, Carrie read *Pilgrim's Progress*. Evangelist warned Christian and Faithful about evil Vanity Fair, established to entice pilgrims on their way to the Celestial City. Vendors specialized in selling vanity—items with only worldly value. Folks could buy houses, land, titles, lust, or pleasure.

Christian and Faithful were arrested. So-called witnesses took Faithful before the Judge, Lord Hate-good, who charged them with causing a commotion. The jury included Mr. Blindman, Malice, and Mr. Cruelty. Faithful was found guilty, then stoned to death.

"Oh, my," Mrs. Gordon gasped. "What good did it do Faithful to be faithful?"

"He arrived at the Celestial City sooner than later," Janie said. "With his Robe, Mark, and Roll."

Mrs. Gordon crossed her arms. "Christian only has a mind

for the Celestial City. Like fairy tales, where forlorn heroes proceed on their journey, viewing a kingdom from afar."

"John Calvin said, 'Faith is not a distant view, but a warm embrace of Christ.'"

"Who's this John Calvin to me?" Mrs. Gordon snapped.

"A sixteenth-century church reformer. He inspired Mr. Bunyan."

"Yet there's no guarantee of an easy life."

"Right." Carrie tapped the book. "But this warm embrace is what John Bunyan knew firsthand. He wrote this story sitting in jail for preaching."

Mrs. Gordon balked. "Jail? Who needs *that* kind of warm embrace?"

That evening, Carrie walked the neighborhood, admiring Victorian homes. Trees arched over the road. Evening shadows fused with flashes of zinnias and snapdragons. Someday she'd renovate her own Victorian—if she could convince Brian. He preferred modern.

A shrill whistle pierced the air. "Kruisselbrink," Dirk yelled from down the street.

"You stalking me, Vandenakker?"

"Guilty as charged." Dirk jogged over. "Your oma pointed me in your direction. I brought you something. In the car. You'll like it."

"A caramel sundae or Zip Strip?"

He chuckled. They walked down Hickory Lane. Which house had been Aunt Sophie's? When Carrie pointed out her favorite Queen Anne home, Dirk hatched a tale about the family who once lived there, prompting laughter.

"That's why you came," she said. "I laugh at your stories."

"Again, you inspire me to my best efforts."

Being with Dirk felt like—how'd Mrs. Gordon put it? Like indulging in chocolate fudge after months of porridge.

At his car, Dirk presented a gift wrapped in newspaper comics. Brian's gifts were embellished with shiny, floral paper tied with ribbons. Wrapped at the store or by his mother.

She opened it, revealing *The Annotated Wizard of Oz* by Michael Patrick Hearn. "I love it!"

"I noticed that at Mrs. G.'s tea party."

"You're too sweet. Thank you." She set the book on the car and hugged him, not expecting such a thrill.

He returned the hug, arms gradually sliding around her. She relished his whiskers brushing her cheek, Old Spice cologne wafting. His shirt smelled woodsy, like the dunes. Warmth prickled through her.

Hot, she pulled back and grabbed the book. Surely her face turned one of those hardware store paint colors. Pink Plunge, Rose Frenzy, or Fire Engine Red.

"You're welcome." His grin widened.

"Wanna come in? Oma made cobbler."

"Sure. Magic words for me."

"Cobbler? Or *come in*?"

"Both."

Inside, she waved the gift. "Look, Oma! A book from Dirk."

"*Nou breekt m'n klomp!*"

Dirk leaned toward Carrie. "*Klomp?* Is she gonna hit me with her wooden shoe?"

Carrie laughed. "Brush up on your Dutch. She means that wins the prize."

Oma set out spoons. "Instead of 'That takes the cake,' we say, 'That breaks my clog.'"

"At least I'm not in trouble," Dirk said.

Oma served blueberry cobbler. "Winkie Surprise. Surprise refers to which berries."

"Do they break your clog, Mrs. Groothuis?"

Oma chuckled. They perused pages of the annotated *Oz*, noting photos, footnotes, and Denslow's illustrations.

"Better than Zip Strip?" Dirk winked.

That night in her bedroom, Carrie noted the inscription.

To Carrie,

Whether escaping locusts, witches, dragons, or the Slough of Despond, you're on a journey that rivals Dorothy's with many adventures to come. I wish you hours of bliss as you read—and hopefully think of me.

Fondly, Dirk

Fondly? What did *that* mean? Think of him? What adventures?

The man was deluded. But oh, so sweet.

Oma knocked on Carrie's door, then sat on the bed. "What a *schat*, that Dirk. Such a sweetheart. Does he know you're with Brian?"

"Oma, he knows. He's just a friend."

"Why hasn't Brian visited? That *gladjakker*. All talk and no substance."

"He's busy. I'll see him in two weeks."

"Maybe it's time *om* Brian *achter het behang te plakken*."

"Glue him behind the wallpaper?" Carrie bristled. "Why?"

"He should be more attentive. He doesn't care for you at this distance."

"I know. We'll talk things over."

Oma touched Carrie's arm. "*Liefje*, just talking is like *dweilen met de kraan open*. Mopping up while the faucet's running."

Thirty-Seven

Tuesday, June 17, 1980

The next day at Mrs. Gordon's, Carrie copied the recipe for Cap'n Bill's Hot Buttered Rum Cheesecake.

Seated with a plate of figure-eight *achjes*, she sipped Lemon Lavender Tea. "Dirk gave me *The Annotated Wizard of Oz*. I love it."

"Does Brian buy you books?" Mrs. Gordon asked.

"Sure. Self-help books, devotionals."

"So, Brian gives self-help books, and Dirk gives you a book you love."

"Is the jury done? Also, I finished reading *Wendolyn and the Gatekeeper of Merrimack Castle*. Keeping Gretchen Trumbauer in the running for favorite author."

Mrs. Gordon winced. "My denouncements made you bound and determined to read it."

"You probably don't like it because it parallels your life. The three creepy dragons chase Wendolyn, enticing her from the castle, like your parents did. The castle's a place full of wonder, where anything Wendolyn paints becomes real. Mr. Baum could be the Gatekeeper with the paintbrush, showing how to create the magic. But she can't escape dragon voices wooing her to go back outside. Like your parents haunting you."

Mrs. Gordon blinked several times.

"Wendolyn's friend Jipper goes to magical places with her, but betrays her in the end, luring her back to the dragons." Carrie frowned. "Not sure who that is."

"Is there a parallel for *your* life?"

Carrie froze. "I don't know." Her parents played the dragon role, squelching her interests. Especially since sixth grade. Did Teddy or Walter betray Mrs. Gordon?

"I hope you're happy now." She stirred tea as if whisking away melancholy. "By eleventh grade, the entire community supported the Wolcott High School newspaper."

Carrie took another *achje*. "Did you write a *Fairylogue* review?"

"Yes, under a pseudonym. Then, I instigated a risky venture. Today, I bring you into the foray of Mrs. Bilkins's admirers by introducing Captain Bilgewater and Mr. Taradiddle."

<hr>

Janie, 16: Autumn, 1908

The newspaper staff embraced Janie's idea. They'd write anonymously about forbidden topics—problems with school policies, curriculum, or personnel—by submitting pages signed *Captain Bilgewater* or *Mr. Taradiddle*.

Janie established their personalities. Bilgewater, a brash, retired Navy sailor turned intermittent janitor, was in everybody's business, liberal with his complaints about school protocols. Mr. Taradiddle was a know-it-all substitute teacher with more savvy about maneuvering school politics.

Mrs. Bilkins would be proud. So would Nellie Bly and Matilda Joslyn Gage.

For two months, the faculty and community welcomed the column's humorous take on daily schedules, field trips, or the merits of nickelodeons as feats of artistry versus questionable entertainment. Then came November. Time to address serious issues. Janie took the paper to the printer, but Mr. Graham hadn't bothered proofreading. Two days later, he stormed into the classroom and escorted Janie to the principal's office.

Principal O'Reilly looked up from his desk, jowls shaking. His voice dripped pomposity. "Miss Broderick, where might I contact the elusive Mr. Taradiddle and Captain Bilgewater regarding the audacious articles about unequal pay between men and women teachers?"

"The writers want to stay anonymous, sir."

"Obviously. They agitated the entire community." He leaned forward. "Has anyone confessed to submitting these articles by our beloved janitor and substitute teacher?"

"No, sir." She'd written them herself.

Mr. O'Reilly shook a paper. "*Somebody* better speak up to prevent the *Eagle*'s demise."

"What about freedom of the press?"

"That doesn't apply to students who want to graduate from this school."

"We're giving students a voice, sir."

"And insulting the board of education. Our formerly content female teachers are flocking to the board, demanding pay increases." Jowls vibrating, Mr. O'Reilly ripped a page in half.

Janie caught her breath. "Sir, these columns provide wider readership. Citizens are engaged, donating to the paper fund. Besides, aren't women worth equal pay?"

Mr. O'Reilly tore another page as she cringed. "Our school's reputation is at risk."

"These columns enhance the school's reputation by encouraging open discussion," Janie said.

"Single women teachers don't support families, thus don't need more money. The culprit has till Monday morning to come forward. Otherwise, no more papers." His jowls wobbled. "Your editorship is also in question."

After school, Janie met the newspaper staff at Gordon's Pharmacy. Ceiling fans didn't cool her anger. Peppermints offered no consolation.

Walter Gordon cheerfully made milkshakes for all.

Frazzled, Janie plopped on a stool. "On Monday, I'll confess they're my articles."

A barrage of responses ensued. "No!" ... "O'Reilly's bluffing." ... "Don't back down."

Janie cast a glance at mirthful Walter. His eyebrows arched as he filled a glass with sarsaparilla.

She lowered her voice. "We could lose the paper. I'll take the fall."

No amount of discussion changed her mind. As students filed out, Janie caught Walter's eye. "Please don't tell anyone about this meeting."

"I'll remain silent to the very end, Miss Janie." He winked, hand on his heart. "I never told a soul about your propensity for Dr. Pepper Black Cows."

He remembered! From five months ago. "Thank you."

"Sounds like trouble brewing. I hope there's a satisfactory resolution." He handed her a Dr. Pepper. "On the house. My wish for your good cheer."

Monday morning, she walked into the principal's office with her confession. Her punishment was removal from the newspaper staff for two months and stepping down from editorship. She was devastated. Did Mr. Baum get in that much trouble as Mrs. Bilkins? How'd her wonderful Baum-inspired idea go so wrong, so quickly?

The principal published her formal apology in the paper.

She confessed to writing half of the articles published under the pseudonyms. Appalled and ashamed, her parents scolded, then indulged in stony silence.

Janie finally understood. *A dreamer is one who can only find his way by moonlight, and his punishment is that he sees the dawn before the rest of the world.* The world wasn't ready for women to stand alongside men as equals. So much for starting out like Nellie Bly. Or Matilda Joslyn Gage, for that matter.

A week later, she received a letter from the Wolcott *Town Crier*. Trembling, she read it.

Dear Miss Broderick,

I've never read The Eagle *more eagerly than these past two months, with Mr. Taradiddle and Captain Bilgewater onboard. Your staff used clever means to communicate issues nobody wants to endure but must. According to your regrettable, induced confession, you're the author of multiple columns. I believe I can identify your distinctive voice. I'd be delighted to meet you in person to confirm my conjectures and invite you to join my staff as a columnist, in efforts to gain a younger readership. You have wit and ingenuity with proficient writing skills. Please set up an appointment to meet me.*

Sincerely,
Mr. Charles Ferguson, Editor

Poetic justice! Like Nellie Bly's journalistic beginnings after replying to a newspaper column. No cranky principal could shut Janie down. Mr. Ferguson had a reputation as a fair, honest man, fastidious about sources. Maybe this was her pathway to feature writing.

The next week, Mr. Ferguson shook her hand as if priming a pump. She verified her articles. He admired Mrs. Gage, Mrs.

Anthony, and Mrs. Stanton. Wanting a woman's voice in the paper, he offered Janie a job. She stipulated her criteria: writing under a pseudonym. Her parents wouldn't approve. Nor would the school. He proposed the same entry-level pay as newer male employees. Thrilled, she would have worked for free.

At home, she wrote out her new signature: *Isabel Louisa Girard.* Isabel for the author of the Pansy books she'd read as a girl: Isabella MacDonald Alden. Louisa for Louisa May Alcott—admired author, abolitionist, and advocate for women's rights. And Girard because it fit.

After a two-month suspension from the school paper, Janie returned while secretly writing for *The Town Crier*. She tucked earnings into the bank.

1980

"Excellent," Carrie said. "One closed door opened another. Did you employ Captain Bilgewater and Mr. Taradiddle again?"

"Their dubious reputations could only bungle the task. But I'm grateful they caught Mr. Ferguson's attention."

"You were a daring, headstrong girl." Carrie smiled, considering her own secret writing, recorded nightly. Had Mrs. Gordon's writing endeavors ended at the tearoom?

Later, Carrie read more *Pilgrim's Progress*. Christian and his new companion, Hopeful, encountered By-Ends, also headed to the Celestial City. By-Ends embraced religion for materialistic gain, more zealous in his Silver Slippers, with sunshine and applause. Christian told By-Ends he must own Religion in his rags as well as his Silver Slippers, whether bound in Irons or bombarded with praise. Pursuing both Riches and Religion led to ruin. Inadvertently proving Christian's point, By-Ends dug for treasure at the silver mine, got lost, and was never seen again.

"Silver slippers, like Dorothy's silver shoes," Mrs. Gordon said. "Is Mr. Bunyan saying everyone should become monks?"

"No. He's saying not to seek religion for power and wealth. He practiced what he preached, holding onto faith in difficult times. Even writing from prison."

Mrs. Gordon frowned. "Embracing religion in rags."

THIRTY-EIGHT

Wednesday, June 18, 1980

Carrie and Mrs. Gordon made The Wizard's Magical Chocolate Cake and Caramel Nougat Tea laced with hazelnut. Carrie copied the recipe for Jack's Pumpkin-Jinjur Mousse.

"Saturday, I'm going to Holland and Macatawa Park," Carrie said. "Dirk and I are sailing on Black Lake—rather, Lake Macatawa."

Mrs. Gordon peered over her glasses. "Does Brian know?"

Carrie dropped her fork on the Blue Willow plate. "It doesn't matter. Dirk's a friend."

"A friend who gives you well-loved gifts."

"Look, there's nothing between us. Brian canceled twice. I'll see him in two weeks."

"Then you'll tell him about no diploma?"

"If I muster the courage."

Mrs. Gordon added sugar. "You're almost engaged. Why keep secrets?"

"*Your* whole life's full of secrets."

"By sharing mine now, I'm encouraging you to take a different path."

Carrie sighed. "Everyone will be furious. But I'm hoping my parents approve my Plan B. Which has been Plan A all along, unbeknownst to them."

Mrs. Gordon pursed her lips. Reaching for wise words or a reprimand?

"I know," Carrie said. "Am I going to live by passions or fears?"

"Ralph Waldo Emerson said, 'To be yourself in a world that is constantly trying to make you something else is the greatest accomplishment.' I say, it takes all your courage."

"Did *you* have that kind of courage?"

Mrs. Gordon stared her down. "Why do you think I became Isabel Girard?"

The same reason Carrie wore a satin face. "What'd Mr. Baum say? Living with fairies takes more courage than jumping down a dune. Even Glinda won't change into a different form."

"Transformations aren't honest. Nor pretending to be what you aren't. Don't hide your true self from those who matter, those who accept you." Mrs. Gordon stirred tea as if dissolving the heaviness of childhood. "Besides Isabel's column, I wrote about mundane events under my own name, so I told my parents. But they'd no idea about Isabel Girard. Nor equal pay."

"They didn't oppose your newspaper job?"

"They viewed it as an opportunity to redeem myself from the humiliating Bilgewater-Taradiddle fiasco." She rapped the table. "Now for my last visit to Macatawa Park."

Janie, 17
1909

When Mr. Baum's invitation arrived for the regatta—a whole week—Janie wept. Her parents would never allow it. Sparing Aunt Sophie more duplicity, Janie could go alone, leaving a note. *I'll return in a week. Don't worry. I'm safe.* But her parents would know. They'd show up and make a scene. The Baums would be horrified.

One evening, she approached her parents. "Father, Mother, I'm asking for one week off in August to attend the regatta on Black Lake. With the Baums." She handed them an envelope of hard-earned newspaper cash, withdrawn that day. "I'm paying you the wages you'll need to hire help in the tearoom that week, so I can go with your blessing."

Mother's eyes widened. "The Baums again? How dare you ask—"

Father stifled Mother with a hand clasping her shoulder. "Wait. The girl shows some shrewdness." He took the envelope.

Janie's heart raced. Had her father just complimented her?

He removed bills from the envelope. "Another two dollars will do it."

Two dollars? She swallowed. She'd been more than generous, considering he'd never paid her a cent. "Then I may go to Macatawa for the week?"

"Yes, but no riding the interurban unescorted. Your aunt must accompany you."

Whew! "Yes, sir."

Mother started blustering. "Now just a minute."

"Stop it, Elsa. You'll bring on another headache. The girl's seventeen, not a child." Waving the cash, he eyed Mother as if silencing her. Money was a language they understood.

On the interurban in August, the only thing marring the anticipation was the *Fairylogue*'s closing after four months. Surely Mr. Baum was devastated.

Strolling Macatawa's boardwalk was as magical as taking the road of yellow brick into Oz. Every visit proved just as enchanting as before. Grasses swayed, vibrant companions for periwinkle sky and emerald treetops. Was this the road that rolled into Mr. Baum's story, from that dreamy place between sleep and wakefulness?

Though careworn, he offered effusive salutations and lemonade. He lorded the Cubs' World Series victory over the Tigers, the second consecutive year, thanks to Mordecai Brown's stupendous pitching. Aunt Sophie countered with Ty Cobb's accomplished batting and double base stealing. They each spouted their teams' unalienable rights to supremacy until Aunt Sophie declared the Tigers the American League Number One this year, unchallenged since April.

Janie was determined to break up the rivalry. "I loved your *Fairylogue*, Mr. Baum. The *Tribune* called it worthwhile and whimsical, winning everyone's affection."

"Twenty-seven delightful songs," Aunt Sophie said. "Newspapers compared you to Mark Twain."

Mr. Baum sniggered. "Only because I wore a white suit. One reviewer likened me to Peter Pan as the eternal boy." He waved away coiling smoke. "Crowds expanded in the Midwest, then New York City in December." He sighed. "Where it closed."

"Such a shame." Aunt Sophie sipped lemonade.

His face darkened, forehead creases deepening. "I took financial responsibility, giving me the final say-so in everything. But with salaries, theater rentals, projection equipment, and freight, ticket sales weren't enough."

"Yet it's the most inventive undertaking I've ever seen," Aunt Sophie said.

A wave of melancholy engulfed him. "To pay off

considerable debt to the studio, I turned over my books' film rights to Mr. Selig." He looked at Janie. "I hate being the bearer of such dismal news, but I must sell this lovely cottage."

Janie gasped. "No!"

"Oh, dear." Aunt Sophie jostled her drink, nearly spilling.

"To reduce expenses and live in a better climate, we're moving to southern California."

Janie numbed. The sky's vibrancy drained, diffusing, as if pouring from a pitcher into a deep well.

"My dear girl." Mr. Baum took her hand. "I share your distress. Miss McKinnon, may we still write to Charlotte?"

"Of course." Auntie looked as pale as Janie felt.

"We still have this week together. And I've a special parting gift." He picked up a book. "Hot off the press." *The Road to Oz.*

Trembling, Janie browsed through it. Colorful pages blurred.

Aunt Sophie noted the dedication. "To your first grandchild, Joslyn Stanton Baum. Congratulations!"

"Thank you. 'Tis an extraordinary delight to have a grandson. Frank's boy." He tapped the book. "You'll meet Polychrome, the Rainbow's daughter. And the Shaggy Man."

"Did you use children's ideas?" Janie asked.

"I can't escape them. They blend with mine till they're indistinguishable. Now, further from Oz, I'll have the opportunity *you* have, weaving your own ideas as you see fit. If you still want my commentary, mail me your chapters. Will you write as Mr. Taradiddle?" He winked. "My boy adventure stories are reissued as *The Boy Fortune Hunters* series by Floyd Akers."

"Whatever happened to Captain Fitzgerald?"

"It's a publishing decision. It's hard enough keeping my loving child tyrants satisfied. Including you, with your tenacious insistence on a chicken companion for Dorothy."

"Is Billina in this story?"

"As feisty as ever. What about Captain Bilgewater?"

"Now I write as Isabel Girard. Pen names give me a voice I've never had."

"Remember, Charlotte, you've no reason to hide who you are."

Yet she did. "What about your next Oz book?"

"You're holding one of the last, with an idea underway for one more."

"You *can't* be done with Oz."

"Don't fret, dear. Are you in league with all those others?" Mr. Baum smiled. "I'm constantly being dictated what I must do. But Dorothy hasn't contacted me lately." He handed Janie another book, *Aunt Jane's Nieces at Work*. "Edith Van Dyne is working hard, too. Another reason I cannot produce Oz books yearly." As Schuyler Staunton, he published *The Last Egyptian*, a romance novel for adults. He had a story idea about a girl pilot and was collaborating with Paul Tietjens on *The Pipes of Pan*, a comic opera. He relished creating another musical comedy with Montgomery and Stone, perhaps *Ozma of Oz*.

"I'm dizzy listening to all your projects." Aunt Sophie set down her glass. "Well, Mr. Akers, or is it Captain Fitzgerald? I must go."

Janie lifted her chin. "So you don't miss any nickelodeon shows?"

Aunt Sophie chuckled and left.

Mr. Baum checked his pocket watch. "Tell me about your newspaper venture."

She shared how the Bilgewater-Taradiddle fiasco launched Isabel Girard's career as the voice of young women, taking on issues of equal pay. She showed him *The Eagle* and *Town Crier*, pointing out her columns. "I get paid for doing something I love. Father pays me nothing."

"I paid Frank for his work on the *Fairylogue*. Perhaps your parents will pay you after high school."

"But I aspire to greater things."

"Ah, yes. The next Nellie Bly. I wonder which evil plot you'll expose. Don't invite more trouble by making typographical errors. You might be challenged to a duel." He chortled. "In Aberdeen, as newspaper editor, I inadvertently insulted a new bride, describing her smile as *roughish* instead of *roguish*. The groom set out to horsewhip me."

"Oh, no!"

"We settled on dueling instead. Fortunately, we were both cowards. I ran away, pistol in hand, and found out he did too."

Janie laughed. "I also want to publish fairy tales. About Camellia." She handed him three chapters from her satchel. She couldn't take her eyes off him as he read, the last week on this porch together—his mustache twitching, his clear, gray eyes crinkling right before laughter.

"A superb revision and exciting additions. You incorporated my recommendations. Camellia's stubbornness could be her downfall. Poppi has run out of excuses. Camellia's in a pickle. I wonder how they'll get out of this jam."

"Jam? Or pickle?" Janie giggled. "That's from raising the stakes in each chapter."

"By revising, you've done what I often fail to do. Listen to others."

"You take readers' suggestions."

"But I don't revise much. The story works its way out from the germ of an idea. I pad it between chapters until complete. Later, when typing, I make improvements."

"Does the publisher ask you to change things?"

"Sometimes. Conceding to his demands usually improves the story. It takes an objective eye. And somebody responsible for my paycheck. Now, where will you attend college?"

"Western Michigan University has English and writing classes."

"Remember, knowledge from *any* source is a treasure no one can steal. Pursue your dream. Even now, with the *Fairylogue* debacle behind me, I can't stop thinking of ways to tell more stories through books or stage." Sadness rippled over his face. "Though it'll take time to overcome this collapse, most risks are worth it and breed wisdom. After multiple failures, folks pay me for my view of modern fairy tales and authors. Imagine that! Better yet, my stories never send children to bed with nightmares. And virtue reigns supreme over evil."

"You've accomplished much."

"But happiness doesn't rest in accomplishments, Charlotte. It's found in family and friends, in everyday wonders. Call it magic or science, there's much joy in a flower blooming, a cow making milk, or a wave rushing to shore." He gestured toward the lake.

Together they named everyday marvels, a rich reminder of beauty she'd neglected while sinking in mire at home. *A hundred magical reasons to be here.*

He fastened his gaze on her. "Dorothy achieves, too. Not from magical powers, but for being a sweet, simple girl, honest to herself and to all. Simplicity and kindness are the magic wands that work wonders. Just keep walking, even if baby steps. 'It is a long journey ...'" His voice cracked.

"'Through a country that is sometimes pleasant and sometimes dark and terrible.' You said that the first day I met you. The chicken ornament reminds me daily."

"Your mother had no place for fairies, but I couldn't bear seeing your lively imagination smothered." He struck a contemplative pose. "Remember, Charlotte, only imagination and faith keep man above the commonplace. Now what would Captain Bilgewater say about that?"

Janie smiled. "I like the cut of your jib."

THIRTY-NINE

1909

After a whirlwind week of swimming, eating ice cream, and watching boat races, Janie, Kenneth, and his parents took Angel's Flight, the incline railway, up Old Baldhead Dune for a picnic. From Lookout Pavilion, Lake Michigan stretched like taffy to the horizon. Bunting and Japanese lanterns strung across hotels like necklaces. Onlookers on crowded piers cheered boaters.

Mrs. Baum served sandwiches, peaches, and General Jinjur cookies. They watched boat races, screamed for winners, and belted out "Blow Ye Winds" and "Heave Away, me Jollies."

Mr. Baum tended to regatta duties in the late afternoon. As evening settled in, bands entertained from ferries. Bonfires flickered on shore. After sundown, the glittering boat parade progressed across Black Lake.

Fireworks spangled the sky, reflected in water—cannon crackers and pinwheels lighting the darkness. In the *Maybelle* next to Kenneth, Janie clutched a popcorn bag, each minute closer to goodbyes. Kenneth's hand plunged into her bag.

"Catch!" He tossed her a kernel. When she caught it in her mouth, the Baums clapped. Kenneth wolfed a handful.

For the first time, Janie attended the ball at the yacht club. With no dance experience, she trusted Kenneth to lead her steps. They spent as much time laughing as dancing.

The next morning, when Aunt Sophie arrived, Mrs. Baum produced a gift—a framed piece of muslin embroidered with words: *You must walk. It is a long journey, through a country that is sometimes pleasant and sometimes dark and terrible.* The border represented a variety of terrain, weather, and seasons. The quote was enclosed by stitched snowflakes, autumn leaves, buds, blossoms, a gnarled tree from an enchanted forest, and clouds with silver linings.

Janie embraced her. "It's lovely. Thank you."

Aunt Sophie teared up. "You've meant the world to my chinchilla."

Kenneth hugged Janie. "I hope to see you again. But you'll sooner see Robert or Harry. Robert's Edna is here. Harry's sweet on a girl, too." He smirked. "He's practically married, all grown up. He won't snatch your popcorn anymore."

"Unlike you. You've been a brother to me, annoyance and all."

"If that's what makes a good sister, you've been one too." He grinned, blinking hard.

She leaned in, whispering, "I hope you always get the best chicken leg."

"I hope you climb more dunes and sail to distant places." His voice cracked. "But hide your Cracker Jack better so nobody steals it."

Her eyes widened. "You were always my prime suspect." He laughed.

Janie took Mrs. Baum's hands. "Thank you for many kindnesses, cooking together, and beautiful handiwork. I'll never do justice to your patient teaching of embroidery."

"You'll do fine if you practice. Oh, dear, I'll miss you

terribly." Mrs. Baum hugged her, then wiped her eyes. "You've been a daughter to us."

"You've been a mother to me." Janie sniffled. "Your General Jinjur cookies and Welsh rarebit are the best."

Finally, quivering, Janie stood before Mr. Baum, her head level with his shoulder. Through the fog of tears, she saw his kind, gray eyes. She threw herself into his open arms, burrowed her face into his cigar-scented chest, and sobbed. His tears dropped on her hair.

When she stood back, he retrieved his handkerchief. "Why'd the Tin Woodman want a heart anyhow?" He dabbed the hanky on Janie's cheek. "Remember, dear, make room for fairies every day. I'll write you without fail."

"We'll all write," Kenneth added, tears streaming.

Mrs. Baum sniffed. "A fine soggy lot we are."

"A *hyperooden rostratus*, for sure." Laughter erupted. But what Janie's future landscape held without Mr. Baum, she'd no idea.

Aunt Sophie squeezed her shoulder. "Time to go, dumpling."

Janie couldn't bear it. She let the wizard of her imagination fill her view one last time, then spun and dashed down the steps.

<hr>

1980

Carrie blinked tears away. "Was that the last time you saw him?"

Mrs. Gordon nodded. "They sold the cottage and moved to California the next year. Harry stayed in the Midwest. The others went west, Rob a bit later. We maintained steady correspondence for ten years until Mr. Baum passed away in 1919, at nearly sixty-three."

"I'm glad you two corresponded."

"He wrote faithfully. Ken had the first Baum daughter. Mr. Baum insisted she be called Ozma. Robert and Edna returned to Macatawa often, to her family's cottage. In 1932, Mrs. Baum visited the area with Robert. She lived to be ninety-one."

"They brought out your best. Love, wisdom, and courage."

"Mr. Baum once said, 'Stunt, dwarf, or destroy the imagination of a child, and you've taken away its chances of success in life.'" Mrs. Gordon looked away.

Dragons not yet slain. What happened to that sweet girl with a promising future, nourished by Aunt Sophie and the Baums?

"In 1910, he wrote *The Emerald City of Oz*. He sent a copy." From the drawer, she withdrew the book, full of vibrant green ink illustrations.

Carrie read the inscription.

Dear Charlotte Rose,

I've a solution for those who babble too much. Remember talking about this? If someone can't talk clearly and straight to the point, they are sent to Rigmarole Town, whereas in the U.S., they roam free and torture innocent people. Surely, Mr. Taradiddle has plenty to say about that. And remember, dear, simplicity and kindness are the only magic wands that work wonders.

Ozily, Mr. Baum

"Simplicity and kindness." What happened after 1910?

Mrs. Gordon presented a colorful Ozian map and led Carrie to the porch. "My garden's a tribute to Oz." The map's blue, purple, yellow, and red regions corresponded to the garden's triangular sections: blue forget-me-nots, purple dianthus, yellow lupines, and red poppies.

"Too bad the neighbors can't enjoy this. Have you considered removing the fence?"

"I've lived my entire life behind fences. Why change now?"

"Why not? You've been giving me glimpses."

The old woman shook her head. "It's not safe."

Carrie read *Pilgrim's Progress* on the porch. Christian and Hopeful's easier path led to Giant Despair, ruler of Doubting Castle. Bones and skulls littered the yard. The giant threw them in the dungeon for trespassing. Christian and Hopeful prayed for deliverance until Christian realized he had the key called Promise in his pocket. It unlocked any door. They escaped the dungeon and returned to the King's Highway.

Mrs. Gordon removed her sunglasses. "How'd Christian forget he had a key?"

Carrie swayed on the swing. "In the pit of despair, there's no recalling such things."

Mrs. Gordon frowned. "Perhaps Mr. Bunyan's saying that if you believe the promises, you'll have peace in spite of unslain dragons."

Carrie stopped swinging. Though her hair fluttered with the breeze in the sweetness of freesia, her mind backed into a dark corner no dahlias could brighten.

Before more questions came, Carrie left.

FORTY

Saturday, June 21, 1980

Dirk pulled up, radio blasting Bruce Springsteen's "Born to Run." Playing air guitar and singing as if part of the E Street Band, he somehow set Carrie's cooler and bag in the trunk. In the car, he plopped a case of tapes on her lap. "Consider me your own personal deejay."

The case held a musical array: Linda Ronstadt, Neil Diamond, Stevie Wonder, Motown. Christian, bluegrass, and classical. "Such variety. What're you in the mood for?"

"Making you happy. You decide."

His reply touched her. "No disco?" She read labels. "*Finger-Snapping Toe-Tapping. Lemons & Vinegar. Melancholy Part I: Affirming Your Bad Mood. Melancholy Part II: The Abyss.* What on earth?"

"My sister Greta wanted tapes for different moods. These are copies."

"What's *Lemons & Vinegar?*"

"An angry tape, with heavier rock and roll."

"*Morning Coffee?*" She scanned titles, including Chicago tunes and Jimmy Buffet.

"Mood lifters. Light-hearted, energetic songs."

"*Rock & Eagle*?"

"God metaphors. Christian praise songs."

"'Green, Green Grass of Home,' 'Candle in the Wind.' *Melancholy* I understand. But *The Abyss*?"

"Where you plunge to when love doesn't work out. Or anything."

She was curious about his dives into love.

In Saugatuck, Dirk turned onto 64th Street, heading north.

"We're taking country roads?"

He offered a sly look. "The more direct route to my plan for a wonderful day."

Smiling, Carrie played Elton John's song "Goodbye, Yellow Brick Road."

"Seems adventures aren't substitutes for home," Dirk said. "Thinking of the Carrie version of Oz. Permission to meddle?"

"Okay."

"Will your book café require your yellow brick road going a different direction than Brian the accountant's American dream?"

She stewed, skimming titles. "Amazing how Baum's story lives on in different forms and contexts, part of popular culture."

He shrugged. "It's a rhetorical question anyhow."

She replaced Elton John with *Finger-Snapping Toe-Tapping*. Billy Joel's "Scenes From an Italian Restaurant" began. They sang along. Even while driving, Dirk played a mean air saxophone. Brian would never loosen up like that.

"We're here." The street sliced through woods, no lake. "Let me set the stage." He lowered his voice ominously. "Before us, a Victorian castle. Some say Baum modeled Glinda's castle after this one. A German immigrant built it in 1890. His family lived like recluses to avoid the evils of Holland's city life. One daughter fell in love with a Dutchman. You know how *they* are." He winked. "The daughters weren't happy here, so they moved to Holland in 1892. The castle became a children's summer camp, then a resort—Castle Park. In 1896, it was transformed into an inn with surrounding cottages. Supposedly, the Baums ate here often."

He drove through the lot. Trees and flower gardens surrounded the ivy-covered German castle. "This weekend, the International Wizard of Oz Club meets for their twentieth annual gathering. *Here,* since 1967. They have displays, lectures, auctions, quizzes, and more."

"Wow, an Oz convention. Now I've heard everything."

"No, you haven't. They also have Munchkin conventions in the east, Winkie Conventions in the West. Gilliken ones up north. Last year, for the MGM movie's 40th anniversary, Margaret Hamilton who played the Wicked Witch showed up here."

They drove a mile north to Macatawa Park. Dirk's friend Gerrit hosted a walking tour. Black Lake's name changed in 1935. From Lake Macatawa's harbor, he pointed out previous south shore sites of Jenison Electric Park, Angel's Flight up Old Baldhead Dune, and Macatawa Hotel, replaced by Point West Restaurant. On the north shore were Mt. Pisgah and Ottawa State Park, former site of Hotel Ottawa.

They meandered among cottages, including the possible site of the Baum house on the south end. Fire consumed many homes in the 1920s. Pavement replaced boardwalks. Some cottages clung to Victorian vestiges: sprawling wrap-around porches, turrets, and peaked roofs.

Gerrit said the Dutch started digging the channel in the 1850s. In 1907, a steel tower and fog signal replaced the first lighthouse. A light tower was added in 1936. Twenty years later, it was painted red, then christened Big Red during a 1974 campaign to save the lighthouse.

In late morning, Dirk and Carrie waded along Lake Michigan's shoreline. In deliciously clear detail, she imagined the porch where Mr. Baum and Charlotte talked about stories, overlooking breezy treetops. Eating Welsh rarebit and Jell-O dished out with riddles and puns. The wired step buzzed, the typewriter plinked, the printing press whirred. The fob watch ticked, the rocker creaked, the ice cream maker cranked to hearty renditions of "Oh Susanna."

Mr. Baum gulps lemonade. Harry and Kenneth tumble onto the porch. Charlotte scampers down the stairway. Mr. Baum dips in water with his hat and cigar ...

"Reminiscing?" Dirk said.

Carrie startled. "Yeah, for Mrs. Gordon." She shared her reverie.

"How fast do you think they ran into this water?"

"Watch." She jogged in, knee-high. "Race you to that buoy."

They swam, splashed, and laughed until Carrie traipsed from the water, shirt clinging to skin. A pang of guilt rippled through her. What would Brian say?

She didn't care. Dirk was a friend, and available. Brian kept canceling.

In the car, Dirk said, "Let's play Mr. Baum's three-object game. Name three things."

"How 'bout the three-lyric game?" She cited three random Billy Joel lines.

He fabricated an animated tale, then pointed out Hope College in Holland. "Remember the 1871 Chicago fire? It was here, too. Downtown went up in flames. But not a flame touched Van Vleck Hall, comprising all of Hope College then. Any miracles like *that* ever happen at Calvin?"

She rolled her eyes.

At Captain Sundae, they indulged in Tammy Turtle and Fudge Overboard sundaes.

On a bench, Dirk took a bite. "I predict this place will be the *wave* of Holland's future. Every seadog, scallywag, and son of a biscuit eater will drop anchor here."

Carrie snickered. "Son of a biscuit eater?"

"Mild insult. Pirate talk."

"Don't tell me piracy is another pastime of yours."

"Hardly. But we tossed around our share of pirate lingo sailing to South America." He adopted a throaty tone. "Ahoy, me mateys! All hands on deck. Heave ho!" He shaded his eyes, as if scanning the ocean. "Shiver me timbers! Batten down the hatches, you salty sea dogs. Thar she blows! The most dangerous creature known to mankind."

"Whales?"

"No. Woman!" She punched him, but he continued undaunted. "Sirens luring sailors to their death. Women known to melt your heart, cut it from your chest, and suck you dry. Only one solution. Get me my rum, or you walk the plank." He leaned her way, eyebrows raised. "Savvy?"

"Blimey!" She aimed for vicious. "Careful, or you'll be three sheets to the wind."

"That's the point. I'm pretending I can escape her wiles."

"Too late." She lowered her voice. "I'll cut your heart out, and no one will ever know. Dead men tell no tales." They laughed and high-fived. Brian would give her the evil eye for jesting about alcohol. Or pirates.

Dirk lifted a spoonful tantalizingly close. "Want a bite, me hearty?"

She closed her lips over the creamy spoonful. "Good, but not much fudge."

He squinted. "Finagling me for more?"

She smiled and took the next bite he offered, then wrinkled her brow.

"You scalawag," Dirk said. "You're gonna hornswoggle me out of more?"

She lifted a spoonful of Tammy Turtle to his mouth. "Better than rum, I promise." Her arm against his sent a sweet tingle down her spine.

Dirk unhooked the rope from the sailboat in Macatawa Harbor, Gerrit at the rudder. They were off. Carrie hoped the thrill she felt showed more than her fear. After five minutes on the four-seat daysailer, she wished she'd had more adventures. But she'd followed Brian to games like a puppy dog, leaving time for nothing else.

Sunshine bounced on the water. Between glides and turns, her mind zipped to 1905, Charlotte riding with the Baums on the *Maybelle*. Reeling in fish. Racing Lilliputian boats. The ferryboat *Gladys* dropping off summer folk at the yacht club. The *Lizzie Walsh* happily steaming to downtown Holland. Crowds cheering regatta races. Venetian Night fireworks.

After an hour, Gerrit maneuvered through the channel, past Big Red, and onto Lake Michigan. Gladly wearing the required life vest, Carrie gripped the handle. Water sprayed as the boat tilted precariously on choppy waves. She jumped around as the sail swung back and forth during turns. She got flustered when he shouted instructions about starboard or port, bow and stern, jibbing and tacking. Finally, she yelled, "Just say left or right, front or back!"

Dirk laughed. "Don't worry. If you fall in, I'll rescue you."

She braced herself against the fiberglass edge. "This must seem tame for you."

"Tame but not boring." He grinned.

She would've smacked him but didn't dare let go.

"About face!" Gerrit tightened the rope as they turned from the wind. The boat tilted nearly perpendicular to the water. They capsized. *Splash*! Carrie tumbled into the lake. Frigid water swallowed her. Limbs circled in panic. The life vest popped her up, mouth full. She spit water out and laughed, bobbing on waves, catapulted from terror to exhilaration in mere seconds.

Dirk and Gerrit scrambled to upright the boat and climbed in. Dirk pulled Carrie up with a firm hand. "You okay?" He touched the small of her back, sending a comfortable shiver from shoulder to toes.

She shook water from her hair. "Batten down the hatches!" Whatever that meant.

"Prepare for trouble?" He grasped her shoulder. His strength steadied her.

"No, blimey! I'll have to work on pirate talk. Heave ho instead. All hands on deck."

He laughed. "Okay, let's give it some muscle. Try again?" His hand slid off her shoulder.

"I'm game." She took the rope Gerrit offered.

Dirk winked. "See why it's anything but dull?"

"Get to work, sailor," Carrie said. "Lest you become shark bait."

"Whoa." Gerrit whistled. "She's telling you."

"Not worried," Dirk said. "I'm her ride home."

Later, coasting on the smooth channel, Dirk handed her a Dr. Pepper from the compartment.

"Thanks." Carrie grabbed it. "I like the cut of your jib."

The guys exchanged perplexed glances. "You like his sail?" Dirk said.

"No. It means good idea." She popped the can open and took a swig. "You might know pirate talk, but I know old P.E.I. lingo."

FORTY-ONE

Saturday, June 21, 1980

Stepping inside his parents' house, Dirk yelled, "Mom, Dad, batten down the hatches!"

"Calling me trouble?" Carrie said.

Dirk chuckled. "Nope, that's me."

The kitchen featured Delft lace, tiles, and plates. His mom breezed over, hugged him, then took Carrie's hand as Dirk introduced them.

Alice smiled, blue eyes like Dirk's. "Hope you didn't endure much pirate talk. That's been running rampant since age three. We should've sunk that pirate ship we bought him."

Carrie laughed and offered muffins from her cooler. "From the 1900 Broderick Resort secret recipe file."

Alice set the muffins in a basket. "Lovely! We'll have them tonight." She grasped her son's shoulders. "Your father bought a new grill."

"Seriously? Grill number three, eh?"

"Four. But only three work."

Roy Vandenakker popped in, an older version of Dirk,

distinguished by gray-streaked hair. "Figured I'd try it out on company. Welcome!"

"Dad grills through every season—rain, shine, sleet, or snow. Like the mailman."

"Are vegetarian family members cut from the will?" Carrie asked.

"Absolutely," Dirk said. "And get thirty lashes with a wet noodle."

"Or with a slab of steak." Roy waved his tongs.

Carrie giggled. "Why three grills? For parties?"

"On holidays, I cook side dishes that won't fit in the oven with turkey, and I take all three for the church picnic. Each grill has its own purpose. Come here."

Roy led them outside to a new grill sizzling with sirloin steaks. It stood proudly between two others, one cooking potatoes and asparagus. "The broken one was best for shish-kabobs, corn, and other vegetables. This one has wood chips for smoking meats, that one's for rotisserie. It also cooks a mean prime rib roast." Roy pointed. "This grill makes the best herb-crusted lamb chops, salmon with maple soy glaze, and skewered bacon-wrapped shrimp."

Mrs. Gordon would be flabbergasted. "Amazing!"

"That one specializes in turkey and Birmingham barbecued spareribs. It has a larger indirect cooking area. I sear the meat over the flame, then turn it off. Grill turned oven."

"Which grill makes the best pizza?" Carrie expected only a laugh.

"That one." Roy pointed again.

"Once, I grilled Hawaiian style with ham and pineapple," Dirk said. "Working my way up to the forbidden grill."

Roy raised his tongs. "Around here, Carrie, you don't mess with a man and his grills."

Carrie surveyed the yard—a modest home, much smaller than her parents' extravagant house. Tidy flower borders exuded contentment from loving care. Like his family.

A dark-haired young woman joined them. Dirk introduced Greta.

"We're finally good enough for you, bro?" Greta said. "What's so exciting about Wolcott that you can't come home more often?"

"*That* should be obvious." Alice glanced at Carrie.

Dirk blushed. "Just friends, Mom. Remember?" To Carrie, he mouthed *sorry*.

"Iced tea, Carrie?" Greta placed a full glass in her hand and led them to the screen porch.

The decor was homey, inviting, unlike her mother's pretentious matching table runners and placemats. Alice's attention to detail was touchable, much like the conversation.

Alice offered the vegetable platter. "How long have you been in Wolcott, Carrie?"

"Just this summer. I'm living with my grandparents." *Get it over with.* "An elderly woman hired me to record family history."

"We don't value that generation enough," Alice said. "They've much to say before it's lost forever."

"What have you learned, Carrie?" Roy stood in the doorway, still minding the grills.

"Mrs. Gordon had a friendship with L. Frank Baum." She explained how Janie became his yearly guest. "That's why Dirk invited me here. To see Macatawa Resort and Castle Park." They remarked on Ozmapolitan Conventions.

"Where'd you go to school?" Alice asked.

"Dirk didn't warn you? Calvin. Just kick me out right now."

"We'll overlook it this time." Roy winked.

Greta asked, "Did you go to Hope-Calvin basketball games?"

"Some." Too busy following Brian to his own college games.

"What was your major?" Alice asked.

"Elementary ed. Only to discover I don't want to teach."

"How frustrating," Alice said. "But education's still a solid stepping stone, one of those intangibles you can't put a price on."

"Then why'd we fork over so much money to Hope?" Roy asked, prompting laughter.

Dirk munched on crackers and cheese. "Carrie's opening a book café."

"Honestly?" Alice said. "What do you envision?"

Carrie winced. "It's nothing, really."

"Baloney," Dirk said. "She's got the whole thing planned. It'll open this fall."

Carrie tightened her jaw, then explained the café's literary focus, nooks highlighting authors or time periods.

Greta's eyes widened. "I'll go weekly!"

"Sounds irresistible," Alice said. "What's on the menu?"

"Grilled food, I hope." Roy raised his grilling fork.

"Are you for hire?" Carrie asked. "I'm serving food reminiscent of time periods or books. Capturing the setting's flavor."

"Like a Dr. Seuss book nook for green eggs and ham," Dirk said.

"That's Dirk's hangout." Greta punched his arm. "He never grows up."

"Thanks for the compliment," Dirk said. "Don't wanna turn into a stuffy, old codger." Though living the dream of codgers at the hardware store.

"Fat chance, son." Roy checked the grill again. "Ready to roll."

They sat in the screen porch, table spread with potatoes, asparagus, and sirloin marinaded in citrus and soy sauce, topped with mushrooms, along with salad and Broderick muffins.

"Delicious muffins," Alice said. "You love baking?"

Carrie's comfort with them empowered her. "I was

resident baker of my dorm, even made *olliebollen* in the bathroom."

Greta snorted, eyes mirthful. "Seriously?"

"I feel vindicated," Roy said. "And you thought having three grills was obsessive."

"Desperate times call for desperate measures," Carrie said. "You obviously understand following your *passion*, with four-season grilling." She said the word *passion* for Dirk's benefit.

He grinned at her. She blushed.

Seeking menu tips, Carrie picked Roy's brain about grilled food, then asked, "What do you do, Mr. Vandenakker? When not grilling."

"I've owned a real estate agency for eight years."

Greta snickered. "Which came about to avoid paying a huge fine."

Roy explained. "My brother John and I used to fix houses—"

"Akin to running slave labor in old money pits," Dirk added.

"Slave, nothing," Roy said. "You were well paid."

"Money doesn't compensate for such harrowing experiences." Dirk pointed with his knife. "Falling through steps, rewiring rooms five times."

"At least you weren't electrocuted." Alice took a bite of steak.

Roy continued. "For years, John and I fixed and sold houses, running our own construction crew and sales, until I got a warning from the state. We'd have to pay a fine or establish ourselves as brokers, since we passed the sales limit."

"What'd you do?" Carrie reveled in sprightly dialogue.

"In 1966, John bought the Wolcott hardware store. I got my real estate license, kept fixing houses, then started my own business. Instead of paying a fine, I passed the broker exam."

"And hasn't been in much trouble since." Alice smiled. "Except around here."

More laughter. Carrie marveled at their ribbing. She asked Roy about reputable construction workers, then said, "Your flowers are gorgeous, Mrs. Vandenakker."

"Too bad she couldn't cultivate green thumbs in us kids," Greta said.

"So, I shouldn't leave potted plants with you if I go out of town?"

"Only if you want them put out of *our* misery while you're gone," Dirk quipped. "Greta hasn't mastered the watering technique."

"Look who's talking," Greta said. "Dirk can't even keep cactus alive."

Dirk shrugged. "Plants don't like me."

"It's your rock and roll they don't like," Roy said. "Plants are sensitive to loud music."

"They prefer classical," Alice added. "Or bluegrass."

"Did you do a scientific study on plants and music?" Carrie asked.

"Honey, I don't need science for that," Alice said. "Walk in the room when Dirk's playing his Boston records. Or Doobie Brothers. Then watch the plants cower, blossoms closing in midday. Utterly depressed."

Dirk straightened. "On the contrary, 'China Grove' is their favorite song."

"They also wilted when certain folks practiced their violin and trumpet." Roy turned to Alice. "But when *you* play the piano, darlin', the plants sing along."

Alice leaned a bent arm on her husband's shoulder and kissed his cheek.

Roy chuckled and kissed her hand. Their affection moved Carrie. Dirk certainly had a wonderful role model of a loving husband.

Dirk went for round two. "Look, nobody else named the plants, proving I care more."

Greta whooped. "Naming them makes up for killing them?"

"Maybe naming them is what killed them," Alice said. "Who'd want to be called Larry, Curly, or Moe? Or Ringo? Not to mention Springsteen."

Carrie wanted to float away in the delirious flood of friendly banter. Even outspoken disagreement about community programs was accompanied by respectful acknowledgment of differing opinions. Maybe this was how Janie felt at the Baums' dinner table, basking in acceptance, humor, and idiosyncrasies.

Perhaps Dirk's difficult time put life in perspective for his family. More love and acceptance filled this small home than even one room of her parents' three thousand square-foot house.

FORTY-TWO

June 21, 1980

After multiple card games, Dirk and Carrie left at dusk. In the car, Carrie sputtered, "Why'd you bring up the café plans I *confided* in you?"

"Whoa!" Dirk balked. "Back up the train. Didn't we just have a fantastic day together?"

"Ninety-seven percent."

"What happened to three percent?" He looked bewildered. "Just round up to 100. I don't recall classified information."

"That's where you could be more astute. I don't tell just anyone about my book café."

"You told me the first night we met." He seemed more astounded than angry.

"But I asked you not to tell anyone. I was upset when you told Mrs. Gordon."

"But your book café's the coolest thing. Incidentally, you did great hiding your irritation. You're one class act, Miss Carrie."

She bristled. "You need one to compensate for your clodhopping."

His voice quieted. "Hey, are you afraid they'll think it's beyond your reach?" She stared out the dark window. Dirk sighed. "Guess I hit a raw spot."

"I'm afraid of not getting the loan. The fewer people who know about it, the better."

"Are you afraid of failing?"

Critical words from Brian and her parents flooded. "I worry about what people think."

"There's a cure for that."

"Right. Stop caring."

"Hey, I don't understand your secrecy, but I'm sorry for blabbing. I was wrong."

Would she ever get used to receiving apologies? His kindness softened her. "It's okay. I'm sorry for yelling."

"Incidentally, please excuse my mom's assumptions. I told her we weren't dating."

"It's fine. She's adorable."

"She's great," Dirk said. "Despite putting her foot in her mouth. Runs in the family."

Carrie relished his parents' mutual affection, jabs over plants, music, and multiple grills. "They didn't critique my summer job or aversion to teaching."

"Why would they?"

"It's what I'm used to at home."

"Time to surround yourself with different people."

She looked at him. "I am."

"I'm sad to hear about your family's criticism. Must be tough."

"My parents think my sister Amy's the actress, the starlet, but *I'm* the one pretending I'm not angry. Or hurt."

"Why pretend?"

"To survive. To keep the peace. Otherwise, I get the cold shoulder."

"So, they don't have the privilege of knowing the *real* Carrie, like I'm starting to." He paused. "During my rough patch, I learned it's better to put the truth of raw feelings on the table, before God and people you trust, to deal with them honestly. Being fake doesn't give you the chance to know real grace and acceptance."

That would never fly at home. Even Oma and Opa didn't know her true feelings. Or what happened in sixth grade.

He cleared his throat. "Take the mask off. Don't be afraid to be yourself."

Had he been conferring with Mrs. Gordon?

Dirk's voice was steady, warm. "You probably hate not being heard or seen. Yet you're *afraid* of being heard or seen." She looked away. "Hey, look at me, Carrie."

Grateful for the shield of darkness, she stiffened.

The car slowed. He pulled over, put on flashers, and faced her.

She looked at him. His brow wrinkled in sadness. He touched her cheek, as if to hold her in place. "I'm sorry it's been that way for you."

She blinked back tears as he drove again. Her cheek tingled where he'd touched her.

"May I cheer you up?" He tapped the cassettes. "Pick *Finger-Snapping Toe-Tapping*."

Ready to change moods, she complied. "What's next after your summer gig?"

"Gerrit and I will backpack in Appalachia at the end of August. In September, I might head back to camp. They have great weekend retreats for kids. Gotta decide soon."

Why'd her heart sadden? "Or keep playing gigs at the café. If you weren't addicted to scenery changes."

"You're a settled old soul," he said sweetly.

Euphemism for dull. Wolcott was a sleepy town. The whole kingdom slept, waiting for someone to kiss the princess, break the spell, wake everyone up.

When Aretha Franklin's "Respect" blared from the

speakers, Carrie snapped her fingers. Dirk joined in. They sang and danced as much as seat belts allowed.

At home, Dirk walked her to the door. "Thanks for joining me today."

"I had a great time. Your air saxophone rivals none."

He grinned. "Sailing on the Atlantic is nothing compared to sailing with you."

"I'll lie awake wondering if that's a compliment or not."

"A compliment. Look, don't take this as encroaching on Brian's territory, but if you don't have plans for the Fourth, I'd love to take you to fireworks over Lake Macatawa. I have friends with a cottage. We'll sail again." He winked. "A little more Mrs. G. nostalgia."

"Still strictly business?"

"Let's call it friendly business."

Friendly. Then why'd she feel such pleasant electric shocks when he touched her at Captain Sundae, on the sailboat, or in the car?

"I'm getting to know you, Carrie. I enjoy our time together. Will you consider it?"

She hesitated. "Yes."

"Thatta girl. I like the cut of your jib."

The day's fun washed over her in the muggy air as he walked away. Through the screen door, she watched him drive off, waving.

Fireflies dotted the yard with fuzzy illuminations. *Darkness is just as alive as daylight.* Little Janie Broderick found solace in the face of Mr. Baum, the only man who saw her with the tenderness of a father. And tonight, for the first time, Carrie shared a sliver of her pain with Dirk. He'd looked at her with acceptance, kindness. As if he felt her pain, wishing he could remove it.

She shivered. She'd never entrusted her pain to Brian.

Instead, she trusted Dirk. But their lives were night and day. She relished well-decorated places, infused with homeyness, permeated with personal taste. She craved a beckoning porch, a welcoming kitchen, a place to inhabit, inviting you to pick up your feet after a long day and stay for years. Claustrophobic Dirk yearned for places far away, new vistas and explorations.

Ripples of moonlight swirled through clouds, imprinting webs over the grass. *A dreamer is one who can only find his way by moonlight.* She winced. Janie, the dreamer. Where did her dreams get her? Would Carrie's fear of failure and criticism overwhelm her own dreams?

In the kitchen, she held the chicken ornament. *For your journey, through pleasant and dark places.* What about confusing places?

Dirk's words echoed Mr. Baum's. *Take the mask off. Don't be afraid to be yourself. Even Glinda, with all her magic, won't do transformations.*

Only Brian would provide a stable future. Security. But at what price? What if the loan fell through? If her only link to parental approval was Brian, could she continue not being seen or heard?

FORTY-THREE

Monday, June 23, 1980

Over John Dough & General Jinjur's Banana Jinjurbread and Chai Tea, Mrs. Gordon asked, "How was Holland?"

"Wonderful!" Carrie described Macatawa and sailing, then Dirk's family, his dad's grills, and how sweet everybody was.

Mrs. Gordon squinted. "If you don't stop smiling, I'll need sunglasses. Dirk certainly elicits a chipper mood. Hmm."

"Look, it takes more than fun to make relationships work. He's too unfocused."

"Not enough like Brian."

Carrie sipped tea. "Cinnamon, cloves, and ...?"

"You're clumsily changing the subject."

"Yup." Carrie mentioned the Castle Park Oz Club conventions.

"Harry lived in Knox, Indiana. He and his wife Brenda hosted yearly conventions on Bass Lake, starting in 1961. Their lodge was called Ozcot. After he passed away in 1967, Brenda hosted conventions at Castle Park for years."

"Did you attend?"

Mrs. Gordon stirred her tea. "Such conventions are akin to standing in line to see the king, when the king is your uncle."

"What about journalistic pursuits?"

"Today, I'll share my first journalistic venture. Teddy was relieved Mr. Baum moved, lest his lack of churchgoing influence me. But I listened plenty as the preacher talked about love, how love wants the highest good for someone, even at great sacrifice. I had a plan."

* * *

Janie, 18
1910

In April, Janie proofread her letter to Teddy's mother:

Dear Mrs. Callaghan,

> *Your son Teddy works for my father. We've courted for two years. Teddy wants you safe. I found a way to bring you here —alone—feasible with an anonymous donor. I obtained a lawyer in Syracuse specializing in international law and immigration. He can meet you in New Brunswick after sending travel fare. He'll escort you to Syracuse. I'll meet you there with Dr. and Mrs. Weaver, then travel to Michigan. You can board with my aunt, Sophie McKinnon.*

Janie included Auntie's address and signed the letter, pleased with her Nellie Bly efforts. Dr. Weaver had recommended the Syracuse attorney. She sent the letter to Mae's neighbor, the MacFadyens, the address on Teddy's letters.

Like Nellie Bly's asylum venture, Janie labored undercover, telling nobody. Her father would never approve, nor give Teddy time off work. Teddy accepted stringent boundaries, for

Sawyer Broderick offered the chance to pursue business aspirations. Janie's newspaper wages and the pittance from her father would pay the lawyer and travel expenses to bring Mae Callaghan to Wolcott. She'd go to Syracuse, her own adventure. Despite postponing college, the opportunity to rescue Mae was the greater good.

Six weeks later, mail arrived at Aunt Sophie's.

Dear Miss Janie,

I'm so taken by your generous offer that tears are wetting this paper. Due to worsened circumstances, your letter is most welcome. This is truly God's gift, to see my son again after five years.

You said to come alone, but alas, Teddy doesn't know of his four-year-old sister Beatrice, born the spring after he left. She'll be no trouble and require little fare. All correspondence must be directed to my neighbors, the MacFadyens.

Beatrice—like her fairy friend! *God's gift.* Janie overlooked that notion. Wouldn't a better gift be living without torment? She couldn't imagine Mother missing her the way Mae missed Teddy. Would Mae love Janie? Like a daughter? Then later, as a daughter-in-law.

That evening, after wiring money and writing letters about final arrangements, Janie waved Mae's letter at Mrs. Weaver, who left her with Teddy in the parlor.

Janie joined him on the couch. "I have a surprise! Read this."

"My mother's handwriting." He read through tears. "How's this happening?"

"I arranged it. I know how badly you want to see her again."

"Beatrice, my little sister." Anxiety shadowed his face. "What if my father hurt her?"

She touched his arm. "That's past now."

"Janie, how's this possible? Lawyer, train fare."

"First, I'm going to Syracuse to meet her. I proposed this trip to Mr. Ferguson as part one in a series to hometowns of popular authors. This year is *The Wizard of Oz's* tenth anniversary. Mr. Baum's from the Syracuse area. Mr. Ferguson's paying me for three *feature* articles, written as me, not Isabel."

"He'll cover your expenses?"

"Partial reimbursement. The articles are about Mr. Baum and his roots. Your mother moving here is pure bonus."

"You're becoming Nellie Bly. But who's funding the remainder?"

"I am, with money saved from the newspaper job. Please don't tell anyone."

His words stumbled out. "Your own money? Why didn't you tell me?"

"You wouldn't have let me spend it. It's my gift. Everything's set. Dr. and Mrs. Weaver will accompany me."

He embraced her, then kissed her cheek, her chin, her mouth. She returned his passion. His fingers combed her hair. Pulse raging, she pressed her hand to his chest.

"Care for tea?" Mrs. Weaver asked from the doorway.

The two lovers jumped apart as if a firecracker exploded beneath them. Discombobulated, Janie smoothed her hair as he checked his shirt buttons.

Teddy handed Mrs. Weaver the letter. "My mother's coming to Wolcott!"

Mrs. Weaver and her husband rejoiced with Teddy as Janie fanned her face, trying to cool down.

Mesmerized, Janie drank in views of farms, towns, and summer's emerald green rolling hills as the train chugged east. Newsies sold newspapers, sandwiches, and soda pop. Artists sketched, anticipating inspirational beauty of New York's Finger Lakes. After supper, the sun lowered behind her, the moon rose. *A dreamer is one who can only find his way by moonlight.*

This trip stirred the pot of such aspirations as Janie finally began to live her dream. Syracuse, as the first of many destinations, mirrored Nellie Bly's "around the world" adventure.

In Syracuse, Janie took Kodak snapshots on every block. Such amazing architecture! Sunlight reflected in the canal that split Clinton Square in half. The Salina Street bridge rose as yellow, red, blue, and pink barges passed below—all sights Mr. Baum saw when he'd lived there. The new Soldiers and Sailors Monument soared over five stories tall. Dr. Weaver pointed out the Jerry Rescue Building. Storefronts belied the turmoil occurring after runaway slave William "Jerry" Henry was jailed, where abolitionists took a bold stand against the Fugitive Slave Act. Finally, Janie stood on the brink of her own rescue opportunity.

A window display caught her eye: Baum's Castorine Oil, the *LF Baum* signature on the bottle's label. She snapped another picture. Where had the Cardiff Giant been displayed?

The salmon-colored bricks of the Syracuse County Savings Bank formed a Gothic facade with pointed arches and spires, a triangular flag waving overhead. Janie imagined a princess watching from its tower. Long ago, that princess was she, locked in her decaying home until Mr. Baum dashed in to release her. Now the prisoner was Mae, waiting for Janie's arrival.

Janie had written to Mrs. Mary Louise Baum Brewster weeks earlier to arrange lodging. Eight years older than her brother Frank, Mrs. Brewster greeted her warmly. Over tea, Janie bombarded her with inquiries about Syracuse and her childhood. Finally, Mrs. Brewster said, "You certainly are a journalist, my dear. So many questions!"

Janie stirred sugar into her tea. "Your brother inspired me."

She chuckled. "His enthusiasm is contagious. He still encourages me to persevere with my poetry. But my efforts only met dismal failure."

"Your Rose Lawn Alphabet was published in *The Rose Lawn Journal*. It was the impetus for creating my own ABCs for Macatawa Park. And my first newspaper." Janie told her about working the printing press with Mr. Baum.

Mrs. Brewster poured more tea. "Frank's such a dear, even as a pesky little brother. Perhaps he's making it up to me by immortalizing me in his stories as Annabel's sister and Aunt Jane's niece." Mrs. Brewster plucked *Mother Goose in Prose* from the shelf. "Read this."

Janie read Mr. Baum's inscription, dated 1897:

"When I was young I longed to write a great novel that should win me fame. Now that I am getting old my first book is written to amuse children. For aside from my evident inability to do anything great, I have learned to regard fame as a will-o-the-wisp which, when caught, is not worth the possession; but to please a child is a sweet and lovely thing that warms one's heart and brings its own reward."

Deeply touched, Janie copied his words to quote in her article.

"He'd been so worried about money, weary of his traveling sales job," his sister said. "He forsook many creative but fruitless endeavors. This book launched a new course."

Later, Mrs. Brewster showed Janie where young Frank met Maud Gage. Facing the house, Janie placed herself decades back. *Consider yourself loved, Miss Gage.* And she was, even after four children and myriad mishaps. Janie craved that devotion from Teddy.

The next three days spun a thrilling whirlwind as Mrs. Brewster accompanied Janie through an itinerary planned with feature articles in mind. Mrs. Brewster showed her various residences: Rust Street, where the Baums moved when Frank was five, houses where Frank and Maud lived as a young couple, and the family's axle grease business in the Weiting Block.

That evening at the opulent Weiting Opera House, they watched *How the Vote was Won*, a humorous popular suffrage play. Janie imagined Mr. Baum on stage in *The Maid of Arran*. Afterward in Clinton Square, milky clouds skimmed the sky as moon and electric lights reflected in the shimmering canal. What had it looked like when only kerosene lamps lit the square?

On Thursday, Janie and Mrs. Brewster took the interurban to Chittenango, Mr. Baum's birthplace. They strolled by the Baums' first home near a barrel factory. Their father had been a cooper by trade. They rode to Rose Lawn in Mattydale, where the Baums moved when Frank was ten. The house was gone, but Janie filled the space with her imagination: young Frank reading on wide porches, running the printing press with Harry, writing about the Cardiff Giant hoax, trotting through acres of rosebushes, trees, and fields, dodging scarecrows.

"My father sold this property at public auction to pay off debts," Mrs. Brewster said. "Frank bought it back and sold it to my mother for one dollar. It stayed in the family several more years." Nearby was Spring Farms. "My father and brothers raised chickens here."

Janie delighted in her role of populating Oz with those winsome creatures. "Were any named Billina?"

On Friday, Mrs. Brewster arranged for her young neighbors to take Janie to the resorts along Lake Onondaga's shoreline. The seven resorts were considered the Coney Island of central New York, inspired by the Columbian Exposition.

They hit highlights of Long Branch, Lakeside Park, and Pleasant Beach, each bearing similarities to Holland's Jenison Electric Park. The final resort, The White City, advertised as "$1.50 worth of amusement for 50 cents." Painted white, it gleamed with late afternoon sun. Janie and her newfound friends enjoyed the Old Mill, Johnstown Flood, Temple of Mirth, and the miniature scenic railway. They braved the Shoot the Chute ride, splashing into a manmade lagoon. When dusk settled into darkness, twenty-five thousand lights sprang to life in a dazzling display.

Magnificent! Surely like Mr. Baum's first view of the Columbian Expo's White City, with Emerald City visions dancing in his head.

FORTY-FOUR

Monday, June 23, 1980

"You orchestrated the reunion *and* a grand travel adventure," Carrie said.

Mrs. Gordon's jaw tightened. "Some resorts disappeared by 1915. The only thing left is a carousel, preserved in a mall. Like things we grasp, yet they slip through our hands like a sieve."

Carrie leaned in. Another teaser going nowhere. What disaster marred this memory?

The next morning, Carrie handed Mrs. Gordon a recipe. "From Oma. For *stroopwafels*."

"I had these with Katje. Let's make some." She retrieved a pizzelle pan from the cabinet. Soon they indulged in peppermint tea and cookie-like sandwiches oozing with cinnamon-flavored syrup. Carrie placed a *stroopwafel* over her steaming teacup to warm it up as Mrs. Gordon shared benefits of peppermint.

They returned to Syracuse through Mrs. Gordon's reverie.

Janie, 18
July 1910

Janie and the Weavers waited at the train station for Mae. Janie's heart pounded. Surely, Mae would be grateful to see her son. But would she love Janie?

An auburn-haired woman disembarked the train with a red-headed girl.

Janie approached her. "Mrs. Callaghan? I'm Janie Broderick."

Mae's face brightened, her weary, tentative expression melting into joy. Crying, she embraced Janie. "Bless you, dear girl." She lifted Beatrice, who buried her face in her mother's shoulder. The lawyer, Mr. Simmons, appeared behind them with luggage.

At the Brewsters' house, Beatrice seemed plastered to Mae. But a smile emerged as Janie enticed her with a stuffed bear, wooden top, and Mr. Baum's *Father Goose, His Book.*

Gradually, Beatrice joined Janie on the floor, then cuddled with her as Janie read. The girl's leggings scooted up her leg, revealing large bruises. Janie shivered.

The next day, they met with Mr. Simmons to complete immigration paperwork. He had documents to protect Mrs. Callaghan from her husband. A divorce would elicit repercussions, so Mae had left without Owen's knowledge. Mr. Simmons, having done due diligence, knew how to handle this delicate situation when women had no recourse to act alone.

In Michigan, at the Weaver home, mother and son tearfully embraced. But when Mae introduced Beatrice to her big brother, the girl huddled in her mother's skirts, sobbing. Did he resemble his abusive father?

In the parlor, Mae shared news of home and neighbors while Janie engaged Beatrice. Teddy asked about his father.

Mae's eyes darted across the room. "He's the same."

"Has he ever laid a hand on Beatrice? Or harmed *you*?

Mae stared at the table. "Never mind. We're here now."

Teddy popped up. "I knew it! I never should've left." He stamped across the room.

Mae went to him. "I *sent* you away to flourish. And we're safe now. Let's thank God for Janie and this wonderful occasion."

Mae and Beatrice moved in with Aunt Sophie. Janie admired their close-knit family. Teddy would do anything for his mother. Seeing their love was rewarding enough, but mostly, Janie was grateful she'd ended the abuse, its residual effects ever-present. Mae never let Beatrice out of her sight, going to bed when her daughter did, no matter how early. She insisted that doors be locked. Both mother and daughter startled easily. Beatrice often woke the household, screaming from nightmares. Weeks passed before restless Mae achieved a good night's sleep.

Mae was strict about routines: Bible reading after supper, prayers at bedtime, rest on Sunday—like the Brodericks. Yet Mae's rules were conducted with kindness, even when disciplining. Besides Bible stories, Mae read fairy tales and nursery rhymes from Janie's collection. Beatrice cuddled on Janie's lap, too.

One summer evening, Teddy and Janie sat on Aunt Sophie's porch swing. "What happened yesterday?" Janie asked.

Teddy's jaw flinched. "Ron's telling around town that I chew tobacco."

Janie giggled. "If everybody listened to him, we'd all hibernate in caves. He's nothing but a windbag."

"Some folks believe him."

Janie looked at him askance. "So? You know the truth. So does Father. Your morals aren't in question."

"Some denounce tobacco." His jaw tightened. "You don't understand."

Janie touched his arm. "I do. But you're too bothered by appearances." Like her father. There, she'd said it, an observation gnawing for months. "I'm going to ask Father to help pay for college classes."

"Why? I promised to do that after we marry. After a raise." Teddy wanted funds for their own place before proposing.

She'd used her money for rescuing Mae. "I want classes *before* marrying. Western Michigan or Kalamazoo College. It'll give me an advantage at bigger newspapers."

"How, Janie? If you take a better job, you'll have to move. I'm in business *here*."

"I thought you wanted to be with me as I blossomed."

"Yes. In Wolcott."

"What?" she sputtered. "You know I want to travel, do investigative reporting. I assumed we'd travel together. Can't you envision it?"

He shook his head. "Not after investing in business here."

"Working with Thomas, you can leave periodically. Hire managers."

"That's far down the road." His tone had an edge. "You expect me to forfeit my own work to follow you around the globe? I already gave up my dreams once."

She caught her breath. *What about my sacrifice for your mother?* "I have goals, too." Fireflies darted about, lighting the darkness like kerosene. Crickets chirped. The moon rose, like dreams racing to dawn.

"Asking your father for money reflects poorly on me," Teddy said.

"Stop worrying. He trusts you with his business."

"He doesn't value a woman's education or pay you what you're worth."

"Taking a semester before marrying will solve one problem."

"That's not our only problem." Voice rigid, he stared ahead. "Ma's asking why you're so unhappy in church."

Janie froze. "What'd you say to her?"

"Church is hard for you. Your folks were harsh and hypocritical. She wonders if you have faith of your own."

Janie clenched her fists. "She probably doesn't like my stance on women's rights. And now I'm wicked because my faith isn't as strong as yours?" She stewed. "Look at me!"

He turned her way. She searched his eyes for compassion and, fortunately, found it. He caressed her cheek. "Sweet Charlotte."

Trembling, she rasped, "What's *really* wrong?"

"Mother's concerned about us being unequally yoked. You're not a believer."

Janie closed her eyes. Glowing church attendance was merely an act, her flagging faith obvious. "Are *you* concerned?"

"I know your heart, your pain. You're good, kind, and generous. Beautiful inside and out, full of life and imagination. Showing such love for my family. But you doubt God's goodness. You don't seek Him."

"For good reason." Her muscles tensed. "Maybe *you're* unequally yoked to my father, the hypocrite. Doesn't *that* bother your mother?"

"He's a good businessman. Honest and hardworking. That's different from marriage."

Janie fumed. "I can't grasp the idea of God as father, when my own father despises me, and your father horsewhipped you daily. And God watching children like Beatrice get beaten."

"He allows evil for purposes we don't understand."

"The only good father I've seen is Mr. Baum loving his

sons. He loved me as a daughter. If God is like Mr. Baum, I could serve such a God."

"That's wicked to say."

"He knows how to love better than some Christians do!"

Teddy shook his head. "He poisoned you. Don't talk that way."

"Don't deny it. Your wicked father attended church weekly. Mr. Baum never poisons my thinking about God."

"You're blind to the contamination."

Janie gaped. "Contamination?" Tears squeezed out. Words choked. "At least I'm honest about my doubts. Can't you see? I'm on a journey." *You must walk ...* "Point to any church, and you'll find doubting Thomases. They play the game, pretending they don't struggle." She wept in his arms, unable to speak. She never should've told him about her doubts—or about Mr. Baum. But she needed to be her complete self with at least one friend. Especially one she planned to marry.

"Your Aunt Sophie's a strong Christian. Take encouragement from her."

"She never endured hatred from her parents like I have."

Teddy held her as she calmed. His breath ruffled her hair. "I love you, Charlotte. More than anything. We'll always be together." He quietly sang, "Let me call you sweetheart ..."

FORTY-FIVE

September 1910

Residing with Aunt Sophie, Mae took a sewing job for a shop downtown, working at home with Beatrice nearby. Janie kept her doubts about God to herself. One evening, she stayed late at Auntie's, mending with Mae by the hearth. It was one of the first times Beatrice had gone to bed first, without her mother. Aunt Sophie was in bed, too.

Janie jabbed at Beatrice's torn pocket. "What was it like, sending Teddy away?"

Mae startled, and her fingers stopped. "Worse than any strap across my skin." She stared at the fire. "Only God Himself sustained me. And knowing I did the best thing for Teddy's future."

"Did you ever regret it?"

"No, I couldn't afford for us both to leave. And me with child."

"Would a neighbor have taken you in?"

"Perhaps. But Owen would've found us, making it worse." She dropped her mending. "I talked to the minister, but he only saw a decent, hardworking man who tithed every Sunday."

Janie scowled. Another hypocrite. An irony that Teddy worked for her father.

"I knew Teddy'd find a better place." Wind rattled the windowpane, and Mae jerked. "He hated giving up school. But we had no money for it."

Janie pictured Teddy walking away from home in the thick of night under the moon, leaving dreams behind. "He said if he stayed there, he'd be considered an orphan."

"Though treated better than illegitimate children." The fire crackled. Mae jumped. Her face widened in fright before relaxing.

Janie had never seen someone so skittish. "He told me. One can never rise above one's station, even if adopted. But it's not their fault. It's not fair."

Mae tilted her head, firelight reflecting in her eyes. "Been that way for centuries."

Janie barely kept the bite out of her voice. "Didn't Jesus say, 'Let the little children come unto me, for of such is the kingdom of God'? Or was he only referring to legitimate ones?"

"All are welcomed by the Savior, dear. But on earth ..."

Janie finished Mae's sentence. "On earth, people have standards. Higher than God's. No hope for the illegitimates."

"We've improved lately in attending orphans' needs, but protesting does no good."

Appalled, Janie reined in anger and managed a gentle response. "Did you try?" She didn't want to believe Mae was blind to this cruel bias.

"I helped much at the orphanage." Mae picked up her needle. "I was grateful Teddy could grow without the stigma of being an orphan, without the hatred of his father."

Yet he carried it with him. "He also had the gift of a mother's love for fourteen years prior." Envy gripped Janie as words stumbled out.

"That's why I sent *Pilgrim's Progress* with him. The only way to send a tangible part of myself, my faith, something I tried to impart his whole life." Mae eyed her. "To remind Teddy that God is his true Father."

But how could a true father passively watch so much evil? "He showed me the book, his most prized possession." Had Teddy told Mae about his temper and intermittent fights? "Though he still feels his father's hatred, he clings to what you've taught him about God."

"I'm thankful. Without it, we've nothing that lasts beyond this world."

Janie stabbed a needle through cloth. Mae exuded inner strength, unwavering in the face of hardship. Admirable, but Janie couldn't grasp it.

"I hope you never have to send a child away," Mae said.

Would Teddy ever treat his own child how he'd been treated? Or harm Janie?

"Janie." Mae's tone forced eye contact. "You're such a lovely girl, so vibrant, talented, and generous. Yet you carry sadness. I see it in your eyes."

Could Mae possibly understand the pain of Sawyer and Elsa's condemnation of everything she did? It surely didn't compare to what Mae endured. She replied with silence.

Mr. Baum answered Janie's interview questions in a letter, then applauded her articles—written as herself, not as controversial Isabel. The success sparked more trips. Thus, she postponed asking Father for college help. In October, she traveled to Hull House in Chicago for a piece on Jane Addams. In spring, she went to New York again to interview authors Isabella MacDonald Alden and Frances Hodgson Burnett. Between trips, she planned her Unconventional Careers series by Isabel, featuring physician Rose Talbot Bullard and explorer

Harriet Chalmers Adams. Too bad Pinkerton didn't still hire female detectives.

In July, a year after high school graduation, she moved in with Aunt Sophie, Mae, and Beatrice, and received a package from Mr. Baum. Inside was a re-issue of *The Twinkle Tales* in one volume and trading cards of Dorothy and her companions for Beatrice. Earlier, he'd reported that Harry remained in Chicago with his bride. Robert had graduated from Cornell the previous year. Kenneth lived with them in Hollywood, a quiet neighborhood. Frank dropped in from time to time. With Mrs. Baum's inheritance money, they built a comfortable house.

Your letters are a highlight. After many busy hours, I'm sitting in my garden, surrounded by dahlias and chrysanthemums. Our house—aptly named Ozcot—suits us well. We've room for a fine library and a garden of winding gravel paths. In my study, I hung the framed pencil with which I wrote The Wizard of Oz, *one of my links to Chicago and fond memories, including those with you. The camellia bushes make me wonder what your Camellia's next escapade will be.*

Odd sights here are now commonplace, as filmmakers use street corners and shopfronts as settings for their moving pictures. Recently, I was nearly knocked over by a fellow dressed as a policeman and another in a horse costume.

I hope your father softens. You'll benefit from classes. Regardless, the money spent transporting Mrs. Callaghan was not wasted, bringing to mind Oscar Wilde's fairy tale, "The Happy Prince." He gave until he had nothing left. Though nobody knew the gifts were from him, there was One who noticed. And it mattered.

Continue to wring experiences from each day as grist for the mill. Who's to say you can't first endure some Castorine Oil —or dishwashing—on the way to Oz? As I did. What would Captain Bilgewater say about that?

Alas, following my own dream led to financial ruin. Consider what you're willing to risk, my dear, if you're as bullheaded as I am.

Despite the bankruptcy devastation blasted in June's newspapers, we are managing. The Fairylogue *was both my delight and my undoing, plunging us into insurmountable debt. I had to list my assets. Such a sorry, humiliating affair! They are as follows (I can easily tell you, for it won't require much space or ink): two suits, eleven books, an old typewriter.*

Most of my debt belongs to Mr. Selig, the filmmaker. Fortunately, I'd already transferred property and book rights to my wife. The remainder goes to Mr. Rountree so that royalties will go toward debt. Mr. Selig had a fine time of it, fully taking advantage by creating four one-reeler Oz films. They lack the magical film effects of the Fairylogue, *but still exude charm. I wish I'd been part of their creation.*

I tell you this, dear, to encourage. There's no valley so deep or sorrow so great that one cannot keep moving forward. Don't live in the cellar, away from the sun. You must walk. It is a long journey ...

Janie gazed at Mrs. Baum's embroidery over the bookcase, then read more. *The Wizard of Oz* extravaganza ended. He was done with Oz, now working on plays and other series: Aunt Jane's Nieces and The Boy Fortune Hunters. He published *L. Frank Baum's Juvenile Speaker,* an anthology of his works, for classroom use and stage productions. A new series began with *The Daring Twins* for older children, featuring a girl detective. The publisher hoped the ambitious female pilot protagonist in *The Flying Girl*, by Edith Van Dyne, didn't thwart sales.

There was talk of my wife receiving visits from my accomplice, Edith Van Dyne, who devised The Flying Girl's *adventure right in the Ozcot garden!*

After selling 20,000 copies of Emerald City, *I received innumerable complaints from dear readers about cutting off Oz. Perhaps it's akin to killing off Sherlock Holmes— unthinkable. Surely Captain Bilgewater and Mr. Taradiddle can relate to such devastation, due to their own unfortunate disappearance into oblivion. Though Sherlock returned, my new fairy tale series—with Ozzy flavor— beginning with* The Sea Fairies, *must suffice as an Oz replacement. The ocean near La Jolla and Coronado inspires daily. Ah, there's much yet to do!*

1980

"Unfortunately, he never saw another penny from *The Wizard of Oz*," Mrs. Gordon said. "Mrs. Baum didn't get rights back till around 1925, when Frank Joslyn made a film."

"Yet nothing squelched his imagination," Carrie said. "Like a fire you can't put out." Who smothered Janie's fire? Mae's disapproval of the marriage? Teddy's temper? Walter Gordon? "You had good reason to be concerned about Teddy becoming abusive."

Mrs. Gordon squinted, as if tricked into revealing a secret before its time. "A little patience goes a long way." Patience was tiresome.

After gardening, they settled into wicker chairs with *The Pilgrim's Progress*. Nearing the Celestial City's Gate, Christian and Hopeful arrived at the Delectable Mountains. Shepherds warned: beware of Hypocrites who try to lure pilgrims away.

Soon the deceivers—Ignorance, Flatterer, and Atheist—assailed. The Flatterer was disguised as an Angel of Light. Christian and Hopeful got tangled in his net, unsnarled by The Shining One. Along came Atheist, laughing, claiming their travels would bring them to naught, for there was no such place as the Celestial City. He'd searched twenty years.

Mrs. Gordon tilted her head. "Folks like Ignorance and Flatterer have the appearance of belonging to the king, but they don't."

"Right. They would hate the Celestial City anyhow, because it's a land that praises the king. They only care for themselves."

For three days, Mrs. Gordon had Carrie organize, read mail, weed, and run errands. Carrie followed her upstairs and dusted two of four bedrooms. In the hallway, passing one of two closed doors, Carrie reached for the knob. "Shall I dust here?"

"No!" The voice was sharp.

Carrie withdrew her hand as if a BB pellet had struck it. "Okay, but when will we continue your story?"

"When dragons come to rest."

FORTY-SIX

PART THREE: FINDING HOME

Friday, June 27, 1980

After supper, Dirk arrived in his uncle's truck. Bob Seger's "Old Time Rock and Roll" boomed from the radio. Leaning against the truck, Dirk alternated playing piano, guitar, and drums. Carrie threw her bag in back. Off to Barrowdale. In the truck, he handed her the tapes.

"Got one for jitters? I'm only looking forward to Henry's ice cream. I dread seeing my parents without any teaching prospects." And no diploma. Making her private summer rebellion known. Anxiety festered. She'd wanted to secure the loan first but needed to come clean.

"Have you told Brian yet about no teaching?"

"No." Brian scorned her job as if it were a swamp of mosquitoes. "I know. I'm terrible for not telling him, but I can't bear his snarky comments."

"Whoa! That makes *you* terrible? Back up the train." He mimicked pulling a whistle cord. "Permission to meddle?"

She crossed her arms. "Okay."

"If you're almost engaged, you shouldn't be afraid. What do you like about him?"

She balked, then calmed, noting his kind expression. "Fair question. Okay. He's responsible. Has career goals. He's hard-working, persevering, great at saving money." Everything Dirk wasn't. She regretted her response.

He smirked. "Looks good on a resume. But how does he treat you?"

She needed a quick recovery. "My parents love him. We enjoy ballgames."

"Detroit Tigers?"

"No, *his* games. Basketball and baseball. I never missed a game till now."

His jaw twitched. "That's being *together*?"

"We love Win Schuler's and fancy restaurants. Together. He brings flowers. Chocolate." She preferred caramels. "Books."

"Fairy tales?"

"No. Inspirational, self-help—he's not into fiction."

He let her words sink in. "What do you two talk about? Numbers and accounting?"

"Don't be silly. We talk food, family, baseball ..."

"But you're no sports enthusiast." He let that sink in, too.

She squirmed and held up the *Lemons & Vinegar* tape.

"So, you're angry. One more question while I'm on a roll. Brian still doesn't know Billy Joel's your true love?" He winked.

Carrie shoved in the cassette, launching the piano staccato of Billy Joel's "Angry Young Man." Already bracing for Brian's criticism, she felt shame flush her cheeks. As usual, she was a hedgehog rolling into a self-protective ball. With a fraction of Janie the dreamer's vitality, she'd lasso the world, conquering fear of disapproval.

"Hey, sorry for hitting a sore spot," Dirk said. "How 'bout Finger-Snapping music?"

They sang Carly Simon tunes, the Eagles, Chicago's

"Questions 67 and 68." Brian would be furious. But she didn't care. Dirk was comfortable. And safe.

In Kalamazoo at his apartment, Brian looked handsome in khakis and a rust polo shirt. Clean shaven. Carrie hugged him.

He kissed her. "Hey, sweetheart. I've been missing my number one fan."

Rare to hear a term of endearment without a reprimand. "Missed you, too." She glanced at Dirk. *Yes, I really have a boyfriend.* She introduced them.

Dirk's shaggy hair seemed shaggier. The men shook hands, Brian eyeing Dirk's tattoo. Carrie cringed. "Nice meeting you," Dirk said. Surely, he wanted to add *phantom boyfriend, who keeps canceling and only buys self-improvement books for gifts.*

Brian cocked his head as if discerning Dirk's fatal flaws. "Carrie says you're from Holland. A Hope grad?"

"Lasted two years there," Dirk said. "Escorted out the back door."

Brian's eyes widened. "What?"

Carrie's face heated. "Dirk's quite the kidder."

"I really was booted out," Dirk said. "In fact—"

"Let's get the chair." Guessing Brian's thoughts, Carrie grimaced.

"Do I have a surprise!" Brian led them to a hunter green recliner, brand new.

"Green fits your beige color scheme," Carrie said. Boring Bland Mushroom Beige.

"For us, sweetie. With each paycheck, I'll buy a new piece. Take it with you."

"I want the one I'm reupholstering." She scanned the room. "Where is it?"

"Going to someone in need." He patted the chair. "It's at Goodwill."

"What?" Carrie gaped. The room seemed to vanish.

"That chair was a piece of work. Your mother couldn't wait to get rid of it."

"You took my favorite reading chair to Goodwill? The one I asked you to keep?"

"That monstrosity will look out of place with new furniture."

"I don't *want* new furniture!" Her blood boiled. Dirk scowled, arms crossed. "Do you mind?" she snapped. "Wait in the truck."

Shuffling toward the door, Dirk arched his eyebrows.

Carrie's voice rose. "I can't believe you *did* this!"

"What's the fuss? This chair wasn't cheap. I thought you'd be pleased."

"You've *no* idea what makes me happy." Tears flowed.

"That's absurd. Stop crying. Try this out. It's really comfortable."

"I don't want this stupid chair. I'm going to Goodwill."

"Don't be ridiculous, sweetheart. It's just an old chair."

"Give me twenty bucks to buy it back."

"I already spent hundreds."

She stomped toward the door where Dirk waited.

In the truck, he handed her tissues. "Where's the Goodwill? Certainly not *here*."

She ignored his double meaning and blew her nose. Sobbing, she directed him to Goodwill. She wiped her eyes, but couldn't camouflage the red, teary visage reflected in the mirror. "I only have five dollars."

"Got it covered."

"What if the chair's not here?"

"We'll find it."

"I can't go in. I'm a wreck."

He touched her wrist. "It's okay to cry."

More tears spilled. After she calmed, they walked inside.

There it was—scratched maple wooden base, orange and rust plaid fabric. "That's it! Oh, Dirk." She hugged him.

He hugged her back. "Memories and all. Everything's intact."

What a darling! They purchased the chair and heaved it into the truck. He snapped the covering over the flatbed. On the road, Carrie said, "Thank you. I'll pay you at home."

"Nope, it's my gift."

"I'm sorry for making such a big deal."

"It *is* a big deal. No apology needed."

"But I overreacted. I've surely botched things with Brian."

"Whoa! Back up the train. Mind some more meddling?"

She stared at the landscape. "Okay."

"It's not about the chair, but what it represents. Brian botched things, not you. Your lucky guy doesn't know how lucky he is. He doesn't value your feelings or opinions." His mouth twisted. "You're just his number one fan."

Brian's *fan* comment bothered her, too, but she couldn't admit it. "That's not true. He's trying to make me happy. He spent hundreds on that chair."

"The Carrie I know prefers old stuff. He didn't buy that for *you*." He played Melancholy I. Joan Baez crooned, "Will the Circle be Unbroken?" Then Neil Diamond pined about a "Song Sung Blue."

FORTY-SEVEN

June 27, 1980

Carrie sat with her parents in the den. Mom's jubilation about new wallpaper and furniture masked the awkwardness of Carrie's angry departure last month. While Mom knit, Dad read the newspaper, smoking his pipe.

"Any bites on teacher applications?" Dad's eyes stayed on the newspaper.

"No."

"Did you find a summer job?" Mom asked. "After leaving Ophelia's in a lurch."

The Burger Flipper. "I'm doing historical research." Carrie inhaled. "We need to talk."

Mom fiddled with knitting needles. Dad turned a page. No eye contact. Typical.

Fear gripped her. "There's a reason I didn't want a grad party."

"You don't like the attention." Mom's needles clacked busily. "It's easier getting a big fat check from us instead." She was all about huge parties, impressing guests.

Anger pushed up, but Carrie buried it. "There's another reason."

"What then?" Dad studied the paper as if he had no time to spare from world updates.

Tempted to rip the newspaper and grab knitting needles, Carrie expelled words. "I never got my diploma. I failed a class fall semester and couldn't retake it."

They looked up, aghast. Mom's needles stopped. Dad frowned. Silence.

Dad pursed his lips. "They didn't offer a summer class to finish it?"

"No. It's a higher-level one in my major. Philosophy of Education."

"You *failed* it?" Mom paled. "You got an *F*?"

Carrie gulped. "Incomplete."

"You dropped out?" No daughter of hers did such a thing. "Send the work in. Professors make accommodations."

"I was overwhelmed with a full load. When I studied, I barely saw words."

Glare penetrating, Dad lowered the paper. "Kruisselbrinks don't quit." Shame burned. Carrie studied her feet. "You could've gotten tutoring."

"I didn't need help. I needed sanity. I *hated* teacher aiding sophomore year. I'm not like you, Mom. You thrive in the classroom, the more the merrier." Carrie fought unacceptable tears.

"Why didn't you quit intra-murals instead?" Mom said as if the solution were as simple as dividing candy among quarreling kids.

"I quit everything to stay afloat."

Jaw tight, Dad tapped his pipe. "You're finishing this fall?"

Carrie swallowed. "I'm not retaking it. Ever."

"Kruisselbrinks don't fail." Dad slapped the paper on his knee. "How do you expect to get a teaching job?"

"I hated student teaching. I never want to teach. *Never.*"

Mom gasped. "You failed student teaching too?"

"No. I did everything required. But I don't love the classroom like you do, Mom." Her palms sweated.

"Why didn't you tell us before?" Mom sputtered.

"Because of how you're acting now!"

Dad leaned forward, elbows on knees. "Let's get this straight. You're planning on life without a diploma. One class short. Even though we paid for your education. Thousands."

"I'm grateful."

"Not grateful enough," Dad snarled.

"Look, you stipulated my major. You want us to be one happy family of educators, movers and shakers in the school system, but I only did it—"

"For the free education."

"No. I didn't have much choice. I did it for your approval. To make *you* happy."

Mom snorted. "That obviously didn't work."

Carrie blinked. "It *never* works. I've tried my whole life."

Dad rapped the chair arm. "You're failing to appreciate how expensive and prestigious a Calvin education is."

"I *hate* teaching."

He grunted. "That's irrelevant."

"Like every other thought and feeling I've had."

Dad shook his head as if Carrie spoke Swahili. "With a degree, you'd have *something* to show for four years at Calvin. What're you going to do instead?"

Carrie hesitated. She hadn't wanted to divulge anything yet, but facing two vultures changed her mind. "I have a plan already. In a few years, I'll pay you back every penny."

"Please do humor us." Her father's heated glare belied the coldness of his voice. "How will you do that?"

"Humor you?" Carrie stood, needing the upward force to go beyond defensiveness. "That's impossible. So, I'm doing something I'm passionate about. I'm buying Dunham's Diner in Wolcott so I can run my own café."

"What?" Mom flung her arms up. A ball of yarn flew from her lap.

Might as well have said spelunking. "I'm waiting for the loan to go through."

Frantic, Mom waved knitting needles. "You've got to be kidding."

Dad flicked his pipe. "How will you pull that off? If you think you can waltz in here, tell us you've quit school, and expect our stamp of approval for some crazy venture while scorning your education, you're dead wrong. You don't value what I've given you."

"*You* don't value what *I* care about. *My* goals. I'm not a paper cutout of Mom. Or Amy." Her voice rose. "You don't *see* me. You don't even know who I *am*!"

"Are you living a double life?" Mom stared wide-eyed. "Beyond this café caper?"

Masks. "The Stranger" lyrics cycled through her. "I can't be myself with you. Can't have my own opinions. Like not believing me in sixth grade. When you took Miss Nieuwenhuis's side to keep your reputation intact with the school board." The forbidden topic.

"That's different," Dad barked. "With no diploma, you lack commitment. You can't play two sides of the fence."

"Why not? *You* did." Carrie seethed. "And I don't mean careers."

With a sharp glance at her mother, he reddened. "You're mistaken, Carrie. You were a child. That was long ago."

Her pronouncement plunged downhill. Instead of growing like a snowball, picking up speed, it was cast to the realm of oblivion. Her parents sidestepped to dodge the blow, her words null and void. As expected.

"We put your name on the cake with Brian's as a surprise," Mom said as if that covered a multitude of offenses.

"Throw the cake *out*." Carrie headed to the doorway.

"Does Brian know about the ... café?" Mom cringed as if *café* was an expletive.

"Yes, but not about the dropped class. Don't tell the Wiersmas. I'll tell Brian first."

"Don't worry." Mom frowned as if the idea were akin to reporting a stock market crash.

Carrie ran upstairs and slammed the bedroom door. A first. The floodgate of tears broke. She sobbed on the bed. *Kruisselbrinks don't quit. Kruisselbrinks don't fail.*

She shouldn't have unveiled the café plan till after starting renovations—success in action.

She should break up. Brian gave away her chair. She feared talking to him. But he might be her last chance for finding acceptance with her parents. The only buffer.

It's okay to cry. Dirk didn't mind her tears.

Yet she couldn't tell Dirk about no diploma. Dirk, the drop-out, drifting without purpose. She couldn't let him know her inner turmoil. Or that she'd lied to him.

FORTY-EIGHT

Saturday, June 28, 1980

At the Wiersmas' house, Brian's mom hugged Carrie. "We haven't seen you in weeks. Did you notice the cake?" She nodded toward the counter.

In their respective college colors, the words *Congratulations Brian & Carrie* sparkled amidst frosting diplomas. Tempted to punch the cake, Carrie mashed guacamole instead.

Brian sneaked behind her and kissed her cheek. She stiffened. "What's the matter?" he asked.

"A certain *matter* of a missing chair."

"I thought you went to Goodwill with—what's his face? Oh, yeah. Skippy."

She spun around, hips thunking into the cabinet. "Skippy?"

Brian grabbed a cracker. "Seems a brick short of a full load. Why'd he announce his expulsion as proudly as if winning the Pulitzer Prize?"

If only she knew. "In some ways, Dirk's more grown up than you'll ever be." She charged to the bathroom and locked the door.

Brian knocked. "Come on, Carrie. Don't make a scene." *Carrie* used in reprimand.

She turned the water on full blast, like the steam of anger. "Go away."

He left. Mellow music piped through outdoor speakers, seeping through the window. Maybe she'd snatch a Billy Joel tape from home, crank it up, and blast it out.

Guests arrived. Outside, Carrie fielded questions from people playing the One-up Game. They reiterated comparable situations, back in the day—but funnier, scarier, more challenging, more death-defying. After two hours, Carrie felt invisible.

Perfectly groomed, Brian wore a collared shirt, and brown hair dipped across his forehead. Carly Simon's song "You're So Vain" rolled through her.

One lady grumbled about builders constructing their new five-bedroom house. Community-minded women bragged about pet projects, turning concerns into excuses for gossip, spoken in condescending tones for down-and-outers.

Dirk would see through these people in a nanosecond.

Why'd he lead out with his college fiasco as if it were his defining moment? Though unbound by fear, he definitely had a streak of stupidity.

At five o'clock, Trudy Wiersma rattled a glass with her fork. "We have an announcement before cake cutting." Brian strutted over to her, darling son that he was.

Henry Wiersma lifted a glass. "A toast to my son. We're so proud of him, already thriving in a new job." He nodded to Carrie's father. Mom pulled Carrie to Brian's side. Looking smug, he slid his arm around her. She stiffened.

Dad raised a hand. "Brian and I agree that after six months in his current firm, he'll transition to my company, acquiring our accounts as well. In five years, he'll become partner."

Carrie numbed as the crowd erupted with cheers. How

long had her dad and boyfriend conspired behind her back? Whatever happened to Wolcott?

Brian hugged her. "Great surprise, eh?" He was off, making the rounds, shaking hands.

Women flocked to Carrie. "How'd you keep *that* secret?" ... "You didn't even drop a hint." ..."You're one lucky girl."

Carrie stewed silently. A recipient of lavish praise, Brian never looked happier. Why hadn't he consulted her?

Back home, after dark, Mom puttered in the kitchen, washing platters. Dad chatted with Brian. Two decades of invisibility bubbled over. Carrie slammed the Betty Crocker cookbook on the table so hard, Betty might have cracked a rib.

Mom dropped silverware. Everyone stared as if Halley's Comet appeared.

"How come nobody consulted me?" Carrie yelled.

Brian stepped away as if expecting the cookbook to hit him next.

"Why didn't anyone ask my opinion about you two working together?"

Dad puffed his pipe. "We assumed you'd be onboard."

Brian took her hand. "We wanted to surprise you."

"That you did." Carrie shoved his arm away.

Mom wiped her hands on a towel. "You should be thrilled."

"Well, I'm not. I'm humiliated to find out when everyone else did."

"Nobody realized." Mom hugged the cookbook, as if the book had more value than Carrie's broken heart.

"I thought we were going to Wolcott, Brian. Instead, you're scheming behind my back."

"Scheming? Really?" Mom shelved the book. "Calm down."

Carrie seethed. "No. I need you to know my feelings."

"We know plenty already." Mom pursed her lips.

"Next time, we'll tell you first," Dad said.

Carrie smacked the table. "How about asking my opinion?"

"Carrie," Brian said, "it was talk between two businessmen. Out of your realm."

"Am *I* out of your realm? I'll be running a business too. In Wolcott. Where we'd planned to move."

Brian's eyes widened, his first time hearing her mention café plans in front of her parents. "Come on, sweetie—"

"Don't call me sweetie!" She pointed to herself. "I have opinions, too."

"That's why we asked if you wanted a grad party," Mom said. "And if you wanted to make guacamole or salad."

Unbelievable! Carrie fled upstairs.

Sunday, June 29, 1980

After church, Carrie's family ate pot roast and potatoes in typical Christian Reformed Sunday dinner tradition. Amy, her husband, and their toddler joined them. Chatter about Amy's life belied any turbulence. Finally, Carrie packed literature class books and notes. Her thousand-plus book collection for the café could stay here till after renovations.

She waited in front with her bike.

Dirk arrived. "Bicycling in your future?"

"After a tune-up."

"Let the hardware guy take care of it. I only charge a bike ride with me."

Her parents stepped out. *Rats.* She hoped there'd be no more exchanges about college degrees or lack thereof. She introduced them.

Smiling a cheerful greeting, Dirk extended his hand. Her father noted the tattoo before hesitantly reciprocating.

Mom eyed Dirk's shaggy hair and whiskers. No doubt a hippie in her estimation. "Thanks for bringing Carrie home."

"My pleasure. Your daughter's a real gem."

Carrie cringed at the negative ways her parents might interpret that.

In the truck, she slid in Melancholy I and forwarded to Elton John's "Don't Let the Sun Go Down on Me."

"Did you two break up?" Dirk asked gently.

"No."

"Oh."

Disappointed? She eyed the landscape. Could she train Brian to be more sensitive? Was she loyal or stupid? Did her parents' disapproval prevent her from taking drastic action?

After she played the song three times, Dirk suggested *Melancholy II* for variety.

"Sorry I'm such miserable company. Hey, why'd you blurt out about getting expelled?"

"You needed to see how he'd react."

"That was humiliating. Brian thinks I'm hanging out with some noodlehead dropout."

"Wow." He gripped the wheel. "Loser's one thing, but noodlehead?"

"You're turning this into a joke."

"Only because I'm pretending it doesn't hurt."

She stared at him. *You expect an apology?* "You can't judge Brian based on one time."

Dirk bit his lip. "He doesn't treat you how you deserve."

"Well, now he thinks even less of me. You'll forever be Skippy to him."

Dirk chuckled. "That's a good one. Skippy?"

"You laugh at Skippy, get hurt by noodlehead."

"It's all in who does the name calling." His jaw flinched.

"He branded you."

"So what?" He glanced her way. "I'm more concerned that I hurt *you*. I embarrassed you. I'm sorry."

She was stunned.

"I ran off at the mouth, an exceptional skill of mine," Dirk said.

A flutter of warmth swept through her. *He* was apologizing to *her*, though she'd called him a noodlehead.

"I'm angry at how he treats you. Angry that you're afraid to be yourself. Angry that he gave away your chair and gives you ludicrous books."

Her insult hovered in his eyes. "I'm sorry for calling you a noodlehead."

"I hope that's not how you view me."

"I don't." Not a full-blown noodlehead, but short in the responsibility department. Should she confess to not having her degree? "I stood up for you to Brian."

His face brightened. "You did?"

"I told him, in some ways, you're more grown up than he'll ever be." She simpered. "I'll bet that just butters your biscuit."

Dirk laughed. "Butters my biscuit, all right. It takes the cake. Breaks my wooden shoe, too. This rooster's gonna crow." His shoulders straightened. "So, how was it telling your folks about not teaching?"

"Awful. As predicted, Henry's ice cream was the weekend highlight." Dirk had no clue her parents hadn't known about the café. She did the safest thing. Divert. "I might climb Mt. Everest. Go scuba diving. Find the Titanic." No wonder Dirk didn't have relationship problems.

"There's a difference between running *to* and running *from*." His voice was tender. "You gotta be with people who see you, hear you. The *real* you."

Dirk hadn't shamed her for crying, but he didn't know she'd cried enough to overflow Lake Michigan.

"May I cheer you up now?" After his anecdote about a sailing mishap, they sang *Finger-Snapping Toe-Tapping* selections from Neil Diamond's *Hot August Night*.

Late that afternoon, Dirk and Opa carried the chair downstairs. Oma beamed. "Ed, remember Arlene reading to the girls? How they loved *Madeline*."

"See?" Dirk said. "Memories intact."

Oma invited Dirk for The Wizard's Magical Chocolate Cake, Mrs. Gordon's recipe.

Opa handed Carrie a slice. "Your oma's getting over her Broderick paranoia. A few good recipes, that's all it took."

"Paranoia?" Dirk lifted an eyebrow.

"When Oma was eight," Carrie said, "Mrs. Gordon approached her in downtown Wolcott and quoted a line from *The Wizard of Oz*. And one from Dickens about fairy tales. Oma was scared. Didn't even know the lady."

"Odd." Dirk took a bite. "Mmm. Magical. Frankly, she's more charming than her reputation allows."

"You met her?" Oma paused mid-bite.

Dirk hesitated. "I was invited for tea."

"You invited yourself," Carrie said.

Dirk grinned. "It was delightful. That's what you say about a proper tea, right?"

You don't strike me as the tea party type," Opa said.

"I'm quite versatile."

Oma leaned his way. "So, how was she? Carrie won't say much."

"She's an amazing storyteller. So full of opinions you don't have to ask for one. They come right out with the biscuits. I learned a lot."

"How's Amy?" Oma asked Carrie. "And the party?"

"Sorry you weren't there." Mom hadn't requested to put them on the guest list. Carrie shared about Amy, careful not to relegate her to the realm of Wonder Woman. "Typical Wiersma event, perfection incarnate. Tons of guests. Delicious food."

"Nothing like this cake." Dirk raised a forkful. "It breaks my wooden shoe."

Carrie flashed a smile, head swimming with the notion of Dirk gracing their table daily.

"How's Brian?" Oma asked.

Carrie hesitated. "He's ... starting a job at Dad's business."

Opa clapped. "Wonderful! Things are shaping up. Peas in a pod, you two."

Peas in a pod. *Too crowded, too confined, too limited. Too green.* Like accounting books, Brian's nose stuck in them. Green dollar bills spent on new green furniture she hated.

"You never mentioned that, Carrie," Dirk said.

"Brian'll take over your dad's business," Opa said. "You're set for life."

Stuck for life. Panic set in. Carrie's heart thudded. The room shrank.

Oma touched Carrie's hand. "Ed, you're forgetting. Carrie's café is *here*."

Dirk's brow furrowed. "Did you know the plan, Carrie?"

"No. But it's a done deal."

Opa's eyes about popped out. Oma sputtered, "*Nou breekt m'n klomp.*"

"Breaks my clog, too," Dirk said.

Oma dropped her fork. "They can't make plans behind your back. Brian needs *een koekje van zijn eigen deeg.*"

"*Koekje?* He needs a cookie?" Dirk frowned.

"A cookie of his own dough," Carrie said. "Meaning a taste of his own medicine."

Oma clucked her tongue. "*Ze doen knollen voor citroenen verkopen.*"

Dirk finished his coffee. "Thanks, Mrs. Groothuis. I should go."

Carrie followed him to the door, where he lingered, his mouth a grim line. "They didn't consult you. And Brian knowing your café plans. That's wrong, Carrie."

"I know. I slammed Betty Crocker on the table."

"Ouch!" He gave her a high five. "What'd your oma just say?"

Carrie swallowed. "It means they're selling turnips as lemons. Making false promises, feeding impossible dreams."

Like a humbug wizard. Undependable. Dreams of living happily ever after with Brian dissipated.

"I hope you can work it out."

"Not sure what that looks like. Thanks for the ride. My weekend highlight."

"What about Henry's ice cream?"

She smiled. "It's a tie."

"My highlight was you belting it out like Aretha Franklin." He left.

Don't fall for him! He probably had ten bucks in the bank. A shared love of pop music wasn't solid ground for a serious relationship. She and Brian had deeper ties—entwined memories, challenges overcome, woven through the years.

Yet with Dirk, she was seen. She was herself, the girl who liked old furniture.

In bed, she fingered *The Annotated Wizard of Oz* and reread his inscription. *Whether escaping locusts, witches, dragons, or the Slough of Despond, you're on a journey that rivals Dorothy's with many adventures to come.*

Which adventures? With him? But he was leaving this fall. And he didn't invite her.

He craved the next challenge. New vistas. Biking, hiking, climbing, sailing, rafting. She sought security, a home to put down roots, a place for the decades. The café. But without Brian, she wouldn't have her parents' approval. Anxiety threaded through her like a needle.

Forty-Nine

Monday, June 30, 1980

Over Polychrome's Dewdrop Mist Trifle and Trot's Papaya Mango Tea, Carrie rehashed the weekend's debacles, circling back to Brian giving away her chair.

"The chair's merely a symptom of the problem," Mrs. Gordon said.

"I know. He's selling turnips for lemons. Especially now that he's made arrangements with my dad as if our intentions together were null and void. As if there was no café." Carrie frowned. "They don't have confidence I can do anything substantial."

"They surely thought you'd be a good teacher."

"They just want me to do something that makes the family look good. A respectable career until we have kids. My dad always talks about how much blood, sweat, and tears restaurant owners pour into their work. How stressful and risky it is. That's why I wanted to tell them *after* the café was up and running. So they could see my success."

"And be proud of you. On your own terms." Mrs. Gordon

set down her teacup. "Carrie, I'm afraid you'll never please them, no matter how successful you are. Because this venture wasn't *their* idea." The woman took her hand, her touch surprisingly soothing. "Unfortunately, they haven't bothered getting to know you well enough to see your vision, skills, and passion."

Mrs. Gordon sat back. "Don't seek praises of those who love you conditionally. Don't do what I did." A shadow crossed her face.

Janie, 19
August 1911

Mr. Ferguson applauded Janie's idea, a series about women in nontraditional careers. She longed to return to New York to interview Michigan native and journalist Harriet Quimby, the first American woman airplane pilot to get her license, this very month. But school enticed, too. Was this how Mr. Baum felt, torn by myriad un-produced plays and unwritten stories?

But newspaper earnings and Mr. Ferguson's partial reimbursement for trips didn't cover a semester of tuition, books, room and board. She'd depleted her savings bringing Mae to Wolcott.

One evening, Janie approached her father, his newspaper open to Isabel Girard's column. What would he do if he learned she was Isabel? He only knew about her feature articles.

He smirked. "This Isabel Girard says women should be paid the same as men, but tell me how chopping onions compares to chiseling through lake ice or pruning trees."

His words chagrined her, but she smiled. "I agree with her. I've worked diligently in the kitchen four years but receive half of hired hand wages." As of one year ago.

"A business needs a high profit margin, and you're not supporting a family." He flicked his hand, intoning sarcasm. "You've enough for gallivanting around the country."

"The newspaper pays." Partially. "I want to take writing classes at Western Michigan."

"You have the newspaper job. Ask this Isabel by what unseemly methods she gets *her* pay raises. Ha!"

She clenched her fists. *Stay calm.* "With some backpay, I'd have enough for college."

"You'll be married soon. Babies will come." His wave dismissed her. "Better to reinvest in business or give to charity."

Charity? She squelched a scream. Despite his generous community donations, he didn't have a charitable bone. "Teddy says you'll give him a raise after we marry."

"If Teddy supports you in reckless writing ventures, he's crazy."

"I've earned my keep. I'm asking for fair—"

"Fair? I run a family business." His voice ruffled like Lake Michigan waves lathered up for a brewing storm. "I'm not obligated to pay you. Consider every penny a gift."

She stewed. "Then Teddy and I will marry sooner than later." She spun around, fancying herself a young, spirited Maud Gage whose mother protested marriage to Frank.

"No wedding for two years. He's my apprentice. I need more confidence in his abilities."

"Teddy *has* proven himself." Franticness etched her voice. "Why two years?"

"It's reasonable. You're only nineteen."

"My sisters married at nineteen." Their husbands didn't join the business. Thus, the new stipulation about the next son-in-law. "There's no reason to wait. We're in love."

"In love, eh? You just want his pay raise for your silly classes."

Soon, she was crying on her aunt's shoulder.

Auntie stroked Janie's hair and handed her a letter, news from Mr. Baum.

A skedaddle of chickens accompanies us at Ozcot. One featherhead I've named Billina. I've opted for Rhode Island Reds, not Hamburgs. They add their squawks to the music of my songbirds and fountain, serenading me during my writing or weeding.

Miss Van Dyne is devising her next adventure for Louise, Elizabeth, and Patsy. They'll establish their own newspaper, proving that women are just as capable as men—a nod to your own accomplishments. From Syracuse to Chicago and back to New York, you're incomparable to all but Nellie Bly herself! Watch for the title Aunt Jane's Nieces in Journalism.

Janie wondered if the girls would receive equal pay for their efforts.

On Saturday, Teddy finagled a way for them to escape to the meadow alone.

"Your Aunt Sophie thinks we're at the Weavers'," he told Janie. "The Weavers think we're at Aunt Sophie's."

On a blanket under an oak tree, they unloaded fruit, bread, sausage, cheese, licorice, and Dr. Pepper. Teddy stretched his legs. "You're as 'sad looking as the sun in the day of mist, when her face is watery and dim.'"

Janie smiled. "One of your Scottish poets?"

"Adapted from James MacPherson."

"You've still no use for British poets."

"I could say 'sad as a lump of lead.' That's British. Edmund

Spenser's epic poem 'Faerie Queen.'" He brought a grape to her lips. "Eat, love."

She accepted the grape as his fingers outlined her mouth, sending sweet ripples over her skin. "Will you be serenading me?"

"Another Scottish favorite, Robert Burns." He sang, "'O, my love is like a red, red rose, That's newly sprung in June ...'"

"Lovely."

"Not bad coming from one who couldn't carry a tune even if it had handles. Thus said my schoolteachers." His fingers traced her jawline. "What's this melancholy?"

"My father." She shared details.

"Selling your fairy tale to *St. Nicholas* will open bigger doors. I'll help with classes."

"With the pittance he pays you?"

"Made up for in expertise. When we're married, he'll double my pay." He swallowed some Dr. Pepper.

"He says we must wait two years."

He nearly blew out the drink. "I can't wait that long."

Her heart thudded. "You won't wait for me?"

"Of course I will, but two unbearable years ..."

She leaned her head on his shoulder. "There must be poetic justice." No response. She sat up. "What's wrong?"

"Ma loves you, but she doesn't want me unequally yoked."

Janie's throat tightened. "I go to church."

"Only because I go."

"Who helps you control your temper? Are you a better sinner than I?" She blustered. "My father wants you to work two more years. Like Jacob in the Bible, working for Rachel. See? I know my Bible, every blasted story. My father's making you work for me, your prize, his piece of property."

He tipped her chin up. "Like a king wanting his daughter's hand to go to the worthiest. You're the beautiful princess I'm willing to wait for."

His words diffused her anger. Transforming her from

property into princess, what she wrote about in fairy tales. "Oh, Teddy …"

He leaned closer, cupping her cheek. "'As fair art thou, my bonnie lass, So deep in love am I.'" He kissed her tenderly, then hungrily, sending a thrill down her spine, igniting a flame deep inside her belly. His whispers echoed the breeze. "Poetic justice, after all."

He pressed her to his chest, grasped her shoulder, fingers sliding under her neckline, seeking skin. His touch fanned the flame inside. Like brandy for a sore throat, liquor heating and spreading through her, enticing. No more waiting.

The next few weeks, Janie thought only of Teddy, lying together in the sunshine. Minutes apart seemed like hours, hours together like minutes. Several times, they dodged watchful eyes, basking in each other's love, skin against skin.

Janie got morning nausea. Her monthly flow stopped. The realization jolted her like a wheel dipping in a pothole. Daily she prayed. *Please let me bleed.* After two months, she couldn't deny it. She discreetly went to Dr. Weaver's one evening when Teddy was home alone. In the parlor, holding her shoulders, he searched her eyes. "You're shaking. What's wrong?"

"I'm … pregnant."

His face paled, head shaking. "What?" His hands went to his forehead. He walked away. "How can this be?"

"You know very well how this can be! Maybe now my father will let us marry." Though no chance for Janie's education.

He paced. "No, your father'll kill me. Or fire me. I've worked too hard."

"Then let's leave. You can work anywhere."

"I don't have money to move. I have my mother and sister

to care for." He pivoted, arms flailing. "Illegitimate children never rise above their stations. We can't have this child."

"Then we tell Father. If we marry, our baby will be legitimate."

"But it's shameful." Trembling, he picked up *The Pilgrim's Progress*. It hung limply before dropping on the table.

She stepped toward him. "Our love is stronger than this."

"I can't tell your father. Ma would die. No one can know."

"Yes, we sinned. Now we pay for it. But we can give this baby a loving home."

He gaped. "The whole town will know. You must end this pregnancy."

"That's illegal!" Janie squawked, invisible fingers squeezing her throat. "Akin to murder."

"If you miscarry, we'll wait till we're properly married."

"I can't kill life growing inside me. How could you claim to follow God?"

He grabbed her sleeve. "My mother will die of grief, humiliated beyond repair. It's more shameful than fighting. She knows the shame illegitimate ones bring. Permanently."

"Doesn't God's grace cover this sin?"

"God forgives, but nobody else will." His voice burned. "You *can't* tell your father."

The scarlet *A* flashed before her. "Then you're dooming me. I thought you *loved* me!"

His eyes darkened. "Nobody can know," he growled. "All my life, I've run from shame my father heaped on me."

Janie gritted her teeth. "Isn't God your father? He *forgives*!"

His words choked. "I can't bear more scorn."

"You want me to wear a big red *A* while you keep working for my father?"

He glared across the room. "They'll suspect me. Just ... discard the child."

"Like trash?"

Face scarlet, he slammed a fist into his hand. "I *won't* be shamed again. I won't disgrace my mother. I've been running from shame my whole life." He turned away. "You drag me down. All your questions, all your doubts. You wooed me on purpose, hoping we'd marry sooner."

"How *dare* you say that! Who planned a picnic alone?"

"You're always doubting. Your imagination distracts you from important things."

"You *supported* my writing aspirations. You're dooming me to be what you despise. Unmarried mother, servant for life." Janie stamped to the window and back. "*You're* the hypocrite. If God's your Father, do the right thing. You want to kill our unborn child for the sake of your future?"

"You drive me to desperation." He shook her shoulders. Locked in his grasp, she panicked. Would he strike her? "Ma's right, we're unequally yoked." He let go. She stumbled back. He waved *The Pilgrim's Progress*. "You're the Slough of Despond to me!"

"The Slough of Despond?" Her voice wobbled.

He threw the book against the wall. "You lure me in without escape. Trapping me."

Dizzy, she grasped the chair.

"I can't be with you. You're the Slough of Despond, sinking me in the mire, far from God's light." He turned away.

The wall of contempt toppled over her. She groped for words. "So be it." In one last act of desperation, she snatched *Pilgrim's Progress* and fled from the house before he noticed she had it. Pride and that book were his most favored possessions. More than she was.

Mae was out when she reached Aunt Sophie's. Janie confessed all as her aunt held her. They cried together.

Janie sniffled. "I must leave Wolcott."

"Teddy will do what's right. He loves you, chinchilla."

"No." The damage was done. *You're the Slough of Despond to me!* Such venom. Irrevocable. His treasured book, espousing that God was his true Father, meant nothing.

Aunt Sophie wrung her hands, muttering. "They'll blame me for negligence."

"Oh, Auntie ..." Janie ran upstairs and wailed on the bed. She'd always fancied herself a Cinderella, living through hard times to someday marry the prince. Now she was Red Riding Hood, aghast to find a wolf in Grandmother's clothing. Or Hansel and Gretel in the woods, birds eating the breadcrumb trail, offering no way back.

Though furious and heavyhearted, Janie couldn't be vindictive. Dear Mae might break. Perhaps Mae's trust in God would engender forgiveness, but Janie couldn't humiliate her.

Auntie made arrangements with her Holland friends, Dena Vanderlaan's sister Katrina—Katje—for Janie to live with.

A week later, Janie told her parents she was taking a better-paying job in Holland in two days. That she and Teddy were parting ways, for good. She let them think it was her own doing.

Her father was livid. Her mother was distraught about needing to find her replacement in the kitchen. "Family doesn't walk out on family," Elsa sputtered.

But Janie's family already had. She quit her job at *The Town Crier*. Mr. Ferguson countered with bonus pay and another literary trip, but she declined. He wrote a recommendation and asked for more columns. She made no promises.

That evening, Janie picked up the Macatawa stone from the day Harry told her about Ethical Sunday School. His talk about living honorably without God had snaked into her stomach, writhing and squeezing, pressing against everything she'd learned. She'd kept the stone as solace, a link to what she believed was true.

But where was God now? The all-loving God Teddy claimed to follow.

Staggering to the lake, she squeezed the rock. The day clouded with swatches of gray. The beach resembled the Great Sandy Waste and Impassable Desert surrounding Oz. Wind whirled through her hair and stung her eyes. She flung the stone over the water.

Janie embraced her duty to her unborn child. After all, wasn't love wanting the highest good for someone, even at great cost? Love lavished on her by Aunt Sophie and the Baums would flow out to her child. Along with her worn Dorothy doll, she packed nursery rhyme and fairy tale books, leaving plenty for Beatrice. She held Mr. Baum's chicken ornament, recalling pleasant porch chatter—to help her through dark times. *You have all the brains, heart, and courage you need, wherever the road takes you.*

This road she hadn't anticipated. She tucked the ornament into her bag, then shoved Teddy's *Pilgrim's Progress* into a drawer.

Janie said goodbye to Mae and Beatrice, leaving them dumbfounded. Aunt Sophie took her to the home of Jakob and Katje Kloosterman and their four children: twins Henrik and Niels, Pieter, and daughter Mariet. Jakob had obtained a job for her at the Heinz factory where he worked, a mile from their 16th Street home near downtown Holland.

Janie sought employment at *The Holland Daily Sentinel* and *Holland City News*, but nothing was available, despite Mr. Ferguson's positive letter. Perhaps for the best. At the factory, she'd be invisible, better suited for an expanding stomach.

Watching Jakob and Katje interact with their lively children in loving yet stern ways, Janie agonized. How could she raise a fatherless child?

Nightly, they read the Bible—as refreshing water, rather than a club. While Jakob's readings intoned reverence for God, he also laughed at the children's antics, tousled their hair, invited them onto his lap. Janie's heart ached, missing what she never had, lamenting what her child would never experience.

She wrote to Mr. Baum with her new address and the devastating news. Worried about his response, she didn't mail it.

1980

Carrie wiped her wet cheek. Mrs. Gordon scowled without a tear. Surely, she'd been wrung dry over the decades. But pain imprinted her face. Carrie frowned at Teddy's tattered book. "I'm so sorry he called you the Slough of Despond. That's awful. As if he was without fault."

Mrs. Gordon's voice trembled. "I was the questioner, the doubter."

"You were honest. Did he take responsibility later?"

"Never."

Carrie squeezed Mrs. Gordon's hand. "I understand why you never read this book. You're brave to do it now."

"Now you see why I couldn't pursue my Nellie Bly dream. Charlotte Rose and Isabel Girard disappeared."

"What about the baby?"

"We'll get to that." Misery laced her words. "I saw no point for churchgoing after that."

"There *is* no point without dropping off your burden." Carrie tread carefully. "Christian dropped off his heavy load of sin first."

"I've a bigger burden than Christian."

"No, you don't. All sin has the same antidote."

Mrs. Gordon faced the wall. "I sacrificed much for Teddy's sake. Even later."

Like what? They tended the garden, burgeoning with delphinium and hydrangeas. Sunflowers continued their climb as William Blake's poetry took on new meaning. *Ah, Sunflower, weary of time.* Janie, the jilted lover, bound to earth and emptiness.

Later, on the porch, Carrie tapped *Pilgrim's Progress*. "Shall we skip reading today?"

"No sense stalling."

Carrie read, scrutinizing Mrs. Gordon's responses. Christian and Hopeful reached the Enchanted Ground, its air causing drowsiness. They talked to avoid sleep. The lad Ignorance followed them. Christian emphasized that True Faith was flying for refuge to Christ's righteousness, not one's own. But Ignorance trusted his own ideas and good deeds. Christian and Hopeful talked until past the Enchanted Ground, safe from its spell.

"Enchanted Ground," Mrs. Gordon mused. "Like Mr. Baum's Poppy Field, the same drowsy effect. Hmm. Are good deeds worth nothing, according to Mr. Bunyan?"

"Not to gain favor. We can't do enough good. The Robe from the Shining One is a gift, remember? Like 'a warm embrace of Christ.'"

Mrs. Gordon crossed her arms. "As warm as a jail cell."

FIFTY

Thursday, July 3, 1980

Carrie and Mrs. Gordon baked Cayke's Magic Dishpan Cookies, an oatmeal-butterscotch variation. Carrie copied another recipe—Rinkitink's Jolly Berry Trifle. She added sugar to Ceylon tea. "Brian called last night."

"Any apologies about his clandestine career decision?"

"Nope." Hearing his rich, chocolatey voice had reinforced her preference for caramel. "We need to talk face to face. Away from his turf. If he doesn't understand, I might break up."

"Break up with Mr. Polite, Money-in-the-bank, Baseball Star who brings Chocolate?"

Carrie offered a wry smile.

"What does your oma say? Mopping up while the faucet's running ..."

"I know." Carrie bit her lip.

"Better to endure heartache now than after you're married and miserable." Mrs. Gordon's face darkened. "You have choices I didn't have."

Janie, 19
Fall 1911

Katje Kloosterman's home was as charming as she was: a tidy brick cottage, Dutch lace, kitchen brimming with Delft touches. The kitchen smelled like smoked sausage and rye bread baking. Laughter pervaded despite mischievous boys.

The bookshelf bulged with theology, history, and fiction, mostly Dutch, including *Pilgrim's Progress*. The Kloostermans spoke primarily Dutch at home, except to Janie. A Dutch-English Bible topped the coffee table. Snuggling with Mariet, Janie told Dutch stories in English, according to illustrations: "The Entangled Mermaid," "The Boy Who Wanted More Cheese," and "The Princess with Twenty Petticoats."

Weekdays, Janie walked to the Heinz factory, mustering a positive attitude, but tedious repetition of bottling pickles bored her. A pioneer in technological innovation and product purity, Mr. Heinz used the pickle assorter to guarantee uniform pickles. Supervisors were meticulous about quality and cleanliness. Janie and food handlers received weekly manicures. They filled beautiful glass jars for displays.

During long, boring hours, she devised marketing strategies, then relayed suggestions to the unimpressed shift manager. Women's ideas weren't welcome. She asked about product demonstrations at the grocer's, but that job was for salesmen.

Inspired by Mr. Baum's *Show Window* magazine, she offered to create downtown window displays, but nobody wanted her help. Years ago, young Charlotte did printmaking with Mr. Baum, sharing stories and dreams. But look at her now. What would he say?

After family bedtime, watching kerosene light the darkness, Janie wrote fairy tales, recalling lessons from Mr. Baum about characters, dialog, and plot. She composed tales about Camellia of Lavender Lane, then revised, incorporating his tips, planning to submit to *St. Nicholas* before giving birth.

Though the Kloostermans were rigid about Sabbath keeping, they found delight in God's Word and creation. At suppertime, they marveled at God's faithfulness in Bible stories. They pointed out the beauty of leaves turning color, the intricacy of snowflakes drifting from the Creator's hand. Janie's mother had viewed leaves as a nuisance and tracked-in snow as another sad reason to mop the floor. Sandy puddles likened to apostasy.

Katje offered riddles at breakfast and books after supper, before tucking four kids into bed with a sweet good night. Would Janie have energy for her own child? Pregnancy wearied her. And the shame of deflecting judgmental looks.

Janie learned Dutch favorites. Potatoes for most meals, boiled for lunch, mashed for supper, leftovers for breakfast. *Stamppot*—mashed potatoes mixed with vegetables—was served with *rookworst*, a Dutch smoked sausage. A variation was *hete bliksem*—hot lightning—boiled potatoes with green apples, served with *stroop*, or syrup. Katje and Janie sliced extra potatoes Saturday night, to avoid Sunday work. Janie had never had so many potatoes in her life.

Such fare made her crave *snert*, for variation, a pea soup so thick one could stand a spoon in it, like Mr. Baum's coffee. Katje served it with *rookworst* slices and *roggebrood*—rye bread —and Gouda or Edam cheese. The children loved *pannenkoeken*, the Dutch pancake. As a treat, Janie bought them Dutch licorice *griotten* or the salty *zoute* drops.

Janie made morning coffee since Katje needed her *bakje troost*—little cup of solace. Katje insisted it kept her "chicken-delicious"—*kiplekker*. Mr. Baum would love that term. But Janie needed more than coffee to make her feel fresh as a chicken.

On Saturdays, Katje woke early to bake bread and start chores. Sometimes, Janie made blueberry cream cheese muffins. Jakob worked Saturdays, then did house repairs. She envied how he'd brush by Katje to steal kisses, then gather the children with bear hugs.

After errands, Janie often wandered downtown, around Centennial Park and the big white church started by Dominie Van Raalte in 1856. Viewing Hope College, she yearned for writing classes. The school opened to women in 1878, but Janie had neither time nor money.

Out of courtesy, she attended Fourteenth Street Christian Reformed Church with the Kloostermans. As if church hadn't been difficult already, services were in Dutch. Afterward, they only ate, rested, visited, and read. The Kloostermans invited Janie to accompany them to their parents' or friends' houses, but Janie declined, thereby avoiding the evil eye and judgmental tones. For as winter approached, her belly grew, her purpose at the Kloostermans' no secret.

After supper, Jakob played his mandolin and sang with the children. They played games and read till bedtime. Katje mended while Janie fumbled through knitting a bonnet. Jakob read, sometimes aloud.

"I can't keep a book out of his hands," Katje said. "He likes it as much as dessert."

Jakob replied without looking up. "Not as much as your blueberry muffins, Janie."

If Jakob went to bed early, Katje sought her for conversation. Janie was reticent, hesitant to trust. Small talk prevailed. How would happily married Katje understand Teddy's rejection? How could Katje, contented mother of four, understand Janie's fizzling dreams?

On November 6, 1911, a penumbral lunar eclipse occurred. Shadows swallowed the moon. But Janie's dreams might be vanquished forever. Along with the dawn.

Poetry fed her melancholy, especially Thomas Gray's Elegy:

> Full many a flower is born to blush unseen,
> And waste its sweetness on the desert air.

Janie, a flower meant to bloom in the world, vanished, unseen. Except to be scorned.

March 1912

One late evening, Katje found Janie washing dishes. "*Nou breekt m'n klomp.*" She guided Janie to a chair and poured tea. "Prop up your feet. Baby still needs a month in the oven."

Janie sighed. "How do you manage? You're so calm when Niels whines, when Pieter tracks in mud. I'll never be that patient."

"*Zwammen!* Nonsense. I'm on my best behavior with a live-in guest. Plenty of times I snap." Katje picked up mending. "Janie, I want to understand. You are polite when we read scripture, go to church, and pray, but I see your distress. You don't believe this for yourself. You are full of *angst en vrees*. Fear and dread."

Finally, like a bursting dike, Janie told Katje about critical, demeaning parents and how close she came to believing God was good until Teddy abandoned her.

"Do you still hope Teddy will marry you?"

"It's too late. Too much damage."

"*Ja*, like mustard after the meal." Frowning, Katje jabbed her needle. "He was *knollen voor citroenen verkopen*. Selling turnips as lemons. Making false promises."

Bracing for condemnation, Janie examined flames writhing in the hearth.

"Oh, Janie." Katje's fabric dropped to her lap. "People don't always reflect God's light. He should understand forgiveness and do the right thing."

"His father beat him. Teddy still suffers from that."

"So do you now. It doesn't excuse him." Katje took Janie's hand. "Life seems unfair. I know. In 1845, my grandparents left work, property, and family in the Netherlands to come here with Dominie Van Raalte, to freely live their faith. They dug the channel, built the city of Holland, and started businesses. Such hard work. Yet three decades later, in 1871, a fire destroyed the city. My grandparents lost everything again and had to start over. That time was an endless prayer. Yet they held on to their faith. I was born fifteen years later. They taught me that God provided for our deepest eternal needs. He's still trustworthy. We're pilgrims on this earth."

Though touched, Janie winced at the word *pilgrim*. "Sounds like you had a loving home. I was condemned for reading fairy tales."

"Fairy tales?"

"As a child, I read fairy tales in secret. Fiction was evil. Mother only allowed the Bible, the primer, and *Pilgrim's Progress*."

Katje strode to the bookshelf and found *De Gemene Gratie*. "By former *Nederland* prime minister, Abraham Kuyper, a Christian. He founded the Reformed Churches in the Netherlands. Ten years ago, he started writing about common grace."

"Common grace?"

"*Ja*, how to explain ..." Katje riffled through pages. "It's God's preserving work in creation, how He oversees this world, by bestowing gifts to all people." She lifted Janie's Delft teacup. "See the beauty? Common grace is the reason for good and lovely things. It's why men who don't follow God still love others and serve their neighbors."

She picked another book, *De Gemeene Gratie in Wetenschap en Kunst*. "*Common Grace in Science and Art*. Many good people, believers or not, make discoveries or inventions and become doctors or architects." She retrieved Jakob's mandolin. "Jakob plays this beautifully. In the park, an unchurched man plays just as skillfully. See? Talents bless us all with the beauty of God's character." She strummed a chord. "Very bad. My talent is cooking. I know forty-two ways to make potatoes."

Giggling, Katje handed her the book, pointing to a passage. "I'll translate. Dr. Kuyper says, 'As image bearers of God, man possesses the possibility both to create something beautiful and to delight in it ... The world of sounds, the world of tints, and the world of poetic ideas, can have no source other than God ... and it is our privilege as bearers of His image, to have a perception of this beautiful world, artistically to reproduce it, and humanly to enjoy it.'"

"That's lovely. But how does this apply to fairy tales?"

"It means we enjoy stories of all kinds. God made us creators, too, with imagination. It's why Thomas Edison invents the light bulb, Henry Ford builds the automobile, and the Wright brothers the aeroplane. It's why I read many tales to my children, not just Bible stories. It's why American authors, like Mark Twain, write stories that delight. All God-given gifts."

"I saw no grace in my house."

"My dear, you've experienced plenty of grace. You just didn't attribute it to God. Aunt Sophie, for one. Mr. Baum's another. All the stories you enjoyed. All the talents you possess."

Quivering, Janie fingered the paper. "Teddy rejected me, after all I did for him. I lost my journalism career." She patted her belly. "I'm alone, losing my dreams, every blessing a curse. I've sinned against this child I bear."

Katje closed her eyes, as if picking the right words. Her eyelids fluttered open. "Janie, my God is a God of redemption. He can redeem the years the locusts ate."

"What?" A shiver of hope rippled through her.

Katje took the Dutch-English Bible. "God speaks to his people after decades of idolatry and oppressing the helpless.

He allowed enemies to take them into captivity. The Israelites were full of shame for their sins. But listen to what God says." She read from Joel, chapter two:

> *"And I will restore to you the years that the locust hath eaten ... And ye shall eat in plenty, and be satisfied, and praise the name of the Lord your God ... and my people shall never be ashamed."**

Janie listened, eyes closed. "Never ashamed. How? They were captives."

"*Ja.* The Lord planned to richly bless them again and remove their shame. He restored them to their land." She clasped the Bible to her chest. "He does the same today when we acknowledge our sin."

Janie frowned. "I've sinned, but I can't trust God as you do. I only see my father's scowling face. I tried to be good, seek peace, and love others, but to no avail."

"Finding peace apart from God is like *dweilen met de kraan open.* Mopping up while the faucet's running. It doesn't address the real problem."

1980

"God redeems the time the locusts ate," Carrie murmured. Had Janie lived with Dirk's ancestor?

In the garden, marigolds and shasta daisies dazzled. Blue morning glories climbed the trellis. Sunflowers proudly stood four feet tall.

After watering, Carrie and Mrs. Gordon sat on the porch.

"Today, we'll finish Christian's story." Carrie read about

---

* Joel 2:25 (KJV)

Christian and Hopeful's last barrier: the River of Death. Christian floundered in deep water, swamped by anxiety and doubt. Hopeful's passage in shallow waters was easier. At the Gate, they gave their certificates to the Shining Ones and entered the brilliant Celestial City.

"What does Mr. Bunyan mean by the River of Death being both deep and shallow?" Mrs. Gordon asked.

"When Christian was fearful, the river seemed deeper. Both he and Hopeful reached the City, not because of great faith, but because the King keeps his word."

Mrs. Gordon appeared contemplative. "Dorothy was admitted to the Wizard because of the Silver Shoes, and the kiss from the Witch of the North."

"Like the Robe, Mark, and Scroll."

"But the Wizard's a humbug, a trickster. Dorothy wanted to go home. The others had their own requests. Things they already possessed."

Carrie smiled. "Perhaps common grace?"

"Oz says we have everything we need inside us." Mrs. Gordon folded her hands in her lap. "But Mr. Bunyan would say that's poppycock. Christian can't remove his burden. Only the King can give him the Robe."

"Right."

"But I've a bigger burden than Christian. I haven't told you my worst sin."

That evening, Carrie found the café manager. "May I look for the dune picture?"

"Miss Kruisselbrink, I'm busy."

"Which day works?"

Pearl squinted. "What's the rush?"

"Your aunt's eighty-eight, for one thing."

"And healthy as a horse."

"I'd like to give her some happiness." Did Pearl know about the illegitimate baby? Probably not. She might have mentioned it with the pharmacy scandal.

"What's your number? No promises."

Carrie scribbled the number, then settled into a booth. Dirk caught her eye with a merry glint during James Taylor's "Carolina on My Mind," as if *Caroline* occupied his mind rather than the state. Two days ago, Dirk had tuned up her bicycle before they took a bike ride together. He could have ridden to Holland in the time it took her to pant across Wolcott. Forget dance aerobics.

Dirk beelined over after his set. Carrie told him about Janie and the locust prayer. He confirmed his great-grandmother was Katrina Kloosterman.

After marveling, he said, "I made you two tapes, as requested. One's called 'Soggy Pretzels,' named for the woeful Neil Diamond song, then 'Footloose and Fancy Free Aerobics.' Hey, got plans for the Fourth tomorrow?"

"Brian invited me to his family shindig. There's a new event, Battle Creek's Field of Flight Air Show and Balloon Festival."

Dirk's mouth twitched. "Permission to meddle?"

"Sure." She avoided rolling her eyes.

"Carrie, if he hasn't seen how he's hurt you by now, talking face to face won't help."

"It'll help if he's *here*, on *my* turf."

"Okay. But if you're not going, wanna join me tomorrow? We're sailing again. There's a cookout with a bunch of scalawags. A friendly crew. Then fireworks on the beach."

"I'd be a fifth wheel."

Dirk held up his hand. "I, Dirk Vandenakker, do solemnly swear to see that Carrie Kruisselbrink has the day of her life."

"Will you keep the boat from capsizing?"

"No guarantees, but I'll be your hero to the rescue. I'll introduce you around. Boating, jet skiing, swimming. Food galore. Watching fireworks from boats, shore, or inner tubes. Planes and balloons will pale in comparison. Like the cut of my jib?"

She smiled. "Yes. I could use your powers of persuasion on Pearl. I don't have any."

He chuckled. "You have more than you think. What do you want from *me*? Name it."

Invite me on the Appalachian Trail. "I'd like to visit Captain Sundae without you finagling me out of my ice cream."

"Ow!" He put a fist to his heart. "You aim right for the summit. How about me toning down the pirate talk instead?"

"I'd better brush up on it if I keep sailing with you."

"Good point. What do you need from Pearl?" After her explanation, he replied, "I can help. She's in the over-forty crowd—"

"I know. Older women love you."

He glanced at his watch. "Any requests?"

What captured Mrs. Gordon's heartache? "'Fire and Rain.'"

FIFTY-ONE

Friday, July 4, 1980

In Holland, buoyed by Morning Coffee music, Dirk showed Carrie Centennial Park, the Heinz factory, the Kloostermans' former house, and church—now Maple Avenue Christian Reformed.

Sailing on Lake Michigan, Carrie demanded a crash course in directional terminology. She verbalized acronyms to remember port, starboard, stern, and bow. In a precarious turn, Carrie pitched into the water with screams and laughter. Dirk toppled in after her for a swashbuckling rescue.

While kayaking, sparkles of sunshine teased. But while Dirk chattered about bailing out a dinghy near the Bahamas, Carrie slipped into melancholy while pondering Teddy's rejection. What happened to her baby? Dirk finally asked what was wrong. How could he pick up on her moods when Brian didn't?

Minutes later, they strolled Lake Michigan's shoreline. "What's up?" he asked.

Her feet squished in wet sand. "Janie couldn't measure up in her family. Neither did I." She shared incidents she'd told Mrs.

Gordon and more, gauging his expressions. "Life revolved around Amy. She was spunky, witty, smart. I was awkward and shy." Dare she say more? "This sounds so trivial. I should be over it."

Dirk squeezed her hand, radiating strength. "That's your mom's voice."

"I wanted to run a restaurant. They required a four-year education degree at their alma mater. Everything I cared about was frivolous to them. So, listening to Mrs. Gordon's stories, I'm realizing how I've been manipulated, blamed, and shamed my whole life. Like her."

"So, you came to Wolcott to find yourself. Become the hero of your own story."

"Sometimes I feel more like a damsel in distress."

"You're more heroine than you realize, pursuing your café. Plus, from the day we met, you told me what's what."

"My anger was starting to spill out."

"But you've accomplished much. Pardon the sailor talk, but instead of navigating oceans, you've had the superior adventure of plumbing the depths of a person's soul, maneuvering through Mrs. G.'s life, understanding her loneliness and despair. That's admirable."

His words touched her. "Withhold your praise. I only came to Wolcott to launch my private rebellion. I wanted to work at The Burger Flipper to spite my parents. When I landed the job with Mrs. Gordon, it seemed like perfect retaliation. They'd never value such a thing."

Dirk's friendly chuckle rumbled. "Your silent rebellion makes Mister Rogers look like Mick Jagger."

"That's funny to you, but I've spent my whole life being squeezed into different shapes."

"Do your parents know you're rebelling?"

"They know now. I told them about the café, too, waiting on the loan." She set her jaw, on the verge of revealing the failed class and no diploma. "I never had courage to stand up to them. If I did half the stuff you did or got pregnant, I'd be kicked out for good."

Dirk stopped and wrapped his arms around her. His chin nestled on her head, his strength bolstering her. When she pulled back, his eyes riveted to hers. "Carrie, real strength isn't making yourself into a wall that's never hurt. It's being transparent with genuine emotions. Stepping forward as yourself. You're doing the hard thing."

"Mrs. Gordon said that too. But I risk losing the only family I've known." Had she shared too much? She pulled away and forged ahead. He fell in sync beside her. They sidestepped the ghost of a sandcastle, softened by waves, the way her parents washed away her identity, her confidence. Like Charlotte years ago, diluted with time.

"Here's why that chair's so important. When we were little, Amy was bossy, always picking on me. But at night, the playing field leveled. We'd scramble into the reading chair with Mom and a pile of books. We'd read an hour or two."

"The Tasha Tudor book?"

"You remembered! Yes. In the reading chair, Mom took her time. No competition. No criticism. A magical hour." A tickle crept up her throat. "In that chair, for that hour, I felt loved. Other times, Amy was the star. In school, church plays, at the dinner table. Conversation revolved around *her* friends, *her* plans, *her* good grades."

"As if you weren't there."

"My main image of my dad is him reading the newspaper or turning to Amy or walking out while I'm talking. He never looks at me. Still." She sought the vast blueness of sky as if it could swallow her. "I was invisible." Her voice cracked.

Dirk planted himself before her. "Carrie, you're not invisible to *me*." He squeezed her hands. "The problem was them, not you."

"I couldn't be an Amy."

"I'm glad you're not Amy." He grinned. "At the risk of sounding like Billy Joel, I like you just the way you are."

Nobody'd ever said that to her. Not even Brian. "Without Oma and Opa, I'd be a lost soul."

"Your oma is your own personal Aunt Sophie." His tone stiffened. "Your parents had a false measuring stick."

"I haven't even told you the worst thing. In sixth grade. My dad was on the Christian school board. He brought in a new teacher with a great reputation, my sixth-grade teacher, Miss Nieuwenhuis. Problems started immediately. She pegged me for a daydreamer. When she caught me doodling, she'd tear it up in front of class and march me to the wastebasket. After she bonked a kid's head on the desk, I told my parents, but they didn't believe me. After all, she came highly recommended by Dad, backed by the school board."

"Wow."

"My capital punishment research paper contradicted my parents' politics. Mom was appalled. She tore it up and rewrote it. It sounded more adult than sixth grade, so the teacher accused me of plagiarism, gave me an *F,* and called Mom. Instead of admitting her part, Mom told Miss Nieuwenhuis she'd support the chosen consequences."

His brow furrowed. "Then what?"

"It took a week to rewrite it. I still got an *F,* for lateness. Mom was furious I'd kept my viewpoint. Didn't speak to me for a week."

"Whoa ..."

"Miss Nieuwenhuis found fault with everything, from yawning to messy penmanship. She took away recess for ridiculous reasons. She made me wash chalkboards and desks, then rewash them. My parents didn't believe me. The thing is, Miss Nieuwenhuis gave our humble school prestige. Test scores prevailed. If Dad told the board my complaints, he'd look foolish for endorsing her. So, they stood by the teacher."

"Unbelievable."

"In January, she pulled a kid's ear. He'd been bullied enough, so I slammed my desktop to distract her. She punished me. My parents accused me of disrespect and retaliating due to the *F*. So, I wrote the school board."

"You're kidding."

"Nope. I wanted to be anonymous but signed my name. That was a huge mistake. The principal called my dad. There were lots of meetings. But I couldn't throw Mom under the bus for writing my paper. So, the plagiarism accusation made me an unreliable witness."

"That's rotten. Did the board talk to other students?"

"Yes, but kids were too scared to be truthful. Mom didn't budge either. So, it boiled down to me being a big liar. The mayhem continued. My parents rewarded me with silence. Lots." She swallowed. "I've never told anyone. It's not worth opposing them. I toed the line to stay on their good side."

"*What* good side?" Dirk spun her toward himself, his eyes sad, absorbing her pain. He pulled her into a sweet, strong embrace. His lips found the top of her head. "I'm so sorry. That's awful. They're blind to the treasure you are."

Did he just kiss her?

His hands wove through her hair. What was happening? Actions he probably intended as a comforting, assuring friend felt like much more as his touch flooded her body with warmth. But he was leaving in August. *Don't fall for him!* Yet she was aflame, quivering in his arms.

"Another thing." She pulled back. "In May, I had after-school detention. Miss Nieuwenhuis left the room. My father was late. I needed to call him, so I walked to the office. I heard talking in the copy machine room. The closed door had a window ..." Her voice faltered. "My dad and Miss Nieuwenhuis were ... hugging. They kissed. Several minutes. I stood frozen, then knocked."

"Oh, man."

"My dad rushed to the door and said, 'Honey, your teacher

just found out her brother passed away. She's very upset.' As if it were normal for dads to comfort teachers this way. Miss Nieuwenhuis played the part and pulled out a tissue. I said, 'Does Mom know? When's the funeral?'"

"Now you're the quick thinker."

"Dad drove me home, insisting that he'd tell Mom about the brother. Dad said he was comforting Miss Nieuwenhuis because her family was in Massachusetts. Almost had me convinced I'd only seen a handshake."

"Horrible. Did you tell your mom?"

"No. That would backfire. Miss Nieuwenhuis was gone the next week, supposedly at the funeral. Afterward, she overpowered me so I'd stay quiet."

"Did you?"

"Yes. Unfair punishment was one thing. But this was my heart and soul being wrenched from my body." Carrie's voice hitched. "Fortunately, Miss Nieuwenhuis was gone the next year."

"And you've been silent ever since."

"Perpetrating our perfect veneer in town."

"Wow. Maybe this incident explains your aversion to teaching."

She blinked as the words sank in. "Maybe that's why I'm queasy every time I walk into an elementary classroom. I'm back in sixth grade all over again."

"That makes sense. It must be hard to trust people."

She eyed the horizon. His gaze was too intense. "Yes."

"Why do you want your parents' approval? You put them too high on a pedestal."

"I don't know. So much hypocrisy forced me to evaluate faith in God. Believe in something bigger than my parents. But it's hard for me to trust Him, too."

"You carried that alone too long." Dirk held her again as waves washed their feet, his heartbeat thumping in her ear. "Carrie, please don't ever pretend with me. I only want the genuine Carrie. No wonder you identify so much with Mrs. G.'s childhood."

"It's making me face my own dragons. See things as they were. Are. Silence, hypocrisy … lies."

"I wish I could take away the hurt." He led her to a spot in the sand. Late afternoon sun hovered, the lake's vibrant beauty belying her turmoil. He stroked her fingers, resting their hands on his knee. His touch sent shivers. Deep in her belly stirred a new warmth for Dirk. A combination of moments folded into this one: talking at the café, wanting to meet Mrs. Gordon, sharing his rough patch, hiking, sailing, finding the reading chair. Letting her cry. Though fragile as rose petals, she felt safe.

Brian might know how to fold his napkin at Win Schuler's, but Dirk could hold her heart with tenderness. She wanted to curl into him, but she couldn't succumb to gestures that seemed like invitations. Or was she misreading?

"Carrie, I realize you're with Brian, but I enjoy being with you more than anyone else. That's the real Carrie, not just a satin face. When I'm with you, I feel like a sailboat headed to harbor, to a sweet and safe place." He leaned closer. "With you, I also feel like a sailboat headed to sea." His fingertip trailed across her hand. "To an adventure."

But he was leaving soon. She sighed. Would he ever stop traipsing across the globe? "With you, I feel like a sunflower opening to the sun." Not William Blake's doomed sunflower. "Like a rose opening its petals." The flower in the Wendolyn treasure box.

She wanted him to kiss her. He looked like he wanted to.

Fifty-Two

Friday, July 4, 1980

At the party, Dirk introduced Carrie, served her food and drinks, roasted her marshmallows. They tossed a Frisbee and played water volleyball. A provocative conversation with Susan and Teresa prompted her musing. Having known Dirk since grade school, they shared tidbits to inquire about on the way home.

Dirk asked her to Jet Ski. Could the guy ever sit still? As the Jet Ski surged, she threw her arms around his waist. He drove like a crazy man with stops and starts. She squeezed tighter, pressing her cheek against his back, bracing for bounces and wave slaps. Ever conscious of his smell, her lips could easily have grazed his back. "Trying to throw me off?" she asked.

"Never. Just hold on tighter."

She laughed. "Ha! I'm on to your strategy."

Soon, holding soft drinks in inner tubes, they watched the sunset unfold in all its grandeur, catching them in its glittering enchantment. Dirk entertained her with stories of scuba adventures in Belize. She reveled in his expressions, his laughter, his animated storytelling. Above all, his attentiveness. She swatted thoughts of Brian away. With Brian, she was autumn's leftovers.

Dirk proposed a toast. "To Carrie and her bravery for spending the day with me."

Rocking in waves, she smiled. "Bravery or lunacy?"

"With me, you gotta be a little crazy. Did you mind?"

She raised her drink. "To Dirk and the wonderful day. You kept your promise."

His bottle met hers. "See? I don't give turnips for lemons."

At dark, they watched fireworks from the boat. Amidst mental images of Charlotte with the Baums, dazzling color displays stunned Carrie. Dirk's boyishly handsome face brightened as lights exploded above. She caught him watching her, and the images of Charlotte Rose faded.

***

"I learned a lot about you from Susan and Teresa," Carrie said on the drive home.

He smirked. "Take everything they say with a pound of salt."

"You're not as great as they claim?"

He chortled. "They've known me for years. The good, the bad, and the ugly."

"So … maybe you gallivant to avoid getting attached."

"Whoa, back up the train. That's what those troublemakers said?"

"Are they right?"

He cleared his throat. "Here's the deal. You entrusted me with something important. I'll reciprocate. Ready?"

"You have my undivided attention." She wrapped her arms around bent legs in the seat.

"I've had two relationships end badly. One right after high school, in my tailspin. The other one started three years ago in Grand Haven, where I managed the restaurant. A sweet girl named Monica worked at the *Y*. We dated eighteen months after a guy broke up with her. She's the reason I stayed so long." His voice slowed. "Then she went cold. Turns out she'd started dating another guy. Her soulmate, she said." He gripped the wheel. "We'd talked about marriage. But I was only the rebound guy."

"That's terrible."

"She used me. I was naive. And devastated. I swore I'd never be the rebound guy again. A grieving lover needs a year."

Sadness rippled through her. If she broke up, Dirk would disappear? Even if she was his safe harbor? "After eighteen months, that's brutal." She popped an Eagles tape in. "Permission to meddle?" Piano chords introduced the tune of "Desperado."

"Why the meddling and sudden change in music?"

"When you sang this at the café, I wondered if you were singing to yourself."

"I don't follow after diamonds."

"Maybe diamonds are your adventures." The song played out, an exhortation to receive love. Carrie admired his silhouette, the cut of his jaw, his mouth, whiskers that had brushed across her hair. Had he restrained himself because of Brian—or his own fears?

"Carrie, here's the deal. I'm afraid of having a relationship. Afraid of rejection. Afraid to risk it." Like a searchlight, Dirk's eyes swept back and forth between her face and the road. "Until ... I find a girl I can't get my mind off, with the qualities I adore."

Could she be that girl? Why the mixed messages?

"I'm sorry for taking advantage of your vulnerability. I overstepped when I kissed you."

So, she hadn't imagined it. "That's taking advantage of me?"

"I had no right to kiss you, even like that."

"Leading me on when you have no intentions," she stated flatly. "All those things you said, safe harbor—"

"I meant it. But you're with Brian." The word thudded between them.

"And if I wasn't?"

"You'd be on the rebound," he rasped, eyes on the road. "If you break up, do it because it's the best thing for Carrie. Not for me."

She'd shared her deepest feelings. Now he was pushing her away. Hadn't he sung "You've Got A Friend"? Friendship through all seasons, not just summer.

"Carrie, *you're* the girl I can't keep my mind off, with the qualities I adore."

Really? They turned onto her street. He pulled over and faced her. "Okay, I just went out on a limb. And I mean it. But I know you value Brian's financial stability and a secure future. I can't compete with that." He caressed her cheek, sending shivers down her back. "I care about you deeply."

Carrie's heart leaped. *You mean love?*

"You honored me by sharing your pain today. I want to be equal to your trust." He brushed back her hair. "But I have to let you be with Brian."

Her blood rushed at his touch. She wanted to kiss him, leaving Brian in the dust. Forever. But what kind of girl would that make her? And Dirk didn't want to be the rebound guy.

"Hey, I've meddled before," Dirk said, "but I won't tell you what to do. You've been bossed around your whole life."

"Respecting my right to make a decision sounds like apathy right now."

His voice dropped. "Believe me, there's no apathy." His hand formed to her cheek. "But if you tell me to get lost, I understand." His gaze melted her.

She latched on to his wrist, confirming his presence. "I'd never tell you to leave."

He outlined her lips with his finger, radiating warmth. He

traced her eyebrows, her jaw. She soaked in his touch, relishing his tenderness. But ... Brian. She interlocked his fingers, removing his hand from her face. They clutched hands in mid-air, still gazing.

He clenched the steering wheel. "This is too hard."

She'd never sleep tonight, yearning for what didn't happen.

Standing under the porch light at home, she asked, "Which qualities?"

He smiled. "You bring out my best, make me want to protect you. You're sensitive and kind and care about people. You know how to plumb their depths. You rival me in air keyboard. You're smart and down to earth. You're creative and generous. Not afraid to talk pirate lingo."

She giggled. "That's a criterion?"

"Number fourteen." She laughed. He added, "I love your laugh."

"You're glad I think your jokes are funny."

"That too. Number twelve."

"How about a college degree?"

"Seriously? Not on the list."

But she still couldn't tell him.

He left. In the dining room, she sat at the table with the Wendolyn treasure chest, pulling out objects as Oma used to, looking for solace, hope, answers.

Carrie fingered the locket, Wendolyn's assurance of being loved. The magic ladder for climbing over obstacles. The paintbrush for opening doors of imagination. Which object spoke to her right now?

Besides his dismissiveness, Brian was a faucet of legalism that would never shut off. Did she want to spend her life mopping up the mess? Dirk called her a safe harbor, but his boat wasn't ready to drop anchor. Yet she knew where her heart rested.

She picked up a silk blossom representing the story *Of*

Lilacs and Lavenders, the tale where Wendolyn went back in time, stuck in her mother's childhood. Wendolyn had to discover strength, grow in elusive self-confidence. She had to choose between staying in the comfortable past or risk returning home in the full "bloom" of who she'd become.

Amazed at the parallel to her own life, Carrie stroked silk leaves and blossoms. Dirk made her feel alive, but she couldn't depend on him. She might have to face the future alone, without Brian *or* Dirk. Without her parents' approval. Step forward as Carrie. Her true self.

She grabbed a Wendolyn book from the hutch and found a picture of the three dragons: Lieso, Shamea, and Fearat. Maybe she couldn't expect to exile dragons first. She had to move forward, no matter the terrain, pursuing dreams despite them.

In the kitchen, she clasped Janie's chicken ornament. *You must walk. It is a long journey through a country that is sometimes pleasant and sometimes dark and terrible.*

Time to dispel the dragons. She couldn't let them weigh her down anymore.

FIFTY-THREE

Monday, July 7, 1980

Monday's menu featured Glinda's Elegant Eclairs, plus General Jinjur's Royal Chocolate Fudge recipe for Oma. "Guess what," Carrie said as she copied them onto index cards. "Katje Kloosterman is Dirk's great-grandmother."

Mrs. Gordon's face lit. "Such a fine piece of serendipity."

"Providential." Carrie explained Dirk's rough years, how his mother prayed the prayer about redeeming the time the locusts ate, how God started redeeming his time.

"I'd like to hear about that straight from Dirk."

"Another tea party?"

"Not yet." Her mouth formed a grim line. Fear of revealing more about her baby?

Carrie shared literature class notes: Leland Ryken's *Triumphs of the Imagination*, C.S. Lewis's musings, and Tolkien's essay comparing the gospels to a fairy story, encompassing the substance of all such stories. She cited theologian Louis Berkhof on common grace.

After five minutes of Carrie's treatise, Mrs. Gordon asked, "Does this validate your college education?"

"It shows how many Christians value imaginative, creative works. Paintings, novels, music, both sacred and secular."

"It doesn't erase scars. That issue stirred heated debates at Katje's church. Everything invites controversy. What's the use?" she snapped as if Carrie were responsible for the rift.

Later, Carrie sanded and primed the peeling porch railing. What mundane tasks awaited while postponing talk about painful memories? Nobody to knit for, yet pregnant in 1911. Did the baby die? Did she give it up for adoption?

Finally, late morning, Mrs. Gordon said, "No more procrastinating. I must tell you about my baby. She was born in spring, 1912. I named her Dorothy Gail. G-A-I-L."

"Of course." Carrie smiled. "Beautiful. With great meaning for you."

—

Janie, 20
1912

In April, newspapers reported American Harriet Quimby as the first woman to pilot an airplane across the English Channel. Janie longed to interview her for the proposed Unconventional Careers column. Instead, she joined the ranks of motherhood.

Holding the babe, Janie gazed, counted tiny fingers, bore through hours of nursing, as overflowing with milk as with love while the hungry baby latched on.

Katje celebrated with traditional *beschuit met muisjes*, Dutch rusk covered with sugared anise. Then colic, crying, and feeding in wee night hours took over. Frazzled, Janie paced the parlor, soothing inconsolable cries. No amount of coffee or the new Postum drink mix offered energy. Katje watched Dorothy for minimal pay so Janie could keep working. *Servants for life.*

Aunt Sophie visited often, bringing food and gifts. She snuggled with Dorothy, helped around the house. Janie's parents were still angry over her sudden departure. Mae and Beatrice missed her. When Dorothy was three months old, Auntie reluctantly revealed Teddy would soon take over Broderick businesses and was engaged to another girl.

How dare he! Bitter tears stung Janie's eyes. She cradled Dorothy tighter. How could Teddy ignore this darling girl he'd fathered? "I'll never abandon you, Dorothy," she whispered.

Work and baby swallowed Janie's hours. In September, she finally wrote Mr. Baum about five-month-old Dorothy. How would he respond?

A package arrived two months later with gifts: *Father Goose, His Book* and a bonnet knit by Mrs. Baum. Janie eagerly read on Oz stationery:

My dear Charlotte Rose,

A new child has come into the world, and she's yours—Dorothy Gail. Oh my, if you'd seen the 1910 census! But even with myriad Dorothys this past decade, yours is matchless.

Take every opportunity to read to her, to keep her eyes open with wonder for sunsets, flowers, insects, and milking cows. Surely, she'll be lively with imagination as you are. Her circumstances are not as favorable as you'd wish, but she's just as precious.

I hope we meet her someday. Meanwhile, you have fears for her future, raising her alone. Go forward one step at a time and take heart.

For every gesture of judgment you encounter, take care to heap one more spoonful of love upon her. Hold her hand and give her that wise advice we've clung to over the years: 'You must walk. It is a long journey ....'

One more evidence of Mr. Baum's acceptance, despite her sin.

I told you about writing Aunt Jane's Nieces in Journalism. I was excited about the proposition of showing those three young ladies in the throes of printing their own newspaper. Imagine my shock upon discovering my book with a different title! My publisher changed it to Aunt Jane's Nieces on Vacation, claiming the previous title would prohibit sales. It doesn't bode well for female protagonists to be industrious and independent. I was furious. Why should women be confined to such rigid roles?

Lest you think me insensitive to your plight, read on. On the brink of motherhood, you believe you've lost your Nellie Bly opportunities. But now you have the occasion to nurture Dorothy to become a woman of the twentieth century. If you only impact one child in your lifetime, don't deem it less of an achievement than reaching thousands with feature articles.

Mrs. Baum left college to marry me. Heaven only knows why. She devoted herself to raising four rambunctious boys, who have grown into fine young men. They wouldn't be who they are today without their loving, assertive mother.

So, you still have the world in your hands, Charlotte—literally, as you hold your sweet babe, guiding her through the years. Before Oz, I wrote to my sister: 'I have learned to regard fame as a will-o-the-wisp which, when caught, is not worth the possession; but to please a child is a sweet and lovely thing that warms one's heart and brings its own reward.'

Though Oz and other books have brought fame since penning those words, I hold to its sentiment. It captures your opportunity with Dorothy. Making children happy and stirring their imaginations brings more joy than personal accolades.

Janie smiled at the familiar quote from Mrs. Brewster's book in Syracuse.

Modern authors must write for girls, too, he said. Thus was born Phoebe Daring, a girl detective, and Orissa Kane, a female pilot protagonist. He'd written *Sky Island* after *The Sea Fairies.* Two Oz characters appeared, and he hoped that satisfied readers who clamored for Oz. Each story exalted the merits of Coronado or La Jolla.

She reread the letter, its message suffusing. *If you only impact one child in your lifetime* ...She resolved to capture those mother-daughter moments—reading, stitching, baking. Whether Dorothy wanted to be a pilot, journalist, or mother, Janie would prepare her for a vibrant future.

Janie, 21
1913

Janie followed Mr. Baum's advice. When Dorothy started toddling, they picked dandelions, tossed leaves, played in snow. Janie sang and read to her daily. She conjured stories and finger plays. Dangling the chicken ornament, she read *Father Goose* rhymes. "Where do the chickens go at night? Heigh-ho! Where do they go?"

The year was also full of long, restless nights, tantrums,

and precociousness. Dorothy's first word was *mama*, her second word was *no!* Work and Dorothy sapped Janie's energy.

When immigrants were pressed to Americanize and use English in public schools, the Kloostermans balked. Even so, they attended the first English-speaking Christian Reformed Church in Holland—Maple Avenue CRC—for Janie's sake. To compensate, Jakob and Katje spoke more Dutch at home, reveling in Dutch menus and traditions.

That summer, Mr. Baum sent the Little Wizard series, a six-book miniature set for young readers. Included was a new Oz book, *The Patchwork Girl of Oz*, following a three-year respite. Janie was thrilled. After greetings and family news, he wrote:

May you and Dorothy share many fond hours reading together. I imagine her sweet face brightening with each poem, story, and illustration, with each tickle and tweak of the nose. She sounds delightful.

Don't grieve over so little time for writing your own stories. Of course you're bone-weary each evening. Consider this season as fodder for later, while seizing every spare moment to jot ideas. Rhymes assailed me as I chugged along the railroad track to Missouri or Iowa to sell china. I grabbed envelopes and scraps to capture words before they escaped into oblivion. However, I don't recommend using wallpaper for midnight inspirations. Somebody will be upset.

Smiling, Janie riffled through her journal, untouched for days.

Mr. Baum described his new stage musical, *The Tik-Tok Man of Oz*, playing from California to Chicago. He'd written the libretto and lyrics.

Even with current stage success, I'm obligated to return to Oz by way of pencil. The children have pleaded, the publisher insists, and frankly, I must pay the bills. At a fan's suggestion, I've reached Oz through wireless telegraphy, resuming my role as Royal Historian. Thus was born the enclosed book about Scraps, a crazy quilt girl endowed with brains, without a 'cross patch.' The Scarecrow loves her. I'm committed to writing one Oz book yearly.

With so much busyness, I relish time at Ozcot. I write in the garden on my clipboard. The flowers flourish, but I miss my chickens. Unfortunately, they went against code. But I easily imagine their hearty squawks rivaling the songbirds.

Many children come to call, neighbors and school groups. Sipping lemonade together, I fondly recall our Macatawa porch chats. In fact, my drinking has given me quite the reputation. The L.A. Evening Herald dubbed me 'the champion long-distance lemonade consumer of the local Rialto.'

Janie read *Patchwork Girl* over the next few nights by kerosene. In Oz, the jailkeeper, Tollydiggle, explained to the prisoner Ojo that they treated him kindly so he wouldn't become hard and bitter. Thus, he'd resist doing further wrong, for "It is kindness that makes one strong and brave." Was that why Mr. Baum so easily accepted her and Dorothy?

Janie, 22
1914

The May 2 headline in the *Grand Rapids Press* sports page was "Wolfgast Knocked Out by a Suffragist: Former Champion Goes Down in Three Rounds in Battle of Words."

Janie eagerly read the article. For one day, suffragists took over the newspaper. Women made their mark using journalism—like Isabel Girard, but without hiding behind pseudonyms. Mr. and Mrs. Baum would be thrilled! But what was Janie accomplishing? Her days trudged by with tedious pickle packing. Though she and Dorothy shared hugs, books, and nature exploration, most days fused to Dorothy's crankiness and outbursts. Exhaustion pervaded. Evenings produced occasional story chapters, with Janie nodding off, pen in hand.

Maybe she should reapply for a job at *Holland City News*. Risking another rejection.

She stared at the hearth. *To please a child is a sweet and lovely thing.* Janie had the chance to love a child. Her child. She'd do it right. Yet each day proved difficult. Without Katje's love and patience or Aunt Sophie's weekly food, hugs, and helping hand, Janie would be lost.

One October evening, Janie opened a package from Mr. Baum: *Tik-Tok of Oz.* Endpapers featured a colorful map of Oz and beyond. Settling with tea, she read.

Dear Charlotte,

> *I wonder if Dorothy Gail plays with the same fairies you did. I've enclosed words of wisdom from my dear wife. In our Chicago years, she managed four unruly boys while I traveled—hardly a picnic. To make ends meet, she taught embroidery. As the Scarecrow said during General Jinjur's revolt: 'The women must be made of cast iron.'*

Janie felt more like an empty pillowcase than cast iron.

Seems Dorothy has your charm, humor, and wit. But things don't bode well when a toddler's favorite word is 'no.' Mrs. Baum would sooner spank and send a child to bed with no supper, while I preferred rocking together, spinning yarns. Our boys needed both bedtime stories and a firm hand. You fulfill those two roles yourself, but surely a balance will prove successful in the long run.

I applaud you for snatching late-night moments to pen another fairy tale. Hopefully, St. Nicholas will publish it. Remember my 'File of Failures,' with more rejections than paychecks? That's long before any legacy of success. Send me chapters; I'll attempt a helpful critique.

Our family expanded with another grandson (Frank's second), and Robert's and Kenneth's weddings. Kenneth married a Dorothy! Robert married Edna, our Macatawa friend. If war in Europe encompasses the U.S., Frank and Robert may have military obligations.

The Tik-Tok extravaganza ran ten months, though not equal to *The Wizard of Oz's* musical success. The producer closed the show, still in profit. At least Tik-Tok continued in print. The preface alluded to health concerns—*oh, dear!*

Many readers have given me grief about the map's switch of Munchkinland and Winkie Country, despite my claim that their inhabitants have no qualms about it. But to avoid trouble, you might consider keeping detailed notes on the lands your characters trample through, to maintain consistency.

Such a fine idea! She'd start tonight. He also mentioned Edith Van Dyne's two new books in the Aunt Jane's Nieces series—one set in Hollywood. Additionally, he and some friends formed a social club which he christened the Lofty and Exalted Order of Uplifters, dedicated to brotherhood, the sharing of artistic talent, and just good plain fun.

My Uplifters friends and I formed the Oz Film Manufacturing Company. We have a large studio, one of many here. I designed a concrete tunnel for creating magical effects and transformations, along with trap doors, concrete tanks for water scenes, and papier mâché properties. When I wear overalls to work, Mrs. Baum mistakes me for a farmer.

I've oft lamented the regrettable turn of events forcing me to over rights to my Oz books, but no time to wallow. Thus, I've created new Oz stories for film. No pessimism here. We posted a sign: "The man who says it can't be done may go to the office and get his paycheck."

After one month, we finished a five-reeler of The Patchwork Girl of Oz. I wrote the scenario myself, my first attempt at a film script. Mr. Gottschalk wrote the musical score. In September, we released it to Paramount Pictures. Alas, we were sued by American Motion Picture Patents Company. They claim to own Edison's patents on all motion picture making equipment. They're targeting numerous independent companies for patent infringements. Thankfully, we settled out of court. That was expensive enough.

I hope sharing my disappointments encourages you in some way, if only to commiserate. We all have challenges.

Paramount showed the picture in theaters nationwide. Despite good reviews, audiences were too small to make money. It was recommended as children's entertainment.

*Some demanded money back. Paramount wants no more.
The world isn't ready for my fairy tales on screen.*

*Nevertheless, we filmed His Majesty, the Scarecrow of Oz,
then The Magic Cloak of Oz, adapted from Queen Zixi.
Paramount declined it due to Patchwork Girl's failure. So
much anxiety—no wonder my health is compromised.*

Janie paused. How disheartening to have such efforts disregarded.

*Not all is lost. My dahlias thrived. I alternated cultivating
flowers with creating new Ozzy adventures and answering
children's letters. Despite my sundry roles over the years,
who could have predicted my fame as the Chrysanthemum
King of Southern California? I kid you not. Yet, I prefer to be
known as a filmmaker rather than a gardener. I fear my
biggest successes are behind me.*

Janie bemoaned not seeing *Patchwork Girl* in the theater. Mr. Baum's striving despite rejection amazed her. Did she possess a fraction of that stamina? But motherhood lay in a different realm altogether, stakes higher than declining careers. Every evening, she counted more failures than successes. More mistakes than proud, happy moments. Self-doubt sent her reeling. *If only I'd thought before spanking. If only I'd smiled instead of scolded. If only ...*

Mrs. Baum's note suggested routines and discipline. Janie marked helpful tips, recalling Harry's and Kenneth's mischief and skirmishes. Janie stayed up late making a detailed map of Camellia's Lavender Lane neighborhood where fairies capered.

She read *Tik-Tok of Oz*, reveling in Mr. Baum's wise tidbits sprinkled throughout: one who masters himself is always a king. Accept others' peculiarities, whether preferring onions or brimstone. Mimicking book lines, Janie ambled about the house reciting, "'For the love of sassafras.'" She teased Dorothy: "'I'll turn you into a potato and make Saratoga chips of you!'"

Janie, 23
1915

At age three, Dorothy's auburn hair resembled Mae's and held hints of Teddy's. Her blue eyes called to mind how Teddy once looked into Janie's—*like amethysts*. Their first kiss. Aching with loss, she repressed the memory.

Dorothy sat on Janie's lap with the old Dorothy rag doll and books, *Father Goose* a favorite. Swaying the chicken ornament, Dorothy recited, "Where do the chickens go at night —Heigh-ho! where do they go? ..."

Spying geese at the park, she'd chant, "There was a Goose in Syracuse, And full of fun was he ..." She squealed at bees alighting on flowers: "A Bumble-Bee was buzzing, On a yellow holly-hock ..."

Janie read folktales and Aesop's fables. In Baum fashion, she conjured stories from three objects Dorothy picked. When Janie baked pie, she asked how four-and-twenty blackbirds got cooked and still flew away. She kept paper and crayons for Dorothy's imaginings.

Janie sang "Polly Wolly Doodle" and "Hush, Little Baby" from Macatawa days. In summer, they built fairy houses from twigs and whirligigs. They took nature walks and watched boats on Black Lake. At Centennial Park, they picnicked under maple trees, fed squirrels, made penny wishes, and watched fish swim in the coral rock fountain.

At nighttime, Janie lit the kerosene lamp so Dorothy could watch darkness come alive. She formed shadow shapes as the girl giggled with silly guesses.

That year, near Centennial Park, Janie watched construction of the women's literary club building. For three years, she'd read only Oz, nursery rhymes, and fairy tales. Yearning to meet other women and discuss books, she joined the club. When the building opened, she and Katje attended. But when the women realized she was an unwed mother, their staccato greetings turned monotone. Cheery faces hardened to aloof stares. Three days later, Janie received a letter stating she wasn't welcome. Teary, Janie handed it to Katje. "Have I committed the unpardonable sin?"

Katje skimmed the note. "Such foolishness!" She tossed the letter. "I refuse to return without you." Her proclamation restored a measure of Janie's dignity. But even in church, no service lacked a haughty chin or a prim nod. Janie was as out of place as dandelions in a blizzard.

Maple Avenue CRC was abuzz with arguments about the doctrine of common grace. Recent immigrants came from Dr. Kuyper's movement and joined the CRC, sparking a stir, besides debates over the worth of public schools.

One evening, Jakob, a church elder, explained everything to confused Janie.

Katje sighed. "A shame so much breath goes to quarreling while building God's kingdom." Such disputes only cemented Janie's view of church folk as hypocrites, focused on trivialities, like scripture readings administered by an aloof father. Haughty faces scrutinizing her and Dorothy. Was *that* building God's kingdom?

Janie finally wrote her parents about their granddaughter, no mention of Teddy. They could assume Janie's sin occurred in Holland, not Wolcott. Perhaps they'd invite her and Dorothy home. Weeks passed without response. Reluctant Aunt Sophie eventually revealed her parents were too infuriated to reply.

Janie cried into her pillow. She'd never be forgiven. Dorothy would always bear condemnation. At least Mae would be spared. One look at Dorothy's auburn hair and complexion, there'd be no mistaking her parentage.

On her next visit, Aunt Sophie sadly reported that Teddy, married a year, had a baby boy. Janie wept again.

She applied to stores, offering to create shop window displays, then the bakery and newspaper offices, all in vain. In November, Mr. Baum sent *The Oz Toy Book* with character cutouts for Dorothy. He included *Aunt Jane's Nieces in the Red Cross* and *The Scarecrow of Oz*. Janie read family updates, which included a new grandson, Robert Allison Baum. His niece Matilda was soon coming for an extended stay, promising fine companionship: golf with him, movies with her aunt.

Your writing improves with each Camellia installment!
You've taken advice to heart. I enjoyed Rossi's and
Maxwell's antics, incessant squabbling of Beatrice and
Estella—giving new meaning to the word feisty. Like your
characters, mine still won't do what I want them to do.
With minds of their own, there's no telling what disasters lie
in store. Ah, the joy of writing.

He shared suggestions for improving scenes. He wasn't consulted regarding the *Toy Book*, but worse worries prevailed. The country might join war efforts in Europe, impacting Frank, Robert, and the economy. Oz books sales decreased. Future ventures might fail. In merry contrast, the Uplifters produced two plays he wrote and acted in. He'd written song lyrics for the Whooping Cough Quartet. He and Mr. Gottschalk were working on a farce. He hoped to collaborate with illustrator Maxfield Parrish again for a *Snow White* production.

Say goodbye to Edith Van Dyne and Aunt Jane's Nieces,
closing after a ten-book run. Enclosed is the final book,
inspired by the war. But say hello to number eight, The
Scarecrow of Oz. *I reused episodes and characters from the*

film His Majesty, the Scarecrow of Oz, *thus creating a novel from a film script.*

That five-reeler combined plots from three earlier books. We opened an office in New York City, run by Frank. The Alliance Film Company agreed to distribute the film if we changed the title to The New Wizard of Oz. *That failed at the box office, too.*

How aggravating! The OFMC made four more one-reelers, based on his *American Fairy tales*, and another full-length one, *The Last Egyptian*, based on his anonymous 1908 novel for adults. But Alliance wanted no more, even after OFMC changed its name to Dramatic Features. They closed the studio, then re-opened once more to film Frank Joslyn's story about a Roman Catholic sister helping Allied soldiers escape behind German lines.

The Gray Nun of Belgium *had a strong plot and climax, but went the way of* The Woggle-Bug, *the* Fairylogue, *and previous films, refused without offers to review it. Instead, the world wants Charlie Chaplin. We closed, rented the studio, and sold it to Universal. Such gargantuan disappointment, yet my sweetheart Maud encourages me daily. As the Scarecrow says, one only needs brains, not wealth, to live comfortably. Thus, with the film company closed, I spend refreshing hours at Ozcot, tending my garden. I still write there, squeezing in golf games periodically.*

Apparently, my most important works are my fairy tale books, not musicals or films. Numerous Oz Reading Societies and daily letters from children affirm that, despite librarians' scathing disapproval. I still attempt to answer each child, whatever the age. For Oz is the domain of children, young and old.

So true. Janie savored each new Oz book as if a child, never mind the librarians. She delved into *The Scarecrow of Oz*, appreciating Cap'n Bill's philosophy about dipping the oars of knowledge. The Bumpy Man's humorous expressions inspired hers and Dorothy's: Watermelon and waffles! Jumping jacks and gingersnaps!

FIFTY-FOUR

Janie, 24
1916

When Katje's daughter, Mariet, began school, Katje had to work. She gave Janie a month to find help for Dorothy.

One night, Janie gazed upon her, asleep, auburn curls against the pillow, softened by moonlight. Dorothy embodied the Father Goose rhyme about a girl who appeared sweet when sleeping but romped like multiple boys when awake. On her knees, Janie prayed. *Help me be a good mother.* She envisioned them together, singing and laughing through the years. Yet mornings filled with whining, tangled hair, and spilled milk, turning Janie's weary heart cold. Dorothy deserved a better mother.

Growing despondent, Janie couldn't find a babysitter for her illegitimate child. Katje took sewing jobs at home but couldn't give Dorothy full attention. What if Katje evicted them? When Dorothy upset Katje's sewing basket, Janie screamed and thrashed the child. Dorothy's wailing sent Janie crumpling onto the floor, weeping.

Janie dragged herself to church with the Kloostermans, still meriting scowls from the self-righteous. Was God paying attention to her plight? Every evening, Katje invited Dorothy into her lap for Bible stories. At least Dorothy heard about God from someone who loved her.

The factory fired Janie for mistakes, tardiness, and absenteeism. She asked Jakob for an extension of rent. Nightly, darkness covered her like a blanket of lies, like truth extinguished, squelching promises of a good future. Selling turnips for lemons. Was that parenthood? Dissipating dreams. Like Teddy's betrayal. A humbug wizard.

She clung to Mr. Baum's words: *If you only impact one child in your lifetime, don't deem it less of an achievement.* But what impact did she have? She was depleted. Dorothy was naughty. Would she only remember a mother who frowned and scolded?

After sleepless nights, dawn wasn't welcome. Night's darkness stalked her in daytime. Not the night beautifully illuminated by fireflies or kerosene, but a crosspatch of black and gray, like dusk that never succumbs to stars and moonlight. Dawn without hope of sun. Stuck between two voids, in a netherworld of drab, stony skies, each day an ashen cloud. Seeing dawn before others turned from inspirational metaphor to bleak reality. Janie's depression pinned her to bed, as if a beast pressed her. None of Katje's home remedies worked.

One day at market, Dorothy skipped through the store, peeking over fabric rolls and into canisters. Janie was too fatigued to take chase. Eventually, Dorothy dashed from the store into the street. An automobile cranked down the road, headed toward her.

Janie screamed, charged toward the vehicle, and snatched her in time. On the sidewalk, Janie yelled and spanked her. Dorothy spewed choking sobs. The store owner ran out.

Several heads turned her way. Janie was horrified. She'd become her mother. Again.

At home, Janie broke down. Caressing the chicken ornament conjured long-ago words. *You must walk …* She must move forward, through dark and terrible landscapes. Dorothy must too. She needed two parents—a stable, loving home, to grow up strong and imaginative.

Katje told Janie about a local couple wanting to adopt. After several miscarriages, they'd recently immigrated from the Netherlands, sponsored by their church. Janie spoke to Mr. Kluin, the liaison to the DeVries adoption agency. He assured her the couple was kind and loving, eager to welcome her little girl after years of loss. They'd been in the country two months but knew some English. For privacy, he shared no names.

Janie wrote to Mr. Baum. He sent *The Snuggle Tales* for Dorothy, and *Rinkitink in Oz*.

> *We read your letter with much anguish. If Dorothy can flourish better in another home, this will be the hardest decision you've ever made and the biggest sacrifice. But take comfort, dear. This act demonstrates your selfless love for her.*

And wasn't love wanting the highest good for someone, even at great cost?

How had Mae sent Teddy away? Was it easier that he'd been older, after seeing glimpses of the man he might become? Janie once delivered the battered to safety. But now she was relinquishing her own child. She prayed Dorothy would have no memory of it.

Janie explained Mommy was too ill to care for her. She promised her a new mommy and daddy who'd love her forever. Dorothy protested, then ran off to play, surely not comprehending. Janie packed Dorothy's belongings, including fairy tales, but no inscribed Baum books revealing the birth mother's identity or the child's original name.

At Mr. Kluin's office, Dorothy blinked in perplexity. When Janie stood to go, the girl's eyes widened. A shadow crossed her face. "Mommy, don't leave. I don't want a new house. I don't want a new mommy!"

Janie gave Dorothy Gail one last kiss. "I'll always love you." She ran down the hallway, sobbing, drowning Dorothy's wails. *Please redeem the time the locusts ate from Dorothy's life.*

Those locusts had been Janie herself.

———

Janie obtained a bakery job. Every evening, she cooked, cleaned, and mended for Katje.

A month later, while Janie sat knitting, Katje said, "Someone's here to see you."

Father. Grayer, eyes creased. "Hello, Janie." Even his voice was wrinkled.

Gritting her teeth, she knit faster, dropping stitches.

"Your Aunt Sophie tells me you gave up the child." The *child.* Nameless. Words delivered as if reporting grain statistics. "She'll be in good hands."

"You mean *better* hands." He'd never know how it felt to hold your little daughter one last time, kiss her, knowing it's your last time, knowing you can't be the parent she deserves.

Feet shuffled. "Your mother's headaches are worse. She needs help in the tearoom."

Stunned, she stared at him. "How dare you." Her gut clenched.

"With her frailty, it's hard to keep things going. You're a good worker, knowledgeable about tearoom business."

"What about Josephine and Maggie?"

"They're busy with their families."

"And I have *none*."

"You're the best qualified, with experience and know-how."

"Because I can no longer shame you with my child?" She blinked tears away. "Why didn't you come last month when I still had my daughter? *Now* you're willing I should join the family?" Boiling anger overtook shame. "You didn't come to meet your grandchild. Not once."

Silence, his mouth a grim line.

"Don't folks speculate why I left?"

"There's only speculation. I never told them what happened *here*. I'll pay you double from before. Hired hand wages."

She glared. "You think you can buy me."

"You wanted fair treatment." More shuffling. "A man's earnings."

"Fair? I wanted you to treat me as a *daughter*."

"The Broderick name was at stake."

His words felt like a stomach punch. "Do Josephine and Maggie know?"

"We told nobody. In Wolcott, your reputation is unstained. Nobody will *ever* know." Words exuding more command than comfort. "When refrigeration was introduced, I lost my ice business. I fought the competition but then moved on, like you should do. I'm offering you a job."

Janie's eyes widened. Her knitting dropped. "You're comparing your ice business to my *daughter*?" She stood. "Her name's Dorothy Gail. She loves paging through newspapers, like you do. She loves nature, like you. She watches farmers at the plow." Her shoulders straightened. "She bakes cookies, like Mother. Her eyes are blue like mine, her nose like Josephine's, curls like Maggie's. She loves stories and rattles off rhymes like Aunt Sophie. She imagines rainbows in thunderstorms, like me, and giggles like fairies in the meadow." Her voice grew ragged. "She has bits of everyone in our family." *And Teddy's red hair and tenacity.* "She's a Broderick, above all. A *real* person."

Awkwardly, he cleared his throat. "I see you'll need time to think about my offer."

FIFTY-FIVE

Janie, 24
1916

In Holland, Janie's questionable reputation was ironclad, as if she wore an *A* on her chest. But in Wolcott, helping her aging parents, she could start over. And wasn't love doing the highest good for others, even at great cost?

A week after Father's visit, Janie asked Mr. Kluin for permission to send a yearly gift to Dorothy through the agency —a book of fairy tales. He soon reported that Dorothy's new family agreed to one fairy tale book yearly, sent anonymously.

Janie moved to Aunt Sophie's. Mae was happy to see her. Heart aching, Janie again befriended Beatrice, now ten. What would Dorothy look like in six years at Beatrice's age?

One evening, as she walked from the tearoom to Aunt Sophie's, feet shuffled behind her. She turned to a man's silhouette. Teddy.

"Janie." They stood on the lamplight's rim. His features took shape. Images she'd squelched for five years swirled, how it might have been. "My mother said you returned."

"Are you ready to tell our parents of your part?"

"No ..."

"Then we've nothing to say." She kept walking.

He grabbed her arm. "Listen. I'm married now, with a son. I wish to heap no shame on my wife about the past. I know I hurt you terribly."

"You can't possibly know."

"I'm sorry."

"Not sorry enough. You could've found me."

He bowed his head. "Please forgive me."

"You obviously didn't need my forgiveness to start over."

"Tell me about our child."

"The one you rejected?" Her jaw clenched. "Our daughter's name is Dorothy Gail. She's beautiful and full of life. But her best chance was with *two* parents. They probably changed her name."

He sighed. "So, she's in a good home."

"I sacrificed my future for you to go your merry way. With no father, she suffered as much judgment as I. And now you'll never see her."

July 7, 1980

Carrie dabbed her eyes. "I'm so sorry you had to give up Dorothy."

"I've second-guessed myself often," Mrs. Gordon said. "I hope she's not haunted by that awful day I left her."

"Her adoptive parents would've explained your motive, wanting the best for her. Teddy's apology hardly qualifies. And I'm furious your father compared Dorothy to his icehouse business." Carrie cringed. "Family honor, no mistakes allowed. So unlike Mr. Baum, honest about failures. Kept right on walking. Like you taking over the inn."

"I felt like Oscar Wilde's statue of the Happy Prince, an

eyesore in town, stripped bare of value, giving without people knowing. Regarding Dorothy, I felt like the king in 'Shall Joy Wear What Grief Has Fashioned?'"

"So, you didn't travel or write for the newspaper again?"

"Isabel Girard vanished. Running the inn took all my time." Mrs. Gordon picked up *Pilgrim's Progress*. "Mae sent Teddy away with this book, a reminder of her, his direction. I wanted fairy tales to connect Dorothy and me somehow. I scoured through books—Grimm, Lang, Anderson. Mr. Baum's too."

"What'd you send?"

"I'll tell you soon."

<hr>

Back home in the kitchen, Oma greeted Carrie with a hopeful smile, handing her an envelope.

Return address: Wolcott Bank. "Oh, my word!" Nerves buzzing, she clasped it to her chest, examined both sides, then waved it like a fan, cooling down.

"Well, if *you* don't open it, *I* will!"

"Hold on." Carrie's trembling fingers eased it open. She unfolded the one-page letter.

Dear Miss Kruisselbrink,

> *We regret to inform you that your loan request has been denied. Even with outstanding references and a calculated, thorough business plan, your youth and lack of experience work against you. We encourage you to try again in a few years.*

Sinking into a chair, Carrie wilted. "This can't be happening."

Oma wrapped her arms around Carrie's shoulders. "Oh, *liefje*. I'm so sorry."

"There's no way to purchase the diner now. The owner has a second offer on standby." Tears burning, Carrie barely managed words. "Brian will be relieved. And my parents will *gloat*." They'd never respect her now.

"Never mind them. You must pursue what's right for *you*. No matter the obstacles." Oma picked up the Wendolyn treasure box from the hutch, pulled out the tiny paintbrush, and brushed the air. "Look. It's your imagination, still going strong. Nothing squashes it." She withdrew the miniature ladder. "Use this for climbing over that big rock in your path."

Oma wiped a teardrop from Carrie's cheek, then presented the locket. "But most important, you are loved, through rain and shine."

Tuesday, July 8, 1980

Teary, Carrie told Mrs. Gordon the bad news. "Sorry. I thought I finished crying last night."

"Better to have your feelings out in the open."

"You sound like Dirk."

"I prefer thinking Dirk sounds like me." Mrs. Gordon patted Carrie's arm. "I'm so sorry. What did Brian say?"

"I didn't call him, but he'll rejoice."

"Hmm." Mrs. Gordon tilted her head as if projecting additional words.

"I know what you're thinking. Why are we still together?"

"I only want you to listen to the right voice, follow the right path. Doing the thing that gives you wisdom, heart, and courage."

"I was." Carrie waved the envelope. "Until this happened."

"You're not done, young lady. Meanwhile, grist for the mill. And success is not what matters most."

"But my parents ..." Carrie sniffled. "They won't respect me now."

"Nor will they ever." Though Carrie balked, the woman barreled on. "You want the kind of regard that comes and goes with the wind?" Mrs. Gordon took the letter. "Make a File of Failures like Mr. Baum's. Put this in it. But this rejection isn't failure. You need wisdom, heart, and courage to take off the mask for the journey, to step forward as yourself. You only fail by *not* doing so." She handed the letter back. "You don't need pinnacles and acclaim. You need people to walk with you on that journey. Through both pleasant and dark, terrible places."

Wednesday, July 9, 1980

After savoring Ojo's Lucky Strawberry Crepes and sipping Raspberry Nectar Tea, Carrie copied the recipe for Emerald City Mint Squares.

Mrs. Gordon went to the parlor and faced the window, squinting, as if forcing herself to bear the light. She opened the drapes wider, then sat.

Janie, 24
1916

Janie had plans for the tearoom. She'd keep favorites—Blueberry Cream Cheese muffins and her mother's culinary legacies. But make way for Welsh Rarebit, Baked Alaska, and fruit-filled Jell-O desserts. Every idea Elsa had smothered.

If Janie couldn't travel the world, she'd bring the world to Wolcott, through Dutch *rookworst* and *snert* and recipes from the *Pan-Pacific Cookbook: Savory Bits from the World's Fare,* introduced at the 1915 San Francisco exposition. The updated stove and commercial refrigerator brought advantages. She designated chickens for egg-laying, one named Billina. Father had sold acreage but kept dairy cows. Teddy managed the cranberry bog and peach orchards, requiring minimal interactions with Janie. She developed a tough core around people. Her daytime escape from pain was work. Her nighttime escape was writing stories.

New and familiar faces dominated: the Morton Salt girl, Kellogg's Leyendecker girl, Dr. Pepper, Planters' Mr. Peanut. The grocer stocked Graham crackers and Quaker Oats in a new round package. She shuddered at Heinz products, especially pickles.

Nellie Bly aspirations had dissipated. But Aunt Jemima's pancake flour slogan infused her. *I'm in town, honey.* And, for better or worse, *I'm here to stay.*

After a week in Wolcott, Janie went to Gordon's Pharmacy for Mother's pain medication. Her last visit was the high school newspaper staff meeting, eight years ago.

The new facade featured bay windows and a double door. The sign announced *Gordon Apothecary, Walter Gordon, Licensed Druggist,* as if surpassing mere pharmacy. Inside, the renovated sight bedazzled. Tiled floor and marble countertops offset Tiffany glass-doored, cherrywood cabinets, bookending a baroque-style soda fountain with fancy spigots. Brass light fixtures hung under an arch before a huge mirror.

She and Teddy once sat at the countertop, now marble, when life was a happy promise, sweet as peppermint. Only ceiling fans and candy jars, now with shiny scoops, remained from those days. Shelves featured myriad confectionaries: penny stick candy and licorice ropes. A root beer barrel overpowered one corner under competing signs of Coca-Cola, Pepsi-Cola, and Dr. Pepper.

Dark-haired Walter Gordon merrily engaged a customer. Janie admired his handsome face, then gazed about like a child mesmerized by Christmas lights. The new menu tempted her with chocolate frappes, banana splits, and ice cream sandwiches. It sported five-cent ice cream sodas with pure juices, phosphates, and Moxie in flavors of sarsaparilla, vanilla, ginger, and fruits.

Old Mrs. Emery leaned on her cane, shaking her finger. "Listen, young fellow." Her voice grated like sandpaper. "The pharmacist always puts cannabis in my soda water for my rheumatism. You're refusing me?"

"Mrs. Emery," Walter replied calmly, "My father stopped doing that over ten years ago."

"Then give me opium."

"No, ma'am, or I'd be in jail. Illegal since 1914. No drugs without a prescription."

"No wonder nobody comes here anymore. They're all in Saugatuck getting their cannabis." Mumbling, the woman hobbled out.

Janie stepped forward. "Quite an afternoon's entertainment, Mr. Gordon."

His eyes lit. "Why, Miss Broderick! You've returned to humble Wolcott?"

"For now." No committing as if she'd nothing better to do.

"Fortunate for us. May I make you a Dr. Pepper Black Cow?" He brandished an ice cream scoop. "On the house."

Janie smiled. "You remember."

"Nobody else ever asked for one. Please give me the pleasure." Walter scooped vanilla ice cream into a glass. "How can we keep you in Wolcott?"

"I'm managing the tearoom for my mother."

"The muffins weren't the same after you left."

Flattery? "The secret ingredient makes the difference."

"Baking powder, no doubt. Which, incidentally, your mother never bought from *me*."

Janie surveyed the room and menu. "Now I see what we're up against."

"Wonderful, eh? Five years ago, I traveled to New York, visiting pharmacies. Look." He placed a glass under the spigot and jerked on the cherub Greek figure. "Arctic Soda Apparatus revolutionized the soda fountain." Out flowed a stream of bubbly seltzer. He poured a bottle of Dr. Pepper over ice cream. "For you, Miss Broderick." As she lifted the tulip-shaped glass to her lips, he smiled. "You're bound to fall in love. Again."

Double meaning? She hesitated, then sipped. "Delicious."

"Even without cannabis and opium." He laughed with his eyes, too.

"Mmm, refreshing. I'll *definitely* be adding Baked Alaska to my menu. I must compete."

Black hair crossed his forehead, kind eyes intensifying. "Let's not consider ourselves adversaries, Miss Broderick."

"We vie for the same customers."

"They enjoy your braised beef and dumplings, then see me for dessert."

"We serve dessert too. Ice cream's our specialty."

"Your tearoom doesn't have Black Cows, Moxie, and carbonated drinks." He lifted a bottle. "But *you* have plenty of Moxie. Courage, daring, and spirit. Like this drink. And your brave decision with the newspaper staff. I never told a soul. Poor Mr. Taradiddle and Bilgewater, gone as quickly as they arrived." At her blush, he changed the subject. "We'll get hit hard if our president sends us to war in Europe. But with prohibition coming, it might double business for both of us."

"Hopefully, you don't have plans to make alcohol on the sly."

"Not me." Walter chuckled, raising seltzer and Dr. Pepper. "Options for those who'd rather not drive to Canada or sneak into illegal establishments."

"You've chosen your weapons well. Now, I must pick up Mother's medication."

He retrieved a bottle. "What caught your fancy so strongly that we never merited one visit from you in five years?"

"I took a job in Holland."

"Must've been a doozy. Do you need baking powder? Your mother uses a secret source, but commercial brands aren't reliable. Mine's better than any from Percell Grocery or Sears catalog. You'll have the lightest, most feathery cakes. Try a free sample."

"I'd have to hide it from my mother."

"I'll throw in a free spatula. Other promotions include a cookbook, but who am I to offer a cookbook to the town chefs?"

"I won't take anything for free." Ha! What a lie. She'd done nothing but accept charity for five years. The Kloostermans' generosity far exceeded rent.

The register drawer popped open. "No charity, Miss Broderick. Consider it exchange for a promise to join me for dinner Saturday night."

Fiddling with her coin purse, she startled. Dinner? Why? She'd spare herself another rejection. She was damaged goods, unworthy of his affection. "I'm indisposed then." She picked up the medication.

"Any night next week?" He held baking powder toward her.

"I'm at the tearoom, Mr. Gordon." She waved the powder away. "Nightly."

"When do you close?" He slid the powder toward her.

"Eight o'clock." She gingerly picked up the box.

"How about eight-fifteen Monday evening?" He slid the spatula over.

"Now I know why Mrs. Emery's so cranky. You can't take no for an answer."

"If you want your change, I suggest you take the spatula too."

She sighed. "All right. I'll meet you Monday evening."

"You won't regret it."

Monday night, Walter Gordon took Janie to Dunham's Diner. He didn't pry into reasons for her sudden move away. She mentioned the factory, bakery work, and assisting a friend as nanny and cook, with no more time for journalism.

Walter owned his slice of the world through travel and college. Though kind, thoughtful, and attentive, he'd be hard-pressed to discuss Twain novels, preferring nature, science, and soda fountain trends. When Janie commented on unwed mothers, his response confirmed she couldn't be transparent about Dorothy. Not yet.

She enjoyed his humor and charm, but were his attentions a disguise for his interest in the resort? Warily, she agreed to see him again. So, her time filled with tearoom duties, Walter Gordon outings, books with Beatrice, evenings with Aunt Sophie and Mae, then writing. She'd weep often, missing Dorothy. She mailed her first fairy tale book, *The Book of Elves and Fairies*. Yet it hardly sufficed for reaching Dorothy with a piece of herself, a remnant of their life together.

One afternoon near closing, Walter gestured to the apothecary menu. "Order whatever your heart desires."

Could he send Janie back in time? Serve second chances?

She savored a milkshake, he a Tin Roof Sundae, offering bites. Janie laughed so much, she forgot they were rivals. But guilt needled her. With Dorothy, she'd not have the consideration of such a good man.

Affection for Walter wouldn't rule her. "You win. I'll purchase baking powder from you."

"What?" He drew back.

"Count on my monthly order." She stood to go.

"Janie." Walter touched her arm. "Please stay."

She sat. "Why are you bribing me? I sense your unspoken motive."

Walter's face fell. He took her hand. "Then I've utterly failed. Haven't you enjoyed our time together? Shows, concerts, rides in the country?"

"Of course. Otherwise, I wouldn't be here." She tried to still her trembling hands.

"Janie, I don't want to compete. Please see the value of … joining forces."

She flinched. "So you *do* want the tearoom, after all."

"No, Janie." His voice was warm. "I want *you*."

She gazed as if hypnotized. "How can I be certain?"

"I'll draw up papers stating the tearoom will only be yours. But I don't want to be rivals. I want to marry you, Janie, take care of you." He leaned in, inches away, "And you may buy your baking powder wherever you choose." He kissed her gently. Their first kiss.

She didn't expect such a thrill. He kissed her again. She fought the magnetizing pull, repressing fears. Could she ever listen to him without thinking of Teddy's false promises?

Surely, he'd reject her if he knew about Dorothy or her spiritual doubts. She couldn't risk telling the truth. Not even with Walter Gordon.

He held a spoonful to her lips. She let its sweetness linger. "Walter, I must tell you …" Her voice was ragged. "I'm a fairy tale writer, hoping to be published someday. Every evening, I work on my novel. That's something I can't give up." She held her breath as if she'd just told him about Dorothy.

"Do what you're made to do, Janie. I applaud your success. Why'd you wait so long to tell me?"

She pushed the dish aside, stood, and wrapped her arms around the man giving her a second chance at love. After a long kiss, she leaned on his shoulder. She'd do her best to love Walter Gordon. He deserved the best.

Fifty-Six

Fall, 1916

Broderick family gatherings increased Janie's envy and heartache as nieces and nephews romped about. She compensated by exerting tearoom dominion over her sisters with subtle jabs and bossy tones. No other realm was under her control. Contributing to her melancholy, market days drew mother-and-daughter pairs to the tearoom.

Janie's previous letter to Mr. Baum revealed the dilemma of Dorothy's future. Time to reveal her final decision.

You said if I only impacted one child rather than reach many readers, I could be satisfied. Which makes my news even more regretful. I fell into such despair I couldn't care for Dorothy. Katje directed me to an adoption agency that found a fine two-parent family for her. Nothing like the so-called Christian home I grew up in. They permit fairy tales.

A gaping hole remains in my heart where Dorothy lives, the only place where I see and touch her. Neither college nor travel would bring joy now. No pleasure is savored without guilt—and the sadness of not knowing each other.

In person, I'll never be able to open her imagination to landscapes of possibilities, as strange and intriguing as a hyperooden rostratus, the way you did for me. But I discovered a way to reach her heart.

I've embraced your sentiment that dismisses fame in lieu of pleasing a child, bringing its own reward. Dorothy's the only child I wish to please—to hold, to know, to impact. Now I know how.

Thank you, Mr. Baum. For this new aspiration began with that indelible fifteen minutes under the maple tree the day we met, when you first touched my heart, giving me a hundred magical reasons to stir and invigorate my imagination, while reveling in your companionship.

Because of you, I learned to create a story world, complete with an engaging plot, suspense, and amusing, bumbling characters. Only the annual critiques and encouragement on your Macatawa porch spiraled me above the realm of acceptable school papers. You elevated me to a fantastical place that enables me to reach my Dorothy ...

A story was forming in Janie's mind, from tales written years ago, shared with Mr. Baum—with a different audience now. As part of her yearly fairy tale gifts, Janie would pour her own life into a tale, publish it, and mail it. The story was about ten-year-old Wendolyn—formerly Camellia—who woke to find her dear mother gone, no explanation. After being sent gifts and clues, including a locket with her mother's picture, Wendolyn searched for her. Though her mother was under a spell cast by the wicked sorceress Nefaria, Wendolyn learned that evil couldn't stop the stronger power of love reaching over time and space.

Thus, Janie might someday receive a fan letter from her favorite reader. Dorothy's parents nor Mr. Kluin need ever know. The tale was titled *Wendolyn and the Lost Locket*, penned by Gretchen Trumbauer. The story was dedicated "To Dorothy, who will always be loved."

July 9, 1980

Carrie clasped her hands. "You wrote the Wendolyn stories!" Images of Oma's treasure box and its beloved objects whirled through her mind. "Unbelievable!" She brought all seven books to the coffee table. "Are Wendolyn and Camellia the same?"

"Wendolyn's the same character, developed over time."

"Tell me more about the story backgrounds."

Mrs. Gordon described the second book, *The Meticulous Meddling of Madame Throttlemeier*. The sorceress Nefaria threatened the safety of Nickelboggen citizens unless they found her magic bracelet. Wendolyn and her adoptive siblings searched, while Madame Throttlemeier thwarted their efforts. "Read the dedication."

"'To Dorothy who trades lemonade for vinegar, a kitten's meow for a lion's roar, and picnics for storm clouds.'" Carrie looked up. "Referring to activities you did together?"

Mrs. Gordon smiled. "Metaphorically. She rode challenges like riding buffalo. The story shows feisty Wendolyn facing troubles head-on but learning to handle disputes wisely."

Regarding *Of Lilacs and Lavenders: Wendolyn of Fairy Chasm*, Mrs. Gordon explained how Wendolyn learned secrets of her mother's life. She must choose between staying in the comfortable past or returning to Nickelboggen with newfound skills. Either came with sacrifice.

"I remember. 'To Dorothy, full of sunshine, who blossoms in woodlands or deserts, in sun, rain, or shade.' How'd that apply to Dorothy?"

"I wanted her to find contentment in being herself, whether life offered sunshine or rain." Mrs. Gordon explained the fifth book, *The Noodleheads of Nickelboggen*. When two scorned but harmless Noodleheads from the bordering country visited incognito, Wendolyn took them in, causing great embarrassment. The story demonstrated using humor to rise above flaws.

Had Mrs. Gordon learned that lesson herself? She picked up the next book. "'To Dorothy who sees the world upside down and inside out and laughs just the same.'" Carrie looked up in question.

"Dorothy laughed at everything. She'd point out ironies I never saw."

After more explanations, Carrie said, "What about the *Gatekeeper of Merrimack Castle*? Why was it only in circulation a month?"

"Perhaps you know now."

Pondering, Carrie sat back. Due to Wendolyn's bravery, the king and queen invited her to Merrimack Castle. But jealous Nefaria sent her shape-shifting dragons—Lieso, Shamea, and Fearat—to lure her back with deception. Wendolyn and Jipper finally arrived at the castle, a place of wonders. The Gatekeeper introduced Wendolyn to wondrous sights, opening myriad possibilities with a magic paintbrush. The brush painted anything she wanted, making it real.

Meanwhile, the three dragons taunted and beckoned from outside. In the castle, Wendolyn was safe. Yet because of Jipper, she was lured outside into the dragons' clutches.

The last time they'd discussed this book, Carrie identified the dragons as Janie's parents, Mr. Baum as the Gatekeeper, the castle as the Realm of Imagination. But knowing Mrs. Gordon's pen shaped it, a light dawned. "Jipper, the betrayer, is Teddy. He *gypped* you." Carrie stared at an illustration—Lieso, Shamea, and Fearat. She jolted. "Why didn't I see this? The dragons chasing Wendolyn aren't just evil beasts. They're the voices of Lies, Shame, and Fear. You added letters to those words for names."

"Exactly. Since the story was my life's metaphor, *I* insisted it be pulled from circulation, fearing discovery."

Carrie ruminated. "Lies, Shame, and Fear. They're attacks on brains, heart, and courage."

Mrs. Gordon raised her eyebrows. "I knew I did well hiring you. How do you see it?"

"Lies attack the facts, the truth of the situation. Fear attacks courage." Carrie swallowed. "Shame goes after the heart. Shame stands between you and others, disconnecting you. Makes you feel unlovable."

"Until love overpowers it."

"Yes, they're intertwined. It starts with lies. Lies bring shame too. They both cause fear. It takes courage to tackle all three. Dorothy got her own copy, right? Through Mr. Kluin?"

"Yes. Look inside."

Carrie found the dedication. "'To Dorothy whose imagination is bigger than a HR, whose paths of possibilities lead skyward.'" She looked up. "*Hyperooden rostratus*! Of course. How many books did you send her?"

"Fourteen. Through age eighteen, alternating Wendolyn books. As author, I was loved from a distance." She folded her hands. "Dorothy might like being related to Gretchen Trumbauer, not to Janie Broderick, sins and all."

"Oh, Mrs. Gordon ... Did Dorothy write you? And how would you know?"

"She wrote. I discovered her name." Jaw tightening, she withdrew a crayon tulip drawing from the drawer and gave it to Carrie. "The first letter from my Dorothy."

Carrie took it, dated July 1920.

Dear Miss Trumbauer,

I was so happy reading Wendolyn and the Lost Locket. *I got scared, then sad, then happy again. I wish I could meet Wendolyn. She's brave with good ideas. She makes a scary situation better.*

When Wendolyn got lost, I worried. She missed her mother so much. But she outsmarted the sorceress. I'm glad she found out her mother loved her. Nobody could destroy that, not even Nefaria.

I can't wait to read your next Wendolyn story. I hope she'll take her new sister and brother on her next adventure. Can you write about that?

Sincerely,
Tantje De Haan, age 8

Carrie gaped at the signature. *Tantje De Haan.* Ink blurred. She looked from the page to Mrs. Gordon, back and forth. "Oh, my." Her voice quavered. "How'd you know it's Dorothy?"

"I'll explain soon."

Carrie's stomach coiled as her body seemed to detach. Muscles numbed. "The rhymes you taught her ... Was one 'There was a boy from Kalamazoo' And a rabbit climbing a tree?"

"From *Father Goose, His Book.*" Mrs. Gordon went to the kitchen.

Queasy, Carrie stumbled after her. Mrs. Gordon gazed out the window, facing the light. Again. Carrie's voice rattled. "Your Dorothy ... is my oma."

"Please don't tell her yet. I want to tell her myself."

"She doesn't even know she's adopted."

Two hours later, after organizing cabinets in slow motion, Carrie sighed. "Mrs. Gordon, I have to go. I'll return tomorrow." She hugged her. "I won't tell." She walked home, told Oma she'd be out late, then drove to the hardware store in a daze. She dropped her keys. Twice.

Inside, Dirk strode over. "Carrie, you're pale as a fish. Are you ill?"

Her voice wavered. "I'm not as Dutch as I thought."

Dirk took an early lunch. They walked to Dunham's, his hand on her back. "In case you tip over." At the booth, he handed her a menu. "My treat. What's going on?"

Stammering, Carrie explained the adoption, the Wendolyn series, the dedications, the letter from little Tantje De Haan. All making the bank rejection fade into the background.

"Mrs. G.'s your great-grandmother?"

"Supposedly. Oma's her Dorothy Gail. It explains why Oma has no baby pictures."

"Did you tell her?"

"Mrs. Gordon wants to. Oh, my. No wonder she was sharing recipes. But what if she's fabricating this whole thing?"

"Doesn't your oma have all the Wendolyn books?"

"Yeah, but ..." One book still had the original envelope. With the return address.

"We'll verify this. Holland City Hall."

Dirk got the afternoon off. In City Hall, they asked for Dorothy Broderick's 1912 records.

The man flipped through files. "Here's a birth certificate for Tantje De Haan filed in 1916, attached to one for Dorothy Gail Broderick. An adoption and change of name."

They left with copies of each document. In the car, Carrie played Fleetwood Mac's "Landslide" on *Melancholia I*. Soon, they waded on Macatawa's beach under silvery gray skies. Her mind fluttered back decades to Charlotte's age of innocence, building sandcastles, discussing stories on Mr. Baum's porch. Tales that later wove into books that reached her distant daughter.

"How's Oma gonna feel?" Carrie said.

"How do *you* feel?"

"This affects her more."

"Nope, back up the train. Empathy's great, but not at the expense of honesty. Feel duped?" Dirk let her take the word in, as if seeing what she'd do with it.

"She reeled me in with that crazy contract, then dumped this on me."

"Used you to get to Dorothy." He grabbed her arm to dodge driftwood.

"I'm a descendant of the town recluse." Carrie squinted at sunlight peeking through gray strands. "She'll finally meet Dorothy Gail, all grown up."

"Her chance to redeem the locusts."

"Redeem *time* the locusts ate." Carrie shook her finger. "Nobody wants to redeem locusts." He chuckled. She explained the dragons in Wendolyn's tales, how the castle story exemplified Janie's life. "I don't know if I'm angry or sad. Mrs. Gordon drives me crazy."

"And you tolerated all the craziness just to know her. Driving Pearl crazy trying to locate that picture. Sounds like love to me."

Carrie splashed through waves. "It was my job."

"More than that. You have the benefit of knowing the whole person."

Carrie wiped her wet cheeks. Dirk hugged her as she wept. "All summer, I've tried to figure out who I am, separate from my family, and now I've got a different history altogether."

"And Mrs. G.'s a wonderful part of it." His voice soothed, like his touch.

She eyed distant sailboats. "You're right. I love her. Dearly. Because I *know* her."

They talked through supper at a restaurant. Carrie swirled her teabag through hot water, watching it darken. Stupid teabag. Nothing like Mrs. Gordon's flavorful tea leaves. She'd never look at tea without thinking of Mrs. Gordon. Great-grandmother.

At home, her grandparents were sleeping. Carrie found the Castle book envelope. Return address: DeVries Agency. In the dining room, she pulled out the treasure box locket with Great-grandma De Haan's photo. She pictured her giving the box to young Tantje, with objects for each tale. Surely, Great-grandma knew the books came from Janie. Why didn't she mention the adoption?

Carrie started to call Brian, then hung up. She'd spent her emotions on Dirk. Dirk who listened, looked her in the eye, accepted her feelings. Dirk who didn't play games to keep her confined to self-protective mode.

Lies, shame, and fear. The substance of her relationship with Brian.

She couldn't lead a double life anymore. She couldn't seek approval from people she'd never please. She couldn't earn love. Brian didn't want to change. And she already had.

Pros and cons of marrying him would register in the red on a ledger, scales off balance. Ha! Dragon scales, to make a pun. Sure, she'd have financial stability, her family's praise—filling two lines of assets. The liabilities column flashed big letters: No Carrie. No love. No Dirk.

But did Dirk love her? Beyond summer? On to his next adventure, *de wind in de zeilen hebben*, as Oma would say. Catching the wind in the sails. No safe harbor. No rebound guy.

Even so, she was finished with Brian. On Saturday, she'd break up. No more mopping up while the faucet runs. Only one way to turn off that faucet. She'd be the heroine of her own story, casting off the dragons of Lies, Shame, and Fear, stepping forward into her future.

FIFTY-SEVEN

Thursday, July 10, 1980

Mrs. Gordon's house was infused with light. Drapes open, shades up. Carrie hugged her. "When do you want to meet Oma?"

"*You* must adapt to the idea first."

"I need time, but you've waited sixty-four years," Carrie said.

"I don't know how she'll take it."

"Neither do I. But it helps that she loves your muffins and scones."

In the parlor, Carrie read young Tantje's letters aloud with Mrs. Gordon's commentary.

During the third one, Carrie said, "She told you about the treasure box!"

"She always wrote about the object she and her mother picked for each book. I'm touched to know she still has the box."

After lunch, Carrie strolled the neighborhood. *You must walk. It is a long journey* ...Every hero's journey. Dorothy maneuvered through haunted forests, wicked witches, and

430

flying monkeys. Christian battled lies fed by Mr. Legality, Vanity Fair, Apollyon, and the Giant of Despair, all contradicting the King's ways. Wendolyn tried to outrun the dragons Lieso, Shamea, and Fearat. Like Janie did. Like Carrie.

Gretchen Trumbauer wielded her pen through Wendolyn's adventures, using fiction as the vehicle for aspects of truth. All summer, Mrs. Gordon shared her life, imparting wisdom—without her pseudonym, without her pen, without her masks. Outrunning dragons of Lies, Fear, and Shame. Spurring Carrie to be herself. Live by passions, not fears. Reject conditional love.

———

Friday, July 11, 1980

At suppertime, Carrie sniffed. "Smells like Scarecrow's Corn and Potato-Sausage Hash."

"With Mrs. Gordon's scones." Frowning, Oma thumped a pot on the stove. Opa winced.

"Her recipes usually make you smile, Oma. What's wrong?"

A hearty knock sounded on the front door. Opa seemed eager to leave. "I'll get it."

The door squeaked open. Two pairs of feet padded to the kitchen.

"Got a visitor, Carrie." Opa stood next to Brian.

Carrie balked, her emotions wreaking havoc. "What're you doing here?"

"Surprising you." He approached with a hug and kiss. "Business popped up for tomorrow. Figured I'd come tonight."

Stunned, Carrie faced Oma. No wonder she was grumpy. Distress signals.

"He swore us to secrecy." Oma's pot-stirring accelerated.

During supper and small talk, distraught about break-up plans and Oma's adoption, Carrie felt lightheaded. At meal's end, Brian spoke in his chocolatey voice. "I've a special dessert plan, just you and me. Let's go."

"Where?"

He stood and took her hand. "Trust me."

No way.

Oma turned on the faucet. "*Dweilen met de kraan open.* Enough mopping."

Carrie changed into a sundress. They left in his new blue Oldsmobile Cutlass Supreme.

Brian opened the sunroof. "Best feature of all. I see our future driving together, open to the sun, the wide road before us."

"Flatbed trucks have the same open-air distinction." She held her voice in check. "You don't know your way around here, do you?" Meaning, *this is your first visit all summer.*

"I have directions." He kept up lively chatter, but her replies were feeble, the shock of Wednesday's revelation still fresh. He approached Mulberry Street. *No Brian-Dirk collisions, please.* He turned onto Mulberry and parked at the café.

She went numb. "Why *here?*"

"You talk so much about it. Seems like a decent place."

Relegated to one step above fast food. "Beyond decent. It's a historical marker." Despite its 1960s interior. "My friend Dirk works here." *Skippy.*

"I know." He slid his arm around her as they walked in and got seated. Dirk's mellow voice and guitar picking of "Both Sides Now" greeted them. Two months ago, she kept comparing him to Brian. Now, it reversed.

Carrie buried her face in the menu, blocking Dirk from view. Letters blurred.

"Any recommendations?" Brian asked.

Dunham's Diner. Or maybe not. Too painful. "Depends on your mood." *Do they serve Gloom and Doom?*

While waiting for dessert, Carrie pointed out family portraits. Brian gave appropriate nods, an occasional "nice," so far removed from Carrie's life, from Mrs. Gordon, Macatawa Park visits, Oma's adoption. "Too bad you haven't met Mrs. Gordon."

"She sounds like a curiosity."

A slow burn pierced her heart. "Listen—"

Alberta dropped off pie. Carrie stammered. "The thing is—"

"Wait." Brian checked his watch. Eight-fifteen. He gestured toward the corner.

Strumming, Dirk spoke into the microphone. "By special request, for a very special young lady, Carrie, from one *very* lucky man, Brian."

Her face warmed as Dirk sang Billy Joel's "Just the Way You Are." Hearing the song on guitar, not keyboard, strangely expanded the surreal moment. His face exuded tenderness, his eyes riveted to hers, reminiscent of his arms surrounding her after she'd bared her soul.

Had Brian told him to cast the look of love her way too?

Brian took her hand. It felt like stone. "Carrie, that song's how I feel about you. I love you and want us together forever."

Her heart thumped, his words twittering like an echo. Behind Brian, Dirk picked his way through Jim Croce's "Time in a Bottle." Though she stared at Brian, Dirk's face dominated.

Brian opened a tiny box revealing a diamond ring. "Carrie, will you marry me?"

What was happening? *Don't look at Dirk.*

After six years, Brian deserved an explanation. So many issues. The failed class. No diploma. The chair. The job with her dad despite her dreams of Wolcott. Above all, his inability to see her, hear her. Did he think playing this song negated years of dismissiveness?

She blinked. "How can you marry someone you don't know well?"

"I've known you my whole life."

"You know facts, but when I tell you my thoughts and feelings, you shut me off."

"No, I don't. I love you, Carrie."

"I can't be myself with you."

"Are we back to this *stranger* business, that song about masks?" He leaned forward. "How can I prove my love? I requested this song five days ago and stopped by earlier today to tip the guy. Generously."

Five days ago—two days before Dirk drove her to City Hall. Without hinting of Brian's plan, Dirk dropped everything to help her.

Brian continued. "I work hard preparing for our future. You're my motivation."

Normally, she'd apologize for ruining the evening. "You only want to live for who you *think* I am." She exhaled. "I'm not signing any teaching contracts."

"What?" He plunked back as if kicked in the chest. The water glass wobbled.

"See?"

"Oh, you're kidding." He wiped spilled water with a napkin. "You're postponing teaching a year."

"No. I never want to teach."

"Then why'd you get an education degree?"

"To please you and my parents. I have no diploma because I failed Philosophy of Ed."

His face paled as if she'd reported a death. "Retake it."

"No. I don't want to teach. I never did."

"I knocked myself out getting you through student teaching."

"Do you even remember my plans to buy Dunham's Diner?" Though she had no intention of telling him about the denied loan application.

Dirk walked toward their table. *Don't stop here.*

He did. She stared at Brian, blinking to shut down tears.

"Congratulations to the happy couple." Dirk took Carrie's

hand. Startled, she looked up. He gripped her fingers. "I hope you enjoyed that song, just for *you*." His eyes burrowed into hers. As if he'd sung from his own heart.

"It was beautiful." Her voice flattened. "You remember Brian."

The men exchanged curt greetings with a handshake. Dirk left.

"Good guitarist," Brian said, "though Skippy doesn't have much ambition."

Carrie gaped. "Don't *ever* call him Skippy again. Ambition is defined by more than college degrees and forty-hour workweeks."

Face reddening, Brian scanned the room. "Sweetheart, let's talk on the beach."

To avoid a scene. A few women smiled at her. Congratulatory waves from others. The fishbowl effect in action. Better to spill her emotions onto sand and waves.

On the beach, the sky's beauty belied the ache thickening in Carrie's chest.

"Gorgeous sky." He grabbed her hand, but she withdrew it.

She fumed at his ability to obliterate everything by changing topics, deflecting the mood, nullifying her feelings.

"You're not yourself tonight," he said. "You love sunsets."

"I *am* being myself. You just don't recognize me."

"Right. What's eating you?"

"You took a job with my dad without consulting me. You gave my favorite chair to Goodwill. You shut down my feelings."

"You're not the sweet, loving Carrie I've always known?"

"I also tried a strawberry margarita. I love Billy Joel music. I enjoy refinishing furniture and shopping garage sales, not Macy's."

"You've had a strawberry margarita?"

"See! You didn't hear one word after I mentioned alcohol."

"Why don't you want to teach?"

"I hated it. I had a meltdown and couldn't finish one course."

"Meltdown?" He frowned, as if this were akin to bank robbery. "Do your parents know?"

"I told them two weeks ago. They're furious. We haven't spoken since."

"Carrie, you need to show more respect—"

"Respect?" Her eyes widened. "They shaped me into their own mold, but it's not *me*. Then you and Dad planned my life behind my back. You *knew* I wanted to run a café in Wolcott."

"Working with him is a fantastic opportunity."

"What about being with *me*?" She swirled her arms. "You broke your promise about moving here."

"If you don't get the loan, what'll you do?"

She stewed at his reckless change of topic. "Bike cross country. Sail to South America."

"Ludicrous." He rolled his eyes.

"Really? I missed fun things in college because I followed you like a puppy dog."

"We can travel wherever you want."

"You also reneged on supporting my book café."

"No, I just thought it better to have a safe teaching job."

Her fists clenched. "You don't like any idea that's not *yours*! You don't wanna be with a college failure. Or anywhere near a risky restaurant business."

He grabbed her hands, whirling her to face him. "Enough. How is such talk helping? Just say yes, and let's begin our new life together."

She pulled away. "You think proposing wipes out all our problems?"

"No, but we'll be together."

"You're not listening." She continued walking.

"When you told me to listen to that Stranger song, I got the album from your parents' house."

She was stunned. "Really?"

"The guy's talented. But I wasted an hour listening to secular music."

"Can't you see how his lyrics reflect truth?"

"I saw how I got sucked in. So I threw the record away."

"It's at Goodwill?"

"No. Threw it in the garbage."

"You threw *my* album in *your* trash can?" She swung her arms up. "Then why'd you request a Billy Joel song tonight instead of 'Amazing Grace'?"

"It's a love song."

"How dare you have someone sing me words you don't even mean."

"Of course I mean them."

"But you harp on me. I daydream too much. You give me self-help books, but I love fairy tales. And guess what? I went to a second Billy Joel concert. And thoroughly enjoyed it."

"What?" His brows shot up.

"I couldn't tell you, or you'd flip out."

He pulled her to a stop. "I'm concerned about this deception."

"When I'm honest, you chide or ignore me."

"And this obsession with secular music—"

"Don't forget the margarita."

"Stop it."

"See? I'm a bad influence. You need to fix me."

"I can't let you take *me* down that path."

Long-ago words wheedled in. *You're the Slough of Despond to me!* She stumbled backward. Teddy's words entwined Brian's. *Sinking me in the mire, far from God's light ...* "You'll always be superior. I'm bringing you down." She walked faster. "You think I'm wicked. Well, here's your wickedness. Sometimes, I doubt God's goodness. I fret and stew. I'm judgmental. I'm selfish. But you don't wanna hear about all that, do you?"

"But—"

"You can't deal with my *true* self. You only want problems you can fix, like throwing a prized record in the garbage."

"You don't understand—"

"Yes, I do. *You're* the upright one while the world around you sinks into the Slough of Despond. You think we're all stuck, calling you to join us, but you remain the holy one."

"Slough of Despond from *Pilgrim's Progress*?"

"You're stuck, too, and don't even know it. You're Mr. Legality."

She ran down the beach. Clouds scudded above, reflecting moonlight, affirmation of the next step toward her dreams. No longer bound by expectations or fear of judgment.

He caught up and grabbed her arm. "We're not done talking."

"Yes, we are. We've no future together. I'll always be your Slough of Despond."

His silence said all. Declining a ride, she ran up the stairs and jogged home, weeping, two miles in the dark. *Humbug wizard*. Selling turnips as lemons.

At home, she pulled the flower from the Wendolyn treasure chest. Why was blooming so painful? She grasped the chicken ornament.

Oma's hands warmed her shoulders. "Better to change direction halfway than be wrong all the way."

Fifty-Eight

Saturday, July 12, 1980

On the phone, Mother's voice was silky smooth. "What happened, sweetie?"

Ugh. Like Brian. Pet names only when criticizing or manipulating. Had he marched right over to her parents to report? Carrie braced herself. "Brian's lacking things I value in a relationship."

"Lacking what? He's lauded by his church, has stock in good companies, and serves on a community board."

"That makes him a good citizen, not a good husband."

"Who could be more qualified?"

"Qualified for what? Bookkeeping? Managing baseball stats? Driving new cars?"

"Darling, think. It's not too late to patch it up. Answer his calls. He'll forgive you."

Stunned, Carrie squeezed the phone. "*Forgive* me? I did nothing wrong besides stay with him five years too long."

"Honey, he's devoted to you. His income and resources will make a good life for you."

"A feather in your cap, too. But I'll shrivel up and die."

"No need for melodrama. Just call him." Mom's tone had an edge. "With your college failure, what worthy man will want you?"

"I measure worth by honesty and compassion. Someone I can be my true self with."

"You're losing a strong, financial future. You've broken his heart."

"What about *my* heart, Mom? And my own goals?"

"You'll regret spurning your education *and* Brian's security."

"Only you and Dad will have regrets." She slammed the phone down. She'd actually hung up on her mother.

Oma stood in the doorway. "She had that coming. When you burn your butt, you need to sit on the blisters."

* * *

Monday, July 14, 1980

Carrie added too much salt to the Sunflower Bread dough. It went into the garbage.

"What's wrong?" Mrs. Gordon asked.

"I broke up with Brian Friday night."

"Tarts and tadpoles!" Mrs. Gordon dropped a spoon. "Why?"

"We broke up over Billy Joel."

Mrs. Gordon peered over her glasses. "You don't strike me as the two-timing type."

"He's a popular singer. I'm a fan. It's complicated."

"You couldn't be more vague."

"I wasn't good enough for Brian." Carrie sighed. "I'm the Slough of Despond to him."

Voice ragged, Mrs. Gordon patted Carrie's hand. "I'm so sorry."

"He's Mr. Legality. I wasted six years losing parts of myself.

This rift with my parents, well, now I'm on my own." She shared details of her mother's call.

"Now the door's open for Mr. Vandenakker."

Had Dirk really sung to her from his own heart? "He doesn't want to be the rebound guy. Besides, he jumps from job to job. No stability. No money."

"Everything Brian isn't. But can you be your true self with him?"

"Well, yes. He knows me better in two months than Brian did in six years."

"Can you tell him your biggest sin, and he'll still accept you?"

What were Carrie's greatest sins? Envy? Judging? Criticizing? "I think so."

"That's worth more than money in the bank. Otherwise, you're no better off than Mr. Blake's sunflower."

In the parlor, Mrs. Gordon rocked. "I'd like your oma here for tea next Tuesday. But I've things to tell you first." She discussed Mr. Baum's correspondence from 1917 to 1918. His works included a new series about Mary Louise, named after his sister, plus *The Lost Princess of Oz* and *The Tin Woodman of Oz*. He rewrote *Aunt Jane's Nieces and the Red Cross*, reflecting his angst over war. After an appendectomy and gall bladder surgery, he wrote from bed, finishing two more Oz books for 1919 and 1920, published posthumously.

Carrie read from *The Lost Princess of Oz* preface: "'The imaginative child will become the imaginative man or woman most apt to create, to invent, and therefore to foster civilization.' He sure did his part fostering civilization."

"In that book, the Wizard says, '"Those who are contented have nothing to regret and nothing more to wish for.' But contentment eluded me. Hiding behind pseudonyms and roles, I was the inn's proprietor, never known as mother or author. Parts of me were as displaced as the Tin Woodman's legs."

"Shiny on the outside, hollow on the inside," Carrie said.

"Yet not hollow. Sadness and guilt weighed me down." Mrs. Gordon gave Carrie a paper from the drawer. "His last letter, October 1918."

Carrie read parts aloud:

"As Publishers Weekly noted, 'There is one country where no shadow has been cast by the war; it is the Land of Oz.' But the rest of us are overshadowed by much distress. Frank and Robert are officers, their families left behind, all facing interminable odds and an unknown future. You miss Dorothy terribly. As I recently wrote Frank in France, when we look back on something that seemed discouraging and unfair, we eventually realize that God at all times has been on our side. The eventual outcome is the best solution. So, rely on God and trust in His guidance. Remember, Charlotte, only imagination and faith keep man above the commonplace. Both are vital."

"Imagination and faith," Carrie murmured.

"Don't take for granted the blessings sprinkled throughout your life. I completed The Magic of Oz in bed, propped by pillows, putting me in mind of Cap'n Bill, with only one leg. He says: 'When a person's well, he don't realize how jolly it is, but when he gets sick he remembers the time he was well. Most folks forget to thank God for giving 'em two good legs, till later except to praise God for leaving one.' So don't forsake happiness. Thankfulness brings contentment."

Carrie set down the letter. "Did you rely on God and trust His guidance?"

"I wanted to. But life took another bad turn. Wolcott gave up young men for the war. Economic depression and rationing affected the food industry. And ..." Mrs. Gordon fumbled with a button. "Remember why I hired you?"

Finally. "To help clear your husband's name from a false charge."

"This is the last event I must share." Mrs. Gordon shifted as if settling into a revelation with lethal effects. "Walter and I married, April 1917. That same month, the U.S. joined the war. Dorothy turned five. I moved into this house with him, built by his family in 1883. Walter was good, kind, and honest, a church deacon and town councilman. He looked after me well. We lived comfortably. He supported my writing endeavors, though he'd no idea I was writing for Dorothy. I visited Aunt Sophie, Mae, and Beatrice weekly.

"I never got pregnant, as if there'd only been room in my life for one child. After being married eight months, Walter had an emergency appendectomy in Grand Rapids. The surgeon found multiple tumors in Walter's GI tract. Tests verified cancer, already spread. The tumors he removed would grow back. He gave Walter six months. We were devastated. Walter returned home under Dr. Weaver's care. By then, physicians knew radiation could cause cancer while shrinking tumors, so no treatment was recommended.

"Once more, God seemed distant. I'd lost Teddy, education, career, and Dorothy. Now Walter. I pleaded with God to spare him. Walter still worked at the pharmacy, training his assistant to replace him. Some days, he dragged himself in. I helped as needed."

Mrs. Gordon sighed. "The Great War was just the beginning of death. That fall, Spanish influenza crossed the country, killing thousands. But we had our own disaster."

Janie
July 1918

One evening, Janie played games at Aunt Sophie's with Mae and Beatrice. Teddy was repairing a kitchen cabinet. Walter was home sleeping.

Someone rapped on the front door. Aunt Sophie opened it.

Hands clenched, a middle-aged man in overalls stalked in as if Auntie were a breeze he could walk through. The stench of tobacco and alcohol accompanied him. "I'm looking for my wife and daughter," he snarled.

Mae looked up, face paling. She grabbed Beatrice. "Owen!"

"Mae." The man's face hardened, and his words slurred. "You left me."

Beatrice squirmed into her mother's lap. Mae trembled. "You *know* why."

Aunt Sophie slinked into the kitchen toward the phone.

Teddy walked in with a screwdriver and balked. "What're you doing here?"

"Son!" Sarcasm tethered the man's words. "Well, this is a bonus."

Teddy gritted his teeth. "Why are you here?"

"To fetch your mother and sister. They lost their way home."

"For good reason." Teddy the man spoke with courage he'd surely never exhibited with his father before. "How'd you find us?"

"Saw a letter at the MacFadyens with this address. Took a while to save money for the train." Owen squinted. "Which one is Janie Broderick? The one who brought my Mae here."

Janie froze. Mae leaned over Beatrice, who was swamped by Mae's skirt. In the kitchen, Aunt Sophie spoke in coarse whispers and hung up the phone. Janie's heart raced. "Get out."

Owen lunged at her. She stumbled backward.

Teddy threw a vase. Glass shattered against the wall. "You're never touching—"

Owen sniggered. "You talk as if you've amounted to something."

Teddy's face reddened. "I'm married with a child, run a business, and own a house, no thanks to you," he yelled, becoming Teddy the wounded boy. But without cowering.

"Well, ain't that fine." Owen grabbed Mae's arm. She shrieked. Teddy dashed over and punched his father's jaw. Mae shrank into the couch. Owen staggered back, holding his chin. "A fight you want, is it, boy?" He swung at his son, but Teddy smacked his cheek.

"Teddy, stop!" Janie screamed, knowing the rage boiling up, as if all the fury of his twenty-seven years surged into this moment. Teddy pounded him.

Owen taunted, slicing back. Flailing, he returned each of Teddy's blows. Until the last one that sent Owen spinning. His head cracked against the wall. Limp, he slid onto the floor.

Mae and Beatrice sobbed. Blood dripped from Teddy's mouth, his hands. He stared at his palms, at what they were capable of.

Owen still breathed. An ambulance and police arrived.

With no Holland hospital, Owen was treated in Grand Rapids, then sent to Dr. Weaver's for vigilant surveillance. Besides his office downtown, the doctor had an infirmary in the back of his house, with two nurses. Teddy was arrested for aggravated assault, imprisoned without bail. If Owen died, Teddy would be charged with homicide. According to the doctor, Owen's alcoholism, having ravaged his body for years, would impede recovery.

Janie agonized as Owen's life hung in the balance. If he died, Teddy would be imprisoned. For years.

She'd not brought Mae all the way to Wolcott just to be tormented again.

Two days after the assault, Janie brought a tray of food to Walter, where he lay on the couch and sat down near him. "I'm worried about Owen Callaghan dying."

Walter pulled himself to a sitting position. "Janie, I wish you hadn't seen that miserable fight. Owen's threats and Teddy lashing out at him like that."

Janie curled her fists. "Teddy finally stood up to his father. After years of abuse."

"He did much more than *stand* against him. He nearly killed him. Going way beyond self-defense." Shifting, Walter grimaced. "I hate that I can't … protect you anymore."

Janie embraced him. "You're the best husband. You're so much more than this illness."

He grunted. "If Owen recovers, he's going to threaten you and Mae."

"Mae's papers from the Syracuse lawyer should protect her. Owen can't take her."

"Papers won't keep him from hurting her." He touched her cheek. "Or you."

"I'll be fine, but I'm just as worried about Owen dying as living. If that happens, Teddy will be charged with homicide and go to jail."

He cocked his head. "You still have feelings for Teddy?"

"No, Walter. I love only you. It's just that … Teddy's a good man with a young family." *And father of my daughter.* "It would kill Mae to see him in jail. He was abused fourteen years and finally stood against his father." Janie sniffled. "I'm afraid he'll pay for that mistake the rest of his life."

Walter stared across the room. "Maybe not. Owen's an alcoholic. That doesn't bode well for him surviving this ordeal."

"That's no help for Teddy. What's your point?"

Walter lay down as if contemplating. "Nothing, love. Thank you for the meal."

Fifty-Nine

July 1918

Despite weakening, Walter worked daily. Five days after Owen moved to Dr. Weaver's, Janie helped at the pharmacy. The last customer left.

"Doc Weaver's coming for Owen's medication." Perspiring, Walter leaned on the counter and propped his head on his hand, studying the prescription.

Janie took the paper. Doc ordered Bromo-Seltzer for headache, as well as cough syrup with a chloroform sedative. "Sit down. I'll prepare it." She eyed the back shelf, darting down the *B* and *C* row of bottles in alphabetical order: Bismosal, the bright blue bottle of Bromo-Seltzer, then liquid chloroform, cough syrup, and liquid cyanide—an ingredient often used for pesticides, engraving, disinfecting, photo processing, and metal polishing.

The bell rang. Old Mrs. Emery hobbled in with her cane.

"You tend to her," Walter whispered. "I'll get Doc's med."

Janie smiled through gritted teeth. "How are you, Mrs. Emery? How can I help you?"

"By the time you ask the second question, I forget the first." Her sandpaper voice irritated as much as her words.

"Guess I have my answer for the first." *Fat and sassy.* "What do you need?"

"Peace and quiet." The woman shook a piece of paper. "And this, if you can decipher Doc's handwriting. How do I know he's not prescribing arsenic?"

"You'd recognize the metallic taste and spit it out. No harm done."

"You fancy yourself a comedian, Mrs. Gordon?"

"Hardly. But Dr. Weaver knows what he's doing."

"How would *you* know? When do I get help from the *real* pharmacist?"

Ignoring her, Janie peered at the prescription. "Bismosal. That wintergreen taste."

Mrs. Emery's jaw jutted out. "I'll manage it."

"You certainly will." The woman could probably swallow nails without a hiccup. Janie picked up the Bismosal bottle, next to Bromo-Seltzer. Why was chloroform still here? It was commonly mixed into cough syrup as a sleep aid and pain killer. Wasn't Walter adding it?

Janie handed over the Bismosal. Staggering, Walter brushed past Janie en route to the medicine shelf. Mrs. Emery paid and hobbled out the door.

Walter swayed back to the counter. Sweat dripping, he pressed his forehead.

Janie swiped the cough syrup bottle from him. "Sit down. I'll finish it."

Shaking, he bent over the counter.

At the shelf, she stopped short. Bromo-Seltzer, cyanide, chloroform, cough syrup—a different order. Why was cyanide out of place? "Did you add chloroform to the cough syrup?"

"It's ready ..." His voice withered.

"Why is cyanide out of order?"

"Must've put the chloroform back wrong." Face down, he massaged his forehead.

No, everything else was in place. Except cyanide. An empty spot where it once stood, now crowded between Bromo-Seltzer and liquid chloroform. At the counter, she picked up the cough syrup and unscrewed the lid, sniffing. The familiar almond scent of cyanide. *Oh, my!* She must discard it and remix a new tonic. Walter needn't know. One last jar of cough syrup remained on the shelf. Clasping the toxic bottle of tonic, she headed toward the sink.

Dr. Weaver entered, exhaustion etching his face. "Good evening, friends. Is my prescription ready? Mr. Callaghan's in desperate need of pain relief."

An image of imprisoned Teddy plagued Janie. Owen couldn't die. "Is he improving?"

"No, he's got internal injuries. Broken bones are set, but if I can't stop his coughing, it'll cause more damage."

"Can he talk?" Janie asked.

"There's a head injury, but in between agitated attempts to sleep, he mumbles." Dr. Weaver added quietly, "He's determined to reclaim Mae and Beatrice. And hurt you, Janie."

"The law's on Mae's side," Janie said. "She has papers."

"That won't stop him from injuring them. And you."

Janie's voice dropped. "But if he dies, Teddy will—"

"Teddy's like a son to me," Doc said. "I didn't bring him all the way from Syracuse to see him thrown in jail. I'll do everything I can to prevent that."

Quivering, Janie clutched the poisoned bottle tighter. If the man died, Teddy would go to jail. If he lived, Owen would haunt and harm his family. She met Dr. Weaver's sorrowful gaze.

Nobody would ever implicate Walter for a pharmacy error. Death easily occurred from chloroform, a cough syrup ingredient. Risky for alcoholics, like Owen. If he died from cough tonic, Teddy wouldn't be held liable. He'd serve a short time for assault, not years for murder.

Dr. Weaver placed money on the counter. Nobody would suspect cyanide.

Trembling, heart palpitating, she raised the toxic cough syrup bottle and screwed the cap tightly. "Your medicine's ready."

That evening, Janie answered the front door. "Officer Chandler!"

The police chief strutted to Walter in the chair by the hearth. "Walter Gordon, you're under arrest for the death of Owen Callaghan."

Walter's face fell. Janie covered her mouth before a shriek escaped. Wailing, she followed them to the station where Dr. Weaver waited among policemen. His voice was heavy. "I had to report this. I'm sorry. Walter shouldn't be practicing pharmacy."

Walter stumbled to a chair, Officer Chandler beside him. "Tell them your observations, Dr. Weaver," Chandler said.

The doctor cleared his throat, as if reluctant. "Fifteen minutes after one dose of cough syrup, Mr. Callaghan died an extremely violent death. He convulsed, gasped for air, salivated, and vomited, then collapsed with an ungodly scream. All signs of cyanide poisoning."

Sweating, Janie sank into a chair.

Walter paled another shade. "No ... I mixed in chloroform, as you prescribed."

Dr. Weaver continued. "His skin turned a mottled blue. His throat was burned bright red and his stomach swelled. Chloroform doesn't cause mottling. He would've turned yellow, for jaundice. Only after he drank did I realize. Then I smelled the bottle."

Officer Chandler lifted the cough syrup bottle. "We'll have this tested, but there's no mistaking cyanide's almond odor."

"Obvious when the bottle opens." An officer cast a suspicious glance at the doctor.

"My husband would never do this on purpose," Janie said.

"By law, I must report it, Janie." Dr. Weaver's face reflected a parent's grief. He turned to Officer Chandler. "Walter's on pain medication, which may impact his ability to prepare the proper mixture. That must be considered before making charges."

Janie's vision whirled. This was her fault. She could have prevented it. But then Owen might have died on his own, landing Teddy in jail. "I ... I ..."

"Janie, dear." Mrs. Weaver brushed into the room, her face aghast. Janie barely felt Mrs. Weaver's arm around her, as if her own body wasn't pinned to earth.

"It wasn't his fault," Janie whimpered. "He's sick ..."

"There, there, dear." Mrs. Weaver embraced her.

Janie shrugged away. "He's already dying from cancer. After serving this town twelve years, he's going to jail as an endangerment to the community?"

"The court decides that," the officer said. "He'll have his pharmaceutical license revoked. The judge determines motive."

"Motive?" Janie stood, knees wobbling. "My husband wouldn't hurt a flea. You know that." But if she confessed, she'd end up in jail herself, never reaching Dorothy. Whereas Walter may have only weeks to live.

"Enough." Officer Chandler nudged Walter toward the cells. Walter shuffled with a forlorn glance at Janie, face shadowed by shame.

"No! It's not his fault. Please, it's ... it's ..." Janie stammered.

Mrs. Weaver guided her toward the door. "You're distraught. Let's get you home."

The next few days blurred, the worst nightmare. Walter was charged with homicide. What if the court determined Walter had motive? After all, Owen, the father of Janie's former beau, had endangered her, too. Gossip ricocheted about town.

Due to illness, Walter spent one night in jail, then under house arrest. Walter's assistant took over the pharmacy. The cyanide test revealed the telltale Prussian blue chemical. An autopsy was scheduled. Walter would be implicated upon discovery that poison effected Owen's death. If Janie confessed and went to jail, how would she secretly write, publish, or mail books to the adoption agency?

But she couldn't let Walter sink into this bottomless pit alone.

Love enabled her to retrieve Mae, stay silent for Teddy, give up Dorothy, manage the inn for her parents. Wasn't love wanting the highest good for someone, even at great cost?

Late afternoon, Janie sat at his bedside. "Walter, it's my fault Owen died."

"What?" He tried to sit up but flopped back on the pillow.

Trembling, she knelt, her face near his. "I knew you'd picked up the cyanide, but I said nothing. If Owen died from accidental poisoning, Teddy wouldn't go to jail. Otherwise, he'd leave behind a son." *And daughter.*

"You knew? You chose Teddy's welfare over mine?"

"Not purposely. I wasn't thinking straight. I played God because of how Owen treated Teddy over the years." *He's the father of my daughter!* A secret living in cramped quarters. Smothering her. But this admission would taint these days with betrayal and regret, then haunt her from his grave. "Tomorrow, I'm confessing to the authorities."

His silence estranged her, his mouth a grim line. She buried her face near his arm. He caressed her hair. "Janie, look at me."

She lifted her head. "I haven't much time. Don't go to the authorities. *I* made the error. I'll take the blame."

"But you're ill. It was an accident. Your reputation will suffer."

"Where I'm going, reputations don't matter."

"Reputation is all a man leaves behind."

He grimaced in pain. "You have your whole life ahead of you. You have the tearoom. Stories to write. You'll marry again. You deserve happiness."

"No, I don't, Walter. I won't be happy without you."

"Yes, you will. You have much to live for, Janie. You'll have the family I couldn't give you. Don't go to the authorities. Let me take the blame I deserve."

"I can't live with the guilt."

He squeezed her hand. "I beg you to leave it alone."

"But I was wrong."

His voice took on urgency. "You know *nothing* about chemicals. You're no pharmacist. Listen. I never told your mother when you ordered a Dr. Pepper Black Cow." He offered a weak smile. "I never told about your newspaper staff meeting or buying my baking powder."

"But I must confess." Even if she never reached Dorothy.

He set a finger on her mouth. "No, Janie. I'll deny your part. Don't let this tragedy tarnish your life. Let it fall on me alone ... I promise, I'll be silent till the very end."

Walter was charged with homicide. The autopsy confirmed cyanide poisoning. Teddy was charged with aggravated assault and spent thirty days in jail. Walter died three days later. Nobody knew if the court would have deemed it negligence or manslaughter. Either way, folks shook their heads over Walter Gordon. How could God take her dear husband this way?

Janie dared not tell anybody, not even Auntie, about her

culpability. For nobody could be trusted with one's very soul, the darkest evil imprinted on it like a branding iron. The evil of one who'd let someone else take the blame for her sin. Wasn't this what Teddy did to her? Now she was doing the same to Walter. She'd never known how dark her heart truly was.

No poetic justice after all. This sin she would carry herself, unconfessed.

She'd always wanted to shed light in dark corners, like Nellie Bly. Now *Janie* was the darkness. Though Walter's and Dr. Weaver's words raised doubt, surely they'd never take someone else's life into their own hands. But *she* had.

For weeks, she considered going to authorities to wipe Walter's slate clean. But as time progressed, the more ludicrous it seemed. His name was already clouded with doubt and suspicion. And she, over months, then years, lost herself in tearoom duties.

She escaped by delving into her imagination, writing stories for Dorothy. Yet no fantasy lightened her load of guilt more than a few hours. She had nowhere to go with her burden. Dragons of Lies, Shame, and Fear plagued her, propelled by the dragon of Guilt. By writing Wendolyn's stories, Janie sought ways to overcome dragons through her protagonist, while above all, she knew she was fighting against God.

July 14, 1980

Numb, Carrie blinked. *Can you tell him your biggest sin, and he'll still accept you?* She took Mrs. Gordon's hand. "The dragon not yet slain." She looked her straight in the eye. "You're safe. I'm not going anywhere." A long minute stretched between them.

The woman's pulse clicked at Carrie's wrist. "I don't expect you to understand."

"I do. You feared never reaching Dorothy. But you're not the only one culpable. You're no pharmacist, as Walter said."

"But—"

"How do you know Dr. Weaver didn't smell cyanide before administering it? Maybe they both knew what they were doing."

"Then why'd Dr. Weaver blame Walter?" Mrs. Gordon snapped. "They were friends."

"He followed protocol. He had to prove it was cyanide that killed him, not the fight. He also reminded the officer that Walter's pain medication must be considered. A plea for mercy. Maybe Dr. Weaver knew he couldn't keep Owen alive, no matter what he did. So, he chose the next best route to keep Teddy from jail." Carrie leaned in. "They both had motive." She allowed the words to settle in. "Walter grieved that he couldn't protect you from Owen's violence. As a dying man, this was how he kept you from further harm. Nothing to lose but his reputation."

Mrs. Gordon's mouth twitched.

"Dr. Weaver invested years in Teddy's life. Claimed he hadn't brought Teddy from Syracuse just to see him thrown in jail."

"But they wouldn't—"

"Maybe they wouldn't. Maybe they would. But they each had motive."

Mrs. Gordon folded her hands as if grounding herself. "Even so, I know my part."

Carrie lifted *The Pilgrim's Progress*. "I wonder if John Bunyan feared having no influence in prison. But this book was second to the Bible in popularity. Translated into two hundred languages. Written in jail."

Tears gathered in the woman's eyes. "Where I should've gone."

Carrie stroked Mrs. Gordon's hand. "I mean, John Bunyan

had a difficult life, too. Yet God used his trials and prison time for good."

"He redeemed the time the locusts ate. But I was awful, letting Walter take the blame."

"He *wanted* to take the blame." Carrie nearly whispered. "He really loved you."

"Yes." She sighed. "But I felt worse yearly. Despair. Melancholy. Anger."

Carrie hesitated. "That's because he couldn't carry your burden. *You* carried your guilt, strapped on your back, like Christian's burden." Mrs. Gordon looked away. Carrie patted the woman's arm. "Only God knows us to the depths and still accepts us. Only He has power to conquer dragons of lies, fear, and shame. He already defeated Apollyon." Carrie scooted forward. "Hiding behind different faces, different names, doesn't slay dragons."

The woman's jaw clenched.

Carrie's thumb roved across her great-grandmother's wrist. "You still carry your burden. Time to stop believing the biggest lie."

"Which is?"

"That God hates you. The truth is, He provided the way to drop your burden."

SIXTY

Tuesday, July 15, 1980

The words kept rolling through Carrie's head. *Can you tell him your biggest sin, and he'll still accept you?* Time to find out.

At the hardware store, Carrie asked, "Is Dirk here?"

"He comes at an extremely high price." John Vandenakker chuckled. "He's at Hope Haven working with at-risk kids. Never misses a Tuesday. Oops. Said too much. He prefers doing good deeds on the sly." He winked. "Don't get me in trouble."

"Never." Carrie drove to Hope Haven in Holland. So, this was his secret!

The receptionist directed her to a room where three elementary-aged boys played cornhole. Dirk painted a bookshelf while telling a story about a guy who threw a beanbag so hard it flew around the world and hit him on the head five minutes later. They laughed.

The boys rushed to the door where Carrie leaned against the doorpost, arms crossed. They halted. Dirk whirled around. "Carrie!" His face brightened. "How'd you find me?"

"Happened to be in the neighborhood." She offered a coy smile.

Dirk dismissed the boys. "Hey, congratulations—" She displayed her left hand, ring finger bare. "Getting your ring polished?

"Can we talk?"

Fifteen minutes later, they ordered dinner at Dunham's Diner.

"Why're you working at Hope Haven?" Carrie asked.

"After my rough years, I wanted to invest in kids. Another way to redeem lost time. I'd gone haywire even with a solid, loving family. It's tougher for high-risk kids." He crossed his arms on the table. "How're *you* doing?"

"Not the greatest. I didn't get the café loan." She hated admitting that but embraced her great-grandma's words. *You don't need pinnacles and acclaim. You need people to walk with you on the journey.*

"No!" His face drooped, as if he'd received the letter himself. "What a disappointment."

"I'm still reeling. Got the letter last week."

"So, what's next?"

"I'll figure out another funding source. But I'm going solo now. I broke up with Brian."

"Seriously?" His eyes widened.

"Friday night. After you played ... that song." *With that look in your eyes.*

"I'm sorry," Dirk said. The sentiment seemed to require great effort.

"Really? You're always saying he didn't treat me how I deserved."

"Yeah, but I don't like seeing you heartbroken."

"It's more painful knowing how long this went on." She fiddled with a spoon. "We broke up over Billy Joel."

"Now Billy Joel's your lucky guy?"

"That 'Stranger' song symbolized our relationship. He threw my album in the trash."

"He *what*?"

"No kidding. He just threw it away. Everything crystallized then. He rejected everything important to me. My chair. Our life plans. My career preferences. Only appearances matter to him. How others view him. Why didn't I see it?"

"Maybe you did but couldn't escape." He arched an eyebrow. "Too risky."

"I couldn't share deeper thoughts or fears. Or my true failures." *Can you tell him your biggest sin?* "He thinks my worst fault is my musical tastes. He'd never handle knowing my real struggles." She crumpled her napkin. "I might have broken up sooner if I didn't fear the fallout. My parents. Loss of stability ..."

Dirk shrugged. "At the price of what? Look, it takes courage dealing with Mrs. Gordon's prickly demeanor and telling your parents you didn't want to teach. Exiting a bad relationship, not knowing the future."

"I was trapped by lies. You helped me see the truth."

"*You* combatted those lies. I just gave you ammunition." He took her hand. "Carrie, courage is plunging ahead, with feelings intact. It takes no grit to be stoic. You plumbed the depths of Mrs. Gordon's soul. Tough assignment, with circling sharks, long lifeline to the surface. Little air in the tank. An adventure I never had."

She warmed at his compliment. And his touch.

"By the way, Friday night, that was *me* singing to you." He swallowed. "But I can't be the rebound guy. You need time, so you don't mistake loneliness for affection."

For a whole year?

"I can't make promises. My actions need to speak for themselves."

Time for action, then. Her muscles tensed. "I lied about my college degree."

He folded his hands on the table, waiting.

Her hand lay empty. Cold. "I failed Philosophy of Ed. I was mediocre in student teaching. They let me walk at graduation, but I didn't get a diploma."

"That happens. No big deal." His voice was casual, but his face was sad.

"But I let you assume I had my diploma."

"That *is* a big deal." His jaw tightened. "Nobody knows?"

"I told my parents in June. They're furious because I won't retake the class."

"Why not?"

"Summer of my private rebellion, remember? Also, I had a meltdown. I'd stare at words like hieroglyphics, kept skipping class. I hated student teaching."

Dirk frowned. "Did Brian know?"

"Not till Friday night. He was appalled. But I'm more upset about him tossing my album than him thinking I'm a dunce for failing my class. Why?"

Dirk shrugged. "The class is something others expect you to do. The record's a part of who Carrie is."

His words rang true. "I couldn't tell my family because they valued the degree. That's why I took such a dim view of you when we met. I was wrong."

"So, you're wrong about me but still judge yourself by the same false measuring stick?"

She focused on her spoon.

"You thought *I'd* think less of you not being a college grad?" he asked.

"No. I'd think less of myself. I needed to be better than you, the college dropout."

"Like me, the noodlehead."

"Oh, Dirk, I'm so sorry. I completely misjudged you. I made assumptions because you left college, went globetrotting. Your tattoo ..." Mouth twitching, Dirk cradled his coffee cup. Carrie grimaced. She scooted over, grabbing her purse.

"Where're you going?"

"Home. Sorry I ruined everything." Good thing they'd driven separately.

Dirk was up in a flash. "Please don't go." His voice was tender. "Let's talk this out." They sat. "It's the *reason* for your deception that bothers me. I'm hurt that after all these weeks, you still think so little of me, you couldn't admit you didn't finish college."

"I'm sorry." She forced herself to maintain eye contact.

His spoon tapped the table. "Did you lie about anything else?"

"No. Just not forthright about feelings."

His voice softened. "By caring more about appearances, aren't you doing the same thing to me that your parents did to you?"

The words stung. "I'm so sorry."

"Stop apologizing."

"But you keep telling me how bad you feel."

He fingered his cup. "Look. It's possible to talk through feelings without cutting people off. Without distancing them. Or yelling."

"That's not my experience."

"I know. I've listened to you when you're angry. I'd like the same courtesy." He paused. "I'm more hurt than angry. I thought I'd earned your trust, been a safe place for you."

"You are."

"And I consider *you* a safe place. You care about my feelings. But I don't want you to wallow in them." His blue eyes deepened. "No masks. No ignoring, no changing the subject. Two people can share their hearts, be angry, forgive, and still be cared for."

And loved? His words trickled into her like sunshine on Lake Michigan's shoreline.

"Carrie, anger doesn't mean the mask goes on. Don't be afraid of talking to me. Even if it's as little as a fly walking on your biscuit." He brandished his fork like a sword. "If I *ever* make you fearful of being honest, give me the royal boot."

"Mrs. Gordon's inviting you for tea next Tuesday," Carrie announced.

"Why?" Oma sprinkled salt on a pan of beans.

"It's high time she meets you, since she shared her secret recipes."

"I'd like to meet her, too."

"You're not worried?"

"Well, maybe I've come off my high horse. She's been generous." Oma marked the date on her calendar. Six days away. Carrie unleashed a huge sigh.

The next day at Mrs. Gordon's, Carrie stirred batter to the rhythm of *Five more days, five more days* ... Over Princess Ozma's Birthday Cake and tea, she relayed Dirk's honest but gracious reaction to her no-diploma confession.

Mrs. Gordon smiled. "So, when's the wedding?"

Carrie balked. "He also says a grieving lover needs a year. To avoid the rebound effect."

"Fiddlesticks! He scales mountains and sails oceans. Riding whitewater rapids for him is like eating crackers for us."

Carrie shrugged. "Some things he won't risk."

"Love shouldn't be one of them. What do you like about him?"

"Everything." Carrie grinned. "He's kind and sweet and funny. He treats me like a queen. He seizes each day, never wasting a chance to make someone happy. He's honest, has integrity. Unafraid to discuss feelings. He has depth and loves God. Even with my flaws, he's still my friend. The truest kind."

"Far superior than playing baseball and bringing chocolate." Mrs. Gordon nodded. "He said two people in love learn how to combine their worlds. How far are you willing to step outside of yours? Or change your goals?"

"I don't know."

"If you sacrifice, do it for the right reason. You can love while staying true to yourself. Which I never did." She frowned. "Shortly after Walter died, I legally changed my name to Charlotte Rose. I wanted to be irrepressible Charlotte, instead of a failure in motherhood and marriage. But I couldn't muster Charlotte's identity. My family refused to call me that."

"But your imagination flourished as Gretchen Trumbauer for years."

"I escaped into my fairy tale world, but I went alone, thankful for the pseudonym. Nobody had to deal with the real me."

"But *I* want to." Carrie took her hand. "And I'd like to call you Grandma."

Tears ran down the woman's cheeks.

Thursday, July 17, 1980

At the café, Dirk sang Neil Diamond's "Song Sung Blue." Was he still angry?

Alberta beelined to her booth. "That nice young man cajoled Dirk into serenading you the other night. Honey, what's your secret?"

"Cajoled him?"

"The guy came earlier to tip him. Dirk only cooperated because Pearl insisted. He refused a twenty-dollar tip." Alberta waited as if inviting a revelation of juicy details.

Instead of satisfying Alberta's curiosity, Carrie went to ask Pearl about the lost picture. Pearl darted the other way. So, Carrie ordered tea as Dirk played "Sweet Caroline."

During his break, he slid into her booth. "How're you doing, Carrie?"

"I want that dune picture, but Pearl stormed off at the sight of me."

Dirk grinned. "When shall I turn on my charm?"

"I don't need your charm. I'll get that picture myself."

"No doubt you will." He slugged water and stood. "Shall I play 'You're No Good,' dedicated to ex-lucky guy? Or 'You're So Vain' and 'It's Too Late, Baby.'"

"A new song set for heartbreakers?"

"To unmask guys who give turnips for lemons."

She lifted her chin. "What about 'Desperado'?"

Instead, he sang "You've Got a Friend." He gazed at her as if other customers had disappeared, sending pleasant shivers from shoulders to toes. She was riveted as lyrics promised friendship through the seasons. But he wouldn't be there for fall, winter, or spring.

Sixty-One

Tuesday, July 22, 1980

Clutching her bag beside Oma, Carrie knocked and opened the front door.

Pale Mrs. Gordon waved them in. "Thank you for coming."

Carrie gave an encouraging smile and introduced them. Introductions seemed trite, considering the impending revelation.

Oma offered her hand. "I'm so glad to meet you, Mrs. Gordon. It's long overdue."

Staring at Oma's hand, Mrs. Gordon slowly reached, quivering. They shook. A wince crossed the older woman's face, as if fighting a tear at this first touch. "Yes, it is."

"Thank you again for sharing your tearoom recipes. Here's my not-so-famous peach jam." Oma handed her a jar.

In the dining room, the table displayed the Delft tea set on lace. Carrie poured tea and served Shaggy Man's Irresistible Gooey Caramel Chocolate Bars—hopefully as irresistible as his Love Magnet. The stack of Wendolyn books rested on the fourth chair, as planned. Out of sight.

Oma surveyed the figurines and a cluster of fairy tale prints. "Surely each item has a story to tell. Tell me about them."

Mrs. Gordon studied her daughter's face. "I will. But today, only one story needs telling. A true one awaiting its time."

Tensing, Carrie patted Mrs. Gordon's shoulder.

"Seventy years ago in Wolcott, a young man and woman fell in love," Mrs. Gordon went on. "Unfortunately, she found herself in the family way. She desired to marry and establish a home to raise the child. But he refused. So, she moved to Holland and bore this child alone."

"Devastating." Oma paused her fork.

"For four years, this mother cared for her daughter, but was sabotaged by depression and judgment. She found a stable home for her. Though grieved, the mother knew she'd done best for the child. But no contact was allowed." Mrs. Gordon fiddled with her napkin. "So, she obtained permission to send a yearly gift, anonymously, through the adoption agency."

"What gifts?"

On cue, Carrie handed the first Wendolyn book to Mrs. Gordon, who explained. "She sent a book, dedicated to her, using her birth name." She located the dedication page. "'To my Dorothy who will always be loved.'"

"I have this." Oma's face lit. "I've had the whole series since childhood."

"The mother signed her name in each, for she was the author."

Carrie handed her the second book. Mrs. Gordon pointed out its dedication page.

Oma's eyes darted back and forth. "I have all of these. Also signed by the author."

"The author only signed one set," Mrs. Gordon said.

"How can that be?" Oma mused.

Carrie opened the third book.

"'To Dorothy whose imagination ...'" Mrs. Gordon swallowed. "*You* are this Dorothy."

Oma's face widened. "*Lieve hemel!* I'm adopted? Who is this Gretchen Trumbauer?"

"I am," Mrs. Gordon replied. "That's my pseudonym."

Carrie set out two documents from her bag: Dorothy's birth certificate and Tantje's adoption paper.

Trembling, Oma stared at the papers. "Carrie, how long have you known?"

"A few days. This explains why there aren't pictures of you before age four."

"I have one." Mrs. Gordon pulled a Kodak snapshot from under her plate and handed it to Oma. "You're three here." Little Dorothy stood beside her mother, Janie Broderick, resembling a young Oma.

Carrie set out the 1916 baptism picture from Oma's album, then pulled the chicken ornament from her bag. "You said it seemed familiar." Shaking, Oma fingered the engraved LFB.

Mrs. Gordon quoted, "'Where do the chickens go at night ...'"

Oma's voice was ragged. "'Heigh-ho! Where do they go?' Oh, dear."

Mrs. Gordon folded her hands. "One day in Wolcott, I knew I was looking at my Dorothy, almost eight. I recognized you, your auburn hair. Your adopted mother called you Tantje. I wasn't allowed to introduce myself, so I said the first two things that came to mind. First, the advice from the Witch of the North in *The Wizard of Oz*, about the long journey. The second was Charles Dickens' fairy tale quote."

Grabbing Carrie's arm, Oma gasped.

"I could only love you from afar. Every tale I wrote with you in mind, to teach about love, courage, and perseverance, being strong as a girl. I felt like a failure giving you away, but by writing these stories, I'd reach you, showing you how to grow up."

Mrs. Gordon quoted the other book dedications, explaining each. "I have the letters you wrote." She handed Oma a manila envelope.

Oma held each letter as if fine glass, skimmed faded handwriting, studied the tulip drawing.

Mrs. Gordon clutched the table edge. "Do you have any memory of my leaving you?"

"For years, I had nightmares—a woman walking away. I'd wake up screaming. My mother held me, promising to never leave. Over time, the nightmare faded."

Voice frayed, Mrs. Gordon took her Dorothy's hand. "So, you were *loved*."

Oma nodded. "Greatly."

Carrie stroked Mrs. Gordon's arm. "God redeemed the time the locusts ate."

Mrs. Gordon led them upstairs to a forbidden door. "I made this for you, Dorothy, with all the child delights of imagination." She turned the doorknob.

Inside, light filtered through lace-covered windows, revealing a girl's bedroom. Pastel pink walls caressed framed illustrations: Kate Greenaway's and Randolph Caldecott's nursery rhymes, Walter Crane's fairy tale prints, *Wind in the Willows*, Madeline, and Curious George.

Raggedy Ann and Winnie-the-Pooh attended a child-size tea party. Above hung Maxfield Parrish's illustration, "The Knave of Hearts." Books of poetry, folktales, and Mother Goose topped the bedside table. Wynken, Blynken, and Nod sailed in a wooden shoe mobile, near a poster of "The Owl and the Pussycat." A miniature family occupied a three-story Victorian dollhouse. Behind, as if the books had conjured magic, a painted mural of rolling hills and craggy mountains led to a distant castle, blending into rosy walls.

An appliquéd quilt covered the bed where a stuffed gingham dog nestled with a calico cat, straight from Eugene Field's poem. Beside them laid a tattered Dorothy rag doll.

Oma picked up the doll and hugged it. "I remember this!"

Mrs. Gordon smiled faintly. "I failed to be a good mother, so I loved you from afar. I cared for this room the way I wanted to care for you."

Carrie's gaze swept over the beautiful shrine to a lost daughter, full of sunshine, magic, and castles. But alas, no child ever stepped foot inside. Just a lonely old lady with her dust rag, adding to the shrine as if the child had never grown up.

Oma's voice quaked. "How long have you known I was Dorothy?"

"Besides the incident when you were eight, I didn't know until you moved to Wolcott in 1949. I recognized you at the tearoom. Hearing your maiden name mentioned confirmed it."

"Why didn't you tell me before?"

"I didn't have courage."

Carrie balked. *No courage?* The woman so quick to unleash wrath and sarcasm?

Mrs. Gordon looked away for a moment. "It takes no courage to be cross or critical, to incite an argument, or speak one's mind about teabags and trifles when you don't care what others think. But when you want to love someone and want their love in return, that takes all the courage in the world."

Oma briefly embraced her mother. "I should go. But I'll return. Soon."

———

At home, seated at the table with coffee, Oma said, "My mother always pointed out Wendolyn dedications to this girl Dorothy. We'd talk about it after reading the story. She must've known the books were a gift from my natural mother but never said a word."

"She couldn't have known your mother was the author," Carrie said.

"But she surely knew my given name. Maybe she suspected."

"Hmm. Maybe that's why she never told you."

Oma tilted her head. "What?"

"She couldn't break agency protocol. If you knew the connection, she couldn't allow you to write to the author."

"But this way," Oma mused, "Mother and I could enjoy the books together."

"And you and Gretchen Trumbauer could exchange letters. For years."

Carrie called her mother about the adoption and asked if she'd like to meet Mrs. Gordon. Aghast, Mom cast doubts on the woman's credibility, confirming her dubious reputation.

That afternoon, Carrie reported Oma was adjusting and wanted to visit soon. Mrs. Gordon smiled, the biggest one yet. Hesitantly, Carrie relayed her mom's response.

"When your grandparents moved here," Mrs. Gordon said, "they came to the tearoom regularly. I knew the regulars. Your mother was fifteen, starting at Wolcott High. Six years later, after college graduation, she walked down my street. I was on the porch before work and asked her to water my sunflowers. She didn't recognize William Blake's poetry, as you did."

Carrie was spellbound. "Did you offer her a summer job?"

"The same job I offered you. But she refused."

Carrie smirked. "You needed an anti-tulip-smashing contract."

"Clearly, she wanted nothing to do with an eccentric old woman."

"I'm grateful *I'm* the one who heard your story.

"And I'm grateful I've found a new family. You've seen my shame and bitterness and haven't left." Mrs. Gordon patted Carrie's arm. "Home can be discovered, if not inherited."

Sixty-Two

Wednesday, July 23, 1980

"What do you remember about your great-grandmother, Katrina Kloosterman?" Mrs. Gordon asked Dirk on the front porch. Carrie sat beside him.

"She died when I was ten. We visited her Sunday afternoons. She loved us kids, fixed fried egg sandwiches for supper. She limped from arthritis, but always smiled. Very godly."

"I'm glad you knew her." Mrs. Gordon shared about her Holland years with the Kloostermans, how Katje sustained her and Dorothy through difficult times. "But today, I'm inquiring about *your* locusts."

"I've had plenty." He related his wasted years before turning his life around.

"Fine and dandy," Mrs. Gordon said, "but what about someone who wasted decades? Wasted by fear, guilt, resentment, and lost opportunities."

"God's not limited by wasted opportunities. He brings beauty out of ashes."

"Metaphor from your scriptures?"

"Yes." He quoted from Joel: "'I will restore to you the years which the swarming locust has eaten … You shall eat in plenty and be satisfied … And my people shall never again be put to shame.'"*

"But I did something abominable." Jaw tightening, she explained that fateful day at the pharmacy and its aftermath. "Though it kept Teddy from going to jail, I played God."

"God can forgive *all* sin," Dirk replied.

"What about someone who's the Slough of Despond to others?"

"Grandma." Carrie scooted closer. "So *what*?" She spoke so sharply, Mrs. Gordon startled. "*So what* if you were the Slough of Despond? So what if you were Ignorance, Pagan, or Obstinate at one time? God doesn't care what you were. He cares only what you'll *become* when you believe He loves you." The notion settled gently, like dandelion fluff clinging to clothing.

She took her great-grandmother's hand. "Only God wins over Lies, Shame, and Fear. Someday, in the Celestial City, He'll wipe away all tears. The ultimate poetic justice."

Mrs. Gordon spoke quietly. "The ending to the fairy tale that God Himself wrote."

"Like Frederich Buechner said. And Tolkien. The best fairy tale is the true one." She leaned in. "The Brave and Good Prince left his own beautiful country to rescue us. He came to earth to walk a long, dark road in our own shoes. This land that is sometimes pleasant, and sometimes dark and terrible."

Mrs. Gordon's face brightened at the familiar words.

"Though Mr. Gordon took the blame for you, he couldn't remove burdens. But this Brave and Good Prince did both." Carrie recalled Janie's oft-quoted definition. "He wanted the highest good for us, even at great cost to himself."

---

* Joel 2:25 (RSV)

Friday, July 25, 1980

At Mrs. Gordon's request, Carrie obtained the phone number of Teddy's daughter Lillian in Hopkins, where he lived. After his twenty-year absence, Mrs. Gordon set up a visit.

Carrie's stomach clenched as Lillian led her, Oma, and Mrs. Gordon to Teddy Callaghan's front room. Mrs. Gordon toted a bulky drawstring bag. An old, gray-haired man sat near a tea set, his rugged complexion a remnant of farm life. Lillian went to the kitchen.

Teddy slowly stood, looking at each in turn, then settled on Carrie. "How'd you manage to bring your former self with you? I see you in her eyes, her cheeks." He blinked, as it dawned on him. "Oh, my."

Mrs. Gordon gestured to Oma. "This is our daughter, Dorothy Gail. She goes by Tanna. That young lady is your great-granddaughter, Carrie. They know everything. Since last week."

Teddy reached for Oma's hand. She gingerly took his. At their touch, tears trickled down Mrs. Gordon's cheeks.

His face reddened. "Dorothy Gail. I'm so sorry I never knew you. I was wrong. The Lord had mercy on you, considering how I failed you."

"I had a good Christian upbringing," Oma said. "Very loving parents."

He stared at her. "Good. The truth is, your mother" —his voice cracked— "wanted you to have the best of what two parents can give. She did right by you. *I'm* the selfish one. Sorrowful that our first meeting needs an apology." He took Carrie's hand. "You have your great-grandmother's eyes, that you do. At your age, she was all I could look at. You're fortunate to have this woman as your great-grandmother."

"I know."

"Please sit down. Lillian made tea. Only the finest for Charlotte Rose Gordon. I wish my sister Beatrice was here. She's doing well in Indiana, living close to her daughter."

Over tea, Mrs. Gordon shared how she found Dorothy, then rummaged through her bag. "I must return something I stole long ago." She handed him *The Pilgrim's Progress*.

His face brightened as he found his mother's inscription.

Mrs. Gordon sallied forth. "After eight decades, I finally read this book. Now, my burden is gone. But I must confess a sin I carried for sixty-two years." Teddy cocked his head. "I'm responsible for the pharmacy error and your father's death."

"What?" Teddy frowned. Oma's eyes bulged.

"I saw Walter's mistake but ignored it," Mrs. Gordon said. "Your family needed you to work the farm, not sit in jail for the death of a man who beat you up fourteen years."

His voice was ragged. "How ... why ..."

"Walter insisted on taking the blame. And I let him. Otherwise, I feared never reaching Dorothy. But guilt weighed me down for decades."

"My father was an evil man. He tormented my mother."

"And would've from the grave if you landed in jail. I couldn't let that happen."

"Wow."

"I risk being viewed as the Slough of Despond, but I *must* clear my husband's name."

Teddy went to her. "I was wrong calling you that. I beg your forgiveness, Charlotte." He pulled her off the chair till they stood face to face. "I should've been strong, but I was weak."

They stared at each other, blinking back tears—wondering what could have been.

He squeezed her hand. "Now I understand grace, after facing my own darkness." He turned to Oma. "Please forgive me, Dorothy." He'd had his own unslain dragons.

On the way home, Mrs. Gordon said there'd be no quelling

town gossip, but those who mattered now knew the truth of the pharmacy error. She was satisfied.

Sixty-Three

Tuesday, July 29, 1980

Carrie took cream puff pastry from the oven. "How was your time with Oma yesterday?"

Smiling, Mrs. Gordon spiked whipped cream filling with caramel for Kiki Aru's Piccadilly Praline Puffs—a pronounceable name inspired by the unpronounceable magic word, Pyrzqxgl. "We baked and explored the bedroom. She showed me her treasure box objects. We started reading the first Wendolyn book, accompanied by her questions. I've learned much about my daughter. Though she didn't pursue a career, she embraced traditional roles as wife and mother and volunteered in church and community with simplicity and kindness."

"The only magic wands that work wonders."

"Tomorrow, she'll return for more reading and baking."

"Yikes!" Carrie pouted. "What'll happen to me?"

"There's no shortage of baking opportunities. I've left no stone unturned."

"Or muffin unbaked."

"I've prepared every pertinent prerequisite."

"For what?"

"For you to decide." She led Carrie to the parlor. The room glistened, drapes open, highlighting figurines, woodwork, and tassel-fringed pillows. "What are your autumn plans?"

Carrie smirked. "Fast food."

"If you ever work fast food, don't tell me. Have you pursued other funding for your café?"

"I'm back to square one since the owner sold Dunham's Diner. It'll take a while to find another good location."

"Meanwhile, this photo needs a different frame." Mrs. Gordon pointed behind the French door.

Carrie picked up the frame bordering the enlarged Kodak photo of Charlotte Rose and the four Baum boys by the dune. Charlotte's happiness permeated the image. "Wonderful! Where'd you find it?"

"Pearl brought it last night. She started organizing upstairs and found it."

"Probably tired of my nagging."

"She was. Let's pick a frame from the bedroom."

Upstairs, Dorothy's door stood open, flooded with light. But Mrs. Gordon stopped at the other door. A glimmering shaft seeped underneath. She turned the knob.

Inside, mint green walls gleamed as if Carrie wore the Emerald City's green spectacles. Framed Oz prints dominated: Denslow's and Neill's illustrations, a 1902 Extravaganza poster, Denslow's 1900 poster of a surprised goose trailing a bevy of Oz characters.

A green and white quilt covered the bed, cozy with Mrs. Baum's embroidered pillowcase and a Scarecrow pillow. A framed photo graced the bedside table—Charlotte standing near Mr. Baum, who was seated in a rocking chair. Carrie gazed silently lest she spoil the magic by uttering words that didn't give enough weight to Mrs. Gordon's memories.

Mrs. Baum's embroidered pinafore and apron hung on Merrie Land of Oz hangers. Hooks supported Oz marionettes,

Christmas ornaments, a perky jumping jack, and a mobile of character cutouts. Woggle-Bug and Ozmite Club pins scattered over the stitched handkerchief on the bureau. Oz valentines stuck in the mirror frame, next to stitchery with the well-loved quote, "You must walk ..."

An Oz board game with pewter figurines occupied a table as if mid-game. Nearby were riddle cards from the Woggle-Bug Game of Conundrums, a magnetized trivia game, and Scarecrow spinner beside Little Wizard jigsaw puzzles and trading cards. Shelves bulged with Fabrikoid dolls, puppets, ceramic banks, and the 1934 *Waddle Book* with figures re-enacting their adventure.

Another shelf displayed toys and food promotions: a top, Mattel Jack-in-the-box, drinking glasses, peanut butter pails, and Whitman's Wonderbox candy. Scarecrow and Tin Woodman bookends flanked Baum books, school playlets, scrapbooks, *The Baum Bugle* magazines, and *Ozmapolitan* newspapers.

Mrs. Gordon handed her a string-bound Macatawa ABC booklet, pages curled.

Carrie chanted alphabet sentences, skimmed Janie's hand-printed *Laurel's Lark* newspapers, then surveyed the scrapbook of Kodaks, 1902 to 1909. "What an extraordinary collection! It should be in a museum." Her gaze swept over the room. "It's a *hyperooden rostratus*."

Mrs. Gordon laughed, like merry Lake Michigan waves. "Peruse indefinitely, after settling business."

"Oh, yes, the frame." Carrie held the dune picture next to one. "This works. But there's no wall space." The Victorian *horror vacui*—fear of empty spaces—thrived here. "It would look great in the tearoom, with a makeover, vintage 1900."

"Ironic you should say that. Open that drawer and read."

Carrie set the pictures down, withdrew a document, and read, gaping. "You're buying back the café?"

"Open the envelope."

Carrie complied—a check made out to Pearl Donahue. "You *are* buying it. Why?"

"On one condition. You. You still want to run a book café, don't you?"

"What?" Her skin prickled.

"I'm buying it on the condition that we're co-owners. You'll manage, and I'll deed it to you in my will if you agree to run it for ten years minimum."

"I don't know ..."

"Fiddlesticks! Besides your own knowledge and experience, you'll have training from Pearl for starting in a new venue."

Fearful she'd collapse, Carrie plopped on the bed. "When do you want an answer?"

"The contract's binding for thirty days. After that, Pearl may rescind the offer." Mrs. Gordon pointed. "Your signature goes here."

"I've no money for this."

"I'll take it out of this week's paycheck. You can afford a dollar."

"Don't I have to contribute more to be part owner?"

"Only if you have a hundred thousand dollars."

Carrie felt like a kite jerking in the wind, headed for tree branches. "Was this your plan all along?"

"Never. Pearl wants to retire. Her family's not interested. Three weeks ago, after your loan fell through, I decided to buy it. If you're game. If this is still your passion. Pearl agreed to mentor you for six months."

"How'd you get Pearl onboard? She hates me."

"It's me she hates, not you. Pearl's a good manager. We've both held bitterness for years, but we've made our peace. She did well with business matters, customers, and employees, with little turnover except college students."

What would Carrie's parents say? They'd yank her kite

string, pull it down, jeer if it caught in treetops. Especially for attaching herself to peculiar Mrs. Gordon.

Mrs. Gordon shook a finger. "You're entertaining reasons to say no. But there are a hundred magical reasons to say yes. Remember, 'a dreamer is one who can only find his way by moonlight.' Dawn has arrived. And your home is here now."

Carrie hugged her. "You're amazing." She circled the room, taking in the decor. Book café images flashed. The Dickens corner, the Bronte space, Mark Twain's booth.

"I see your wheels spinning. Create it into whatever you want."

Carrie scrutinized illustrations, hugged a Scarecrow doll, moved game pieces, manipulated marionettes, and caressed gifts from Mrs. Baum. She held the Kodak image of Mr. Baum with Charlotte. "The café must be a tribute to Mr. Baum. A tribute to his books and imagination. Including the menu."

Mrs. Gordon's face brightened.

"The decor too. May I use it all?" Carrie's gesture encompassed the room.

A grin emerged. "It's time for others to enjoy these mementos."

"It'll be a celebration of imagination, a tribute to all children's literature, mainly Mr. Baum." Carrie set the dune picture over the chosen frame. "This'll hang by the window facing the dune." Carrie grasped her great-grandma's hands. "I'll give you my final answer soon."

Carrie called her mentor, Rita, then discussed the offer with Oma and Opa. Not her parents. Nor Dirk. He'd been snapping his fall plans into place without her. Definitely not the rebound guy. Signing the contract committed her to Wolcott for ten years, pushing out any future with him.

Time to follow her passion. But did she have the mettle?

Remodeling costs were high. What if she didn't lure customers? What if she failed? What would people think of her joining rank with odd Mrs. Gordon? Would the same shadow fall over her and the new tearoom?

The next day after work, Carrie drove to the café. Under the maple tree, a vision materialized, Mr. Baum chatting with Janie. His influence trickled through her great-grandmother's life, now touching Carrie. Two months ago, she was like that girl under the tree, unacceptable as she was. But much had changed. For the better.

She eyed the stately brick Victorian home. Her mind raced with renovations. She peeked in windows, ambled onto the porch. Brainstorming, she sat in a rocker then strolled back to the maple tree. Images of Charlotte scrambling up the dune with the boys morphed into Carrie and Dirk's climb, then jumping down, tumbling into a summer of beach walking, hiking, and sailing. Saying yes to the tearoom meant watching Dirk sail into the sunset. Alone. Forever.

She startled at the tap on her shoulder. "Alberta!"

"Food for thought, hon? Or coming for dinner?" Alberta straightened her name tag.

"Food for thought."

"What's on your menu?" Alberta winked. "A certain young man?"

"Thinking about all the Broderick family memories. Little Charlotte running around."

Alberta shuddered. "That's long before the Gordon name was tainted."

Carrie flinched. By signing this contract, she'd legally and publicly unite herself to so-called eccentric Mrs. Gordon, subjecting herself to townsfolk's scorn. Did she want to endure scrutiny and speculations that questioned her own sanity?

Are you going to live by your passions or your fears?

Carrie straightened. "Alberta, there's more to her story than you realize."

"It doesn't negate history. People here don't forget."

"I know. But after working for Mrs. Gordon this summer …"

"Yes?" Alberta tilted her head as if awaiting juicy gossip.

Let people think what they want. No more dragons of fear and inadequacy would taunt her. Carrie smiled. "I learned home can be discovered, if not inherited."

Thursday, July 31, 1980

Carrie's first words were, "Yes! I'll run the café. I'm so excited. Oma will help too."

Eyes dancing, Mrs. Gordon bombarded her with advice. Carrie would meet with Pearl twice weekly to review orders, vendors, budget, hiring, and scheduling. "It's vital you attend training in hygiene protocol. No more *oliebollen* in the bathroom." She lowered her voice. "You've no qualms about being publicly associated with me?"

"None. I'm proud to be your great-granddaughter."

"Pearl doesn't know about our bloodline. Tell her privately as you deem proper. I'll call her to notarize the contract by week's end. That gives you time to back out."

"I'm not backing out. I picked a name. Though primarily a tribute to Mr. Baum, it'll celebrate other authors, too. The Ozcot Café and Tearoom."

Mrs. Gordon beamed a smile.

Carrie arrived at the café as Dirk sang Gordon Lightfoot's

"Cotton Jennie." Perpetually grinning, she mentally renovated back to 1900, redecorating with Oz items.

When Dirk's set ended, he buzzed to her booth. "I could dump ketchup on you, and you'd still say, 'What a wonderful day.'"

"You'll never guess." Carrie could hardly sit still. "Great-grandma's buying the café, and I'm running it."

"No kidding?" Dirk whistled. "Incredible! Better than pirate's gold at Captain Sundae."

She explained how the last few days unfolded. He raised his hand for a high five. When her hand sailed into his, he caught it, holding firm. "*You're* incredible. You always were."

"Thanks." Face warm, she forged ahead. "Guess what's on the menu. Munchkin Delights, Winkie Surprise, Bristle's Welsh Rarebit—"

"Her old menu?"

"It's a tribute to Mr. Baum." She pointed. "Bookshelves on the north wall—"

"Your book café?"

"A tearoom, too, for adults. We'll serve lunch and dinner, pastries, desserts, and stories. At the Ozcot Café."

"Of course! Feeding stomachs and imagination at the same time."

"What could be better?"

"You." He squeezed her hand. "You following your passion."

Could he see through to her soul, the part that yearned for him?

"I see the firelight in your eyes. Feel free to take advantage of my restaurant and house renovation know-how. I've got two weeks before heading south to backpack."

His words fell to the pit of her stomach. "Let the brain-picking begin," she said.

"Just don't smack me if I say that can't be done."

"What happened to Mr. Optimism?"

"That's still me. But if you want to move the kitchen sink from point *A* to point *B* and there's no plumbing, it's cost-prohibitive. If you cross wires the wrong way, it's a fire hazard. Heavy bookshelf placement is limited, considering support and ductwork."

"I get it." Taking notes, she asked about updating appliances, plumbing, construction, and painting. She'd still need a loan for renovations. His dad and uncle knew reputable contractors. "I also want to refinish furniture. Vintage turn of the century, trash the 1960s look. Recapture Mr. Baum's visit in 1900. I'll need a cool sign out front."

"Plus, a cassette for renovations. Ode to Ozcot. Happy finger-snapping tunes."

"Perfect." Like everything at this moment. Except for Dirk leaving.

Sixty-Four

August 1980

Carrie worked at the café full-time, alternating kitchen duties and waitressing. With Oma and Great-grandma, she brainstormed organizing space according to genres. She wanted Ozzy themes to permeate the room with the Broderick portraits. Perhaps a yellow brick road mural, Denslow style, embellished by a rotating exhibit of Mrs. Gordon's relics. Upstairs, Carrie found the original table the Baums ate at. Decades earlier, Janie marked its underside by carving LFB.

Dirk offered to refinish the table and a bookcase. One evening, before closing, he poked his head in the kitchen door. "Are you happy?"

"Immensely. Why?"

"You glow, and I wanna make sure it's not from any other cause."

She laughed. *Five days till Dirk leaves.*

Ideas ran rampant. New landscaping could function as a Secret Garden. Activity lists featuring authors or titles would include word puzzles, news headlines of literary events, and story starters. Upstairs rooms were suitable for special parties and author nooks. People could receive passport books with pages of trivia questions corresponding to respective alcoves. Waitresses would stamp a passport with each visit, ten stamps meriting a prize.

Carrie sketched diagrams to determine locations for her stenciled bureau and a hutch for tea jars. She invited Dirk's parents for brain-picking about grilling and remodeling. She'd eventually alternate monthly menus, featuring different titles, eras, or literary themes.

<hr>

Pearl delegated schedules and vendor orders to Carrie, with oversight. After closing time, they examined inventory. Dirk ran back and forth, up and down stairs, lugging boxes.

Four days till Dirk leaves. After an hour of numbers, Carrie sat back, buggy-eyed. "Wow, finances alone could be a full-time job."

"My son assists me. In money matters, even managers and owners need accountability."

"My mentor Rita feels the same way. Seems prudent."

"Unlike jumping the gun on remodeling." Pearl's eyes darted to Dirk.

"Just cleaning upstairs," Carrie said. "Later, I plan on returning this to vintage 1900. Like your aunt's childhood."

Pearl rolled her eyes.

"What's wrong?"

"That woman drove me crazy for years. Criticism galore. If I made a grocery list, she'd cross half the items out." Her voice escalated. "We constantly butted heads. After she retired, I did my duty, visiting weekly. I couldn't deny Aunt Jane some pity—"

Dirk showed up with two water glasses as if arriving on his steed to rip through tension with his trusty sword.

"Refreshments for you two ladies?" Carrie offered a grateful smile. "Call for a refill." Dirk sauntered away.

"Mrs. Donahue." Carrie folded her hands. "Your Aunt Jane —who prefers Charlotte—had many challenges, things you've no idea about."

"Tough times don't justify bad behavior for decades. It's like expecting my feelings to change just because one day she finally apologizes."

"She apologized?"

"Yes, three weeks ago. Drapes were wide open, too. Very odd."

"Really?" Two days after Dirk's porch visit.

"Said something about a burden dropping." Pearl shook her head. "And locusts."

Carrie chuckled. Dirk fiddled with a roll of tape, surely all ears.

Pearl crossed her arms. "What's so funny?"

"She's referring to a Bible verse. I'm surprised to hear it."

"Bible verse? Aunt Jane? I mean Charlotte."

"Ask her about it. She'll tell you."

Pearl sipped water. "She can't waltz in apologizing and expect years of exasperation to melt away. But I was so touched, the next day I searched for the picture and took it over."

"Thank you. You've no idea how much it means to her."

"Another shock. She said she appreciated how I'd run the café. Her expertise had been business, not people."

"Right. And anger doesn't just disappear, but I hope things improve between you." Carrie pulled out the Ozzy menu. "Later, I want to change the menu back. I'd like help determining a budget."

Pearl took the menu. "Again? Heavens to Betsy!"

"Here's the story." Carrie leaned forward. "Your aunt knew L. Frank Baum personally. He authored fourteen Oz books. They had a friendship, after meeting in *this* room in 1900.

Later, he returned, and she climbed the dune with his family. That picture you found is the four Baum boys and Janie."

"Honestly?"

"She maintained that friendship for years, visiting their summer home at Macatawa Park. Only your Great-aunt Sophie knew because Janie's parents condemned fairy tales. Condemned Janie. Their religious piety tried to squelch every imaginative bone in her body."

"Very sad, but pardon the pun, this menu's a recipe for failure. It's her sentimentality."

"There are more Oz fans than you realize. Also, I want to run a book café." Carrie explained how her idea morphed into the Ozcot Café and Tearoom. "I need your expertise."

Pearl sat back. "Fascinating, but you're so young, with limited experience. Why's she putting so much into your hands?"

Carrie fidgeted, then straightened. "Because I'm her great-granddaughter."

Pearl's eyes popped. "What?" Her hands dropped to the table like dead weight.

Carrie explained Janie's move to Holland, giving up Dorothy Gail, reaching her through Wendolyn books and letters, and finally meeting her.

Tears edged Pearl's eyes. "I'm flabbergasted. I'd no idea. That explains her sharp tongue. Her need for control. She must've been jealous of her sisters with families of their own."

Carrie nodded. "Rooted in grief, more than anything."

Carrie barreled forward without notifying her parents about the café. She'd eventually pay them back for college. But craving their approval was like *water naar de zee dragen.* Carrying water to sea. Never again.

Work and meetings with Pearl offered her little time to fret about Dirk leaving. Yet she thought of him constantly. Nightly, he popped by to sand, stain, or varnish a shelf upstairs or dig through messes as Carrie finished kitchen duties. His Ode to Ozcot tape accompanied them, a collection of mutual favorites: Motown and pop rock.

Wednesday after close, while Carrie swept the dining room, Frankie Valli's Four Seasons' tune played on the sound system: "Can't Take My Eyes Off You." Music tugged. She swayed with its rhythm, broom swirling. Volume rose. She swung the broom out, soft shoeing between sashays across the room. Right before the climactic refrain, she spun toward the doorway.

She faced a grinning Dirk. "Oh!" Her face burned.

"May I?" He set the broom aside and took her hand. During the refrain, he snapped his fingers and performed crazy moves, making her laugh. When the music slowed, he pulled her close, faces inches apart. She could hardly breathe. As the music sped up, they shifted rhythm, side by side. Her heart hammered. Feeling flushed, she grabbed the broom and swept. Had he wanted to kiss her as much as she'd wanted to kiss him? *Three more days.*

The next evening, same scenario. When he clomped downstairs, Stevie Wonder's "I Wish" flooded the room, a lively bass staccato. She danced with the broom. His wild antics resembled a jerky marionette. *Two more days.*

Friday evening, they planned to have dinner after closing. Dirk played his last guitar set, ending with "You've Got a Friend," directed to Carrie. She listened in the kitchen doorway, blinking back tears. *Gone tomorrow.*

Dirk picked her up at home after they freshened up. He carried a bag into Dunham's. After ordering, he handed her a lavender paper-wrapped gift. "A goodbye present."

She unwrapped it to find *The Tasha Tudor Book of Fairy Tales*. "Oh, Dirk!" She read the inscription.

To Her Royal Highness, Princess Carrie,

You're the True Treasure of the Amiable Land of Wolcott,
one I'll always recall with great affection.

Fondly, Dirk

Fondly? Affection? That's all? Fitting for a rambling man.
He took her hand. "Missing you already."

"You'll be fine once you breathe that Appalachian air." She winced, anticipating his dried-up affection. "I have presents for you too." She handed him a paper sack.

He examined the stenciled bag. "Hand-painted. Charming." He peered in. "Muffins!"

"Blueberry cream cheese. Grandma and I baked them. A dozen for you and Gerrit before subjecting yourselves to freeze-dried trail food."

"Hope these last till morning. I'm keeping this bag as a memento of your creativity."

She slid a tiny box his way.

He fumbled through nautical wrapping paper and withdrew a pewter anchor keyring. He whistled. "Classy. I'll think of us sailing, the look on your face before falling into the big lake, your acronyms for port and starboard, your pirate smack at Captain Sundae." He dangled it. "Anchor or no anchor"—he brought a fist to his heart—"those memories are *here*."

She smiled. "It might help you consider where to drop anchor someday."

He grasped her hand. "Carrie ..." He gazed at her until the waitress set plates down.

Afterward, at home, Dirk said goodbye to her grandparents. At the front door, he held Carrie's hands. "I'll be back Thanksgiving weekend."

"What if I'm in Barrowdale?"

"I'll track you down. And I promise to write from camp."

"I know how *those* postcards go. 'Today we went swimming. Weather's great. Food's bad. Having loads of fun. Wish you were here.' But not really."

He chuckled. "I'll write more than that." Their hands swung in rhythm. He embraced her. She relished his taut muscles, whiskers grazing her cheek. He stepped back with moist eyes and left.

Later in bed, Carrie reread Dirk's inscription. His expression when singing "Just the Way You Are" flooded her. Yet he never *said* he loved her. Of course, he'd be the kind of guy who'd equate a declaration of love to commitment. After a year of her rebounding, he'd lose interest or find somebody else.

SIXTY-FIVE

August 1980

Ten days after Dirk left, Carrie watched the penumbral lunar eclipse. Words that once inspired Janie Broderick infused her: *A dreamer is one who can only find his way by moonlight.* Now, Carrie was fulfilling a dream for them both. With or without moonlight. With or without Dirk.

She presented bound typed pages to her great-grandmother. "'The Memoirs of Charlotte Rose Broderick Gordon,' sub-titled 'Musings about a Fairy tale Written by God's Fingers.' My nod to Hans Christian Anderson. I wrote everything you shared, 1900 to 1919, from Macatawa to Dorothy, including your recipes, tea trivia, and tidbits of wisdom. I want permission to share it with Oma and Opa."

Mrs. Gordon gave her assent with an embrace.

September 1980

Most days, Carrie worked the late shift and helped close. She loved staying later, organizing and planning alone. One night, after emptying another upstairs room, she trekked downstairs with hammer, nails, and two framed pictures—Mrs. Gordon's dune and porch photographs—to see how they'd look on the west wall.

Instead of rosy smudges of summer sunset, autumn darkness gnawed the windows but didn't dampen her enthusiasm for landing in the grip of a great adventure.

Yet not a day passed without thoughts of Dirk's smile, laughter, and stories.

He'd been gone four weeks, and his correspondence was a joke. His North Carolina postcard said, "Dear Carrie, Having a great time. Wish you were here. Trail food stinks but views are phenomenal. Hahaha." He mentioned camping, hiking, and bear sightings. "Fondly, Dirk." His second postcard arrived from the children's camp in northern Michigan. Why hadn't he stopped by on his way up north? "Dear Carrie, Weather's great. The oatmeal stinks. Haha. Found the perfect Ozcot sign, sending it special delivery. Please tip the delivery boy."

He had the gift of gab, not writing. How long till Thanksgiving? *Stop thinking about him!* He'd kept his word with two measly postcards. Nothing about undying love.

Snippets of summer memories flitted through her. Sadness slowed her movements after feverish work all day. By now, he was immersed in camp activities. Carrie was a pleasant memory at best. Perhaps time would reveal her own heart growing cold toward him.

Nothing a little Melancholy I music couldn't cure. Ah, another reminder of Dirk.

Carrie held up the dune picture, its brass plate engraved with the date and children's names. Waves of summer rolled over her, all she'd gleaned from Mrs. Gordon's stories—Macatawa Park, Mr. Baum, Teddy, Dorothy—her connection to each.

She climbed a booth, hung the dune picture, then jumped off to admire it. Back on the seat, she pounded another nail in.

A rap on the door startled her. The window revealed a fuzzy silhouette. The door swung open, bells tinkling. Was Alberta wondering why lights were on? Was Oma worried?

Dirk! Her pounding heart leaped.

Dirk. Looking as he did every day, in T-shirt and jeans. Yet he'd never looked better. His face beamed a smile. He held a three-foot mahogany board.

"What're you doing here?" She still stood on the seat.

"I'm the delivery boy. What're *you* doing here alone after hours? Tap dancing in the booths? Figured you could use a helping hand." He lifted the board to reveal burned-in words. *Ozcot Café and Tearoom.* Smooth, precise lettering. Refined, not rustic. For Victorian decor.

"It's beautiful! Where'd you get it?"

"I made it at camp. Wood burning class." He grinned like a kid and set it down.

"Shouldn't you be at camp?"

"I resigned after recruiting and training my replacement."

"What? You anticipated camp all summer."

"I had to come home." He stepped forward.

"What happened? Is your family okay?" She hopped off the seat.

"My family's fine." He took two steps. "*You're* my home."

A flush tingled through her. "Sounds like a Billy Joel song."

"So it does. I've a story for you." He dug something from a tiny drawstring bag. "Once upon a time, there lived the most beautiful girl in the world named Princess Carrie."

Blushing, she swatted dirt off her T-shirt, combed fingers through her hair, surely a wreck.

"Ah, her beauty had nothing to do with clothing or hairdos. She had this uncanny ability to be beautiful no matter what, from the inside out." He dangled a felt ornament, a girl dressed in pink. "She reigned over the kingdom of Four Seasons. Not Frankie Valli's. Then along came this blustering man who relished himself as Sir Dirkus but was more of a court jester. He liked frogs, snakes, sailboats, music, and myriad adventures, especially slaying dragons, which he fancied himself good at." He dangled a boy felt figure.

"Once, in the middle of merry adventures, he had the good providence to meet Princess Carrie and was swept off his feet." The girl figure whacked the boy figure, which flew in an arc onto the floor. Dirk picked it up. "Once he dusted himself off, he did everything possible to serve this princess well, for she wasn't like ordinary royalty. She had the best qualities of a good princess—smart, kind, courageous—and she spoke pirate lingo."

As Carrie reveled in his tale, her head spun in delight.

"They had grand times together drinking tea with Lady Gordon, the noble queen mother, climbing the Dastardly Dune, seeking the lost royal throne in the village of Barrowdale, sailing on the *HMS Macatawa*, listening to regal music, and learning royal family history. Oh—and defeating the hideous dragon, Rian-bay. Among others."

He produced the anchor keychain from his pocket. "They took Ozzy walks along the grand promenade of Macatawa and the shire of Wolcott. 'Twas the best summer ever, sparking thrills greater than scaling heights and fighting dragons.

"One day, he played a song for Princess Carrie on his mandolin, promising to be her friend through all seasons. Then off he went. But alas, he missed her so greatly that he returned to the realm of Four Seasons to prove his worth to her."

Dirk revealed a golden silk leaf. "Sir Dirkus said to the princess, 'Your Highness, I've only had the good fortune to serve you in the Province of Summertime. But I wish to serve you in the Province of Autumn, where your chestnut brown hair rivals trees in their finery, where your courage rivals the gold of sun-touched leaves."

He held a snowflake ornament. "I wish to be with you in Winter, where neither blizzard nor cold quenches my longings for you. Where snow falls on poppies, awakening lions." He lifted a silk daffodil. "I wish to be with you in Spring, when buttercups bloom, tulips sing, and dahlias spout poetry."

Dirk discarded items and took her hands. "Carrie, I want to share all the seasons of our lives."

"That's the sweetest story I've ever heard." Tears trickled down her face.

He wiped her cheek. "This is where I'm dropping anchor."

For the café venture? "What if I sold the café tomorrow?"

"I'd question your sanity, but I'd still wanna be with *you*."

"What about your next adventure?"

"Loving *you* is my next and final adventure. If you'll have me. I love you, Carrie."

As Mrs. Gordon once quoted, his sweetness put honey to shame.

Dirk stroked her hair. "On the trail, I couldn't stop talking about you. Gerrit said I'd better do something about it. After hiking, I rushed north to find my replacement at camp."

"What about the rebound guy?"

"I'm willing to take the risk." He squeezed her quivering hands. "A certain woman put me in my place. She said, 'You've climbed mountains, conquered white water rapids, and sailed the ocean, but you're afraid to tell Carrie you love her? Love overcomes fear, Mr. Vandenakker. Are you going to live by your passions or your fears?"

Dirk touched her lips. "She said it was your love for her that broke through her own wall of fear, dispelled the locusts, slew the dragons. You were her safe harbor. She shook her finger at me. 'I'll venture to say she's your safe harbor, too. If you don't come back and pursue that girl, it'll be the biggest mistake of your life.'"

Carrie gasped. "When was this?"

"Between the trail and camp. I stopped at her house to confess my fears, to find out how you really felt, but swore her to secrecy."

"You scalawag!"

He held her shoulders. "Here's my plan. I'll get my real estate license to work for my dad. We're also renovating another fixer-upper. Meanwhile, Uncle John will keep me at the hardware store. Whenever possible, I'll help you here. I'll save money to support us later, so you can run the café without worries." He cupped her chin. "I'll contact your parents, but no matter how they respond, I'm committed to you."

Trembling, she flooded with happiness.

"The time has come for Happily Ever After." He stuck his tape in the player, inviting Linda Ronstadt's and Aaron Neville's harmony to permeate the room with "All My Life."

He drew her close. Their lips met in a sweet, tender kiss. His fingers wove through her hair.

"I love you, too, Dirk." Their lips met again, his warmth undulating through her.

Mellow music absorbed them, words drifted as an echo. She reveled in his arms, in his exhilarating presence. They swayed in slow rhythm, cheeks together. If Dirk let go of her, she'd sink to the floor.

They melded into another kiss as the tape played Billy Joel's "You're My Home."

"How 'bout a walk on the beach?" Dirk asked.

"Wait." Carrie took the picture of Mr. Baum and Charlotte Rose, climbed aboard the seat, and hung it on the new nail, next to the dune and smiling children. "What do you think?"

Dirk helped her down. "Beautiful. Just like you."

They headed outside, hand in hand, and walked toward the dune. The moon smiled through the darkness, rippling across

Lake Michigan waves. *A dreamer is one who can only find his way by moonlight ....*

This time, she'd face the dawn with Dirk.

... As the three dragons were subdued, the princess and her prince lived long and happy in the land.

Free Recipe Sampler

Dear Reader,

Thank you for choosing to read *A Hundred Magical Reasons*. I am honored.

This novel grew from my fascination with author L. Frank Baum—his humor, family values, resilience, and imagination. If this story has sparked your own imagination or touched your heart in some way, it has served its purpose. Let me know. I love to hear from readers.

I'd be thrilled to visit your book group as a guest author, either in person or via Zoom. Please contact me through my website: lauradenooyer-author.com.

If you've got a hankering for Munchkin Delights, Winkie Surprise, Polychrome's Dewdrop Mist Trifle, or other treats from *A Hundred Magical Reasons*, check out this sampler of recipes selected from *A Taste of Oz Cookbook*, the companion to the novel:

A-Taste-Of-Oz-Cookbook-Sampler.com

Ozily yours,
Laura DeNooyer

Author's Note

Though Charlotte Rose Broderick is a product of my imagination, this story relays how her friendship with L. Frank Baum could have unfolded if she'd lived and met him. Fictional Wolcott, Michigan is right off 196 on exit 34 to M-89, seven miles west of Fennville.

After reading my first Baum biography in 2014, I was smitten. Pairing Baum with my interest in writing a turn-of-the-century novel seemed like a perfect union. That was topped by learning that his family summered at Macatawa Resort—at the opposite end of Lake Macatawa where my own family vacations. This novel idea took root as if destiny.

Karl J. Franson's 1995 essay, "From Vanity Fair to Emerald City: Baum's Debt to Bunyan," suggests that Baum's inspiration and motifs for *The Wonderful Wizard of Oz* were drawn from *The Pilgrim's Progress*. In *The Annotated Wizard of Oz*, Michael Patrick Hearn compares aspects of Dorothy's journey through Oz to Christian's journey to the Celestial City.

Intrigued by the notion of *The Wizard of Oz* as the secular counterpart to *The Pilgrim's Progress*, I wanted to explore this idea further in my novel. This led me to other juxtapositions, such as imagination and religious piety, truth in fiction, and the gospel as fairy tale, as espoused by G.K. Chesterton, J.R.R. Tolkien, C.S. Lewis, Frederich Buechner, and others.

I periodically employed literary license to serve the story. For example, photos indicate no steps on the north side of the Baums' cottage, but I included steps for Janie's and Aunt Sophie's arrival each time. Rob wired their Chicago home so it's feasible he might have done so at the cottage. At age sixteen in 1902, his shenanigans may have been even more elaborate.

Baum's son Harry uses the term *hyperooden buttscoff* for the rental cottage in his autobiography in *The Baum Bugle* (Winter 1985), whereas Baum's son Frank refers to the cottage as *hyperooden rostratus* in *To Please A Child*. I chose *hyperooden rostratus*, Latin for bottlenose whale.

Baum's son Rob wrote that his father obtained their boat, the *Maybelle*, in 1904, and built the pier on Lake Michigan around the same time. In my story, the Baums own the boat in 1902.

Baum loved baseball enough to launch a team in Aberdeen, then enjoyed Cubs baseball games at Chicago's West Side Park in the 1890s. He attended every home game in 1897 when he lived within walking distance, before his move to Humboldt Boulevard. Surely, he continued to love baseball even after his attendance dwindled.

According to the biography *To Please A Child*, only Frank and Robert attended Ethical Culture Sunday School, with no mention of Harry. In the same book, the last summer the Baums spent at Macatawa Park was 1910, not 1909.

Throughout the years, folks have speculated about the origin of Dorothy, the name Oz, the road of yellow bricks, and more. I didn't want to perpetuate any myths or debunked theories. Thus, I relied on information from Michael Patrick Hearn and Sally Roesch Wagner, Founder of the Matilda Joslyn Gage Foundation.

Janie mails *The Book of Elves and Fairies* (Frances Jenkins Olcott) in 1916, but it wasn't published until 1918.

I grew up in southwest Michigan, with one foot in Dutch culture on my dad's side of the family and one foot in English/German ancestry on my mom's side. Our family was a melting pot of its own. In this novel, I give tribute to both sides by using family names of the last three generations. They all worked to achieve the American Dream—the Dunhams and Percells through agriculture, orchards, cranberry bogs, ice houses, and the Old Homestead Tea Room of Grand Mere Park in Stevensville, Michigan (which I renamed and moved north to fictional Wolcott), then the Bellgraphs, the Rhems, and finally, the DeNooyers, who went from raising celery to selling automobiles.

There really were two Billy Joel concerts in Michigan in 1977 and 1978—I attended both. Also, in case you're wondering, my college roommate, Kathy, and I once made *oliebollen* in the dorm bathroom at Calvin. It was her idea.

Discussion Questions

1. Aunt Sophie says, "Sugar sweetens everything it touches. Like books and stories. They flavor your whole life. They sweeten every day." How have stories sweetened your life?

2. Mrs. Gordon says, "Fiction has all the truth I need." How is that a true statement? How is it false? How do fairy tales lead us to reality rather than away from reality? Consider quotes by G.K. Chesterton, J.R.R. Tolkien, C.S. Lewis, and Frederick Buechner.

3. A recurring line is the Good Witch's words: "You must walk. It is a long journey, through a country that is sometimes pleasant and sometimes dark and terrible." What are the journeys in your own life? How do they lead *to* or *away from* a true home? As Mrs. Gordon says, "Home can be discovered, if not inherited."

4. Baum tells Janie, "Even Glinda, with all her magic, won't change into a different form, nor change somebody else." Later, Mrs. Gordon tells Carrie, "Transformations aren't honest. Nor pretending to be what you aren't. Don't hide your true self from

those who matter." So, what is the role of masks in the story? When do you put on a mask? When is wearing a mask necessary and/or self-protective and when is it hypocritical and/or harmful? What is gained or lost by not being real—or by *being* real?

5. Both Mrs. Gordon and Carrie wrestled with the dragons of lies, shame, and fear. Part of that came from feeling invisible—unseen, and unknown. How do we make people feel invisible? How do we make them feel seen?

6. Mrs. Gordon asks Carrie, "Are you going to live by your passions or by your fears?" When have you chosen your passions over your fears? Or vice versa?

7. Which metaphors in the story resonated with you? Light, drapery, sunflowers, the Yellow Brick Road, Oz, locusts, unslain dragons, the Slough of Despond, or other images from *The Pilgrim's Progress* (Mr. Legality, the Giant Despair, etc.).

8. L. Frank Baum said, "Stunt, dwarf, or destroy the imagination of a child, and you've taken away its chances of success in life" and "Only imagination and faith keep man above the commonplace." What is the role of imagination and why is it so crucial? When has your own imagination been stunted?

9. Mrs. Gordon tells Carrie that a true friend is someone you can tell your biggest sin to and he'll still accept you. "Otherwise, you're no better off than Mr. Blake's sunflower, yearning for the sun, but bound to earth." Is that the defining trait of a true friend? Which other traits matter? How did this impact Carrie's understanding of her relationship with both Brian and Dirk?

10. Aunt Sophie said there were a hundred magical reasons for Janie to keep visiting Mr. Baum. What

are some of them? Was Aunt Sophie justified in taking Janie to the Baums behind her parents' backs? Have you ever benefitted from being with someone who others deemed unsuitable or a bad influence?

11. Mrs. Gordon wrote the Wendolyn stories as gifts for her daughter, each one an illustration of life advice she wished to convey. What's a meaningful piece of advice you'd like to pass on to the next generation?

12. In the book, Baum says, "Living with fairies takes more courage than jumping down a dune." Later, Mrs. Gordon says, "It takes no courage to be cross or critical, to incite an argument, or speak one's mind about teabags and trifles, when you don't care what others think. But when you want to love someone and want their love in return, that takes all the courage in the world." What are some of these "quiet" acts of courage in your own life, and why are they sometimes more scary than outright heroic acts?

13. Mrs. Gordon says to Carrie, "Whatever your heart's desire, experiences you encounter along the way are grist for the mill." Which experiences have been your "grist for the mill"?

14. A recurring line is Oscar Wilde's quote: "A dreamer is one who can only find his way by moonlight, and his punishment is that he sees the dawn before the rest of the world." How was this true for Janie and Carrie, and even Baum? When have you found this to be true in your own life or someone else's?

Acknowledgments

Writing a novel takes a village, and this village has many residents. I'm especially grateful to the foremost Oz/Baum scholar, Michael Patrick Hearn, for sharing his wealth of knowledge on top of treasures I discovered in his remarkable book, *The Annotated Wizard of Oz*. He graciously answered questions and helped me unravel discrepancies so I could accurately portray Baum's character, family, career, and timeline. Any errors are my fault alone.

Many folks from the International Wizard of Oz Club (IWOC) shared their expertise or directed me to pertinent articles, books, and sources. Jane Albright endowed me with over three dozen back issues of *The Baum Bugle*, answered random questions, sent photos, and encouraged me to create a companion cookbook. Blair Frodelius located photos and sent articles. Marc Baum answered questions at the All Things Oz Museum in Chittenango. Atticus Gannaway gave an online presentation of California's influence on Baum. A huge thanks to Leah Barber and Chris Kaiser, who read the manuscript.

I'm grateful to Gita Dorothy Morena and Robert Baum, great-grandchildren of L. Frank Baum. Gita put me in touch with Michael Patrick Hearn and offered favorable feedback on my novel chapter and first-place short story, "A Week with Mr. Baum." Robert shared family photographs and kindly answered questions.

Many thanks to my Scrivenings Press publisher, Linda Fulkerson, for championing my story, and a huge thanks to my editor, Susan Page Davis, for her skill, knowledge, kindness, and patience. Thank you to Cynthia Ruchti for her time and thoughtful input that led to improvements. Before that, this novel-writing venture thrived on the feedback and encouragement of wonderful critique partners: Laura Dritlein, Elizabeth Daghfal, Brooke Cutler, Darla Phillips, Mark Stay, Bob Boesch, and Jennifer Schroeder. Kathy Giorgio of All Writers Workplace & Workshop, LLC in Waukesha, Wisconsin, edited the first several chapters.

Valuable input from beta readers shaped later drafts: Elizabeth Daghfal, Anita Klumpers, Rita Trickel, Sue Brinkmann, and Alice den Hollander. Other readers became avid cheerleaders: Laurie Herlich, Ruth Schmeckpeper, and Barbara Britton. Additionally, my entire launch team deserves a huge thanks. Rita Trickel honored me by asking for a novel tour at Lake Macatawa in June 2023. This included kayaking into Lake Michigan for a sailor's view of Big Red and the previous Macatawa Resort shoreline (now Point West).

Thanks to Alice den Hollander and Sue Brinkmann for spotting my out-of-season flowers, Alice for correcting Dutch phrases and explaining Dutch nicknames, Wayne Holubetz for real estate intel, my nephew Brenden Leach for restaurant knowledge, Bob Paffenroth for his grilling proficiency, and Mark Doremus for creating the trailer.

Thank you to my daughter Audrey for creating the image of L. Frank Baum on his Macatawa porch, based on a familiar photograph. Check out her work on Etsy: Audrey Moore Punch Portraits, https://etsy.me/3eLGiDy. Many thanks to my brother Jake and sister-in-law Mary Beth DeNooyer for their gracious hospitality on Lake Macatawa for numerous summers. Such times allowed me to explore the Holland/Macatawa/Saugatuck area and discover details that shaped my novel. Also, thanks to my parents for their interest in my projects over the years and for sharing stories of our Dutch, English, and German ancestors.

Thanks to my sister, Carol, for listening, encouraging, reading my long-winded stories despite her preference for non-fiction, and for dealing with my overactive imagination (if there is such a thing) through the years. Even though she didn't enjoy the times as kids when I made her sit down and write stories together, she grew up using her imagination in other magical ways.

Thank you to my husband, Tim, for his patience in living with a creative and for supporting my endeavors for forty-two years. He started the Baum ball rolling when he and our two sons created a birthday treasure hunt for me in 2014. It ended in a bookstore where I selected my first Baum biography. That opened a whole new world for me. I'm grateful for four imaginative kids, all grown up now but still using their creativity in a hundred different magical ways on their respective journeys.

Above all, I'm grateful to God for being the Giver of all good and perfect gifts—for imagination, for faith, and for the Brave and Good Prince in the one fairy tale that is eternally true.

These books and articles proved helpful:

- *The Annotated Wizard of Oz*, Michael Patrick Hearn (2000)
- *Our Landlady*, L. Frank Baum, edited and annotated by Nancy Tystad Koupal (1996)
- *Baum's Road to Oz, The Dakota Years*, edited by Nancy Tystad Koupal (2000)
- *The Wizard of Oz*, The Critical Heritage Series, L. Frank Baum, Michael Patrick Hearn, editor (1983)
- *L. Frank Baum, Royal Historian of Oz*, Angelica Shirley Carpenter & Jean Shirley (1992)
- *The Wizard of Oz and Who He Was*, Martin Gardner & Russel B. Nye, editors (1994)
- *The Real Wizard of Oz, the Life and Times of L. Frank Baum*, Rebecca Loncraine (2009)
- *To Please A Child, a biography of L. Frank Baum Royal Historian of Oz*, Frank Joslyn Baum & Russell MacFall (1961)
- *The Wonderful World of Oz*, John Fricke (2013)
- *The Oz Scrapbook*, David L. Greene & Dick Martin (1977)
- "From Vanity Fair to Emerald City: Baum's Debt to Bunyan," Karl J. Franson, *Children's Literature*, Vol. 23 (1995)
- *Born Criminal: Matilda Joslyn Gage, Radical Suffragist*, Angelica Shirley Carpenter (2018)
- International Wizard of Oz website: ozclub.org
- *The Baum Bugle* (1960s to present), currently edited by Sarah Crotzer
- *The Wonderful Mother of Oz*, Sally Roesch Wagner (2003)
- *Woman as an Inventor*, Matilda Joslyn Gage (1883, reprint 2004)

- L. Frank Baum's 14 Oz books, published 1900 - 1920 & numerous other children's books
- *The Annotated Anne of Green Gables*, L. M. Montgomery, edited by Wendy Elizabeth Barry, Margaret Anne Doody, and Mary E. Doody Jones (1997)
- *The Poisoner's Handbook: Murder and the Birth of Forensic Medicine in Jazz Age New York*, Deborah Blum (2011)
- *The Wisdom of Oz*, Gita Dorothy Morena (2001)
- *1899: L. Frank Baum's Oz-Inspiring Macatawa Park*, William Bollman (2013)
- *Stevensville & Area: Stevensville, Michigan 1884-1984*, Betty Goetz, editor
- *Triumphs of the Imagination*, Leland Ryken (1979)
- *Telling the Truth: The Gospel as Tragedy, Comedy, and Fairy Tale*, Frederick Buechner (1977)
- *The Magnificent Defeat*, Frederick Buechner (1966)

About the Author

Laura DeNooyer thrives on creativity and encouraging it in others. A Calvin College graduate, she is a teacher, wife, parent of four adult children, and a multi-award-winning author of heart-warming historical and contemporary fiction. Her first novel, *All That Is Hidden*, earned the Artisan Book Reviews Book Excellence Award and was a semi-finalist for the Serious Writer Book of the Decade. She's an active member in her church and American Christian Fiction Writers. When not writing, you'll find her reading, walking, drinking tea with friends, or taking a road trip. For updates, freebies, giveaways, and a free prequel, join Laura's monthly newsletter StandoutStoriesNewsletter.com.

Learn more at lauradenooyer-author.com.

Stay up-to-date on your favorite books and authors with our free e-newsletters.
ScriveningsPress.com

www.ingramcontent.com/pod-product-compliance
Lightning Source LLC
Chambersburg PA
CBHW071532120726
47907CB00014B/1533